I0585112

Elias Lyman Magoon

Orators of the American Revolution

Elias Lyman Magoon

Orators of the American Revolution

ISBN/EAN: 9783337229696

Printed in Europe, USA, Canada, Australia, Japan

Cover: Foto ©Andreas Hilbeck / pixelio.de

More available books at **www.hansebooks.com**

ORATORS

OF THE

AMERICAN REVOLUTION.

BY

E. L. MAGOON.

FIFTH EDITION.

NEW YORK:
C. SCRIBNER, No. 124 GRAND STREET.
1860.

SG

STUDENTS WHO ARE NOT DRONES,

CHRISTIANS WHO ARE NOT BIGOTS,

AND

CITIZENS WHO ARE NOT DEMAGOGUES,

This Book is Respectfully Inscribed.

LIST OF PLATES.

CONTENTS.

CHAPTER I.

CONTENTS.

PREFACE.

— ∿∿∿∿∿∿ —

THE following work is an attempt to present the oratorical features of the American Revolution. The political history of the country has been ably written. Vivid delineations of our early martial heroes are also before the public. All the great leaders in the various departments of statesmanship, literature, science and art, have received the meed of skillful scrutiny and discriminated praise. In view of this general appreciation of our illustrious fathers, it is the more remarkable that so little attention has been paid to the particular merits of the great leaders of the American forum. True, a good deal has been said of them in biographical sketches, legislative history, and traditionary annals; but we are not aware that any work has heretofore been devoted to a critical and comprehensive examination of our great orators as such. Many pointed allusions and partial descriptions lie about in books of various kinds, facts, anecdotes, and fragmentary sentiments, which are to a full analysis of specific traits and the judicious estimate of individual worth, what a confused mass of indefinite outlines are to a gallery of elaborate full-lengths, each distinctly drawn, rounded into symmetrical shape and colored with appropriate tone.

Our leading speakers, in Colonial and Revolutionary times, were distinguished not more for their general ability, than for the wonderful originality of talent with which each in particular was characterized. To indicate this individuality of oratorical excellence, and the results which by a mighty unity in diversity were produced, is the object of the present publication.

Each one of the following portraitures briefly comprehends the earthly career of its subject ; but, in accordance with the above avowal, the reader may expect to meet with historical details, only so far as they are requisite to explain the preliminary training and elucidate the peculiar eloquence of the master under consideration. The dates and circumstances employed for this purpose the author has gathered from all the resources within his reach.

It will be observed that several of the personages herein portrayed do not strictly belong to the Revolutionary period of our history. But, like the great patriots who preceded them in the battles of life and solemnities of death, their merits are worthy of profound study and perpetual emulation.

The last four names in the present series represent an impressive group, more recently departed, from whom we may hereafter turn to contemplate the *Living Orators in America.*

E. L. M.

Cincinnati, July 4th, 1848.

THE BATTLE-FIELDS OF EARLY AMERICAN ELOQUENCE.

GREAT is the power of local association. To none is its influence indifferent, but it is the most thrilling to minds of the most delicate tone. Reverence for the scenes of exalted deeds is a noble instinct planted in our hearts for noble ends. It is inarticulate adoration ad·dressed, not more to the understanding than to the heart. To be in a high degree void of this, is an evidence of personal ignominy and a presage of deserved oblivion.

Doctor Johnson, in a well-known passage, happily refers to those feelings, which local associations awaken in the refined bosom. On arriving at Icolmkill, in his "Tour to the Western Islands," he wrote:

"We are now treading that illustrious island, which was once the luminary of the Caledonian regions, whence savage clans and roving barbarians derived the benefits of knowledge and the blessings of religion. To abstract the mind from all local emotion would be im·possible if it were endeavored; and would be foolish if it were possible. Whatever withdraws us from the power of the senses; whatever makes the past, the dis·tant, or the future predominate over the present; advances us in the dignity of thinking beings. Far from me, and from my friends, be such frigid philosophy as may conduct us, indifferent and unmoved, over any ground which has been dignified by wisdom, bravery or virtue. That man is little to be envied whose patriotism would not gain force on the plain of Marathon, or whose piety would not grow warmer among the ruins of Iona."

The associations which are the most affecting are moral. The venerable monuments of the past, and localities connected with which great events transpired, are invested with irresistible attractions to a susceptible heart and cultivated mind. They snatch the soul away in rapture, as if it had already traversed the tomb, and on the bosom of immensity imbue it with the inexhaustible glories which Jehovah has diffused through the universe:

> "The mind hath no horizon,
> It looks beyond the eye, and seeks for mind
> In all it sees, in all it sees o'erruling."

It was with reference to this power of local association that the ancient poet, when describing the battle of Salamis, together with the temples of their gods, and the persons of those most dear to them, mentioned also the tombs of their fathers as the objects best fitted to rouse the courage and inflame the patriotism of the Athenians in times of peril. Cicero beautifully alludes to the pleasure, which every accomplished mind experiences when exercised on the spots sanctified by illustrious characters. Germanicus visited Athens with veneration; and during his stay, divested himself of every insignia of power. Atticus paused with awe among its tombs and monuments: Julian shed tears, on quitting its bowers and groves: Leo Allatries wept over the ruins of a house which was said once to have belonged to Ho mer. And why are the ruins of that illustrious city so thrilling to a cultivated and reflecting mind? Because it was the focus of intelligence; the arena of the noblest strife of the noblest heroes.

Still do we trace there the bold terrace of the Pnyx; the scene of the stormy assemblies of the free people of Athens, and the battle-ground of her mightiest orators. Hither resorted the intellectual sovereigns of the world; the patriots who

> "Shook the arsenal, and fulmined over Greece,
> To Macedon and ARTAXERXES' throne."

It was thence that Demosthenes spoke, and excited or calmed the sea of popular commotion, more powerful than the Ægean, whose billows, dashing near, mingled their roar with the thunders of his eloquence.

There is a hallowed fellowship existing between all master minds. The most meritorious are always the first to recognize the claims of merit in others, the acutest to feel their excellence, and the most eloquent to proclaim their worth. When Cicero visited Athens, he wrote the following query:

"Shall I ascribe it to a law of our nature, or to a de-lusive habit of mind, that when we look upon the scenes which illustrious men of old frequented, our feelings are more deeply excited than even by hearing the record of

their deeds, or perusing the works of their genius?
Such is the emotion I now experience, when I think,
that here Plato was accustomed to discourse; these gardens around us not merely recall the idea of the sage to
my memory, but place, as it were, his very form before my eyes.   Here, too, Speusippus taught; here
Xenocrates, here his disciple, Polemon; this is the very
seat he used to occupy."

From these words of the great son of Rome, turn for
a moment to the scene of his grandest struggles, that
arena whereon the mightest spirits met in terrible conflict, the Forum.   Here, while Romans were freemen,
all state affairs were debated in the most public manner, ·
and the spot perhaps deserved the praise of being "the
noblest theatre on this side of heaven."   Elevated in
the midst of the great square was the rostra, from which,
with his eyes fixed on the capitol, which immediately
faced him, and the Tarpeian rock, with which the most
impressive associations of honor and infamy were connected, the noblest of orators, "wielded at will the fierce
democracy," filling all bosoms with a passionate love of
freedom and the glory of the Roman race.   Cicero, in
his work *de Finibus*, has indicated a fine trait of his
character in the following remark:

"Often when I enter the senate house, the shades of
Scipio, of Cato, and of Lælius, and in particular of my
venerable grandfather, rise to my imagination."

Every elegant mind will be thus haunted in the same
localities.

The scene that beneficent spirits have visited "remains hallowed to all time," says Schiller; it is still

"blessed, though robbers haunt the place." Southey adds, "He whose heart is not excited upon the spot which a martyr has sanctified by his sufferings, or at the grave of one who has largely benefitted mankind, must be more inferior to the multitude by his moral, than he can possibly be raised above them in his intellectual nature." We are indebted to the influence of local as sociation, for one of the most valuable productions in modern history. It was in the Church of St. Maria d' Ara Cœli, on the Capitoline Hill at Rome, as Gibbon himself tells us: "On the fifteenth of October, 1764, as he sat musing amid the ruins of the capitol, while the bare-footed friars were singing Vespers, that the idea of writing the Decline and Fall of the city first started to his mind."

Why is Pompeii so full of thrilling associations to the thoughtful traveller? It is because he there views a city that was old when CHRIST was a babe, the well preserved homes of a thousand happy circles all of whom perished long before our ancestors had a language or the world a substantial hope. It is a city that reposed twenty centuries in the bosom of the earth, with nations trampling above, while its monuments and decorations have been so well preserved, and now stand out so brightly in brilliant day, that a contemporary of Augus-tus, returning to its streets, its forums, its temple-fanes and tesselated boudoirs, might exclaim:

"I greet thee, O my country! my dwelling is the on'y spot upon the earth which has preserved its form; an immunity extending even to the smallest objects of my affection. Here is my couch; there are my favorite authors. My paintings, also, are still fresh as when the ingenious artist spread them over my walls. Come, let us traverse the town; let us visit the drama; I recognize the spot where I joined for the first time in tho plaudits given to the fine scenes of Terence and Euripides. Rome is but one vast museum; Pompeii is *a living antiquity.*"

On visiting the universities of Cambridge and Oxford, the ingenuous scholar is inspired by the genius of the place. He remembers that within those venerable walls, Hooker and Johnson, Bacon and Newton pursued the walks of science, and thence soared to the most elevated heights of literary renown. It was the same noble emulation that Tully experienced at Athens, when he contemplated the portico where Socrates sat, and the laurel grove where Plato discoursed.

But the most interesting associations we can explore are those connected with the early struggles of our country to be free. This topic is the most important, and we shall dwell on it more at length.

In glancing at the historical events of our Revolution, we escape from the obscurity which invests the "dim and shadowy visions" of a remoter past. We contemplate an age crowded, indeed, with unparalleled and stupendous events, but one perfectly authentic and luminous with the highest degree of splendor. Mr. Alison, describes the era of our national birth in the following high strain of eloquence:

"The reign of George III., embraces, beyond all question, the most eventful and important period in the annals of mankind. In its eventful days were combined

the growth of Grecian democracy with the passions of
Roman ambition; the fervor of plebeian zeal with the
pride of aristocratic power; the blood of Marius with
the genius of Cæsar; the opening of a nobler hemisphere
to the enterprize of Columbus, with the rise of a sociai
agent as mighty as the press or the powers of steam.

"But if new elements were called into action in the
social world, of surpassing strength and energy, in the
course of this memorable reign, still more remarkable
were the characters which rose to eminence during
its continuance. The military genius, unconquerable
courage, and enduring constancy of Frederic; the ardent mind, burning eloquence, and lofty patriotism of
Chatham; the incorruptible integrity, sagacious intellect, and philosophic spirit of Franklin; the disinterested
virtue, prophetic wisdom, and imperturbable fortitude of
WASHINGTON; the masculine understanding, feminine
passions, and blood-stained ambition of Catharine, would
alone have been sufficient to cast a radiance over any
other age of the world. But bright as were the stars of
its morning light, more brilliant still was the constellation which shone forth in its meridian splendor, or cast
a glow over the twilight of its evening shades. Then
were tó be seen the rival genius of Pitt and Fox, which,
emblematic of the antagonist powers which then con-
vulsed mankind, shook the British Senate by their vehemence, and roused the spirit destined, ere long, for the
dearest interests of humanity, to array the world in
arms; then the great soul of Burke cast off the unworld-
ly fetters of ambition or party, and, fraught with a
giant's force and a prophet's wisdom, regained its destiny

ın the cause of mankind; then the arm of Nelson cast
its thunderbolts on every shore, and preserved unscath-
ed in the deep the ark of European freedom; and, ere
his reign expired, the wisdom of Wellington had erected
an impassible barrier to Gallic ambition, and said, even
to the deluge of imperial power, "Hitherto shalt thou
come and no farther, and here shall thy proud waves be
stayed." Nor were splendid genius, heroic virtue, gigantic wickedness, wanting on the opposite side of this
heart-stirring conflict. Mirabeau had thrown over the
morning of the French Revolution the brilliant but deceitful light of Democratic genius; Danton had colored
its noontide glow with the passions and the energy of tri-
bunitian power; Carnot had exhibited the combination,
rare in a corrupted age, of Republican energy with private virtue; Robespierre had darkened its evening days
by the blood and agony of selfish ambition; Napoleon
had risen like a meteor over its midnight darkness,
dazzled the world by the brightness of his genius and the
lustre of his deeds, and ɩured its votaries, by the deceitful
blaze of glory, to perdition.

"In calmer pursuits in the tranquil walks of science
and literature, the same age was, beyond all others, fruit
ful in illustrious men. Doctor Johnson, the strongest
intellect and the most profound observer of the eighteenth
century; Gibbon the architect of a bridge over the dark
gulf which separates ancient from modern times, whose
vivid genius has tinged with brilliant colors the greatest
historical work in existence; Hume, whose simple but
profound history will be coeval with the long and eventful thread of English story; Robertson, who first threw

over the maße of human events the light of philosophic genius and the spirit of enlightened reflection; Gray, whose burning thoughts had been condensed in words of more than classic beauty; Burns, whose lofty soul spread its own pathos and dignity over the "short and simple annals of the poor;" Smith, who called into existence a new science, fraught with the dearest interests of humanity, and nearly brought it to perfection in a single life-time; Reid, who carried into the recesses of the human mind the torch of cool and sagacious inquiry; Stewart, who cast a luminous glance over the philosophy of mind, and warmed the inmost recesses of metaphysical inquiry by the delicacy of taste and the glow of eloquence; Watt, who added an unknown power to the resources of art, and in the regulated force of steam, discovered the means of approximating the most distant parts of the earth, and spreading in the wilderness of nature the wonders of European enterprise and the blessings of Christian civilization; these formed some of the ornaments of the period, during its earlier and more pacific times, forever memorable in the annals of scientific acquisition and literary greatness."

The colonial and revolutionary history in this country comported with the intellectual character of the age just sketched. The founders of our colonies, the Winthrops, the Smiths, the Raleighs, the Penns, the Oglethorpes, were among the most accomplished scholars and elegant writers, as well as the most elevated and pure spirits of their time. They were men of severe morality and unblemished integrity, as distinguished for private purity as for public virtue. Being driven into war, they

2

drew their swords for opinion's sake; having entered
the contest on conscientious grounds, they deemed no
sacrifice too great to be made in defence of their rights

"Such were the men of old, whose tempered blades
Dispersed the shackles of usurped control,
And hewed them link from link: then Albion's sons
Were sons indeed; they felt a filial heart
Beat high within them at a mother's wrongs;
And shining each in his domestic sphere
Shone brighter still when called to public view."

Diodorus Siculus tells us that the forest of the Pyre-
nean mountains being set on fire, and the heat penetrating the soil, a pure stream of silver gushed forth from
the earth's bosom, and revealed for the first time the
existence of those mines afterwards so celebrated. So,
in circumstances of severe trial, intellectual resources
are developed in copious and splendid profusion.

The heroical pioneers of freedom in our land were not
only conscious of the dignity and importance of the immediate consequences of their acts, but they were
prophetic of the future grandeur which their country was
destined to attain. The spirit of lofty and wise patriotism
was diffused through all classes, and the resolute determination to resist oppression was shared by all. American mothers early learned, like the Spartan matron, to
say to their sons marching to battle, "*Return victorious,
or return no more.*"

Another striking feature in our primitive annals was
the unanimity of purpose and action which subsisted
among all the early patriots. The parent colonies teem
with charms "unborrowed from the eye." They abound

with scenes which memory has sanctified, history com memorated, and poetry adorned; every rivulet has its hallowed associations, every secluded lake and untamed forest haunts the imagination with reminiscences of savage times; every field has its tale of blood, every shore its record of suffering, and "not a mountain lifts its head unsung," or unworthy of heroic strains.   Although the external aspect of nature is becoming rapidly changed by the inroads of unexampled enterprise, and many vestiges of primitive wildness are swept away, still

> " A spirit hangs,
> Beautiful region ! o'er thy towns and farms,
> Statues and temples, and memorial tombs."

But one impulse moved our fathers in the great work they were commissioned to perform.   Each one was full of the sentiment of Grattan, " I never will be satisfied so long as the meanest of mortals has a link of the British chain clanking on his limbs; and the declaration is planted, and though great men should apostatize, yet the cause shall live ; and though the public speaker should die, yet the immortal fire shall outlast the organ that conveyed it, and the breath of liberty, like the word of the holy man, will not die with the prophet, but survive him."

That spirit has survived its first propagators, enhanced in value, if possible, by the recollection that, equally in the remotest sections, there was unanimous promptitude for a common defence, and not one recreant among avowed patriots to disgrace their toil.

The blood that was shed in the war of the Revolution

was shed in the defence of essential rights, and to secure
independence for all. The bond of mutual sympathy
was strong, and the interchange of patriotic labors delightful. The most glorious victories of the south, were
won by a northern general; and the greatest achievements north of the Potomac, distinguishes the name of a
southern officer. Patriots did not then stop to calculate
the value of the Union, and strike a balance between
imaginary and substantial allegiance to a common country. Then the richest consolation men enjoyed in life
and in death, was that their sacred trust as statesmen
and fellow citizens had been discharged with equal
fidelity to every portion of the struggling land, and that
the fruits of that fidelity, consecrated with their tears
and blood, were entailed on their latest posterity. Not
yet are statues and columns, and temples dedicated to
each of that immortal band. Perhaps the most appropriate monument and which best comports with their
character and fame, is the one they themselves erected;
the simple and sublime grandeur of our vast Republic.

The influence of local association is strongly felt in
the bosom of every American who visits the crumbling
ruins of Jamestown, "Glorious still in all her old decay;"
or the unwasted rock at Plymouth; the solid shore on
which the Pilgrims first stepped, and which is immortal
like Marathon or Nazareth. Truly said the great statesman of the north:

"We shall not stand unmoved on the shore of Plymouth, while the sea continues to wash it; nor will our
brethren in another early and ancient colony forget the
place of its first establishment till their river shall cease

to flow by it. No vigor of youth, no maturity of manhood, will lead the nation to forget the spots where its
infancy was cradled and defended."

He must have sensibilities dull indeed who can contemplate unmoved the original dresses still preserved in
"Pilgrim Hall;" the very plates from which our ancestors feasted and thanked God, and the venerable records
in which their own hands inscribed the incidents of their
first days on this continent, the most sad and sublime of
history. "Where a spring rises or a river flows," says
Seneca, "There should we build altars and offer sacrifices." We feel the force of this sentiment when we
bend over the " sweet and delicate springs of water," for
which the Pilgrims rendered especial gratitude, and which
are still gushing at the foot of that hill, hard by the
sounding sea, on the dreary summit of which, in that
bleak December, the first germs of our nation sought a
refuge amid drifting snows. Commerce is now busy
there, wealth, science and art are multiplying their monuments all around, but O! let them not encroach on the
sacred precincts of that hill's summit—the first burial-
ground of our land; leave that as a hallowed shrine
where the remotest descendants of the pure and the free
from his hearth far-off by the shore of the Pacific, may
come and listen to the kindred tones of the Atlantic, and
the holy melody of night-winds as they sigh a perpetual
requiem over the graves of the first victims of that
dreadful winter, Carver, White, R.ose Standish, and
Mary Allerton. In the language of a distinguished
poet, now living in New England, may we not
exclaim:

"Oh! if the young enthusiast bears
  O'er weary waste and sea the stone
Which crumbled from the Forum's stairs
  Or round the Parthenon;
Or olive-bough from some wild tree,
Hung over old Thermopylæ:

"If leaflets from some hero's tomb,
  Or moss-wreath torn from ruins hoary,
Or faded flowers whose sisters bloom
  On fields renowned in story;
Or fragments from the Alhambra's crest,
Or the gray rock by Druids blest!

"If it be true that things like these
  To heart and eye bright visions bring,
Shall not far holier memories
  To these memorials cling?
Which need no mellowing mist of time
To hide the crimson stains of crime!

But the most remarkable characteristic of our early history is, that Providence seems to have assigned each man an especial duty, and to have marked each battle-field of forensic strife with distinguished honors. It is interesting to observe how the citadel of oppression was attacked at different points, and a stone loosened here and there, by individual efforts, preparatory to the general storm and complete downfall. James Otis, in his argument against "Writs of Assistance," avowed and triumphantly defended the doctrine, that "taxation without representation is tyranny;" and Samuel Adams, in a college exercise pronounced in the presence of the chief minions of British power, boldly announced for his theme that "Resistance to the Chief Magistrate is a duty, when the Commonwealth cannot otherwise be preserved." These were radical principles and struck at the foundation of all colonial wrongs.

About the same time, Patrick Henry led off the south. ern wing of freedom's young army in a most bold and daring manner. The ruins of the old House of Bur· gesses will be for ever associated with his name. It was on that spot, in 1764, that he originated the great ques· tion which led eventually to American Independence. The whole colony of Virginia was confounded and dispir· ited on the promulgation of the Stamp-Act. It was in that dark crisis that Henry arose, and the thunders of his eloquence were heard, holding up to public indignation the tyranny of Great Britain, and animating his coun· trymen to resist the injustice which in that Act she had presumed to inflict. It was in allusion to the august scene, when this "forest-born Demosthenes" boldly braved the popular feeling of the world and the world's greatest power, that Jefferson declared, "Mr. Henry certainly gave the first impulse to the ball of the Revolution."

The same hand smote down another iniquitous prin· ciple in the old court-house yet standing in Hanover county. We refer to the famous controversy between the clergy on the one hand and the people of the colony on the other, touching the stipend claimed by the former Goaded to a sense of religious freedom by the arrogance of a state establishment and the stings of intolerance, the colonists sought a defender of their rights, and found him in the person of a rustic patriot, then but twenty

four years old. We need not here recour⁴ the splendid
scene when Henry delivered his famous "speech against
the parsons," making the blood of all to run cold, and
their hair to rise on end.

It was thus that Otis, by the flames of his eloquence.
calcined the corner-stone of legal tyranny, and Henry
with a thunder-bolt shattered the key-stone of ecclesiastical wrongs. Like Hercules and Theseus, they were
the avengers of the oppressed and the destroyers of
monsters. These were not men who, as Burke said of
the aristocratic politicians of his acquaintance, had been
"rocked and dandled into legislators." James Otis and
Patrick Henry were, above all others, best fitted for the
emergency to which they were born, because they dared
to say more in public than any other men. They possessed the brawny strength of the giant under whose
massy club the hydra fell, and the ethereal terrors that
rendered Jupiter Tonans dreadful to his foes, rather
than the effeminate ease and elegant locks of Adonis,
graceful in the dance, but inefficient on the field of
severe and solemn conflict.

Every conquest of value is at the price of popular
commotion and heroic blood. Men must dare if they
would win. The atmosphere we breathe would stag-
nate without tempests, and the ocean becomes putrid
without agitation. Galileo fought in the observatory
and suffered in prison while establishing the true doctrines of astronomy. Otis, Henry and Adams struggled
on the rostrum, and pleaded with a price set upon their
heads, while they cleared a space for the sunshine and
growth of enlarged liberty. They were just the men

for the task. They struck for freedom and not for plunder, and were ready to sacrifice everything in behalf of the boon for the attainment of which they fought. To give battle single-handed, like Cocles, against a horde of foes, or, like Curtius, to immolate themselves for the good of their country, was a duty which they courted rather than shunned. Those three men were the Horatii of this nation, and their renown will grow broader and brighter with the lapse of time.

It is interesting to observe what great results sometimes flow from little causes. On November the seventeenth, 1307, three patriotic Swiss met at night on the border of a lake in the bosom of the Alps, and mutually pledged their labors and their lives for the disenthralment of their country. By the blessing of Providence on their efforts, and the vigilance of their successors, Freedom won and has maintained her sublime throne on that spot for six hundred years. Near the same place, three rivulets pour their limpid waters and unite in a stream constantly augmented as it leaves mountain and forest behind and rushes on to linger a while in the placid beauty of Lake Constance ; thence it leaps down the cataract of Schauffhausen, rolls along the bases of the Jura, the Vosges and the Taurus ; traverses the plains of Friesland, waters the low countries of Holland ; and having received twelve thousand tributaries, flowed by one hundred and fourteen cities and towns, divided eleven nations, murmuring the history of thirty centuries and diffusing innumerable blessings all along its course, it stretches its mighty career from central Europe to the sea. But who can measure the length or fathom the depth of that current of good, first opened by the instrumentality of Otis, Henry and Adams?—a stream which, more beneficent than the mighty river of Egypt or the Rhine, is destined to inundate and fertilize the world.

The source of American independence may be traced higher than to the period when, to speak in the verse of Thomson,

> " Strait to the voted aid,
> Free, cordial, large, of never-failing source,
> Th' illegal imposition follow'd harsh,
> With execution given, or ruthless sought,
> From an insulted people, by a band
> Of the worst ruffians, those of tyrant power."

It was not the Stamp-Act that produced, although it immediately occasioned, the struggle with the mother-country.   It has been well said by Mr. Jefferson, that 'the ball of the Revolution received its first impulse, not from the actors in that event, but from the first colonists."   The latter emigrated to America in search of civil and religious freedom; they fled hither with a hatred toward the shackles which feudal institutions and the canon law imposed upon the soul.   The spirit of revolt against oppression originated in England, and went with Robinson's congregation to Holland; thence it emigrated in the Mayflower to Plymouth, and became the basis of all the legislation put forth by the wisest of colonists.   Our Pilgrim Fathers moulded their social compacts and ecclesiastical government in direct opposition to the systems under which they had been so severely oppressed.   But this spirit of freedom, which had been developing from the first planting of the

colonies, England attempted to quell. The chief resistance was made to her aggressive measures in Massa
chusetts, because that colony was selected for the first
trial of tyrannic control. We have seen, however,
that the south was as prompt to resist as her more
oppressed brethren at the north.

The historian of Greece records the names of *ten*
distinguished orators who resisted the Macedonian
conqueror, and the persons of whom he demanded, as
being hostile to his supremacy. Our youthful colonies,
soon after the conflict was commenced by the venerated
patriots already named, presented an array of orators
equal in number and efficiency to those of any land.
Henry, Lee, and Randolph, in the south, and Otis,
Samuel Adams, John Adams, Josiah Quincy, Hamilton,
and others, in the north, rose in grandeur and usefulness
as the storm increased; showing that they were the
voices and the beacon-fires which God had toned and
lighted for the welfare of mankind.

Several coincidences in our early history are remarkable. The first and last battle-fields of the Revolution
are almost within sight of the colleges where our leading
patriots were educated, and the rostra where the first popular debates occurred. All the chief orators of New
England were graduated at Harvard; the popular discussions which led to actual conflict with the mother-
country took place in the public buildings of Boston,
and the first great battle for freedom raged on Bunker
Hill.

The chief leaders of the patriotic party in the south
were educated at the college of William and Ma

Jefferson, then a student, heard Patrick Henry's first eloquent denunciation of oppression almost under the eaves of his Alma Mater, as John Adams, then a young man, heard Otis when he first attacked the principle of unjust taxation in the north. In the immediate neighborhood of Williamsburg, Cornwallis surrendered, and the long struggle of the Revolutionary war was closed. Thus the ball rested near where it received its first impulse. Without those colleges to discipline our heroical fathers, how different would have been the destinies of the world! Long may the venerable halls remain, and there

"Long may young Genius shed his sparkling ray,
And throw his emanations bright around."

The apostles of liberty in America, like the original preachers of our holy religion, first proclaimed their doctrines to a few fishermen; men of toil and enterprise, such as Burke described: "While we follow them among the tumbling mountains of ice, and behold them penetrating into the deepest frozen recesses of Hudson's Bay and Davis' Straits; while we are looking for them beneath the arctic circle, we hear that they have pierced into the opposite region of polar cold: that they are at the antipodes, and engaged under the frozen serpent of the south. Falkland Island, which seemed too remote an object for the grasp of national ambition, is but a stage and resting-place in the progress of their victorious industry. Nor is the equinoctial heat more discouraging to them than the accumulated winter of both the poles. We know that while some of them draw the line and strike the harpoon on the coast of Africa, others run the longitude and pursue their gigantic game along the coasts of Brazil. No sea but is vexed by their fisheries; no climate that is not witness to their toils. Neither the perseverance of Holland, nor the activity of France, nor the dexterous and firm sagacity of English enterprise, ever carried this most perilous mode of hardy industry to the extent to which it has been pushed by this recent people; a people who are still, as it were, but in the gristle, and not yet hardened into the bone of manhood.

"When I contemplate these things; when I know that the colonies in general owe little or nothing to any care of ours, and that they are not squeezed into this happy form by the constraints of a watchful and suspicious government, but that through a wise and salutary neglect a generous nature has been suffered to take her own way to perfection; when I reflect upon these effects; when I see how profitable they have been to us, I feel all the pride of power sink, and all presumption in the wisdom of human contrivances melt and die away within me; my rigor relents; I pardon something to the spirit of liberty."

Such being the spirit of enterprise among the colonists in their efforts to obtain an honest livelihood on the land and on the sea, we cannot suppose that they would long submit to oppressive exactions. Popular discussions of popular wrongs soon became frequent, and one of the most noted places of gathering was around *Liberty Tree.* This was a majestic elm, a species peculiar to America, and one of the grandest trees in

the world. It stood opposite where now stands the
Boyston Market, with its immense branches over-
spreading the street. Governor Bernard, writing to
Lord Hillsborough, in a letter dated Boston, June 16,
1768, gives the following description of the renowned
spot:

"Your lordship must know that Liberty Tree is a
large old elm in the High-street, upon which the effigies
were hung in the time of the Stamp-Act, and from
whence the mobs at that time made their parades. It
has since been adorned with an inscription, and has
obtained the name of Liberty Tree, as the ground under
it has that of Liberty Hall. In August last, just before
the commencement of the present troubles, they erected
a flag-staff, which went through the tree and a good
deal above the top of the tree. Upon this they hoist a
flag as a signal for the 'Sons of Liberty,' as they are
called. I gave my Lord Shelburne an account of this
erection at the time it was made. This tree has often
put me in mind of Jack Cade's 'Oak of Reformation.'"

The towering elm thus referred to was the grand
rallying-point for the ancient Sons of Liberty. On its
sturdy trunk notices of tyrannical movements and calls
to resist the same were wont to appear in the night,
nobody could tell from whence; from its lofty branches
obnoxious functionaries were often suspended in ridiculous representations, nobody could tell by whom.
For instance, on the fourteenth of August, 1765, an
effigy of Mr. Oliver, recently appointed to distribute the
stamps, and a *boot* (emblematical of Lord Bute) with
the devil peeping out of it with the Stamp-Act in his

nand, and various other satirical emblems, here appeared in the manner described. By this time, so strong had the popular indignation become, that the sheriffs, when ordered to the task by Chief Justice Hutchinson, declined the danger of removing the pageantry from the tree. It would seem that on this spot "liberty-poles" originated, and one now marks the site of the tree so dear to our fathers; a locality thrilling indeed in its associations.

To the thoughtful American, as he perambulates Boston and its vicinity, there are many scenes calculated to arrest and strongly to absorb attention; but, all things considered, perhaps no place in New England is more interesting than Faneuil Hall. We have already alluded to several distinguished battle-fields of early American eloquence, each of which is remarkable for the conquest of some grand and specific principle of freedom. The old State-House, the head-quarters of colonial government in Boston, was the arena on which unrighteous taxation was combatted and the true ground won. The House of Burgesses, at Williamsburg, was the field on which open rebellion against Parliament was first declared, and Hanover court-house, in the same colony, was the blessed spot whereon priestly rule was effectually destroyed; but Faneuil Hall will be forever memorable for still more noble and enduring associations. Within those venerable walls transpired not so much the work of destruction as construction; patriots therein not only resisted wrong, but they elicited and moulded into practical use the elements of what is right and good; while they pulled down antique forms of government, they at the same time built up a new order of political and moral architecture the most symmetrical and sublime.

Three prominent features characterize our republican institutions; universal representation. free discussion, and the decision of all questions by majorities. It is easy to demonstrate where these fundamental principles were first established.

The " town-meetings" of New England were entirely a new feature introduced to the world in connection with political reform. A noted one was held in Faneuil Hall on the twelfth of September, 1768. Dr. Cooper opened the exercises with prayer. A letter written to the commissioners of the British government, by one of their spies, gives us some interesting details with respect to the customs and feelings that prevailed in the popular meetings of those times. The informer tells .hem that the people met in Faneuil Hall; that Mr. Otis was chosen moderator, and was received with an universal clapping of hands; that the hall not being large enough to contain them, they adjourned to Dr. Sewall's meeting-house; that after several motions, and the appointing a deputation to wait on his excellency, they agreed to adjourn to the next afternoon ; "the moderator first making a speech to the inhabitants, strongly recommending peace and good order, and the grievances the people labored under might be in time removed; if not, and we were called on to defend our liberties and privileges, he hoped and believed we should one and all resist, even unto blood; but at the same time, prayed Almighty God it migh never so happen."

. Thus was the right of free discussion in a popular assembly asserted and exercised, and the still higher right
of universal suffrage connected therewith. The show
of hands decided every question, and the hard hand of
the laboring man counted as much as that which signed
orders for tens of thousands. Such gatherings and dis
cussions had the most salutary effects. The people be
came acquainted with each other, and felt the need of
mutual dependence as well as mutual restraint. The
influence of every man was estimated according to his
personal worth. In the popular strife for universal freedom, they struck upon the fundamental principle of republicanism, that the majority must rule; it was this
that gave each member of an assembly a pride in maintaining its decisions, as he thereby fortified his own judgment and self-respect. No sooner had these meetings,
actuated and controlled by such original and exalted
principles, began to be held in the "Cradle of Liberty,"
than the sagacious Burke recognized and proclaimed
their superior dignity. Said he of the colonists: "Their
governments are popular in a high degree; some are
merely popular, in all the popular representative is the
most weighty; and this share of the people in their ordinary government never fails to inspire them with lofty
sentiments and with a strong aversion for whatever tends
to deprive them of their chief importance." But what
this magnanimous statesman approved, others maligned.
Governor Bernard vilified the character of the popular
meetings, to which misrepresentations the "Vindication
of the Town of Boston," written by Otis, replied as follows: "The governor has often been observed to dis

cover an aversion to free assemblies ; no wonder then
that he should be so particularly disgusted at a legal
meeting of the town of Boston, where a noble freedom
of speech is ever expected and maintained ; an assembly
of which it may be justly said, to borrow the language
of the ancient Roman, 'They think as they please, and
speak as they think.' Such an assembly has ever been
the dread and often the scourge of tyrants."

The struggle between the metropolis of New England
and the British government was severe, and continued
from the time of the Stamp-Act, in 1765, till the evacua-
tion of the foreign troops in 1776. Every walk of industrious life and every profession, the bar, the pulpit
and the press, combined to give intensity and efficiency
to the civil war. As an indication of the plainness and
power of the latter, the following anecdote will suffice.
A negro, whose principles were like his master's, a tool
of foreign despotism, one day met Mr. Edes, the printer
of the Boston Gazette, which was the devoted organ of
the patriots, and inquired of him what was the news.
The printer replied that there was nothing new. "Well,"
said the sable aristocrat, "if you've nothing new, Massa
Edes, I s'pose you print the same old lie over again."

It is important to remember, that in all the excitements of those times ; the vexations that arrested commerce ; the irritations produced by the presence of mercenary troops ; the menaces of arrogant officers, and
even the massacre of several citizens in open day ; de-
spite all sorts of provocations and the most favorable
opportunities for revenge, during the whole period of the
Revolution not a single life was destroyed by the Bos-

tonians, either by assassination, mob law, or public execution.

In the meantime, the meetings in Faneuil Hall and other large public edifices were spreading the most salutary influence over the country. The town-meetings and provincial assemblies were the arenas wherein the people were trained and armed intellectually for the great battle of independence. It was then that orators, fitted expressly for that preparatory work, like Otis and Henry, appeared, and consummated their exalted task. Driven at the points of British bayonets from Williamsburg, the noble band of Virginia patriots were still loyal to the highest duty. The Old Dominion continued to respond to the Bay State; the "Old Church" at Richmond echoed back in tones of thunder the patriotic cries that rang from Faneuil Hall.

Hallowed are the associations connected with that venerable church in Richmond! Often has the writer sought its precincts alone, and pondered there on the scene when, within the walls yet standing, Henry, as the embodiment of the Revolution and all its sublime results, rose like one inspired, and delivered that speech unequalled in the history of man, ending with the ominous words, "*Give me liberty, or give me death!*" It was in the same burst of transcendent eloquence that the phrase, "After all, we must fight!" first broke on the popular ear, and fired the universal heart. The history of that expression is interesting, as showing the close relations that subsisted between the north and south in all the Revolutionary struggle. They are the expression of a quiet Puritan in the interior of Massachusetts, given

to the world on wings of fire by the bold Cavalier of
Virginia. The facts are stated as follows, in a letter
from John Adams to William Wirt:

"When Congress had finished their business, as they
thought, in the autumn of 1774, I had with Mr. Henry,
before we took leave of each other, some familiar conversation, in which I expressed a full conviction that
our resolves, declarations of rights, enumeration of
wrongs, petitions, remonstrances and addresses, associations and non-importation agreements, however they
might be expected in America, and however necessary
to cement the union of the colonies, would be but waste
paper in England. Mr. Henry said they might make
some impression upon the people of England, but agreed
with me that they would be totally lost upon the government. I had but just received a short and hasty letter,
written to me by Major Joseph Hawley, of Northamp-
ton, containing 'a few broken hints,' as he called them,
of what he thought was proper to be done, and concluding with those words, 'After all, we must fight!' This
letter I read to Mr. Henry, who listened with great attention; and as soon as I had pronounced the words,
'After all, we must fight,' he raised his head, and with
an energy and vehemence that I can never forget, broke
out with 'By God, I am of that man's mind!' I put
the letter into his hand, and when he had read it, he returned it to me, with an equally solemn asseveration
that he agreed entirely in opinion with the writer. I
considered this as a sacred oath, upon a very great occasion, (and would have sworn it as religiously as he
did,) and by no means inconsistent with what you say,

in some part of your book, that he never took the sacred name in vain.

" As I knew the sentiments with which Mr. Henry left Congress in the autumn of 1774, and knew the chapter and verse from which he had borrowed the sublime expression, ' We must fight,' I was not at all surprised at your history, in the hundred and twenty-second page in the note, and in some of the preceding and following pages. Mr. Henry only pursued, in March, 1775, the views and vows of November, 1774.

" The other delegates from Virginia returned to their State, in full confidence that all our grievances would be redressed. The last words that Mr. Richard Henry Lee said to me when we parted, were : ' *We shall infallibly carry all our points ; you will be completely relieved ; all the offensive Acts will be repealed ;* the army and fleet will be recalled, and Britain will give up her foolish project.'

" Washington only was in doubt. He never spoke in public. In private he joined with those who advocated a non-exportation, as well as a non-importation agreement. With both he thought we should prevail; without either he thought it doubtful. Henry was clear in one opinion, Richard Henry Lee in an opposite opinion, and Washington doubted between the two. Henry, however, appeared in the end to be exactly in the right."

It is evident that John Adams and Patrick Henry parted on the above occasion with a perfect identity of sentiment, and returned to their respective colonies to urge on the crisis which they saw was inevitable. Henry acquitted himself of his duty at Richmond, as has been already described. Adams rejoined his distinguished colleagues in the popular movements in Faneuil Hall. To describe the immediate and remote consequences of those movements, we cannot do better than by employing the following extract from Daniel Webster : "No where can be found higher proofs of a spirit that was ready to hazard all, to pledge all, to sacrifice all, in the cause of the country. Instances were not unfrequent in which small free-holders parted with their last hoof and the last measure of corn from their granaries, to supply provision for the troops and hire service for the ranks. The voice of Otis and of Adams in Faneuil Hall found its full and true echo in the little councils of the interior towns ; and if within the Continental Con gress patriotism shone more conspicuously, it did no, there exist more truly, nor burn more fervently ; it did not render the day more anxious or the night more sleepless ; it sent up no more ardent prayer to God for succor, and it put forth in no greater degree the fullness of its effort and the energy of its whole soul and spirit in the common cause, than it did in the small assemblies of the towns."

Those primary meetings, we remark again, which soon began to prevail throughout the country, served to enlighten all classes, and became the firmest cement to bind them together, when a comprehensive and combined effort was demanded. The source and model of those assemblies was in the "Cradle of Liberty," happily yet extant. Long may it remain one of the most hallowed spots on the globe. What men have there spoken, and what events have therein tran-

spired ! What American can ever ascend to that Forum
without standing enthralled by the intensity of thrilling
associations ? Here, as in the famous area where the
masters of the world were wont of old to address the
Roman people, the applause of venerated patriots mingled with the tones of kindred orators, cheered and fortified them in the exposure of crime, the vindication of
justice, and the defence of freedom. Here, too, as there
are palpable reminiscences of the heroic past. Every
foot of the Forum at Rome was hallowed by the memory
of some great domestic or national event. Columns and
arches and temples testified on all sides the devotion of
individuals and the triumphs of the republic. Standing
in Faneuil Hall, one sees not only the colonnades, the
galleries, the floor and the ceiling of the vast gathering-
place of early patriots, the battle-field of consummate eloquence, but there, too, are the artistic forms of some who
mingled in the sternest strife of our country's darkest
days. Would that the walls were all granite, and the
roof iron, firm and enduring as the souls whose memories are for ever linked with the locality, and that, from
niches all round this theatre of most glorious deeds, the
marble forms of all the chief actors might look down
upon interminable generations of American freemen.

We come, finally, to consider the most glorious battle-
field of all ; the Congress of '76. Everything has been
prepared for the grand and decisive blow. Providence
summons the whole country to a general council in Philadelphia, and the choicest spirits of every section are
prompt to obey. What were the thoughts that accompanied those patriots, as they turned their backs upon

every thing dear around home's hearth, and set their faces toward a common altar, journeying up thither with the determination to consecrate everything to the public weal? It is certain that they were capable of properly appreciating the perils that encompassed them, as well as the benefits which might flow from the efforts they designed to make. Never was there a popular assembly of politicians that comprised a greater proportion of highly educated members. Nearly one-half were graduates of colleges at home or abroad. Some were self-educated, in the best school, and to the highest degree. The ancient poets taught that Astræa, the goddess of Justice, had her last residence among unsophisticated husbandmen before she quitted the earth. The Genius of Liberty found a rural home in our land ere she was throned by general acclamation at Carpenter's Hall, in the central colony of America. Twenty-five of the fifty-six immortal men had trod the soil and studied in the institutions of Great Britain. Among those who had not received university laurels, were philosophers like Franklin and jurists like Roger Sherman.

In this connection, we should not forget the stripling surveyor, born on the banks of the Potomac, beneath a farmer's roof, and early left an orphan. No academy aided his youthful aspirations, no college crowned him with its honors. But industry and integrity provided for the best education of his great natural powers " Himself his own cook, having no spit but a forked stick, no plate but a large chip," at sixteen years of age, he is found roaming over the Alleghanies and along the Shenandoah, training himself under the eye of Heaven, one day to be the hope and leader of a nation in arms. Most truly might he have said:

> " To rear me was the task of power divine,
> Supremest wisdom and primeval love."

In the language of Sparks, "Happy was it for America, happy for the world, that a great name, a guardian genius, presided over destinies in war, combining more than the virtues of the Roman Fabius, and the Theban Epaminondas, and compared with whom, the conquerors of the world, the Alexanders and Cæsars, are but pageants crimsoned with blood and decked with the trophies of slaughter, objects equally of the wonder and the execration of mankind. The hero of America was the conqueror only of his country's foes, and the hearts of his countrymen. To the one he was a terror, and in the other he gained an ascendancy, supreme, unrivalled, the tribute of admiring gratitude, the reward of a nation's love—our WASHINGTON !"

The congress of '76 has assembled, and solemn prayer has just been offered for the divine blessing on the country and in behalf of the patriotic cause. Let us enter the hall and contemplate the august assemblage. The first thing that strikes us is, the wonderful diversity of character present, constituting a perfect whole. The quality that is deficient in one, in another superabounds; where one is wise to construct a theory, another is equally skilful to demonstrate its practicability. Whether we desire severe logical deduction, or gorgeous rhetorical expression; whether it be necessary to convince the judgment or inflame the passions: no models can in

3

the world be found superior to those here congregated.

In the President's chair sits Hancock, crowned with
a demeanor graceful and splendid, like "blazing Hype-
rion on his orbed throne." Prominent in the heroic band,
and oldest of their number, is he who at the same time
snatched the lightnings from the skies and the sceptre
from the oppressor's hand. There, too, is Morris, the
financier of the Revolution, whose generous aid, advanced on his own credit, paved the way for the victories at Trenton and Princeton, and in the gloomiest hour
caused the American eagle to soar aloft toward Heaven.
More retired, but not less interested, is that old Puritan, Samuel Adams, "on his front, engraven thought
and public care." He was among the very first to excite
popular rebellion against wrong, and he is here to aid its
progress and pray for its consummation. Of few words,
but abounding in great and beneficent deeds, he sits in
council grave and taciturn, like "gray-haired Saturn
quiet as a stone," his soul firm as granite and unbending
before the storm. His more oratorical namesake, John
Adams. with watchful eye and ear is scanning the proceedings; while every look and motion betrays his readiness to exemplify his favorite maxim, "I would rather be
in the wrong with Plato than in the right with Epicurus."
Lee, with inimitable suavity and elaborate grace, moves
in chivalrous majesty on the scene. Witherspoon, the
divine, "visibly written blessed in his looks," is there,
with the meekness of a minister of Jesus Christ, but
with a firmness that never quailed in the presence of his
country's foe. In the alternative between the sacrifice

of freedom or the loss of life, like the Spartan mother, ne would rather have seen his son brought home a corpse upon his shield, than dishonored by its loss. And Rutledge, the youngest of the patriots, comes forward to illustrate in his own person the ancient apologue of the youthful Hercules, in the pride and strength of beauty, surrendering his entire soul to the worship of exalted virtue. But it is needless any further to specify; all, as one man, are ready to exclaim, our mother is America, our battle is for freedom, purity of purpose is our breastplate, and the favor of Heaven is our shield.

In the momentous proceedings of July 4th, 1776, we miss the persons of several of the most famous men in our colonial and revolutionary history. Their absence strikingly indicates the care of Providence in all great events. Bold and daring patriots, with the most intrepid zeal, had long since roused the colonies and stung them into indignation against tyrannic wrongs. Those pioneers of national prosperity had urged on the fearful crisis, and at length the period had arrived when everything was at stake. But when counsel was needed most, and the action of sublime statesmanship commenced, the men of passion declined, their mission being gloriously fulfilled. He who rules over all withdrew them from the scene. Otis, disabled by a brutal attack made on him by a British emissary, lay secluded from public life. Henry was indeed sent up to Congress, with one effort of almost divine eloquence to break the spell that at first bound the assembly in awful silence, then he withdrew, and was little heard of more The successors of these primitive patriots were not less resolute, but more discreet. A consciousness of the fearful responsibility devolved upon them by their position, seems to have rendered them solemnly reflective and sublimely self-possessed. To describe their eloquence will be the purpose of subsequent chapters ; at present, we will look only at one grand event and its associations—the *Declaration of Independence.*

One whom we have not yet named, but in some respects the most renowned of men, Jefferson, appears before Congress, bearing in his hand that noblest of all documents not the result of inspired wisdom. " Whether we regard it as a specimen of strong and fervid eloquence, of manly remonstrance, or of deep and solemn appeal, it is every way sustained and wonderful. The writer speaks as if he felt himself to be the voice of a great and outraged people, giving indignant utterance to its many wrongs and oppressions, and in face of Heaven, and the whole earth for witnesses, declaring that they shall be endured no longer."

The question was on the adoption of the Declaration. We should consider the character of that document, and the circumstances under which it was reported. It has been called the Chart of American Freedom; but it was vastly more elevated than the famous Magna Charta wrung from King John at Runnymede. There is some resemblance in the original of the two documents, but their spirit is very little alike. John Lackland, as he was called, levied heavy contributions on the barons, and seized at his pleasure their beasts of burden and agricultural implements. This touched the selfish interests of the owners of the serfs and soil. It is a singu lar fact that the great instrument of English freedom had no nobler origin than this. It seems still more strange that one Article of that great charter forbids the destruction of houses, woods, or *men*, without the special permission of the proprietor, who had full power over the life of Englishmen. The haughty slave-holding barons who extorted Magna Charta from King John, did not in the least consult the welfare of the plebeian orders. *Nullus liber homo*, is its domineering phraseology. The vassals who were chained to the soil, were left just where Magna Charta found them. No mistake can be greater than to suppose that the war of the barons against the infamous king was waged for the benefit of the great mass of the people, or that the treaty of Runnymede secured *their* liberties. Certain great privileges were exacted, it is true, but the end designed was far aside from popular freedom.

On the other hand, the first sentence in the American Chart of '76 recognizes the equality of mankind, and the Declaration proceeds to demand the highest privileges for all. The conflicts in which our fathers signalized their courage and their strength were in the defence of exalted principles, and the resources they chiefly relied on were moral. They did not desire to arm themselves in the spirit of those

" Whose game was empires, and whose stakes were thrones,
Whose table earth; whose dice were human bones."

The circumstances under which that Declaration was reported and discussed were of the most impressive character. A proposition was brought forward in favor of separating the colonies from the parent country. The grand question then agitated was between power and right. The orators seemed to feel and speak as if they clearly saw that in the decision then to be made lay the liberties of three millions of colonists, as well as the hopes of all the civilized nations that should thenceforth people the earth. The depositaries of the immediate and prospective rights of mankind were not unfaithful to their trust. They seceded from their age and elevated themselves above it. They emerged from the dubious atmosphere of ordinary views, and stood in calm grandeur on the serenest heights of political prophecy. They assembled around the sacred shrine of liberty, and under the influence of the loftiest inspiration, consulted the eternal wants of man, and legislated for all coming time. Napoleon said to his staff as they entered the battle of the Pyramids, "Think that forty centuries look down upon you from the summits of yonder monuments." But our patriotic sires took a more comprehensive view, from a higher point, and under convictions of a more solemn cast. With a full consciousness of the perils they incurred, they voted for the Declaration.

A classic poet has described Heaven itself as surveying with pleasure the scene of "a brave man struggling with the storms of fate." If this is allowable, we think a much sublimer spectacle is presented by a brave nation struggling for freedom and independence, especially when the odds are so great as in the instance under consideration ; a few feeble colonies on one side, numerous disciplined troops, veteran skill, and all the vast resources of despotic power on the other. But the question was not what is safety to ourselves, but what is duty to our constituents, our successors, the world. Each man of them seems to have set his name to that immortal pledge with the feelings with which Leonidas, in view of inevitable and speedy immolation on the altar of his country, exclaimed:

"But ye rocks of Thermopylæ, free mountains and happy plains, ye will remain!"

The Congress of '76 was a more than Amphictyonic council, in the intelligence and devotion of which one might safely predict the perpetuity of national strength at home and increasing influence abroad. Profound and impassioned consecration possessed every breast, united the Congress in one purpose, and electrified the whole continent. Every faculty of the human soul was summoned to the highest duty, and braced up to the most intense exertion. The light then kindled in Independence Hall seemed to be immediately reflected back from every cottage in America, and at every moment since has gone on spreading wider and brighter over prison and palace round the globe.

The pen with which the several signatures were made on the Declaration of Independence is now in the cabinet of the Massachusetts Historical Society, together with a sealed vial full of tea, caught in the shoes of one of the "Mohawks" who destroyed the obnoxious cargoes in Boston harbor. What American can look upon those memorials without emotions of the purest and most thrilling gratitude?

Those patriots have all passed away, each one deserv-

ing the encomium of Pericles, "No citizen through their
means ever put on mourning:"

> "They were below, ere they arrived in heaven,
> So mighty in renown, as every muse
> Might grace her triumph with them."

The brightest thing about the Congress of '76 was the
integrity which its members pledged in behalf of their
common country. Their lives were dear to them, their
fortunes were ample, but their sacred honor was their
choicest wealth and greatest glory. They encountered
hardships of the most fearful magnitude, and temptations
of the greatest power, but not one of them hesitated a
moment in his allegiance to duty, or swerved in the
slightest degree from the discharge of it. They were
not only all true to their solemn vows, but not a single
stain ever soiled the escutcheon of one of them. They
were republicans to the last. The noble sentiments
proclaimed to the world on July 4th, 1776, their authors
never belied. As a class, they were remarkably frugal
and temperate, and nearly all of them lived to extreme
old age. For intelligence, patriotism, purity of life and
loyalty to country, the history of the world at large has
nothing to compare with the names of the immortal
fifty-six.

If other battle-fields are interesting in their associations, what shall we shall say of that glory of Philadelphia, Independence Hall? "If there be a spot upon
earth," says Doctor Clarke, "pre-eminently calculated
to awaken the solemn sentiments, which such a view of
nature is fitted to make upon all men, it may surely be

found in the plain of Marathon; where, amidst the wreck of generations, and the graves of ancient heroes, we elevate our thoughts towards Him, 'in whose sight a thousand years are but as yesterday;' where the still-ness of Nature; harmonizing with the calm solitude of that illustrious region, which once was the scene of the most agitated passions, enables us, by the past, to deter-mine of the future. In those moments, indeed, we may be said to live for ages; a single instant, by the multitude of impressions it conveys, seems to anticipate for us a sense of that eternity 'when time shall be no more;' when the fitful dream of human existence, with all its turbulent illusions, shall be dispelled; and the last sun having set, in the last of the world, a brighter dawn than ever gladdened the universe, shall renovate the domin-ions of darkness and of death."

But to the free citizens of this continent, the power of local associations is more powerful in the precincts of Independence Hall than on the plains of Marathon. Collisions with a mightier foe, and deeds of daring put forth for richer conquests, took place there, than when heroic Greeks grappled with the Persian host. What history, what picture, could ever tell the half of what is suggested to every intelligent and susceptible mind on entering that venerable hall? Who is not immediately carried back to that day, thenceforth memorable for ever, when an awful stillness pervaded the assembly for several moments previous to voting "that these United Colonies are and of right out to be, free and independent states?" What devotion then filled that consecrated place, and rose to heaven in silent prayer for firmness, unanimity

3*

and deathless resolve! One almost hears Hancock suggesting to Franklin, "We must all hang together now."
"Yes," is the characteristic response of that plain old
Nestor of patriots, "we must indeed all hang together,
or most assuredly we shall all hang separately."

Perhaps the only edifice in the world invested with
associations at all comparable with this, was the old
Parliament House in Westminster. It was there that
the Commons, in their feebleness, sent for the prelates
to aid their consultations. Afterward, when the days
of "the usurping blood of Lancaster" were past, and the
power of the Tudors and the Stuarts were trophies in
their hands, the same "poor Commons" abrogated the
arrogant rights of the peerage, and destroyed the very
prelacy for whose counsel they had once sued. There
Charles had come to seize the obnoxious members;
and in the Chamber adjoining the Commons, Stafford
and Laud had pleaded. There, in 1653, Cromwell
entered, dismissed the attendants, locked the doors, and
made himself, as Protector, the council of a nation upon
whose council chamber was seen inscribed, "This house
to let, unfurnished." That room, the cradle of English
freedom, had witnessed the consummation of govern-
mental power, and its greatest possible restrictions
within regal limits. From 1688 to its destruction it
had been the arena of the greatest eloquence and most
impressive scenes. There, Shaftsbury and Bolingbroke
had spoken; there from 1740, the contentions of successive parties, animated and adorned by the speeches
of Walpole, Windham, Pulteney, Chatham, Burke, Pitt,
Fox and Sheridan, had been fought with a passionate

strength of intellect, and the mighty excitement produced by the conflict of gigantic minds. When that
ancient palace of legislation was consumed, it was
indeed a mournful sight. To all the English nation,
and their colonies in every clime, a link in the chain of
historic interest and thrilling associations was destroyed.
A splendid new palace for Parliament is now rising on
the same site. In accordance with the laws of mind,
and with a wise respect for the distinguished dead, the
commissioners of the realm have recently reported in
respect thereto that, "as St. Stephen's Hall stands on
the spot where the House of Commons was, during
many centuries, in the habit of assembling, it should be
adorned with statues of men who rose to eminence by
the eloquence and abilities which they displayed in that
house."

But the great battle-field whereon our fathers met that
Parliament in its most august display of oratorical talent,
braved that great kingdom with all its consolidated
strength, and won the day under the most fearful odds,
yet remains. The heroes indeed are departed, but here
before us is still open their scene of action. Death has
claimed them, but war and wasting elements have spared
the theatre of their stupendous struggle. We can go
and meditate there, gazing at the places where they sat,
the floor on which they stood, the windows through
which the bright sun looked in smilingly upon their sublime transactions, and may touch the walls which seem
yet to vibrate to the thunders of their eloquence.

Long may those walls remain, the Mecca of a worship
holier than the Saracen's; and when they shall have

passed away, may the genius of American Art, harmonious with the Genius of Liberty, her best patron, and
commemorative of her grandest work, here come, and in
a worthy master-piece heave up a monument which shall
perish only

> " When wrapped in fire the realms of ether glow,
> And heaven's last thunders shake the world below."

Yes, the men of the Congress of '76 have passed away,
but let us hope that the spirit they evoked, and which
guided them to victory, is not yet become obsolete.
Their laurels freshen in eternal bloom on their sepulchres,
and their posthumous influence is busy everywhere dis-
enthralling the world.   May the flame kindled on the
national altar in the first true Hall of Freedom, to illuminate and consecrate the Declaration of Independence
in America, burn with inextinguishable splendor, quicken
every tardy pulse with patriotic zeal, and blast to cinders every fetter and every tyrant's accursed three .

CHAPTER II

JAMES OTIS,

ORATOR OF INTREPID PASSION

THE planting of English colonies in America was the beginning of an influence which stopped not at their original boundaries. The world has witnessed its expansion. The human race has felt its power. To the world then—to the human race—belongs their influence, and in that their greatest glory.

We are becoming a great nation, and already, perhaps, are accustomed to contemplate the Colonial period of our history as a juvenile era. But, in one sense, we nave had no national infancy. We have had no age of barbarism, no gradual transition from an obscure antiquity, with much primitive degradation adhering to our career. America, visited by the Anglo-Saxon race, like the statue of Prometheus touched by heavenly fire, awoke in adult vigor. Her first cry was for freedom, and her first struggle won it. We began with the experience of sixty centuries. We laid our foundations in the results which accompanied and glorified the opening drama of a new world—the sternest battle ever fought by right against power.

About the period of the first settlement of this coun

try, the mental productions before the public in England, were of the highest excellence. The discussion of constitutional principles, and the fervid strife for toleration in religious matters, had called forth the most potent intellectual energies, and produced some of the profoundest works in divinity and politics, to be found in any age or tongue. As in the ancient republics, and as is the fact in every land where the mind of man is allowed freely to act and speak, the most eloquent writers and profoundest orators were on the side of liberty and the rights of the people. As instances and proofs of this, put Locke and Algernon Sidney by the side of Filmer and the other parasitical advocates of the divine right of kings. It is a wholesome lesson and a vigorous discipline, to read the leading authors of England who flourished between the accession of Charles the First and George of Hanover.

The germs of great principles began to spring up abroad, but their first productive growth was in American soil. A great truth was first proclaimed by our hardy Colonists, which has since traversed oceans, and aroused continents. It is impossible to exaggerate its ultimate effects, not merely upon this western hemisphere, but upon the father-land and the remotest east. The first throbs of liberty here created the tremendous revolutions of Europe, the convulsive spasms of which still agitate the oppressed of all lands. The experiment which demonstrated the practicability of establishing a self-governing republic over a vast domain, is an example which it will be impossible for aristocracies, kings, and emperors, either to resist or restrain

It was an era of vast energy, a combinat'on of physical force and profound erudition, exemplified by the French in the prodigies which they executed while truly inspired by the genius of liberty. A little army, composed of soldiers and scholars, subdued cities and penetrated citadels, planted institutes and observatories, schools of agriculture, and all the arts of civilization, from the valley of the Rhine to the Delta of Egypt.

But in the birth-place of that spirit, on the sublimer field of its primitive conflict and most glorious conquest, in the American colonies, the main force was mental rather than martial. Eloquence, then, was fervid, bold, and gigantic. like the Revolution it defended. Then, genius was hailed as a divine gift. No trammels were imposed upon imagination—no drag-chains crippled patriotic aspirations—no limit marked the boundaries up to which daring thought might go.

It should be neither uninteresting nor unprofitable to glance back upon those times, and contemplate a few of the leading minds. In a sense equally elevated, and more relevant to ourselves than Milton expressed, let us—

> " To the famous orators repair,
> Those ancients, whose resistless eloquence
> Wielded at will that fierce democracy,
> Shook the arsenal, and fulmined over Greece
> To Macedon and Artaxerxes' throne."

In considering the eloquence of the Colonial and Revolutionary period of our history, we shall find less variety in the works of the orators than in the orators themselves So absorbed were the statesmen of those days in the immediate and pressing avocations of the crisis, that they bestowed little or no strength on tasks not imperiously exacted by great public duties. But we shall find such men as Otis, and Adams, and Henry, and Hamilton, and Ames, fine embodiments of our early eloquence. They were among the great and gifted spirits of the heroic age of American oratory, and will for ever illustrate the grandeur of its mental grasp, the wealth of its magnificence, and the splendor of its im- perishable glories.

The Otis family, now widely extended in this country and a good deal distinguished, derived their origin from John Otis, who came over from England at a very early period, and was one of the first settlers of Hingham, Mass. He took the freeman's oath on the 3d of March, 1635 By his mother's side, he was connected with the first founders of Plymouth Colony, who arrived in the *May- flower*, in 1620.

James Otis, the illustrious subject of this sketch, de- scended in the fifth generation from the first of the name in this country, was born at Great Marshes, in what is now called West Barnstable, Feb. 5th, 1725. He was carefully prepared for college under the care of Rev. Jonathan Russell, the clergyman of the parish, and en- tered Harvard in June, 1739. The first years of his college course he seems to have devoted more to social en joyment than severe mental discipline; but in his junior year he changed his habits, and by the greatest industry did much to redeem lost time. He graduated in 1743 and in due order took his second degree.

Of his juvenile traits of character, little can now be

gleaned. It is known that when he came home from college, his love of study was intense and perpetual. In general he was meditative and grave, but occasionally was gay and sarcastic. He sometimes beguiled the weariness of abstract speculation by playing on a violin. A company of young people one day prevailed on him to treat them to a country dance. The set was made up, and when in the full tide of successful experiment, he suddenly stopped, as if struck with the folly of the pursuit, and hurling up his instrument, exclaimed, "So Orpheus fiddled, and so danced the brutes!" He rushed into a neighboring garden, and forsook the revel for a nobler occupation.

After completing the usual course of classical studies, Mr. Otis devoted two years to elegant literature, before entering upon the study of a profession. He was very fond of the best poets, and, in the zealous emulation of their beauties, he energized his spirit and power of expression. He did not merely read over the finest passages—he pondered them—he fused them into his soul—and reproduced their charms with an energy all his own. In the skill of pouring the whole spirit of an author into the most familiar extract, making the heart bleed at the sorrows of Hecuba, and the soul quake under the imprecations of Lear—a talent of the highest utility in popular address, and capable of being wielded to the noblest ends —James Otis excelled.

His education was liberal, in the true and noble sense of the term ; in science he was well grounded ; in elegant letters he was an accomplished scholar ; and to the end of his brilliant career he prosecuted his studies with

antiring industry. In the midst of innumerable professional toils, he wrote a valuable work on Latin Composition, and another on Greek Prosody, the latter of which
was never published, as there was then no Greek type
in the country, but remained in manuscript, and perished
with all the author's valuable papers.

In 1745, he began the study of law in the office of
Mr. Gridley, at that time the most eminent lawyer in
the Colony. Having finished his preparation for the
bar, he removed to Plymouth in 1748, and was admitted
to practice. Two years afterwards he removed to
Boston, and came rapidly into notice as an accomplished
advocate. His talents were in requisition far and near.
On one occasion he went to Halifax in the middle of
winter, to argue a very important cause. His private
studies were as incessant as his public labors were
honorable.

In the spring of 1775, Mr. Otis was married to Miss
Ruth Cunningham, the very beautiful and accomplished
daughter of a wealthy merchant. They had three children, one son and two daughters. Mrs. Otis is represented as having been a placid and formal matron, happily adapted to modify the impetuous genius and reck-
less daring which so peculiarly adapted her husband for
the great crisis of national affairs which he was destined
in a great degree both to create and control.

On November 26th, 1768, he addressed a letter to Mr.
Arthur Jones, in which intimations occur of the gathering storm. "All business is at a stand here, little going
on besides military musters and reviews, and other
parading of the red-coats, sent here, the Lord, I believe.

only knows for what. I am and have been long concerned, more for Great Britain than for the Colonies.
You may ruin yourselves, but you cannot in the end
ruin the Colonies. Our fathers were a good people; we
have been a free people, and if you will not let us remain so any longer, we shall be a great people, and the
present measures can have no tendency but to hasten,
with great rapidity, events which every good and honest
man would wish delayed for ages, if possible, prevented
for ever."

During the period of Colonial subordination, Otis was
the constant vindicator of American rights; and when
British usurpation became as burdensome as it was unjust, he defended his countrymen with an eloquence
whose ultimate influence transcended his own sublime
aspirations. He sowed the seeds of liberty in this new
world, without living to see the harvest, and, probably
without ever dreaming what magnificent crops would soon
be produced. But he seems to have felt himself predestined to an exalted public career, and knew that he occupied " a dreadful post of observation, darker every
hour."

Circumstances do not so much form men as reveal
them; they develope the royalty of those who are kings
without the name, and who, elevated by the tempest they
were born to rule, reign by force of character and grandeur of thought. Without ancestors and without pro-
geny, alone of their race, their mission is accomplished
when the occasion which demanded their existence is
passed, and they then disappear, leaving to the world
decrees which are sure to be performed.

In 1760, George the Second suddenly died, and his grandson reigned in his stead. Then were edicts issued which enabled the king's collectors to compel all sheriffs and constables to attend and aid them in breaking open houses, stores, cellars, ships, trunks, &c., &c., to search for goods which it was supposed had not paid the unrighteous taxes imposed by parliament, through the influence of the royal governors, and certain avaricious West India planters. Dreading the "obstinacy" of the Bostonians, the minions of power proposed to try their first experiment at Salem. But the Supreme Court, then sitting there, ordered that the "great question of the legality of the obnoxious measure should be argued in Boston." "The fire in the flint shines not till it be struck," and this was the occasion when Mr. Otis first became famous in history. When the order relating to the "Writs of Assistance," as they were called, came from England, he was Advocate-General of the Colony of Massachusetts. Deeming them to be illegal and tyrannical, he refused to enforce them, and resigned his office. At the request of the Colonists, he undertook to argue against the writs, and met in stern conflict his veteran law-teacher, Mr. Gridley, then Attorney-General. It was on the occasion of that great argument, that James Otis blazed forth, the bold, erudite, brilliant and victorious champion of Colonial rights. Knowing that he stood on the immovable foundation of justice, and conscious that he was fortified by the law, he gave a free rein to his oratorical powers, and soared into regions of patriotic principles new both to himself and the world. The doctrines he broached and the conclusions he deduced, fell like brands of fire on the summits of the political world, and kindled a conflagration destined to sunder every fetter, and enlighten every human mind.

The lucid impetuosity of that great speech, dazzled its antagonists into awe, and inspired a youthful spectator with a spirit of patriotism which lived through the subsequent struggle for national freedom, and on the memorable death-day of two Presidents, cried, amid shouting millions of happy citizens—" Liberty and Independence for ever !"

" Otis was a flame of fire," says John Adams, in his sketch of the scene. " With a promptitude of classical allusions, and a depth of research, a rapid summary of historical events and dates, a profusion of legal authorities, a prophetic glance of his eyes into futurity, and a rapid torrent of impetuous eloquence, he hurried away all before him. The seeds of patriots and heroes were then and there sown. Every man of an immensely crowded audience appeared to me to go away, as I did, ready to take arms against Writs of Assistance. Then and there was the first scene of the first act of opposition to the arbitrary claims of Great Britain. Then and there the child Independence was born. In fifteen years, that is, in 1776, he grew up to manhood, and declared himself free."

That spark kindled where it fell ; and we shall hereafter have occasion to show, how the third President of the United States was in a political sense born simultaneously with the first cry of liberty enunciated in the Colony of Virginia, by the great orator of the South ·

The question is, perhaps, more curious than profitable, which relates to the source and occasion of the first of that series of events which produced the war of the Revolution. Men have often asked, what was its original cause, and who struck the first blow? This inquiry was well answered by President Jefferson, in a letter to Dr. Waterhouse of Cambridge, written March 3d, 1818.

"I suppose it would be difficult to trace our Revolution to its first embryo. We do not know how long it was hatching in the British cabinet, before they ventured to make the first of the experiments which were to develop it in the end, and to produce complete parliamentary supremacy. Those you mention in Massachusetts as preceding the Stamp-Act might be the first visible symptoms of that design. The proposition of that Act, in 1764, was the first here. Your opposition, therefore, preceded ours, as occasion was sooner given there than here, and the truth, I suppose, is, that the opposition, in every colony, began whenever the encroachment was presented to it. This question of priority is as the inquiry would be, who first of the three hundred Spartans offered his name to Leonidas. I shall be happy to see justice done to the merits of all."

Leaving the question as to when and how the Revolution began, let us look at the aspect presented by this era in the career of Mr. Otis. He took the side of his country in the above legal contest, at great pecuniary sacrifice, and under other peculiar circumstances which made his decision irrevocable. He was transferred at once from the ranks of private life to the leadership of opposition against the designs of the British ministry

"Although," says President Adams, "Mr. Otis had never before interfered in public affairs, his exertions on this single occasion secured him a commanding popularity with the friends of their country, and the terror and vengeance of her enemies; neither of which ever deserted him."

In the primitive opposition made by Otis to the arbitrary acts of Trade, aided by the Writs of Assistance, he announced two maxims which lay at the foundation of all the subsequent war; one was, that "taxation without representation was tyranny," the other, "that expenditures of public money without appropriations by the representatives of the people, were arbitrary, and therefore unconstitutional." This early and acute sagacity of our statesmen, led Burke finely to describe the political feeling in America as follows; "In other countries, the people, more simple, of a less mercurial cast, judge of an ill principle in government, only by an actual grievance; here they anticipate the evil, and judge of the pressure of the grievance, by the badness of the principle. They augur misgovernment at a distance; and snuff the approach of tyranny in every tainted breeze."

Mr. Otis was unanimously chosen to the legislature in May, 1761. The chief topic in debate for the session was the currency. Governor Hutchinson and Otis were the leaders. The latter gave proof of great learning and powerful reasoning, mingled with great sarcasm at his opponent, for whom he seems never to have entertained either fear or respect. From his first appearance as a legislator, Otis exhibited such superiority of talent and energy over all others, that, in 1763, we find him in the full lead of all important measures. In this year, Governor Bernard sent a message respecting troops, which was strongly resented by our hero. The Governor replied in another message, to which Otis, as chairman of the committee appointed for that purpose, drew up a response, which contained the following sentence :

" No necessity can be sufficient to justify a House of Representatives, in giving up such a privilege; for it would be of little consequence to the people, whether they were subject to George or Lewis, the king of Great Britain or the French king, if both were arbitrary, as both would be, if they could levy taxes without Parliament."

When this was read, Mr. Paine, a member from Worcester, cried out " *Treason! Treason!*" but after an eloquent speech from Otis, the answer was passed entire by a large majority, and sent to the Governor. We shall have occasion to notice the striking resemblance between James Otis and Patrick Henry in their character and career : the above incident is one of the parallels.

In 1762, a pamphlet appeared, bearing the following title : " A Vindication of the Conduct of the House of Representatives, of the Province of the Massachusetts Bay : more particularly in the last session of the General Assembly. By James Otis, Esq., a Member cf said House.

> Let such, such only, tread this sacred floor,
> Who dare to love their country and be poor .

Or good though rich, numane and wise though great,
Jove give but these, we've naught to fear from fate.

Boston, printed by Edes and Gill."

Instead of copious quotations from this patriotic work, we present the following judgment upon its merits by one best qualified to estimate its worth. "How many volumes," says John Adams, "are concentrated in this little fugitive pamphlet, the production of a few hurried hours, amidst the continual solicitation of a crowd of clients; for his business at the bar at that time was very extensive, and of the first importance, and amidst the host of politicians, suggesting their plans and schemes! Look over the Declarations of Rights and Wrongs issued by Congress in 1774. Look into the Declaration of Independence, in 1776. Look into the writings of Dr. Price and Dr. Priestley. Look into all the French constitutions of government; and to cap the climax, look into Mr. Thomas Paine's Common Sense, Crisis, and Rights of Man ; what can you find that is not to be found in solid substance in this Vindication of the House of Representatives ?"

About 1776, Mr. Otis seemed inclined to a compromise, and labored to conciliate parties at home and abroad. This excited surprise, suspicion and obloquy. But events soon proved, that although he relaxed his opposition for a while, he had not changed sides. At the opening of the legislature in 1765, he resumed his wonted standing, and, in the language of John Adams, "he on whose zeal, energy and exertions the whole great cause seemed to depend, returned to his duty, and gave entire satisfaction to the end of his political career."

In the course of the same year, 1765, Otis produced another work, with the following title: "Considerations on behalf of the Colonists, in a Letter to a noble Lord. London: printed for J. Almon." The manuscript was sent from New England, dated Boston, Sept. 4, 1765. It was written with great spirit and ability, and was the last printed work from the pen of Otis.

On the 19th of October, 1765, the Stamp-Act Congress assembled in New York. Nine colonies were represented. Mr. Otis was one of the members from Massachusetts. Here, as elsewhere, he stood high in the opinion of his colleagues, for extraordinary energy and talents.

On his return to the colonial legislature of 1766, Otis was appointed chairman of a committee to reply to the angry message of Governor Bernard. The answer is characteristic of its author. They do not dispute the governor's right to deliver a speech in any way he pleases; at the same time, when it contained sentiment. which reflected on them or their constituents, they add, "it appears to us an undue exercise of the prerogative, to lay us under the necessity, either of silence, or of being thought out of season in making a reply. Your Excellency says, that these times have been more difficult than they need have been; which is also the opinion of this House. Those who have made them so, have reason to regret the injury they have done to a sincere and honest people." More follows in the same tart strain, which we need not quote.

During the session of this year, an innovation was made in the history of legislation which strikingly ind:-

cates the progress then made in free thought and freedom of speech. On the 3d of June, 1766, Otis brought forward a proposition, which was carried, "for opening a gallery for such as wished to hear the debates." Thus was a harmony first produced between the spirit of a representative government and the masses of the people ; a vast leap in the improvement which tended powerfully to diffuse knowledge and create vigilance among the populace in respect to their inalienable rights. To that little beginning in the patriotic and magnanimous mind of Otis, as in many other particulars, we may trace the stupendous superiority of this country at present over all other nations, in the influence of parliamentary and popular speech.

Repeated revolutions in France have bequeathed to that country two Houses of legislation, and a press partially redeemed from military despotism. But the Peers habitually hold their sessions in secret ; and the Chamber of Deputies can scarcely be called a deliberative body. The members read their orations from a contracted pulpit, to few or no listeners from among the people. Should a debate chance to grow warmly eloquent, any orator who might hazard an obnoxious sentiment against the crown, is liable to be immediately marched out by an armed force.*

The legislature of England is scarcely more propitious to free and effective eloquence. In theory, the House of Commons contains about seven hundred members ; in practice, debates occur and laws are enacted usually in the presence of fifty or sixty. Most of the bills are drafted, not by members, but by clerks hired for that

* A change is going on !

purpose; leaving the dignitaries to relieve the stupidity
of their stammering debates with frequent cries of "hear,
hear!" No popular audience is permitted; only a few
bystanders can gain admittance in an obscure gallery,
and that under very inconvenient restrictions. Reports
of debates are unauthorized, and of course imperfect.
No visitor is allowed to have pen or pencil in his hand
in Parliament. To render the matter worse, by a strange
perversion of the hours, unknown in any other country
or age, most of the important legislation transpires in
the dead of night, when those who are sane and sound,
and who desire to remain so, are reposing in bed, rather
than yawning on the lordly woolsack and the soft chairs
of state.

There are but three legislatures in the world that are
popular, even in form. We have glanced at two of
them, and it is evident that they present a meagre field
for eloquence, compared with the American Congress.
In the British Parliament, for instance, there are not at
present, and never were in its best condition, more than
two or three at any one time, actuated by the great impulses of oratory. When some of the best productions
accredited to the best days of Parliament were praised,
Dr. Samuel Johnson said, "those speeches I wrote in a
garret." But the masterly eloquence of our Congress
has no such origin; it is partly inspired and fully verified by the crowds of freemen who throng free galleries,
a right which James Otis early perceived, and happily
procured.

Another important feature in the unfolding of our
free institutions, was the system of town-meetings which

began to be held as early as 1767. One held in October of that year was presided over by Otis, and was called to resist new acts of British aggression on colonial rights. On Sept. 12th, 1768, a town-meeting was held, which was opened with a prayer by Dr. Cooper. Otis was chosen moderator. The petition for calling the meeting requested, that inquiry should be made of his Excellency, for " the grounds and reasons of sundry declarations made by him, that three regiments might be daily expected," &c. A committee was appointed to wait upon the governor, urging him in the present critical state of affairs to issue precepts for a general assembly of the province, to take suitable measures for the preservation of their rights and privileges; and that he should be requested to favor the town with an im-mediate answer.

In October several ship-loads of troops arrive. The storm thickens. Another town-meeting is called, and it is voted that the several ministers of the Gospel be requested to appoint the next Tuesday as a day of fasting and prayer. The day arrives, and Faneuil Hall is crowded by committees from sixty-two towns. They petition the governor to call a General Court. Otis appeared in behalf of the people, under circumstances that strongly attest his heroism. Cannon were planted at the entrance of the building, and a body of troops were quartered in the representatives' chamber. After the court was opened, Otis rose, and moved that they should adjourn to Faneuil Hall. With a significant expression of loathing and scorn, he observed, " that the stench occasioned by the troops in the hall of legislation

might prove infectious, and that it was utterly deroga-
tory to the court to administer justice at the points of
bayonets and mouths of cannon."

Soon after this, Mr. Otis was violently assaulted at
the British coffee-house in State street, by a miscreant
named Robinson. Five or six bludgeons, and one
scabbard, were found on the scene of murderous attack,
from which the assassin retreated through a back passage. Mr. Otis was cruelly lacerated in body and
shattered in mind by this assault, to a degree from which
he never entirely recovered.

But the bloody 5th of March soon arrived, and with
it, nearly on the same spot, the massacre of citizens was
perpetrated by mercenary troops. This aroused a whole
people to the full atonement of outrageous wrongs.

In 1770, mutilated and dispirited, Mr. Otis retired to
the country in pursuit of health. The town of Boston,
on the 8th of May, passed a special vote of thanks
to him for his great public services, accompanied with
strong solicitude for his recovery.

In the debate on the Boston Port Bill in Parliament,
April 15th, 1774, Colonel Barré referred to the ruf-
fianly attack made on Mr. Otis, and his treatment of
the injury, in a manner that reflects honor on both of
the orators. "Is this the return you make them?"
inquired the British statesman. "When a commissioner of the customs, aided by a number of ruffians,
assaulted the celebrated Mr. Otis, in the midst of the
town of Boston, and with the most barbarous violence
almost murdered him, did the mob, which is said to
rule that town, take vengeance on the perpetrators of

tf.is inhuman outrage against a person who is supposed to be their demagogue? No, sir, the law tried them, the law gave heavy damages against them, which the irreparably injured Mr. Otis most generously forgave, upon an acknowledgment of the offence. Can you expect any more such instances of magnanimity under the principle of the Bill now proposed?"

The allusion here is to the fact that when the jury had awarded to Mr. Otis two thousand pounds sterling as damages, it was all relinquished as soon as Robinson publicly confessed the wrong. Said the noble-hearted sufferer, "It is impossible that I should take a penny from a man in this way, after an acknowledgment of his error." Such magnanimity had ever been a trait prominent in Mr. Otis. He was distinguished for generosity to both friends and foes. Governor Hutchinson said of him; "that he never knew fairer or more noble conduct in a pleader, than in Otis; that he always disdained to take advantage of any clerical error, or similar inadvertence, but passed over minor points, and defended his causes solely on their broad and substantial foundations." When he plead against Writs of Assistance he did it gratuitously, saying, "in such a cause, I despise all fees." But in that contest there was something nobler exhibited than superiority to mercenary consideration. "It was," says the venerable President so often quoted, "a moral spectacle more affecting to me than any I have since seen upon the stage, to observe a pupil treating his master with all the deference, respect, esteem, and affection of a son to a father. and that without the least affectation ; while he

baffled and confounded all his authorities, confuted
all his arguments, and reduced him to silence! The
crown, by its agents, accumulated construction upon
construction, and inference upon inference, as the giants
heaped Pelion upon Ossa; but Otis, like Jupiter, dashed
this whole building to pieces, and scattered the pulver-
ized atoms to the four winds ; and no judge, lawyer, or
crown officer dared to say, why do ye so ? He raised
such a storm of indignation, that even Hutchinson,
who had been appointed on purpose to sanction this
writ, dared not utter a word in its favor, and Mr.
Gridley himself seemed to me to exult inwardly at the
glory and triumph of his pupil."

The ardent devotion to literature which distinguished
Mr. Otis early in life, and characterized his subsequent
career, remained predominant in the evening of his
days. His stores of knowledge were diversified and
extremely abundant. Even after he suffered the shock
which occasioned temporary insanity, he seized with
avidity every opportunity for discussing literary topics,
his strong memory and copious acquisitions always
enabling him to take the lead.

The above sketch of the mental character and political
career of James Otis, will enable us the better to analyse
his eloquence. But, unfortunately, few of his rhetorical
productions are now extant. A sad fatality attended
all his manuscripts. None of his speeches were fully
recorded, and he himself being cut off from act ve life
before the Revolution actually commenced, his name is
connected with none of the public documents of the
nation. His memorials as an orator are rather trad

tionary than actual; we are compelled to estimate his merits chiefly through the imperfect descriptions, but boundless admiration, of his time. But the mutilated fragments that yet survive are colossal, and with these for our guide we can in faint idea reconstruct the noble proportions of the original works, as Cuvier built up the Mastedon from a few relics, and Michael Angelo, with the Torso of the Vatican before him, projected anew the master-piece of Grecian genius on a scale of artistic grandeur which threw into insignificance all the conceptions of cotemporary minds.

There is sublimity in the very idea of one man presuming to brave such perils and power as Mr. Otis was called to face.

"We can admire the man who dares a lion,
But not the trampler on a worm."

The era in which he was born was favorable to the exercise of his peculiar gifts. The time to favor freedom, the set time for the advent of a powerful advocate of popular rights, like Otis, had come; the corypheus appeared and brought the proper talents with him. His eloquence was bold, witty, pungent, and practical. His boldness was a prominent trait, and the sure precursor of powerful changes. Men adapted to the wants of their age are never wanting. When portentous storms are lowering—when the battles of freedom are approaching—when the excited ocean of human thought and feeling waves around some firm, heroical leader, as where "the broad-breasted rock glasses his rugged forehead in the sea"—then are the

4*

unutterable effecus of eloquence produced less by the genius of the speaker, than by the sympathy of the audience. They receive with rapture what their own ardor has half inspired.

From the life and education of Mr. Otis, we should infer that his eloquence would be naturally and extremely bold. The mind grows by what it feeds on ; it becomes invigorated and fashioned both by its aliment and exercise. Every original thought, and every genuine utterance imparts to a speaker new force of will and increased felicity of speech. The more one's mind shapes excellence to itself and bodies it forth in efforts to promote noble ends, the more is its native capacity to create substantiated, and its happy power of execution increased. Our passions are the most potent artists; they surround themselves with fit occasions, assimilate to themselves appropriate materials; and, when wisely disciplined in a sphere commensurate with their ability, they people the void of longing hearts with beautiful forms, and store the kingdom of thought with imagery, familiar or fantastic, radiant and divine, suited to every class and every theme.

Otis communed much with other minds, but more with his own. He was erudite, and yet original; courteous in his deference to the opinions of others, out bold and daring in his own investigations. He was supple as a babe to appeals that were conciliating and motives that were just; but in the presence of arrogance and oppression, he was stubborn as rock Legions of armed tyrants were to his bold and indomitable spirit things to be trampled on in sport, "like forms of chalk painted on rich men's floors for one feast night."

The wit exemplified by Mr. Otis in debate was often keen but never malignant, as in John Randolph. The attacks of the latter were often fierce and virulent, not unfrequently in an inverse proportion to the necessity of the case. He would yield himself up to a blind and passionate obstinacy, and lacerate his victims for no apparent reason but the mere pleasure of inflicting pangs. In this respect, the orator of Roanoke resembled the Sicilian tyrant whose taste for cruelty led him to seek recreation in putting insects to the torture. If such men cannot strike strong blows, they know how to fight with poisonous weapons; thus by their malignity, rather than by their honorable skill, they can bring the noblest antagonist to the ground. But Mr. Otis pursued more dignified game and with a loftier purpose. He indeed possessed "a Swiftian gift of sarcasm," but, unlike the Dean of St. Patrick's, and the forensic gladiator alluded to above, he never employed it in a spirit of hatred and contempt towards the mass of mankind. Such persons should remember the words of Colton, that, "Strong and sharp as our wit may be, it is not so strong as the memory of fools, nor so keen as their resentment; he that has not strength of mind to forgive, is by no means weak enough to forget; and it is much more easy to do a cruel thing than to say a severe one."

The following extract from his Vindication of the

Colony of Massachusetts, in 1762, will illustrate both the boldness and wit of Mr. Otis:

"In order to excuse, if not altogether justify the offensive passage, and clear it from ambiguity, I beg leave to premise two or three da'a. 1. God made all men naturally equal. 2. The ideas of earthly superiority, pre-eminence, and grandeur, are educational, at least, acquired, not innate. 3. Kings were (and planta-ion governors should be) made for the good of the people, and not the people for them. 4. No government has a right to make hobby horses, asses, and slaves of the subject; nature having made sufficient of the two former, for all the lawful purposes of man, from the harmless peasant in the field, to the most refined politician in the cabinet, but none of the last, which infallibly proves they are unnecessary."

Another striking trait in the eloquence of James Otis was its pungency. He was eminently natural, intelli-gent, and in earnest. As completely armed as he was with scholastic tools, yet, in his public speeches he never played the artificial rhetorician. No sooner did he face his audience than he resigned all to the noble impulses of his ardent nature, and sought a connection of ideas more than of words—or rather, he sought no relation, and thus wielded the true one; for passion, when deep and honest, has a logic more compact, and more convincing even, than reason. Figures that are striking, emotions that are fleeting, intermingled with close reasoning and calm repose, constitute a style of address universally popular, because adapted to our nature. Thoughts must not present a dry, anatomical form, allowing the spectator coolly to count the muscles, the tendons, and the bones; they must be clothed with flesh, all glowing with latent heat that gives the body quick motion, and makes it tremble with the energies of immortal life. The fragments of oratorical compositions which remain to us of Mr. Otis, are marked by sudden transitions, bold imagery, rapid reasoning, stern deductions, and overwhelming appeals. He was fear.ess, impetuous, and imperiously independent. These are the mental qualities which constitute a fascinating orator.

One who is accustomed to extemporaneous speech in popular assemblies, and is therefore self-possessed, has a great advantage over the frigid thinker who never looks for strong effects but through elaborate premeditation. When one can create thought rapidly on his feet, and has the grace of confidence in every situation, ascends the rostrum to harangue the multitude on any topic that admits of an appeal to the feelings, the first flash of his spontaneous soul creates a sympathetic communication between himself and his fascinated audience. That which is thus begun in pleasure and continued with a perpetually augmented force, is an agency of great power, and may be subordinated to the most useful ends. At every new touch of feeling, the popular heart swells with enlarged conceptions; at each loftier flight of fancy, a thousand eyes sparkle with delight or swim in emotion. All this tide of feeling in turn reacts upon the susceptible orator and rapidly accumulates around him the force of conviction. In this electrical communication between excited souls, the

whole man is wrought up to the highest pitch of menta,
action, ardent and irresistible as the blazing torrent of
a volcano. The faults of such speakers are palpable,
but their excellences place them immeasurably beyond
the abilities and fame of ordinary men.

It might be said of the fervid style in which Mr. Otis
was wont to speak, as was said of the most renowned
orator of antiquity. It is scarcely possible to divide his
speeches, like those of most men, into argumentative
and declamatory passages. " Logic and rhetoric are
blended together, from the beginning to the end ; the
speaker, while always clear and profound, is always
rapid and impassioned. The vivid feeling displayed at
intervals by other orators, bursts forth in him with every
sentence. We are forcibly reminded of the description
of lightning in Homer :

> " ' By turns one flash succeeds, as one expires,
> And heaven flames thick with momentary fires.' "

There is usually more passion than intellect in the
eloquence which creates revolutions. We are not
much moved by a little flame that burns for a long time
with a steady light. But no one is indifferent to those
conflagrations which suddenly burst through sombre
clouds and then expire as suddenly as they were born.
Pindar long since sang of the astonishing effects produced by that great furnace of nature, Etna, which is
impressive not by an uniform erupt on, but because at
moments of fear and devastation it hurls up, from its
profound depths, cinders, rocks, and rivers of flame. It
is only the grand and extraordinary that is admirable

and surprising. The passions are powerful advocates, and their very silence, when emotion grows dumb from its excess, goes most directly to the soul.

Many of the most effective orators, of all ages, have not been most successful in long and formal efforts. Nor have they always been close and ready debaters. "Sudden bursts which seemed to be the effect of inspiration—short sentences which came like lightning, dazzling, burning, striking down everything before them—sentences which, spoken at critical moments, decided the fate of great questions—sentences which at once became proverbs—sentences which every body still knows by heart"—in these chiefly lay the oratorical power of Mirabeau and Chatham, Patrick Henry and James Otis.

American eloquence has ever resembled our national domain, spontaneous and prolific, grand in outline and rich in tone. The most refined taste in landscape gardening acts on the principle that the greatest excellence consists in the resemblance to nature—nature adorned by a skilful grouping of her own charms around an occasional embellishment of art—but in all her prevailing features nature still. Otis was naturally elevated in thought, and dwelt with greatest delight in the calm contemplation of the lofty principles which should govern political and moral conduct. And yet he was keenly susceptible to excitement. His intellect explored the wilderness of the universe only to increase the discontent of those noble aspirations of his soul which were never at rest. In early manhood he was a close student, but as he advanced in age he became more and more absorbed in public action. As ominous storms threatened the common weal, he found less delight in his library than in the stern strife of the forum. As he prognosticated the coming tempest and comprehended its fearful issue, he became transformed in aspect like one inspired. His appearance in public always commanded prompt and profound attention; he both awed and delighted the multitudes whom his bold wisdom so opportunely fortified. "Old South," the "Old Court House," and the "Cradle of Liberty," in Boston, were familiar with his eloquence, that resounded like a cheerful clarion in "days that tried men's souls." It was then that his great heart and fervid intellect wrought with disinterested and noble zeal : his action became vehement, and his eyes flashed with unutterable fire ; his voice, distinct, melodious, swelling, and increasing in height and depth with each new and bolder sentiment, filled, as with the palpable presence of a deity, the shaking walls. The listeners became rapt and impassioned like the speaker, till their very breath forsook them. He poured forth a " flood of argument and passion" which achieved the sublimest earthly good, and happily exemplified the description which Percival has given of indignant patriotism expressed in eloquence :

> "Its words
> Are few, but deep and solemn ; and they break
> Fresh from the fount of feeling, and are full
> Of all that passion, which, on Carmel, fired
> The holy prophet, when his lips were coals,
> The language winged with terror, as when bolts

Leap from the brooding tempest, armed with wrath,
Commissioned to affright us, and destroy."

We have said that the eloquence of Otis was bold,
witty, and pungent ; we remark, in conclusion, that it
was exceedingly practical. The great body of the
people comprehend thought and genius most easily
under the emblems of force; they are ready to respect
that which they love, and yield willingly to that which
impels them ; they highly appreciate that which is
heard with pleasure, and venerate the heart that has
profoundly moved them. Intellect and emotion constitute the basis of all effective speech ; but the commanding
form, stentorian lungs, and flashing eye, are indis
pensable adjuncts to the popular speaker.

The trait which, perhaps, was most prominent in Mr.
Otis, was his constant and complete forgetfulness of
himself in the themes he discussed. He explored all
the resources at command, and, in defending his position, became entirely absorbed. While engaged in
speaking, he appeared to be absolutely possessed by his
subject, and thought as little of the skill he should
display as an orator, as he who is fighting for his life
thinks of the grace he shall exhibit in the flourish of
his weapons. Enthusiastic sincerity actuated his great
native powers, and gave them overwhelming force.
His was the true eloquence of nature, the language of
a strong mind under high but well regulated excitement.
The disenthralment of the Colonies of America was the
grand ambition of his soul ; and to the attainment of
this he subordinated all the resources he could command. Freedom, of the most exalted kind, was the idol

of his heart, and, as he braved the terrors of rebellion against sovereign power, he saw nothing, loved nothing, with affection more fixed. In this consisted his best qualification for the great work to the execution of which, under Providence, he was assigned;

> " For he whom Heaven
> Hath call'd to be th' awakener of a land,
> Should have his soul's affections all absorbed
> In that majestic purpose, and press on
> To its fulfilment, as a mountain-born
> And mighty stream, with all its vassal-rills,
> Sweeps proudly to the ocean, pausing not
> To dally with the flowers."

In respect to physical ability, Otis was happily endowed. One who knew him well has recorded, that " he was finely formed, and had an intelligent countenance : his eye, voice, and manner were very impressive. The elevation of his mind, and the known integrity of his purposes, enabled him to speak with decision and dignity, and commanded the respect as well as the admiration of his audience. His eloquence showed but little imagination, yet it was instinct with the fire of passion." It may be not unjustly said of Otis, as of Judge Marshall, that " He was one of those rare beings that seem to be sent among men from time to time, to keep alive our faith in humanity." He had a wonderful power over the popular feelings, but he employed it only for great public benefits. He seems to have said to himself, in the language of the great master of the maxims of life and conduct:

" This above all,—to thine own self be true,
And it must follow, as the night the day,
Thou canst not then be false to any man."

Otis was just the person to kindle a conflagration ;
to set a continent on fire by the power of speech.
When heard on exciting local topics, deep feeling,
kindred to the sentiments of the orator, opened each
heart and soul to the stream of his burning thoughts.
Assembled multitudes love that which dazzles them,
which moves, strikes, and enchains them. In the
best orations of the ancients, we find not a multi-
plicity of ideas, but those which are the most pertinent,
and the strongest possible ; by the first blows struck
ignition is produced, and the flame is kept blazing with
increased brilliancy and power, until guilt stands revealed in terror, and tyranny flies aghast. It is indeed
true, as an American poet has said,

" Few
The spirits who originate and bend
All meaner hearts to wonder and obey,
As if their look were death, their word were fate ;"

but Otis was certainly one of this rare class.

His eloquence, like that of his distinguished successors,
was marked by a striking individuality. It did not
partake largely of the placid firmness of Samuel Adams ;
or of the intense brilliancy and exquisite taste of the
younger Quincy ; or the subdued and elaborate beauty
of Lee ; or the philosophical depth of John Adams ; or
the rugged and overwhelming energy of Patrick Henry ;
though he most of all Americans, resembled the latter

Compared with English orators, our great countryman was not unlike Sheridan in natural endowment.
Like him, he was unequalled in impassioned appeals
to the general heart of mankind. He swayed all by
his electric fire; charmed the timid, and inspired
the weak; subdued the haughty, and enthralled the
prejudiced. He traversed the field of argument and
invective as a Scythian warrior scours the plain, shooting most deadly arrows when at the greatest speed.
He rushed into forensic battle, fearless of all consequences; and as the ancient war-chariot would sometimes set its axle on fire by the rapidity of its own
movement, so would the ardent soul of Otis become
ignited and fulminate with thought, as he swept
irresistibly to the goal. When aroused by some great
crisis, his eloquent words were like bolts of granite
heated in a volcano, and shot forth with unerring aim,
crashing where they fell.

No patriot was ever more heartily devoted to the
welfare of his country, nor more practical in his public
toils, than was James Otis. Taking into consideration
the times in which he appeared, and the sublime results
that have flowed from the influence he exerted, the
following language of President Adams seems appropriate and just. "I have been young, and now am old,
and I solemnly say, I have never known a man whose
love of his country was more ardent or sincere; never
one who suffered so much; never one, whose services
for any ten years of his life, were so important and
essential to the cause of his country, as those of Mr
Otis, from 1760 to 1770."

Mr. Otis suffered much in the latter part of his life from the gloomy effects produced by Robinson's brutal assault. He lived retired in the country in the most simple and quiet manner. In the lucid intervals of his mind he conducted some legal business, and habitually devoted himself to literary and religious cultivation. In 1782, his grandson, the distinguished living representative of the family, Harrison Gray Otis,* brought the venerable patriot from Andover on a visit to Boston. There he received great attention from his old friends, and especially from Governor Hancock. What a scene must this have been to the great pioneer of the Revolution! What exciting, but hallowed recollections must have rushed on his mind, as in the midst of a free and mighty people, and encompassed by his old comrades whose youth he had inspired and whose action he had guided, he sat down, the patriarch of freedom at the festive board of honor and wealth! But the exhilaration was too much for his shattered nerves and agitated mind. He was immediately advised by his brother and grandson to return to the quiet of rural life again, which he did with the gentleness of a child.

Six weeks after his return to Andover, his end came in a manner as remarkable as had been his career. When first emerging from insanity, he had said to his sister, Mrs. Warren, "my dear sister, I hope when God Almighty, in his righteous providence, shall take me out of time into eternity, that it will be by a flash of lightning;" and this desire he often repeated. On the 23d of May, 1783, a heavy cloud suddenly

* Recently died.

arose.   Otis, calm and sound in mind, stood leaning on his cane in the front door of the house where he resided. A single flash glared on the family assembled near, and Mr. Otis fell instantaneously dead in the arms of Mr. Osgood, who sprang forward as he saw him sink.   The body was brought to Boston, and his funeral was attended by one of the most numerous processions ever seen in New England.

Peace had just been concluded.   The great battle of the Revolution had been fought and won, when the great mind which had incurred the most fearful affliction in the early strife, permitted at length to gaze in placid joy on the glorious result, was then by a bright bolt snatched to Heaven without a pang.

A cotemporary poet wrote a commemorative ode, which closed as follows:

> "Yes! when the glorious work which he begun,
> Shall stand the most complete beneath the sun;
> When peace shall come to crown the grand design,
> His eyes shall live to see the work divine—
> The heavens shall then his generous 'spirit claim,
> In storms as loud as his immortal fame'—
> Hark, the deep thunders echo round the skies!
> On wings of flame the eternal errand flies.
> One chosen, charitable bolt is sped—
> And Otis mingles with the glorious lead."

CHAPTER III.

———⟨⟨⟨⟨⟨⟨⟨⟨⟩⟩⟩———

SAMUEL ADAMS,

LAST OF THE PURITANS.

ONE of the brightest and most prominent traits in the early history of our country, is presented in the exalted moral worth of many of the leading patriots. It is a feature delightful to contemplate, and one that accounts for whatever is worthy and stable in our free institutions. If our principal men are not men of principle, it is vain to look for enduring excellence in the works they execute. Burke sagaciously remarked, "I never knew a man who was bad, fit for service that was good. There is always some disqualifying ingredient, mixing and spoiling the compound. The man seems paralytic on that side, his muscles there have lost their very tone and character—they cannot move. In short, the accomplishment of any thing good is a physical impossibility for such a man. There is decrepitude as well as distortion—he could not, if he would, is not more certain than he would not, if he could."

The late George Canning, himself a happy example of the association of private morality and political eminence, in an early literary work, enforced the necessity of personal purity, as illustrative of public character, with a vigor of thought and elegance of diction peculiar to himself. He first quotes the following remark from an illustrious master of ancient eloquence : "It is impossible that the unnatural father, the hater of his own blood, should be an able and faithful leader of his country; that the mind which is insensible to the intimate and touching influence of domestic affection, should be alive to the remoter influence of patriotic feeling ; that private depravity should consist with public virtue." " The sentiment is here expressed," says Canning, "with all the vehemence of a political chief, conscious of the amiableness of his own domestic life, and inveighing against a rival too strong in most points to be spared when he was found weak. It has, however, a foundation of truth, and may suggest the advantages resulting from the blended species of biography of which we have spoken. Even in the anomalous cases where no correspondence, or no close correspondence, can be traced between the more retired and the more conspicuous features of a character, a comparative exhibition of the two has its use, and will furnish the philosopher with many interesting themes of reflection. The chief use, however, of such an exhibition resides in the rule and not in the exceptions, and belongs not to the speculative few, but to the active many. By associating, in the view of mankind, whatever is amiable, and, as it were, *feminine* in the human character, with whatever in it is commanding and Herculean, it takes advantage of our veneration for the latter to betray us into a respect for the former. It gives dignity to the humbler virtues and domestic chari-

tics in the eyes both of public and private men, both of
those who aspire to become great, and of those who are
content to remain little ; and thus secures the vital inte
rests of society."

A happy instance and illustration of the above doctrine is before the world in the life and character of

Samuel Adams. He was born in Boston, on the 27th
of September, 1722. The family from which he descended was one that early emigrated to New England,
and commenced the settlement of the Colony. His
father was a man of considerable wealth, of irreproachable character, a magistrate of Boston, and a member of
the House of Assembly for many years, under the Colonial government. Having resolved to give his son a
liberal education, Samuel Adams was placed under the
instruction of Mr. Lovell, a celebrated teacher of the
grammar school in Boston. Under his supervision
young Adams was fitted for admission to Harvard University, at an early age. He graduated with honor in
1740, when only eighteen years old, and took his Master's degree at twenty.

When Samuel Adams graduated, John Adams was
five years old, and Josiah Quincy and Joseph Warren
yet unborn. James Otis was three years after Samuel
Adams, in the list of graduates, and Quincy twenty-three
years after him. John Adams completed his college
course in 1755, which was fifteen years after the gradu-
ation of Samuel. Samuel Adams was distinguished at
the university for a serious and secluded cast of mind.
He at first designed to devote himself to the Gospel
ministry, but read comprehensively, especially in

5

history. The severe writers of Greek and Roman annals were his favorite authors; but Divinity was the
profession he resolved to live and die by.

The year that Samuel Adams entered Harvard, was
the same in which the Earl of Chatham entered Parliament, so that he must have seen the whole of that great
statesman's splendid career. But the greatness he saw
from afar and emulated, neither crippled the expansion
of his own free faculties nor created fear in his breast.
He was early distinguished for great assiduity in study,
and promptness in the performance of collegiate duties.
He was equally remarkable for the uprightness of his
demeanor and the frugality of his habits. From the
stipend allowed him by his father, he saved a sum sufficient to publish an original pamphlet, entitled " Englishmen's Rights." When he took his second degree, the
thesis he discussed was, "*Whether it be lawful to resist
the* SUPREME MAGISTRATE, *if the Commonwealth cannot
be otherwise preserved?*" This he affirmed and maintained with great force, in the presence of the king's
Governor and his Council, in the reign of George the
Second, while Sir Robert Walpole was Prime Minister,
and these Colonies were not only at peace but exceedingly
loyal to England. But in that young bosom lay the elements of glorious rebellion, and in the question he discussed in 1740, lay the whole history of the war of Independence, which dates from 1776.

Samuel Adams must be regarded as the great leader
of our Revolution. As such he was regarded beyond
the Atlantic, where his real character seems to have
been better understood than at home. Mr. Adolphus

in the second volume of the history of England, speaks of him thus : "Samuel Adams, a distinguished leader of the American councils, noted for subtlety, perseverance and inflexibility, boasted in all companies, that he had toiled twenty years to accomplish the measure of Independence. During that time he had carried his art and industry so far, as to search after every rising genius in the New England seminaries, employed his utmost abilities to fix in their minds the principles of American Independency, and now triumphed in his success." A learned commentator on this authority, who thoroughly understood the character of Samuel Adams, asserted that he was "no *boaster*, but a polite gentleman of modest carriage."

The Rev. Dr. William Gordon, another Englishman, who resided a number of years near Boston, as a parish minister, says in his fourth Letter on the history of those times, "that Samuel Adams became a member of the legislature in September, 1765; that he was zealously attached to the rights of Massachusetts in particular, and the colonies in general, and but little to his own personal interest; that he was well qualified to second Mr. Otis, and learned in time to serve *his own political views* by the influence of the other ; that he was soon noticed by the House, chosen and continued their clerk from year to year, by which means he had the custody of their papers ; and of these he knew how to make an advantage for political purposes. He was frequently upon important committees, and acquired great ascendency by discovering a readiness to acquiesce in the proposals and amendments of others, while the end

aimed at by them did not eventually frustrate his leading designs. He showed a pliableness and complaisance
in these smaller matters which enabled him, in the issue,
to carry those of much greater consequence ; and there
were," says the historian, " many favorite points, which
the ' sons of liberty' in Massachusetts meant to carry,
even though the Stamp-Act should be repealed."

Thomas, Jefferson, in a letter to the grandson of Samuel Adams, said : " He was truly a great man, wise in
council, fertile in resources, immovable in his purposes ;
and had, I think, a greater share than any other member
of Congress, in advising and directing our measures in
the northern war.   As a speaker he could not be compared with his living colleague and namesake, whose
deep conceptions, nervous style and undaunted firmness,
made him truly our bulwark in debate.   But Samuel
Adams, although not of fluent elocution, was so rigor-
ously logical, so clear in views, abundant in sense, and
master always of his subject, that he commanded the
most profound attention whenever he rose in an assembly, where the froth of declamation was heard with the
most sovereign contempt."

Again, in a letter written by the same renowned patriot to Dr. Waterhouse, he says :

" Dear Sir—Your letter of the 15th was received on
the 27th, and I am glad to find the name and character
of Samuel Adams coming forward, and in so good hands
as I suppose them to be.   I was the youngest man but
one in the old Congress, and he the oldest but one, as I
believe.   His only senior, I suppose, was *Stephen Hop-*

kins, of and by whom the honorable mention made in your letter was richly merited.

" Although my high reverence for *Samuel Adams* was returned by habitual notices from him, which highly flattered me, yet the disparity of age prevented intimate and confidential communications. I always considered him, more than any other member, the *fountain* of our important measures;· and although he was neither an eloquent nor easy speaker, whatever he said was sound, and commanded the profound attention of the House.

" In the discussions on the floor of Congress, he reposed himself on our main pillar in debate, *Mr. John Adams.* These two gentlemen were verily a host in our councils. Comparisons with their associates, northern or southern, would answer no profitable purpose; but they would suffer by comparison with none."

It will be unnecessary to cite further cotemporary authorities, touching the general outlines of Samuel Adams' character. The idea of the Independence of the Colonies was doubtless more or less cherished from the beginning, but he was the first man who embodied, and, with extraordinary tact and effect, diffused that doctrine from North to South, until it became in '76 the vital principle of our constitution. Many years before ordinary minds dared to hope for such a consummation, Gordon wrote in his history, that " Mr. Samuel Adams long since said, in small, confidential companies, ' *This country shall be independent, and we will be satisfied with nothing short of it.*' "

In turning now to a more specific analysis of the

mental structure of this great patriot, with an effort to estimate the value of his public services, it is proposed to consider the influence of his pen, his tongue and his example.

First, let us glance at what he achieved with his pen. We have seen that he accustomed himself to political writing while at college. He was favorably known as a polemic, during the administration of Governor Shirley, whom he opposed on the ground of his exercise both of the civil and military power. When the intelligence reached Boston, in 1763, of a design to tax the Colonies, and place the revenue at the disposal of Parliament, Adams promptly opposed the measure. At that period, when the town met to choose their representatives to the General Assembly, it was the custom to instruct them respecting their legislative duties. Soon after the ominous news arrived, the people elected Mr. Adams to draw up appropriate instructions. The document is yet extant in his own hand-writing; and in that manuscript is found *the first public denial of the right of the British Parliament to tax the Colonies without their consent— the first denial of parliamentary supremacy—and the first public suggestion of an union on the part of the Colonies,* to protect themselves against British aggression.

Samuel Adams possessed a calm, solid, and yet polished mind. There is a wonderful lucidness in his thought and phraseology ; every thing about his composition is plain, forcible, and level to the simplest comprehension. Above all the men of his day, he was distinguished for sound practical judgment. All prominent statesmen looked to him for counsel. He aided Otis in preparing state papers; and a direction to the printers, attached to some of Josiah Quincy's manuscripts, reads —" Let Samuel Adams, Esq., correct the press." In fact there were few, if any, important documents published between 1764 and 1769, in Boston, that were not revised by the cool and solid judgment of the New England *Phocion*.

The idea of assembling the first Congress not only originated with him, but he early became a conspicuons delegate in that body. He was placed upon every important committee, wrote or revised every report, and had a hand in every measure designed to counteract foreign tyranny. The people of America soon recognized in him one of their most efficient supporters, and the government in England openly proclaimed him one of the most inveterate of their opponents.

Samuel Adams possessed various instrumentalities for promoting political and moral designs, and not the least among them was his versatile and potent pen. He is said to have wielded that almost omnipotent engine, a free press, with the irresistible arm of a giant. Clear and cogent paragraphs, scattered about in newspapers, stung the popular mind to the quick ; while more elaborate essays, like those of Junius, convinced and impelled leading men, and prompted all classes to execute the purposes at which the great patriot aimed.

In the second place, his living eloquence was a powerful auxiliary to the popular cause. But of this orator as of James Otis, there are but few written remains The patriots of those times acted, wrote and spake, as though they felt deeply that they were born for their country and for mankind. They were evidently more intent in laying the foundation of great institutions for the benefit of posterity, than in recording transient memorials of themselves.

Several traits in the eloquence of Samuel Adams are worthy of particular notice; among these were his sagacity, his knowledge of man, his fearlessness of kings, and his devotion to republican liberty.

He commenced his public life as a legislator in 1765, in the General Assembly, as a representative from Boston. He very soon became distinguished in that body for his wisdom, foresight, and ardent support of popular rights. His commanding influence and stern defiance of foreign aggression, soon attracted the notice of the agents of Parliament. Overtures were made to him by Governor Hutchinson, but they were indignantly rejected; and Hutchinson, referring to his discomfiture in a letter to a friend, said: "Such is the obstinacy and inflexible disposition of the man, that he can never be conciliated by any office or gift whatever." No language could express a higher tribute to the integrity and patriotism of Mr. Adams.

During the angry contention which lasted for several years between the citizens and the military force quartered in Boston, and which came to the melancholy issue in the massacre of March 5th, 1770, Samuel Adams, aided by John Adams, Hancock and others, bore a prominent part, in efforts to effect their removal from the town. On the morning after the outrage was committed, a public meeting was held, and Samuel

Adams was placed at the head of a committee to wait on the acting governor, Hutchinson, and demand the removal of the troops. Hutchinson at first evaded the immediate request, by offering some frivolous plea; but, being told by Mr. Adams that the people still remained in session, determined on redress, and that the consequences of his refusal must rest upon his own head, he at last promised compliance with their demands.

Not long after another occasion occurred when the sagacious firmness of this great moral hero was called into profitable requisition. Governor Hutchinson, having refused to receive his salary from the province, and being paid by the crown, was made independent of the people, who saw at once in this move a dangerous innovation. They remonstrated with the Governor, but their memorials were treated with indifference and contempt. On November 2d, 1772, on the motion of Samuel Adams, a large committee of citizens were appointed "to state the rights of the Colonists, and of this province in particular, as men, as Christians, and as subjects; to communicate and publish the same to the several towns in this province and to the world, as the sense of this town, with the infringements and violations thereof, that have been, or from time to time may be made; also requesting of each town a free communication of their sentiments on this subject." This was the original committee of correspondence, out of which grew the subsequent union of the Colonies, and the Congress of the United States.

Governor Gage arrived in Boston in May, 1774, and presuming upon the truth of a maxim which originated among British politicians, and is generally believed there, that "every man has his price," offered a heavy "consideration" through Colonel Fenton, his agent, to Samuel Adams. But those minions of regal power and rotten aristocracy were destined to learn, that there is such a thing as patriotism, which thrones cannot awe nor bribes corrupt. If the sturdy patriot was found to be proof against venality and corruption, then the agent of tyrannical arrogance was directed to threaten him with an arrest for treason. Mr. Adams, glowing with indignation at such attacks upon his honor and patriotism, first demanded of the messenger, Fenton, a solemn pledge that he would return to Gage his reply just as it was given, and then rising in a firm manner, said, "*I trust that I have long since made my peace with the King of kings. No personal consideration shall induce me to abandon the righteous cause of my country.* Tell Governor Gage, it is the advice of Samuel Adams to him, no longer to insult the feelings of an exasperated people."

The Governor having vetoed no less than thirteen Councilors, chosen by the people in May, 1774, and adjourned the General Court to Salem, the Assembly at length advised a Congress of the Colonies at Philadelphia, in September. Samuel Adams was one of the five delegates sent from Massachusetts. In the Continental Congress, as everywhere else, he was indefatigable and earnest in his labors to promote the cause of freedom. John Adams, in a magnanimous allusion to Thomas Jefferson, speaks of his namesake and co-patriot in a way illustrative of our present topic. Jefferson, said he,

"though a silent member, he was so prompt, frank, explicit, and decisive upon committees—*not even* SAMUEL
ADAMS *was more so*—that he soon seized my heart."
Indeed, all cotemporary proof goes to show that in the
committees of Congress, and in the associations of the
"Sons of Liberty," at Boston, he was the soul of their
movements.

Another peculiarity of Samuel Adams was, his profound and accurate acquaintance with the nature of
man. He had studied its secret springs, and could
move them at pleasure. He knew that the human
heart is like the earth. "You may sow it, and plant it,
and build upon it in all manner of forms; but the earth,
however cultivated by man, continues none the less
spontaneously to produce its verdures, its wild flowers,
and all varieties of natural fruits." The spade and the
plough trouble not the profounder depths where innumerable germs are hid. The identity of this planet on
which we live is not more perpetual than that of human
nature. Its latent impulses we must know. Its spontaneous productions we must learn to employ, if we would
toil among mankind with success.

One or two instances will suffice to illustrate Mr
Adams' skill in dealing with mankind. A great "town
meeting" was held in Faneuil Hall, to form an associa
tion against the importation of goods into Boston from
Britain, until certain grievances were redressed. That
the leaders in this business contemplated a limited time
is evident from the fact that at a subsequent period, both
Samuel and John Adams opposed, in Congress, the non-
importation scheme, lest the country should be exhaust

ed of certain necessary articles *when they came to fight.*
The object proposed to the aforesaid popular meeting in
Faneuil Hall was received by general acclamation. But
a Mr. Mc——, a Scotchman and large importer, refused to join the association. The Scotch were uncommonly loyal to George the Third, and are usually not
very slow to look after their own interests. Some were
wroth that this citizen refused to sign the non-importation
agreement; but angry words were by no means en-
couraged by Mr. Adams, for the *suaviter in modo* was a
prominent trait in his energetic character. The committee from the meeting who had been directed to call
on the stubborn Scotchman, and who had been repelled
by him, were directed to call on the recusant again;
they returned with the same answer; when Mr. Adams
arose and moved, that the meeting (about two thousand
persons) should resolve itself into a committee of the
whole house, and wait upon Mr. Mc——, at the close of
the meeting, to urge his compliance with the general
wish ; which being agreed to without a dissenting voice,
they proceeded to transact the business before them.
The sagacious patriot knew that the individual in question had personal friends in the meeting, some of whom
immediately slipped away to inform him, that the *whole
body* would, as a committee, wait upon him at the close
of the meeting. The result was, as Mr. Adams anticipated. In the midst of their deliberations on other
subjects, in rushed Mr. Mc——, all in a foam, and bow-
ing to the chairman and to Mr. Adams, told them that
he was ready and willing to put his name to the non-
importation pledge. Mr. Adams pointed to a seat near

him, with a polite, condescending bow of protection in the presence of the people, which quieted the alarm of the discreet Scotchman, who was struck with dread at the idea of two thousand people presenting themselves before his dwelling, and hastened to avert such threatening honors.

Another sagacious movement on the part of Samuel Adams, and one of the most profitable deeds of his patriotic life, was his enlisting the very rich and accomplished *John Hancock* in the popular cause. The means of accomplishing this have never transpired, but as to the author of the achievement there is no doubt. The cause of freedom throughout the world is greatly indebted to both men. One gave to it his great mind, and the other his splendid fortune ; one obtained cotemporary fame, the other, like all heroes of the highest order, reposed on posterity. But it is easy to suppose that the watchful and diligent votary of liberty felt no little complacency in winning so potent an auxiliary to the cause he most dearly loved. One day John and Samuel Adams were walking in the Boston Mall, and when they came opposite the stately mansion of Mr. Hancock, the latter turning to the former, said, with emphasis, "I have done a *very good* thing for our *cause* in the course of the past week, by enlisting the master of that house in it. He is well disposed and has great riches, and we can give him *consequence* to enjoy them." And Mr. Hancock did not disappoint his expectations; for when they gave him the "*consequence*," so genial to his nature, by making him President of Congress, he put everything at stake, in opposition to British encroachments.

In the third place, Samuel Adams was fearless of all combinations of human power. Pure and exalted patriotism was the boldest feature in his character. The freedom and prosperity of his country; the union of all her sons in a common and national fraternity; and the advancement of moral truth, harmony, and virtue, were the grand objects of his unomitted pursuit. It may be said of him, as Justice Story said of Bushrod Washington, "Few men have possessed higher qualifications, either natural or acquired. His mind was solid, rather than brilliant; sagacious and searching, rather than quick or eager; slow, but not torpid; steady, but not unyielding; comprehensive, and at the same time cautious; patient in inquiry, forcible in conception, clear in reasoning. He was, by original temperament, mild, conciliating, and candid ; and yet he was remarkable for an uncompromising firmness. Of him it may be truly said, that the fear of man never fell upon him ; it never entered into his thoughts, much less was it seen in his actions. In him the love of justice was the ruling passion; it was the main-spring of all his conduct. He made it a matter of conscience to discharge every duty with scrupulous fidelity and scrupulous zeal."

The propriety of applying the above remarks to Samuel Adams will be confirmed by adducing the following emergency and the sentiments it occasioned. When Mr. Galloway and a few of his timid adherents were for entering their protest in Congress against an open rupture with Britain, Samuel Adams, rising slowly from his seat, said, " I should advise persisting in our struggle for liberty, though it were revealed from Heaten that nine hundred and ninety-nine were to perish, and *only one freeman* of a *thousand* survive and retain his liberty. That *one* freeman must possess more virtue and enjoy more happiness, than *a thousand* slaves : let him propagate his *like*, and transmit to them what he had so nobly preserved."

This quotation leads us to consider yet more definitely Mr. Adams' love of liberty, and the peculiarity of his eloquence.

When, on the morning of April 19th, 1775, the volleys of fire-arms from the British troops at Lexington, announced to him and his companions, that the great battle for freedom had begun, he threw up his arms, and exclaimed, in a voice of patriotic rapture, "Oh! what a glorious morning is this!"

Five days before the battle of Bunker Hill, Governor Gage proclaimed pardon to all who should lay down their arms, excepting Samuel Adams and John Hancock. Being thus signalized by superior hate only increased their popularity with the people, in the support of whose dearest interests they had put every thing at stake and incurred royal vengeance.

The exasperation of Gage against Samuel Adams in particular, had been augmented by the bold and effective measures taken by the latter in the assembly at Salem. It was by him and there that a Continental Congress at Philadelphia was proposed, at a time when the popular mind was not maturely decided as to the expediency of the measure, and contrary to the hopes of British emissaries a majority was obtained to act with him. Moreover, in secret session, the five delegates to that Congress were elected, notwithstanding the governor issued his official injunction against the proceedings. In this movement of the liberty party, the authority of the governor was set at defiance, and the doors were bolted against his entrance. His secretary, armed with a commission to dissolve the assembly, was obliged to sustain his dignity on the steps outside, while the key of the hall door reposed in Samuel Adams' pocket.

Mr. Adams took his seat in the first Continental Congress on the 5th of September, 1774, and continued an active and effective member of that great national assembly until 1781, exemplifying wisdom seldom equalled, and an enthusiasm for freedom never excelled. On the 8th of May, 1776, while Congress was in session at Philadelphia, the sound of heavy artillery was heard down the Delaware. It was known to proceed from gun-boats that had been sent to protect the river from British cruisers. Hitherto no sound of actual war had reached that section of country, whose inhabitants were conscientiously more pacific in their tone than suited the ardor and exasperation of New England. As the sound of the first gun burst upon the ear of Congress, Samuel Adams sprang upon his feet, and cried out with exultation, to the infinite astonishment of a few timid members, "Thank God! the game's begun—none can stop it now." In that hall he put his name to the Declaration of Independence, and he never ceased his efforts till the victory was won.

As an orator Samuel Adams was peculiarly fitted for the times on which he had fallen. His eloquence was characteristic of its author, full of massive simplicity and pungent common sense. His ideas were plain, pertinent, and forcible; comprehended by all with ease, and long remembered for their pith and point. He moved much among the masses of mankind, and knew how to sway their thoughts. This apostle of liberty, like the heralds of salvation, began first to preach to the common people, and ultimately attained an influence that made despots tremble on their thrones.

One great secret of the power of his popular address, probably, lay in the unity of his purpose and the energy of his pursuit. He passionately loved freedom, and subordinated every thing to its attainment. This kind of inspiration is a necessary pre-requisite to eminent success.

Samuel Adams had more logic in his composition than rhetoric, and was accustomed to convince the judgment rather than inflame the passions; and, yet, when the occasion demanded, he could give vent to the ardent and patriotic indignation of which his heart was often full.

His education was substantial and thorough; his reading and observation comprehensive and exact. The principal decorative element in his mental culture was music, of which he was a proficient and devoted admirer. Like Milton, whom he resembled in many points, stern and rugged in general character, he could "feel music's pulse in all his arteries," and was accustomed to turn away from exhausting struggles for human weal and seek solace in the luxury of sweet sounds. In him there was a happy blending of strength and beauty of the highest kind. He was not eloquent in the ordinary sense of the term, as his speech nad more of substance than show. His deductions were clear, cogent, and to the purpose; his language was chaste, luminous, and pointed; his fluency seldom impeded, and his action always mpressive; so that, in their energetic union, his great mental and moral qualities possessed a charm which never failed to win upon the confidence and captivate the judgment of his audience. He had little of those coruscations of fancy, transient gleams such as "live in the rainbow and play in the plighted clouds;" but was richly endowed with those more exalted qualities which enabled him to speak in "the large utterance of the early gods." He always steered in the dignified medium between tameness and ferocity. There was a mingling of heroical and Christian graces in him, which showed, that the ambition of his soul, and the symmetry of his thoughts, were fashioned after the sublimest models, and for a better world.

One who knew him intimately has described him as being one of the most ardent of the patriots, before and during the Revolution; a popular writer and energetic speaker. "He was of common size, of muscular form, light blue eyes, light complexion, and erect in person, He wore a tie wig, cocked hat, and red cloak. His manner was very serious." His enunciation is said to have been remarkably slow, distinct, and harmonious. Whenever he arose to address a popular assembly, every murmur was hushed at the first flash of that "sparkling eye beneath a veteran brow." Expectation was on tiptoe for something weighty from his lips, and was seldom disappointed. "Eloquence," said Boling broke, "must flow like a stream that is fed by an abundant spring, and not spout forth a little frothy water on some gaudy day, and remain dry the rest of the year."

The encomium which Ben Jonson pronounced on Lord Bacon's speaking may be justly applied to Samuel Adams. "There happened in my time one noble speaker who was full of gravity in his speech. His language was nobly censorious. No man ever spoke more neatly, more pressly, more weightily, or suffered less emptiness, less idleness in what he uttered. No member of his speech but consisted of his own graces. His hearers could not cough or look aside from him without loss. He commanded where he spoke, and had his judges angry and pleased at his devotion. No man had their affections more in his power. The fear of every man that heard him was lest he should make an end."

The patriotism of Samuel Adams was undoubted, and his personal worth was of the most exalted character. The influence he exerted on the destinies of the country was probably more potent and salutary than that of any other man. He might not cope with some others in the ability to convulse or console an audience in tumultuous debate, but he could privately lead the leaders. Plain, quiet, indigent, sagacious, patriotic old Puritan, as he was, now melting his stern soul into unwonted tears of joy, and pacing the "Common" with exulting step, because that morning he had "won that chivalrous young aristocrat, John Hancock," to the defence of the popular cause; and now glancing, with

a sly twinkle in his eye, at fiery resolutions pendant
from the "Tree of Liberty," purporting to have been
produced nocturnally by the serene goddess herself, but
which, he well knows, first saw the light by his solitary
lamp ; and, anon, ensconced behind the "deacon's seat"
in "Old South," with an immense throng crowding the
double galleries to the very ceiling, he stealthily passes
up a pungent resolution, which kindles some more
excitable mouth-piece, and, finally, inflames the heaving
and swelling mass with spontaneous cries of "Boston
harbor a tea-pot to night!"—why, he was, indeed, a
power behind the throne greater than the throne, he
ruled the winds that moved the waves.

Our third general point relates to the service which
Samuel Adams rendered to his country and the world
by the force of his example. A few words on this
topic.

The character of a man, viewed at large, is the
aggregate of his passions, and his passions are developed
and toned by the circumstances of his situation. The
most striking personages in history are produced by a
great variety of little incidents ; as from an infinity of
minute threads of hemp the mightiest cables are formed.

We have seen that Mr. Adams early became interested
in the welfare of his country ; to promote her weal he
devoted all the wealth he inherited and all the talents
he possessed. From a humble position in life, he rose
through successive gradations of rank until, in 1795,
he became governor of his native commonwealth.
The respect paid him at home and abroad was such

as his extraordinary merits were calculated to command.

George Clymer, of Philadelphia, writing from England to Josiah Quincy, Jr., directed his friend as
follows:

"I beg you will make my particular compliments to
Mr. Hancock and Mr. S. Adams. There are no men
more worthy of general esteem; the latter I cannot
sufficiently respect for his integrity and abilities. All
good Americans should erect a statue to him in their
hearts."

Josiah Quincy, in turn, writing to his wife from
London, in a letter dated Dec. 7, 1774, remarks:

"The character of Mr. Samuel Adams stands very
high here. I find many who consider him the first
politician in the world. I have found more reason
every day to convince me that he has been right when
others supposed him wrong."

General Joseph Read, of Pennsylvania, on being
offered a heavy bribe by Governor Johnson in 1778
returned this pithy answer to the corrupt attempt on
his republican loyalty. "I am not worth purchasing,
but such as I am, the king of Great Britain is not rich
enough to do it." Such integrity was not uncommon,
during our Revolution, but in Samuel Adams it was
proverbial. He might have declared at any time,
without fear of contradiction, with Cardinal de Retz, " In
the most difficult times of the Republic, I never deserted
the State; in her most prosperous fortune, I never
never tasted of her sweets; in her most desperate
circumstances, I knew not fear." During the most

gloomy periods of our national struggle, when others were desponding, he always kept up cheerful spirits, gently rebuking the fears of others, and expressing his unwavering reliance upon the protection of an over-ruling Providence, who he had felt assured from the first, would conduct the country through all its trials to deliverance and prosperous repose. As a patriot, he toiled incessantly, without complaint; as a Christian, he trusted in God, and was not confounded.

Grattan said of Fox, that "He stood against the current of the court; he stood against the tide of the people, he stood against both united; he was the isthmus lashed by the waves of democracy, and by the torrent of despotism, unaffected by either, and superior to both; the Marpesian rock that struck its base to the centre, and raised its forehead to the skies." And such, too, was Samuel Adams. He was the most puritanic of all our statesmen. Others were endowed with the more splendid gifts, and more flexile powers of popular harangue; but he, above all his cotemporaries, glorified with his incorruptible poverty the Revolution which he was the first to excite and the last to abandon.

In 1781, Mr. Adams retired from Congress, with the desire, in the near prospect of peace, to withdraw from all public labors. But he was repeatedly pressed into the service of his country. He was a member of the convention which formed the constitution of Massachu-setts, and of the committee which drafted it. He was successively a member of the Senate, president of that body, and member of the convention which adopted the Federal Constitution. In 1789, he was elected lieutenant-governor, in which office he continued until 1794, when he succeeded John Hancock as Governor of the State. To this office he was annually elected until 1797, when his age and increasing infirmities compelled him to retire from public life altogether. He died on the 3d of October, 1803, in the eighty-second year of his age. At the close of his life, and from a much earlier period, he had a tremulous motion of the head, which probably added to the solemnity of his eloquence, as this was, in some measure, associated with the wonderful melody of his tones.

Samuel Adams was the last of the Puritans—"a class of men," says Governor Everett, "to whom the cause of civil and religious liberty, on both sides of the Atlantic, is mainly indebted, for the great progress which it has made for the last two hundred years ; and when the Declaration of Independence was signed, that dispensation might be considered as brought to a close. At time when the new order of things was inducing laxity of manners and a departure from the ancient strictness, Samuel Adams clung with greater tenacity to the wholesome discipline of the fathers. His only relaxation from the business and cares of life was in the indulgence of a taste for sacred music, for which he was qualified by the possession of a most angelic voice, and a soul solemnly impressed with religious sentiment. Resistance to oppression was his vocation."

He was a Christian. At an early age he was imbued with the spirit of piety, and the purity of his life verified tho sincerity of his profession. The last production of

his pen was in favor of Christian truth, and the light
that cheered him in death emanated from the Cross.

> "He is a freeman whom the truth makes free,
> And all are slaves besides."

CHAPTER IV.

JOSIAH QUINCY, JR.,

ORATOR OF REFINED ENTHUSIASM

THIS distinguished patriot was born in Boston, February 23d, 1744. His temperament was ardent, and his sensibilities were extremely acute. He acquired the rudiments of a classical education at Braintree, and, in 1759, entered Harvard College, where he distinguished himself for upright conduct and ripe scholarship. He graduated in 1763, and in due course took his second degree, with very high reputation. His theme on the occasion was "Patriotism," and is said to have been remarkable both on account of its composition and delivery. "His taste," says his biographer, "was refined by an intimate acquaintance with the ancient classics, and his soul elevated and touched by the spirit of freedom they breathe. His compositions during this period also prove, that he was extensively conversant with the best writers of the French and English schools. Above all, the genius of Shakspeare seems to have led captive his youthful imagination. In his writings, quotations, or forms of expression, modelled upon those of that author, perpetually occur. There still exists among his papers, a manuscript of the date of 1762, he then being in the junior

C

class of the college, of seventy closely and minutely written quarto pages of extracts from that author.

Mr. Quincy read law in the office of Oxenbridge Thatcher, the distinguished advocate who was associated with James Otis against the Writs of Assistance. Mr. Thatcher died in 1765. Mr. Quincy had not then completed his preparatory studies, but remained the residue of his student's term, took a general oversight of the business of the office, and therein succeeded to a lucrative and extensive practice. He early made himself conspicuous by the ardor with which he wrote and spoke against the encroachments of the mother country

The boldness with which Quincy entered upon the great contest is indicated by the following sentiments published by him in 1770, in the midst of great excitement, and only twenty days previous to the Boston massacre:

"In answer to the question, 'What end is the non-importation agreement to answer?' I give the following reply:

"From a conviction in my own mind, that America is now the slave of Britain; from a sense that we are every day more and more in danger of an increase of our burdens, and a fastening of our shackles, I wish to see my countrymen break off—*off for ever!*—all social intercourse with those whose commerce contaminates, whose luxuries poison, whose avarice is insatiable, and whose unnatural oppressions are not to be borne. That Americans will know their rights, that they will resume, assert, and defend them, are matters of which I harbor no doubt. Whether the arts of *policy*, or the arts of *wa*

will decide the contest, are problems, that we will solve
at a more convenient season. He, whose heart is en-
amored with the refinements of political artifice and
finesse, will seek one mode of relief; he whose heart is
free, honest, and intrepid, will pursue another, a bolder,
and a more noble mode of redress. This reply is so in-
telligible, that it needs no comment or explanation."

In August, 1774, at the urgent solicitation of his
political friends, Mr. Quincy determined to relinquish
business and embark for England on a secret mission in
behalf of his country. In this enterprise it is believed
that he accomplished much good. His efforts were unremitting, and his solicitude were both profound and sincere. This is indicated by the following extract from a
letter dated

"LONDON, *December* 14, 1774.

"In the sight of God, and all just men, the cause is
good; we have the wishes of the wise and humane, we
have the prayers of the pious, and the universal benison
of all who seek to God for direction, aid, and blessing.
I own I feel for the miseries of my country; I own I
feel much desire for the happiness of my brethren in
trouble; but why should I disguise, I feel ineffably, for
the honor—the honor, I repeat it—the honor of my
country. If in the trial, you prove, as your enemies say,
arrant poltroons and cowards, how ineffably contemptible will you appear; how wantonly and superlatively
will you be abused and insulted by your triumphing
oppressors!"

On the 16th of March, 1775, Mr. Quincy embarked
for Boston. His health was bad, and grew much worse

during the early part of the voyage. After being five weeks at sea, and yet far from his beloved home, he became convinced that death was at hand, and prepared to submit himself to the will of heaven with heroic calmness and Christian resignation. He repeatedly said to his companions that he had but one desire, which was, that he might live long enough to have an interview with Samuel Adams, or Joseph Warren; that granted, he should die content. But this wish was not granted to his patriotic heart.

As he drew near his native shore, the crisis he had so long expected transpired. The battle of Lexington was fought. According to his prediction, "his countrymen sealed their faith and constancy to their liberties with their blood." But he lived not to hear on earth the tidings of that glorious day. "On the 26th of April, 1775, within sight of that beloved country which he was not permitted to reach; neither supported by the kindness of friendship, nor cheered by the voice of affection, he expired; not, indeed, as, a few weeks afterwards, did his friend and co-patriot, Warren, in battle, on a field ever memorable and ever glorious; but in solitude, amidst suffering, without associate, and without witness; yet breathing forth a dying wish for his country, desiring to live only to perform towards her a last and signal service."

A few hours after his death, the ship, with his lifeless remains, arrived at Gloucester, Cape Ann, where the body of this devoted patriot was interred with becoming respect. Mr. Quincy had no opportunity of communicating to his countrymen the result of his observations

abroad, which was eager y expected. The regret on
this account, was however, merged in the universal sorrow for the untimely loss of a virtuous and gifted advocate of freedom, who was cut off in his thirty-first year,
in the very crisis of the country he so much loved.

We will now proceed to notice more particularly Mr.
Quincy's character as an orator. He was early distinguished at the bar, and has rendered his name immortal
as a patriot. The cultivation of elegant literature sup-
plied his pastime, but love of country was the strong
passion of his soul and the habitual inspiration of his
public toil.

The peculiar excellence of his oratorical character
was refined enthusiasm. The exercise of this was frequent and most effective. In the great debates which he
mainly led in Faneuil Hall, on the Stamp-Act, the Boston
Massacre, and the Boston Port-Bill, the pathos of his
eloquence, the boldness of his invectives, and his impressive vehemence, powerfully inflamed the zeal and
aroused the resentment of an oppressed people. His
lips teemed with those significant sounds and sweet
airs which ever give delight, as in sincerity he could
exclaim,

> "Hail to the glorious plans that spread
> The light with universal beam,
> And through life's human desert spread
> Truth's living, pure, perpetual stream!"

True enthusiasm is no other than the sublime inspiration of an imagination vividly exalted, always united to
reason, which it does not sacrifice, but which it animates
with the interest and pungency of impassioned senti-

ment. It is not to astonish by the scaffolding of his learning, that the true orator addresses assembled multitudes; it is to agitate, instruct, and subdue them. True eloquence dissipates doubt and rends prejudice, as hot shot explode a magazine; it is heat combined with force. Hence Dionysius, of Halicarnassus, compared Demosthenes to a sacred fire kindled on the Acropolis at Athens, to illuminate and warm a people equally blind and careless, upon questions of the greatest moment.

The orator of the people must vividly arouse in his own bosom all the grand sentiments of liberty, equality, humanity, and virtue, which are dormant in the hearts of all men. Before their fixed eyes and open mouths and swelling bosoms he must evoke the gigantic images of religion, country and glory. He must be able to make the meadows smile at their feet, and the shepherd's pipe of peace sound from distant hills; or, if it better suit his purpose, he must banish all pleasing images, and wrap the awed multitude in gloom made doubly fearful by earthquakes beneath and thunders on high. To do this successfully, there must be

> "Holy revealings,
> From the innermost shrine, from the light of the feelings."

The speaker must foster a constant regard for the high principles of truth and justice. He must remember that human beings are composed not of reason only, but of imagination also, and sentiment; and that his energies are legitimately employed only while, with simultaneous force, they give shape to the judgment and open proper springs of emotion in the heart. Speaking thus, he will

command universal confidence while he diffuses universal delight.

> " And aged ears play truant at his tales,
> And younger hearings are quite ravished,
> So sweet and voluble is his discourse."

Quincy appeared at an auspicious moment for the
exercise of his peculiar talents. The statue of Liberty
was not yet cast, but the metal was abundant, was already boiling in the furnace, and how soon the glorious
work was to be consummated, is indicated by the following extract of an address which our orator published
in the Boston Gazette, October, 1767 :

"Be not deceived, my countrymen. Believe not
these venal hirelings when they would cajole you by
their subtleties into submission, or frighten you by their
vaporings into compliance. When they strive to flatter
you by the terms, "moderation and prudence," tell them
that calmness and deliberation are to guide the judgment; courage and intrepidity command the action.
When they endeavor to make us 'perceive our inability
to oppose our mother country,' let us boldly answer:
In defence of our civil and religious rights, we dare oppose the world; with the God of armies on our side,
even the God who fought our fathers' battles, we fear
not the hour of trial, though the host of our enemies
should cover the field like locusts. If this be enthusiasm,
we will live and die enthusiasts. Blandishments will
not fascinate us, nor will threats of a 'halter,' intimidate
For under God, we are determined, that wheresoever,
whensoever, or howsoever, we shall be called to make
our exit, we will die freemen.

"Well do we know that all the regalia of this world cannot dignify the death of a villain, nor diminish the the ignominy with which a slave shall quit his existence. Neither can it taint the unblemished honor of a son of freedom, though he should make his departure on the already prepared gibbet, or be dragged to the newly erected scaffold for execution. With the plaudits of his conscience he will go off the stage. A crown of joy and immortality shall be his reward. The history of his life his children shall venerate. The virtues of their sire shall excite their emulation."

This is a fair specimen of Mr. Quincy's composition. It indicates a power to seize boldly on the attention of an audience. It is a style calculated to arouse its pity, or its indignation, its sympathies, its repugnances, or its pride. It is thus that the popular orator must deal with his fellow men, whether addressing them through the pen or living voice. He must seem to love the public breath and receive its inspiration, while it is himself who communicates to others his own. When he shall have, in a manner, detached all the souls of the community from their bodies, and they have come to group themselves at his feet, and are docile under the magical power of his look, then might it be truly said that all those souls had passed into his own. Behold how they undulate in sympathy with the movements of the oratorical mind, the master whom they rapturously obey. They advance or retire, are raised or depressed, as he wills. They are suspended upon his lips by the graces of persuasion, and by a glorious abandonment to his own strong emotions, he captivates and subdues every listening spirit.

In his popular harangues, Mr. Quincy produced the results of his extensive reading in a simple and most forcible manner. He was familiar with the best writers in poetry and prose, and frequently quoted from them, especially the English dramatists. Tradition says, that in doing this, the execution was extraordinary. He gave forth not merely the verbiage, the cold medium of sentiment, but he vividly reproduced all that his author originally designed to express. He quoted a literary gem as though every line and word had been early transplanted into his heart—had been brooded over in silence and bathed at the fount of tears, to burst forth when called for, like the spontaneous and native growth of his soul.

However severe he was in private discipline, and strictly logical in the construction of his argument, in public, he stood unshackled, and careered over the popular mind on the wings of a free and flexible imagination. We should estimate addresses made to miscellaneous audiences by the circumstances which demand a little license and a good deal of freedom. Who would be so rash as to apply the square and compass to the delicate lyre of Homer, or the sublime one of Pindar? Thus wounded and encumbered, the divine instrument which before was redolent of ravishing harmony, henceforth utters nothing but sharp and discordant sounds.

This refined enthusiasm, so habitually exemplified by Mr. Quincy, constituted the main force of his public in-

6*

fluence. His speech might generally be defined as being logic set on fire. This is true of all effective eloquence. The speaking that is not imbued with the living light and heat of profound emotion, is like the statue of Polyphemus with his eye out; that feature is absent which most shows the soul and life.

About the last of September, 1768, hordes of foreign troops were landed in Boston from fourteen ships of war. With muskets loaded, bayonets fixed, drums beating, fifes playing, and fortified by a whole train of artillery, these mercenary soldiers took possession of the Common, the state-house, the court-house, and Faneuil Hall. It was at this moment of terror and danger that Quincy openly and fearlessly addressed his townsmen in a memorable speech. The following is an extract from his oration, the whole of which was reported in the Boston Gazette of October 3d:

"Oh, my countrymen! what will our children say when they read the history of these times, should they find we tamely gave way, without one noble struggle, the most invaluable of earthly blessings? As they drag the galling chain, will they not execrate us? If we have any respect for things sacred; any regard to the dearest treasure on earth;—if we have one tender sentiment for posterity;—if we would not be despised by the world;— let us, in the most open solemn manner, and with determined fortitude swear,—we will die,—if we cannot live freemen!'

Another fine display of his bold enthusiasm, was occasioned by the arrival of the obnoxious tea in Boston harbor, on Saturday, November 27th, 1773. A town meeting was held on the Monday following, and resolutions were passed, calling on the consignees not to receive it. In urging this measure, Mr. Quincy, with a strong perception of the events which would naturally follow, and wishing to try the spirit and to increase the energy of his fellow citizens, by setting before them in a strong light, the consequences that might be expected from their resolves, addressed the meeting in the following terms:

"It is not, Mr. Moderator, the spirit that vapors within these walls that must stand us in stead. The exertions of this day will call forth events, which will make a very different spirit necessary for our own salvation. Whoever supposes that shouts and hosannas will terminate the trials of the day, entertains a childish fancy. We must be grossly ignorant of the importance and value of the prize for which we contend; we must be equally ignorant of the power of those combined against us; we must be blind to that malice, inveteracy, and insatiable revenge, which actuate our enemies, public and private, abroad and in our bosom, to hope that we shall end this controversy without the sharpest conflicts; to flatter ourselves that popular resolves, popular harangues, popular acclamations, and popular vapor, will vanquish our foes. Les us consider the issue. Let us look to the end. Let us weigh and consider, before we advance to those measures, which must bring on the most trying and terrible struggle this country ever saw."

These specimens are enough to show that, however powerful this orator was with his pen, he was much more potent when seen and heard in the impressive act of living and spontaneous speech.

> " How this grace
> Speaks his own standing! what a mental power
> His eye shoots forth! how big imagination
> Moves in his lip! to the dumbness of the gesture
> One might interpret."

The spirit of eloquence is a social spirit, dwelling in the midst of men, making appeals to their sympathies, beguiling them of their fears, and aggrandizing their minds. It gathered its thousands around the bema and rostrum of old; it nerved nations like the tocsin of war, and made aggressions on the kingdoms of igno- rance and tyranny with the clear clarion cry of perpe- tual triumph. It was heard at the banquet of artists, the festival of authors, and the coronation of heroes. Eloquence was twin-born with Liberty; together they have harmoniously lived through all vicissitudes, and together they have migrated from land to land. The spirit of eloquence is the sun, which from its rising, in- spired the statue of Memnon; it is the flame which warmed into life the image of Prometheus. It is this which causes the graces and the loves to take up their habitations in the hardest marble, to subsist in the emp- tiness of light and shadow on the pictured canvas, or in winged words to bound from soul to soul through con- gregated masses with the potency and impressiveness of omnipotence.

Mr. Quincy possessed, in no ordinary degree, those attributes of voice, figure, look and action, which are essential to complete the full charm of eloquence. His face was instinct with expression ; his eye, in particular, glowed with intellectual splendor.

The lovers of elegant oratory must have keenly enjoyed Quincy's thrilling, imaginative, yet forcible style of address, which broke forth like intermittent flashes of lightning amid the thunders of colonial agitation. When fully aroused in view of the coming conflict, he was "seraphic all in fervency," and was superlatively impressive while "rolling the rapturous hosanna round." He was not less a patriot, for being something of a poet; he was in soul an orator, and his ardent heart fused into the liquid flow of brilliant eloquence the purest elements of democratic power. He had a warm heart and quick perception, organs which are ever on the alert to explore the beautiful and feel the sublime under all their forms, borrowing from multifarious life all its sensations, from nature all its wealth, and from art all its blandishments. If the fastidious condemned his style, the enraptured masses of the people adored his sentiments; some, it may be, pronounced him too ornate, and others too diffuse, but all listened to him with that profound admiration which is always the test and reward of noble and harmonious eloquence, emanating from a generous and honest heart.

> "As I listen'd to thee,
> The happy hours pass'd by us unperceiv'd,
> So was my soul fixed to the soft enchantment."

The popular orator must study the whole nature of man, and learn how to sway his passions, prejudices and sensibilities, as well as his reasoning faculty. The human soul is like a many-stringed instrument, upon which he alone can play with success who can touch with skill *all* the cords. And Hume, with all the ancient critics, has pronounced in favor of the orator who can produce the most powerful effect on the passions. Quinctilian says, logicians can be found every where. " An able argument is not rare ; but seldom has that orator appeared whose eloquence could carry the judge out of his depth ; who could throw him into what disposition of mind he pleased, fire him into resentment, or soften him into tears." Many have constructed arguments as logical as those of Demosthenes and Cicero, but none ever arrayed them before their audiences with such magic power. The greatest men of the age acknowledged the resistless force of such oratory. Even Julius Cæsar once confessed himself subdued by the eloquence of Cicero, and absolved a criminal contrary to his settled purposes.

Abstract speculations and the astute deductions of the metaphysician are very well in their place, but they are not by any means the best part of eloquence. On the contrary, they are utterly subversive of that glow of interest, vivacity of spirit, and richness of sentiment, which it is the prerogative of eloquence alone to create

> " Clear arguments may raise
> In short succession : yet th' *oratoric* draught
> Shall occupy attention's stedfast soul."

From deep and ardent enthusiasm alone, gush up

with irresistible impetuosity those overflowing streams of thrilling emotion, which take captive the popular heart and ignite it with corresponding zeal.

We have said that Mr. Quincy appeared at a time favorable to the cultivation of extraordinary force in speech. All great masters in this divine art are disciplined in storms. When Demosthenes—"the *orator by eminence*"—was thundering his patriotism over the country of his birth, and summoning the "band of the faithful" to resist the encroachments of a foreign and merciless usurper, he made Philip of Macedon quake to the very centre of his iron heart. That this faculty was soon extensively cultivated in ancient Greece, besides a vast quantity of evidence derived from other sources, not only from historians, but, likewise, from actual specimens of oratory yet extant, we may infer from the poems of Homer. This "Prince of Poets" invests his heroes with all the charm of eloquence, and in the third book of the Iliad there is a beautiful comparison between the oratory of Ulysses and that of Menelaus. This comparison cannot be more happily expressed than in the language of the admirable translation, by the illustrious poet of Twickenham.

> " When Atreus' son harangued the listening train,
> Just was his sense, and his expression plain;
> His words succinct yet full, without a fault,
> He spoke no more than just the thing he ought.
> But, when Ulysses rose, in thought profound,
> His modest eyes he fixed upon the ground;
> As one unskilled or dumb, he seemed to stand,
> Nor raised his head, nor stretched his sceptred hand.

But, when he speaks, what elocution flows!
Soft as the fleeces of descending snows,
The copious accents fall, with easy art,
Melting they fall and sink into the heart.
Wondering we hear; and fixed in deep surprise,
Our ears refute the censure of our eyes."

The eloquence of Nestor, of Diomede, of Hector, and of Agamemnon is truly pre-eminent. Of each of these men it may be said, with emphasis, that in this department, at least, he was unsurpassed if not unequalled. Their oratory embraces a union of the most polished elegance, the most glossy neatness, and the most exquisite modulation, with a remarkable purity and originality of mind, and strength and pomp of diction. The reply of Diomede to Agamemnon, in the ninth Iliad, displays the highest order of intellect and sentiment; and it is worthy of frequent and attentive perusal, so rich is it in sublimity and noble pathos.

" When kings advise us to renounce our fame
First let him speak, who first has suffered shame.
If I oppose thee, prince, thy wrath withhold,
The laws of council bid my tongue be bold;
Thou first, and thou alone, in field of fight
Durst brand my courage, and defame my might :
Nor from a friend th' unkind reproach appeared,
The Greeks stood witness, all our army heard.
The Gods, O Chief! from whom our honors spring,
The Gods have made thee but by halves a king.
    *   *   *   *   *   *
The noblest power, that might the world control,
They gave thee not,—a brave and virtuous soul.
Is this a general's voice, that would suggest
Fears like his own to every Grecian breast?

Confiding in our want of worth he stands ;
And if we fly, 'tis what our king commands.
Go thou, inglorious ! from the embattled plain :
Ships thou hast store, and nearest to the main.
A nobler care the Grecains shall employ,
To combat, conquer, and extirpate Troy.
Here Greece shall stay, or if all Greece retire.
Myself will stay, 'till Troy or I expire ;
Myself and Sthenelus will fight for fame :
God bade us fight ; and 'twas with God we came."

The tears which an orator like Quincy compels his audience to shed, make friends and brothers of them all.

"One touch of nature makes the whole world kin."

Faith and feeling become strengthened by diffusion. Each individual feels himself stronger among so many kindred associates, and the minds of all flow together in one grand and irresistible stream. The auditor loves to yield himself up to the fascination of a rich, mellow voice, a commanding attitude, and a brilliant physiognomy. He outruns the illusion. He is thrilled in every nerve, he is agitated with rapture or remorse, with indignation or grief. He blends all his emotions with the speaker, and is subdued or inspired under his power. He soon becomes stripped of all defence, and willingly exposed to every blow, so that the greatest effects are produced by the slightest words adroitly directed and skillfully expressed.

Mr. Quincy died before our national triumph was won. But he saw its glories. He prophetically described them in language worthy of his august theme, and equalled only by the splendid reality when it came.

"Spirits and genii like those who arose in Rome," said he, "will one day make glorious this more western world. America hath in store her Bruti and Cassii,—her Hampdens and Sidneys;—patriots and heroes, who will form *a band of brothers:*—men, who will have memories and feelings, courage and swords;—courage, that shall inflame their ardent bosoms, till their hands cleave to their swords, and their swords to their enemies' hearts"

CHAPTER V

JOHN HANCOCK,

DIGNIFIED CAVALIER OF LIBERTY

The Revolutionary period of our history is exceedingly interesting, whether considered in the object at
stake, the series of acts by which it was accomplished,
or its immediate and remote results. Says Sparks, "it
properly includes a compass of twenty years, extending
from the close of the French war in America to the
general peace at Paris. The best history in existence,
though left unfinished, that of the Peloponnesian war,
by Thucydides, embraces exactly the same space of
time, and is not dissimilar in the details of its events.
The Revolutionary period, thus defined, is rounded with
epic exactness, having a beginning, a middle, and an
end ; a time for causes to operate, for the stir of action,
and for the final results. The machinery in motion is
on the broadest scale of grandeur. We see the new
world, young in age, but resolute in youth, lifting up
the arm of defiance against the haughtiest power of the
old ; fleets and armies, on one side, crossing the ocean
in daring attitude and confiding strength ; on the other,
men rallying round the banner of union, and fighting
on their natal soil for freedom, rights, existence ; the

long struggle and successful issue ; hope confirmed, justice triumphant. The passions are likewise here at work, in all the changing scenes of politics and war, in the deliberations of the senate, the popular mind, and the martial excitements of the field. We have eloquence and deep thought in council, alertness and bravery in action, self-sacrifice, fortitude, and patient suffering of hardships through toil and danger to the last. If we search for the habiliments of dignity with which to clothe a historical subject, or the loose drapery of ornament with which to embellish a narrative, where shall we find them thronging more thickly, or in happier contrasts than during this period ?"

Prominent among the actors in the great drama referred to above, was John Hancock. He was born in Quincy, formerly Braintree, 1737. The grandfather and the father of our hero were both distinguished clergymen. His father died early, leaving him to the care of a wealthy uncle, by whom he was educated and made the heir of great wealth. Young Hancock, at the early age of seventeen, was graduated at Harvard, in the year 1754. Having spent some years in the counting-house of his uncle, in 1760 he visited England, was present at the funeral of George II. and the coronation of his successor—a monarch against whom he was destined to wage a protracted and successful war. When twenty-seven years old, he returned to his native land, and, on the death of his generous patron, came into the possession of an immense fortune.

In October, 1774, Mr. Hancock was unanimously elected president of the Massachusetts Provincial Convention. The next year, the first of the Revolution, he ascended to the highest political distinction then possible, by being made the president of the Continental Congress. It has been well remarked, "that by his long experience in business as *moderator* of the town-meetings, and presiding officer and speaker of the provincial assemblies, during times of great turbulence and commotion, he was eminently qualified, as well as by his natural dignity of manners, to preside in this great council of the nation."

Hancock was chosen governor of Massachusetts in 1779, and was annually re-elected until 1785. After an interval of two years, during which Mr. Bowdoin occupied the post, Hancock was again placed in the governor's chair, which he occupied until Oct. 8, 1793, when he died, aged 56 years.

Mr. Hancock was a magnificent liver, lavishingly bountiful when once enlisted, and splendidly hospitable to the friends of any cause he loved. Mr. Tudor, in his life of Otis, thus speaks of the effect which the sudden acquisition of his uncle's bounty had upon him, and the manner in which his resources were employed.

"This sudden possession of wealth turned the eyes of the whole community towards him, his conduct under this trying prosperity secured universal esteem and good will. It made him neither giddy, arrogant, nor profligate ; he continued his course of regularity, industry, and moderation. Great numbers of people received employment at his hands, and in all his commercial transactions, he exhibited that fair and liberal character which commonly distinguishes the extensive and affluent merchant."

It was natural that the Boston patriots should wish to enlist this ardent and influential citizen in the popular cause. The manner in which this end was attained is described in the following letter from John Adams to the author referred to above: " I was one day walking in the mall, and accidentally met Samuel Adams. In taking a few turns together, we came in full view of Mr. Hancock's house. Mr. Adams, pointing to the stone building, said, 'This town has done a wise thing to day.' 'What?' 'They have made that young man's fortune their own.' His prophecy was literally fulfilled, for no man's property was ever more entirely devoted to the public. The town had that day chosen Mr. Hancock into the legislature of the province. The quivering anxiety of the public under the fearful looking-for of the vengeance of king, ministry, and parliament, compelled him to a constant attendance in the House, his mind was soon engrossed by public cares, alarms, and terrors; his business was left to subalterns, his private affairs neglected, and continued to be so to the end of his life."

Once interested in the cause of his country, he put every thing at stake, and incurred the most violent hatred of England. He was *the dignified cavalier of American liberty*. In the proclamation issued by General Gage, after the battle of Lexington, and a few days before that of Bunker Hill, offering pardon to the *rebels*, he and Samuel Adams were especially excepted, their offences being " of too flagitious a nature to admit of any other consideration than that of condign pun ishment."

When the Declaration of Independence was to be authenticated by the signature of the president of Congress, and given to the world, Hancock wrote his name in a bold character, that was evidently designed never to be erased.

Hancock and Adams, by their station in popular esteem, and zeal in the popular cause, succeeded Otis as the object of parliamentary insult and denunciation, as is evident from abundant instances recorded in the debates of that day. The two following are extracted from the speeches of Mr. Fox. The first occurred in a debate in 1779, on the Irish discontents, when he assailed Mr. Dundas, and illustrated the present subject, by allusions to former measures respecting America :— " What was the consequence of the sanguinary mea- sures recommended in those bloody, inflammatory speeches ? Though Boston was to be starved, though Hancock and Adams were proscribed—yet, at the feet of these very men, the Parliament of Great Britain were obliged to kneel, to flatter, and to cringe ; and as they had the cruelty at one time to denounce ven- geance against those men, so they had the meanness afterwards to prostrate themselves before them, and implore their forgiveness.—Was he who called the Americans ' *Hancock and his crew,*' to reprehend any set of men for inflammatory speeches ?" In the debate on the address to the king, in 1781, speaking of the American war, he said, " They (the ministers) com- menced war against America after that country had

offered the fairest propositions, and extended her arms
to receive us into the closest connection. They did
this contrary to their own sentiments of what was
right, but they were over-ruled by that high and secret
authority, which they durst not disobey, and from
which they derive their situations. They were ordered
to go on with the American war or quit their places.
They preferred emolument to duty, and kept their
ostensible power at the expense of their country. To
delude the parliament and the people, they then described
the contest to be a mere squabble. It was not America
with whom we had to contend, it was with ' *Hancock
and his crew,*' a handful of men would march triumphantly from one end of the continent to the other." This
was the language sounded in that House, and for this
language a learned member of it (Lord Loughborough)
was exalted to the dignity of a peer, and enrolled
among the hereditary council of the realm. He was
thus rewarded for no other merit, that he could discover,
but that of vehemently abusing our fellow subjects in
America, and calling their opposition, the war of
"*Hancock and his crew.*"

Mr. Hancock was indefatigable in his patriotic labors
to the last days of his life. The author of " Familiar
Letters on Public Characters," who was his neighbor
and knew him well, says that Hancock was mainly
instrumental in causing the constitution to be adopted
in Massachusetts. " He had been absent some days,
from illness. On the 31st of January, 1788, he resumed
his place, and after remarking on the difference of
opinion which prevailed in the convention, as he had

seen from the papers, he had to propose that the constitution should be adopted; but that the adoption should be accompanied by certain amendments, to be submitted to Congress, and to the States. He expressed his belief, that it would be safe to adopt the constitution, under the expectation that the amendments would be ratified. The discussion appears then, to have turned on the probability of obtaining such ratification. It cannot be assumed, for certainty, that this measure of Hancock's secured the adoption; but it is highly probable. The convention may have been influenced by another circumstance. About this time a great meeting of mechanics was held at the Green Dragon tavern, situated in what is now part of Union street, and westerly of the Baptist meeting-house. The tavern and the street were thronged. At this meeting resolutions were passed, with unanimity and acclamation, in favor of the adoption. But notwithstanding Hancock's conciliatory proposal, and this expression of public feeling, the constitution was adopted by the small majority of *nineteen* out of three hundred and fifty-five votes.

" The adoption was celebrated in Boston by a memorable procession, in which the various orders of mechanics displayed appropriate banners. It was hailed with joy throughout the States. General Washington is well known to have expressed his heartfelt satisfaction that the important State of Massachusetts had acceded to the union."

The talents of Hancock were useful, rather than brilliant. His personal dignity and great practical skil in business, rendered him a superior presiding officer 'n deliberative assemblies. His voice was sonorous, his apprehensions were quick, and his knowledge of parliamentary forms, combined with his well known devotion to the popular cause, rendered him the object of universal respect.

When Washington consulted the legislature of Massachusetts upon the propriety of bombarding Boston, Hancock advised its being done immediately, if it would benefit the cause, although the most of his immense property consisted in houses and other real estate in that town.

But Hancock was ready to sacrifice more than property, more than life even ; if necessary, he was willing to sacrifice his popularity in aid of the cause of national freedom. Though in this matter he was a man of deeds more than words, yet he shunned not in the most public and forcible manner to express the most ardent and patriotic sentiments.

In the very darkest hour of colonial despair, he came boldly forward in an exercise commemorative of those who fell in the unhappy collision with British soldiers in State street, and in his "Oration on the Massacre," as it was called, poured forth the following terrible denunciations:

"Let this sad tale of death never be told without a tear; let not the heaving bosom cease to burn with a manly indignation at the relation of it, through the long tracts of future time ; let every parent tell the shameful story to his listening children till tears of pity glisten in their eyes, or boiling passion shakes their tender frames.

" Dark and designing knaves, murderers, parricides ! now dare you tread upon the heartn which has drunk the blood of slaughtered innocence, shed by your hands ? How dare you breathe that air which wafted to the ear of heaven the groans of those who fell a sacrifice to your accursed ambition ? But if the laboring earth does not expand her jaws—if the air you breathe is not commissioned to be the minister of death—yet, hear it, and tremble ! The eye of heaven penetrates the secret chambers of the soul ; and you, though screened from human observation, must be arraigned—must lift your hands, red with the blood of those whose death you have procured at the tremendous bar of God.'

In an oration delivered in Boston, on the 5th of March, 1774, Mr. Hancock concluded with the following excellent remarks :

" I have the most animating confidence, that the present noble struggle for liberty will terminate gloriously for America. And let us play the man for our God, and for the cities of our God ; while we are using the means in our power, let us humbly commit our righteous cause to the great Lord of the universe, who loveth righteousness and hateth iniquity. And having secured the approbation of our hearts, by a faithful and unwearied discharge of our duty to our country, let us joyfully leave our concerns in the hands of Him who raiseth up and pulleth down the empires and kingdoms of the world."

The Greeks had a saying that every man lived as he spoke and Quinctilian tells us that it used to be said of Cæsar, that he always spoke with the same mind as that with which he conducted war. Hancock was natu-

rally energetic, and in his happier inspirations he was
very eloquent. Under his oratorical sway, his cotem
poraries were sometimes greatly moved.

> " Their listening powers
> Were awed, and every thought in silence hung,
> And wondering expectation."

New England has ever been fruitful oɩ ᵣipe scholars
and effective speakers. Why is this? Why should
vivid imagination, blended with sound judgment, abound
in that frigid region? We think that several causes
tend to produce the result; and among the first is the
fact of its high northern latitude and rugged soil.

Edward Everett, speaking on this topic, well remarks:
The qualities of our climate and soil enter largely in
ɔther ways into that natural basis, on which our prosperity and our freedom have been reared. It is these
which distinguish the smiling aspect of our busy,
thriving villages from the lucrative desolation of the
sugar islands. and all the wide-spread, undescribed, indescribable miseries of the colonial system of modern
Europe, as it has existed beyond the barrier of these
mighty oceans, in the unvisited, unprotected, and un-
avenged recesses of either India. We have had abundant reason to be contented with this austere sky, this
hard, unyielding soil. Poor as it is, it has left us no
cause to sigh for the luxuries of the tropics, nor to covet
the mines of the southern regions of our hemisphere.
Our rough and hardly subdued hill-sides and barren
plains have produced us that, which neither ores, nor
spices. nor sweets could purchase,—which would not

spring in the richest gardens of the despotic East. The compact numbers and the strength, the general intelligence and the civilization, which, since the world began, were never exhibited beneath the sultry line, have been the precious product of this iron-bcund coast. The rocks and the sands, which would yield us neither the cane nor the coffee tree, have yielded us, not only an abundance and a growth in resources, rarely consistent with the treacherous profusion of tropical colonies, but the habits, the manners, the institutions, the industrious population, the schools and the churches, beyond all the wealth of all the Indies.

'Man is the nobler growth our soil supplies,
And souls are ripened in our northern skies.'

"Describe to me a country rich in veins of the precious metals, that is traversed by good roads. Inform me of the convenience of bridges, where the rivers roll over golden sands. Tell me of a thrifty, prosperous village of freemen, in the miserable districts where every clod of the earth is kneaded up for diamonds, beneath the lash of the task-master. No, never! while the constitution, not of States, but of human nature, remains the same; never, while the laws, not of civil society, but of God are unrepealed, will there be a hardy, virtuous, independent yeomanry, in regions where two acres of untilled banana will feed a hundred men. It is idle to call that *food*, which can never feed a free, intelligent, industrious population. It is not food; it is dust; it is chaff; it is ashes; there is no nourishment in it, if it be not carefully sown, and painfully reaped, by laborious freemen, on their own fee-simple acres."

In hardy industry, the body becomes healthy and athletic; while the mind, by like discipline, grows free and mighty in its freedom. It is to be expected, under such circumstances, that a race of men will spring up in full maturity, as from the sowing of Cadmus. Such persons enjoy the highest liberty, and are prompt to defend their rights, exclaiming,

> " Seize then, my soul! from Freedom's trophied dome,
> The harp which hangeth high between the shields
> Of Brutus and Leonidas! With that
> Strong music, that soliciting spell, force back
> Earth's free and stirring spirit that lies entranced."

New England has a sterile soil and severe clime ; but she also has comfortable school-rooms and a copious literature, and these are the products and proofs of her greatest power. Our distinguished countryman, Mr. Wheaton, in his history of the Northmen, indicates the reasons why they are passionately attached to their bleak homes, and why they are not only happy there, but intelligent beyond the majority of mankind. Before the tenth century, Iceland possessed a national literature in full bloom. The flowers of poetry sprang up luxuriantly amidst eternal ice and snows. Ennobling wisdom and beautifying art were cultivated with success. How so? The Icelanders were free and independent. Their arctic isle was not warmed by a Grecian sun, but their hearts glowed with the fire of freedom. The natural divisions of the country by icebergs and lava streams, insulated the people from each other, and the inhabitants of each valley and each hamlet formed, as it were, an independent community. These were again re-united in the general national assembly of the Althing, which resembled the Amphictyonic Council or Olympic Games, where all the tribes of the nation convened to offer the common rites of their religion, to legislate on general affairs, and to listen to the lays of the Skald and the eloquent eulogy which commemorated the exploits of their ancestors. The best writers of England and Germany have been translated into Icelandic, and when each family pursues its avocations through dreary winters, assembled around the reading and working lamp pendant from each roof, it is the business of some one constantly to read aloud from favorite authors, a practice which explains why the people are free, and their intellects both elegant and profound.

It is not often that education becomes subservient to the cause of tyranny. France, in three revolutions, poured forth her scholars to protect popular rights. Elevated institutions of learning have almost always arrayed themselves on the side of liberty. The University of Oxford presents a melancholy exception, in connection with the era when the spirit of republicanism was extinguished for a time, in the blood of Sidney and Russell. In direct reference to the death of these patriots, while the block was yet reeking with their blood, that institution, in solemn convocation, declared that the principles for which they died—that civil authority is derived from the people—that government is

a mutual compact between the sovereign and the subject—that the latter is discharged from his obligation
if the former fail to perform his—that birthright gives
no exclusive right to govern—were "damnable doctrines, impious principles, fitted to deprave the manners
and corrupt the minds of men, promote seditions, over-
turn states, induce murder, and lead to atheism." But,
when, in the Colonies of America, gathered and burst
the tempest which threatened to "push from its moor-
ings the sacred ark of the common safety, and to drive
the gallant vessel, freighted with every thing dear, upon
the rocks, or lay it a sheer hulk upon the ocean,'' then
did the graduates of our colleges appear in the front
rank of heroes, powerful to "ride on the whirlwind and
direct the storm."

Accuracy of observation is a trait in New England
minds as prominent as that of patient investigation.
An incident in the life of the German poet, Schiller,
will illustrate this characteristic. His father once
found him, perched in a solitary place on a tree, gazing
at the tempestuous sky, and watching the flashes of
lightning as luridly they gleamed over it. To the
reprimands of his parent, the enthusiastic truant plead
in extenuation "that the lightning was very beautiful,
and that he wished to see where it was coming from."
And so of the Yankees, they will climb, if possible, to
the sources of the sublime, and earnestly inquire whence
every thing beautiful is derived.

But, perhaps, that which gives most force and prac-
ticalness to the oratory of the eastern States, is the
influence which the Bible and religious institutions

every where exert on the popular mind. It is unnecessary to multiply proofs of the divine power of religion
in forming an effective style of written language and
living speech. Dryden attributes his excellence in
prose composition, to the frequent perusal of Tillotson's
works ; and Lord Chatham, when asked the secret of
his elevated and eloquent style, replied that he had
often learned Dr. Barrow's sermons by heart.

If we carefully analyze the speeches of the greatest
orators of Christendom, living and dead, we shall find
them indebted for their best passages to the holy Scriptures. The influence of these on the mind of a true
orator is well set forth in the following passage descrip-
tive of Curran. " In the course of his eloquence, the
classic treasures of profane antiquity are exhausted
He draws fresh supplies from the sacred fountain of
living waters. The records of holy writ afford him the
sublimest allusions. It is there he stirs every principle
that agitates the heart or sways the conscience, carries
his auditory whither he pleases, ascends from man to
the Deity, and, again, almost seems to call down to
earth fire from heaven. While they who listen, filled
with a sense of inward greatness, feel the high nobility
of their nature in beholding a being of the same species
gifted with such transcendent qualities, and, wrapt in
wonder and delight, have a momentary relief,—that to
admire the talents, is to participate in the genius of the
orator."

Mr. Pickering has left us the following description of
the personal appearance of the subject of this sketch:

" In June, 1782, Governor Hancock had the ap-

7*

pearance of advanced age, though only forty-five. He had been repeatedly and severely afflicted with the gout, a disease much more common in those days than it now is, while dyspepsia, if it existed at all, was not known by that name. As recollected, at this time, Gov. Hancock was nearly six feet in stature, and of thin person, stooping a little, and apparently enfeebled by disease. His manners were very gracious, of the old style of dignified complaisance. His face had been very handsome. Dress was adapted quite as much to be ornamental as useful. Gentlemen wore wigs when abroad, and, commonly, caps when at home. At this time (June, 1782), about noon, Hancock was dressed in a red velvet cap, within which was one of fine linen. The latter was turned up over the lower edge of the velvet one, two or three inches. He wore a blue damask gown, lined with silk; a white stock, a white satin embroidered waistcoat, black satin small-clothes, white silk stockings, and red morocco slippers."

After having suffered severely for several years from gout, he died, as before stated, in October, 1793, aged fifty-six. His body lay in state at his mansion for some days, and then was interred with extraordinary demonstrations of public grief.

" dear peaceful and how powerful is the grave !"

CHAPTER VI.

JOSEPH WARREN,

TYPE OF OUR MARTIAL ELOQUENCE.

BEFORE proceeding to the main object of the present sketch, let us briefly review the circumstances which compelled our fathers to the employment of military force in the conquest of personal and national freedom. The British cabinet attempted to tax the Colonies, under the pretence of providing for their protection, but in reality to relieve the nation from the enormous debt under which Great Britain was oppressed. In March, 1764, as a prelude to the Stamp-Act, the House of Commons resolved, "That towards further defraying the necessary expenses of protecting the Colonies, it may be necessary to charge certain stamp duties upon them;" and this resolution was followed by what was commonly called the Sugar Act, passed on the 5th of April, prefaced by the following obnoxious preamble : " Whereas it is JUST and *necessary* that a revenue be raised in America, for defraying the expenses of defending, protecting, and securing the same ; we, the commons, &c., towards raising the same, give and grant unto your Majesty, after the 29th day of September, 1764, on clay.

ed sugar, indigo, and coffee, &c., &c., the sum of," &c. This measure, declared by parliament to be so just, was regarded by its subjects here as oppressive and tyrannical, and as such they treated it.   It is literally true that they waged war against a preamble.

Having passed both Houses of Parliament, on the 22d of March, the Stamp-Act received the royal assent. Dr. Franklin, then in England, as agent for Pennsylvania, wrote to Charles Thompson, afterwards Secretary of Congress—" The sun of liberty is set; you must light up the lamps of industry and economy." Mr. Thompson significantly replied, " That he thought *other lights* would be lighted up to resist these unconstitutional measures." The Colonies were immediately and deeply aroused. The pulpit, especially, in New England, labored in the patriotic cause with great zeal and effect. The fires of liberty were kindled in every vale and on every hill, spreading their heat and light from province to province, until the conflagration embraced the whole land.

In Virginia the cry of resistance resounded in tones of thunder. In New York, ten boxes of stamps were seized by the populace, and destroyed. In Massachusetts, the strife was sterner still, and there, under the violence of hired ruffians, the first martyrs to American liberty fell. Otis, the invincible advocate, was mutilated by the bludgeons and dirks of assassins, Gray and other worthy citizens were shot down in the streets, and, in the great battle which these and other outrages had hastened, Warren expired.

Joseph Warren was born in Roxbury, in 1741. When

fourteen years old, he entered Harvard college, where ho bore a high character, and graduated with distinction. Under the direction of Dr. Lloyd, he studied medicine, and in the course of a few years became a distinguished practitioner in the town of Boston.

But he soon became absorbed in the great questions of the day, and sacrificed the fairest prospects for wealth and luxurious ease to perpetual toil in behalf of his country. In 1768, Dr. Warren addressed a letter to Governor Bernard, which the minions of royalty regarded as libellous, and an attempt was made to silence the author by an indictment, but the grand jury refused to find a bill. Nothing daunted, our hero became more busy than ever with both pen and tongue, and as the affection with which he was regarded, especially by the industrious classes, was universal and sincere, his influence upon all ranks was very great.

In the most open scenes and in the presence of the most envenomed foes, he was explicit in the assertion of republican sentiments and fearless in opposition to regal arrogance. A memorable instance illustrative of his character occurred in 1775. Several years before he had delivered the annual oration, commemorative of the massacre of the 5th of March, 1760, and when the time arrived for the appointment of an orator for 1775, he solicited the honor of appearing on that occasion in consequence of a threat uttered by some of the British officers, that they would take the life of any man who should dare to speak of the massacre on that anniver-sary. The day arrived, and the " Old South" was filled

to overflowing; the aisles, the stairs, and even the pulpit, were occupied by a foreign military. The intrepid
orator made his entrance by a ladder at the pulpit win-
dow, and with cool, collected mein, addressed the immense auditory. An awful stillness preceded the exordium. Each man felt the palpitations of his own heart,
and saw the pale but determined face of his neighbor.
The speaker began his oration in a firm tone of voice,
and proceeded with great energy and pathos. Warren
and his friends were prepared to chastise contumely,
and avenge an attempt at assassination.

" The scene was sublime. A patriot, in whom the
flush of youth and the grace and dignity of manhood
were combined, stood armed in the sanctuary of God, to
animate and encourage the sons of liberty, and to hurl
defiance at their oppressors. The orator commenced
with the early history of the country, described the
tenure by which we held our liberties and property, the
affection we had constantly shown the parent country,
boldly told them how, and by whom these blessings of
life had been violated. There was in this appeal to
Britain—in this description of suffering, agony, and
horror, a calm and high-souled defiance which must
have chilled the blood of every sensible foe. Such another hour has seldom happened in the history of man,
and is not surpassed in the records of nations. The
thunder of Demosthenes rolled at a distance from Philip
and his host—and Tully poured the fiercest torrent of
his invective when Cataline was at a distance, and his
dagger no longer to be feared; but Warren's speech

was made to proud oppressors, resting on their arms, whose errand it was to overawe, and whose business it was to fight.

If the deed of Brutus deserved to be commemorated by history, poetry, painting, and sculpture, should not this instance of patriotism and bravery be held in last ing remembrance ? If he

"That struck the foremost man of all this world,"

was hailed as the first of freemen, what honors are not due to him, who, undismayed, bearded the British lion, to show the world what his countrymen dared to do in the cause of liberty ? If the statue of Brutus was placed among those of the gods, who were the preservers of Roman freedom, should not that of Warren fill a lofty niche in the temple reared to perpetuate the remem brance of our birth as a nation ?"

An extract from this oration will be adduced, when we come to speak of Warren's eloquence. We are now more particularly concerned with his bravery. On hearing of the conflict at Lexington he hastened to the bloody scene and shared in its perils. While pressing on the foe, a musket-ball took off a lock of his hair close to his ear. Previous to receiving the appointment of major-general, he had been requested to take the office of physician-general to the army, but he chose to be where wounds were to be made, rather than where they were to be healed. Yet he lent his aid to the medical department of the army, and was of great service in its organization

Several days before the battle of Bunker Hill, the Provincial Congress appointed Dr. Warren to the com mand of their forces. The motive for not assuming the functions of that office, and the manner in which he chose to conduct himself on that occasion, are detailed as follows, in Austin's Life of Elbridge Gerry: "On the 16th of June, he had a conversation with Mr. Gerry, at Cambridge, respecting the determination of Congress to take possession of Bunker Hill. He said that for himself he had been opposed to it, but that the majority had determined upon it, and he would hazard his life to carry their determination into effect. Mr. Gerry expressed in strong terms his disapprobation of the measure, as the situation was such that it would be in vain to attempt to hold it, adding, 'but if it must be so, it is not worth while for you to be present; it will be madness to ex pose yourself, when your destruction will be almost in evitable.' 'I know it,' he answered; 'but I live within the sound of their cannon; how could I hear their roar ing in so glorious a cause, and not be there!' Again, Mr. Gerry remonstrated, and concluded with saying, 'As surely as you go there, you will be slain!' General Warren replied enthusiastically, 'Dulce et decorum est pro patria mori.' The next day his principles were sealed with his blood. Having spent the greater part of the night in public business at Watertown, he arrived at Cambridge at about five o'clock in the morning, and being unwell, threw himself on a bed. About noon, he was informed of the state of preparation for battle a Charlestown; he immediately arose, saying he was wel

again, and mounting a horse, rode to the place. He arrived at Breed's Hill a short time before the action commenced. Colonel Prescott, 'the brave,' (as Washington was afterwards in the habit of calling him) was then
the actual commanding officer. He came up to General
Warren to resign his command, and asked what were
his orders. General Warren told him he came not to
command, but to learn; and having, as it is said, borrowed a musket and cartouch-box, from a sergeant who
was retiring, he mingled in the thickest of the fight,
animating and encouraging the men more by his example than it was possible to do in any other way. He
fell after the retreat commenced, at some distance in the
rear of the redoubt. A ball passed through his head,
and killed him almost instantly. He was thrown into
the ground where he fell."

General Warren may be taken as a *type of our martial eloquence*, as well as a specimen of the highest
bravery. His career was brief, auspicious in its dawn,
diversified in its progress, but glorious in its termination
and subsequent influence on the welfare of man. He
cast himself into the front ranks of the Revolution, and
sacrificed himself the first victim of rank in the sublime
struggle for national independence.

While yet a student in college, he bore the reputation ,
of great talents, undaunted courage, and a generous but
indomitable independence of spirit. His manly life did
not belie the promise of his youth. His magnanimous
spirit soon became tempered in the furnace of national
suffering. His mental vision was therein clarified like

a prophet's, and like one inspired he proclaimed the
triumph for which he was ready to die.

To his friend, Josiah Quincy, jr., then in London,
advocating the claims of his country, he wrote the
following memorable note, dated,

"BOSTON, *Nov.* 21*st*, 1774.

" It is the united voice of America to preserve their
freedom, or lose their lives in defence of it.   Their resolutions are not the effects of inconsiderate rashness, but
the sound result of sober inquiry and deliberation.   I
am convinced that the true spirit of liberty was never
so universally diffused through all ranks and orders of
people, in any country on the face of the earth, as it
now is through all North America."

The times in which General Warren appeared were
calculated to give a martial hue to men's minds, and
powerfully to urge them to deeds of valor.   By a little
effort a fine collection of anecdotes might be made, to
illustrate the determined resolution and ardent enthusiasm, that pervaded the country.   The instance of
General Putnam is well known, who, hearing of the
Lexington engagement while he was ploughing on his
farm, more than a hundred miles distant, unyoked his
cattle, left his plough in the unfinished furrow, and without changing his dress, mounted his horse and rode off
to Cambridge, to learn the state of things.   He then
returned to Connecticut and raised a regiment in the
course of a few weeks.   Among other examples that
might be related, the following is from a living witness:
The day that the report of this affair reached Barnstable,
a company of militia immediately assembled and marched

off to Cambridge. In the front rank, there was a young man, the son of a respectable farmer, and his only child. In marching from the village, as they passed his house, he came out to meet them. There was a momentary halt, the drum and fife paused for an instant. The father, suppressing a strong and evident emotion, said, "God be with you all, my friends! and John, if you, my son, are called into battle, take care that you behave like a man, or else let me never see your face again!" A tear started into every eye, and the march was resumed. It was with this spirit that the noblest heroes of antiquity spoke and acted. "The forests of our arrows will ob-scure the sun," said Xerxes. "So much the better," replied Leonidas, "for then we shall fight in the shade."

Warren was himself but a vivid reflection of the popular feeling and its strong expression. The instincts of a true soul are sure; all the strength and all the divinity of knowledge lie enwrapped in some of the soul's profounder feelings.

Great national commotions, like the American Revo-lution, generally elicit martial orators, whose eloquence is like their profession, full of thrusts the most piercing, and of blows the most deadly. The son of Macedonia and pupil of Aristotle, captivated Greeks and Barbarians as much by his eloquence as by his martial victories. Cæsar commanded the Roman legions by the regal power of his speech. The great military eloquence of France was born amid the first shocks of tyranny and freedom. Napoleon, by a sudden blow of martial fire, embodied in words that spoke like exploding cannon, seized upon the old generals of the republic, upon the army, and upon his nation,—the irresistible empire of victory and of genius.

But Warren aspired only for personal rights and national independence. For this he plead and fought with all the power he possessed, body and soul. He felt the value of the boon, and put every thing, except honor, in jeopardy to attain it. To convince, one must be convinced; he must have something at stake, he must have character.

As the storm thickened, and ordinary souls quailed at its lowering aspect and rapid approach, Warren stood unblenched. When the awful crisis actually had come, he coolly buckled on his armor, and only as he snuffed the hot breath of battle, did he rise to the full height of his native grandeur. Then with bosom bared to the fiercest blows, and with heart throbbing high for his country's welfare, he rushed to the deadliest breach, diffusing animation among friends and consternation to foes. It is easy to conceive him careering amid the carnage on Bunker's heights, like Homer's hero on the plains of Troy:

> "Fill'd with the god, enlarged his muscles grew,
> Through all his veins a sudden vigor flew,
> The blood in brisker tides began to roll,
> And Mars himself came rushing on his soul.
> Exhorting loud through all the field he strode,
> And looked, and moved, Achilles, or a god."

We gain a more distinct conception of the martial spirit of Warren, from the peculiar character of his eloquence yet extant. One extract will suffice.

On March 6th, 1775, he delivered an oration, commemorative of "the Boston Massacre." In that fearful scene an event occurred which it is necessary to mention in order to feel the force of Warren's skillful and terrific amplification. After Mr. Gray had been shot through the body, and had fallen dead on the ground, a bayonet was pushed through his skull; part of the bone being broken, the brains fell out upon the pavement. The orator alludes to this act of needless barbarity in a manner worthy of Mark Anthony.

"The many injuries offered to the town, I pass over in silence. I cannot now mark out the path which led to that unequalled scene of horror, the sad remembrance of which takes the full possession of my soul. The sanguinary theatre again opens itself to view. The baleful images of terror crowd around me ; and discontented ghosts, with hollow groans, appear to solemnize the anniversary of the fifth of March.

"Approach we then the melancholy walk of death. Hither let me call the gay companion; here let him drop a farewell tear upon that body which so late he saw vigorous and warm with social mirth; hither let me lead the tender mother to weep over her beloved son—come, widowed mourner, here satiate thy grief; behold thy murdered husband gasping on the ground, and to complete the pompous show of wretchedness, bring in each hand thy infant children to bewail their father's fate;—take heed, ye orphan babes, lest, while streaming eyes are fixed upon the ghastly corpse, your feet slide on the stones bespattered with your father's brains ! Enough ; this tragedy need not be heightened by an infant weltering in the blood of him that gave it

birth.   Nature reluctant, shrinks already from the view
and the chilled blood rolls slowly backward to its fountain.   We wildly stare about, and with amazement ask,
who spread this ruin round us?   What wretch has
dared deface the image of God?   Has haughty France,
or cruel Spain, sent forth her myrmidons?   Has the
grim savage rushed again from the far distant wilderness, or does some fiend, fierce from the depth of
hell, with all the rancorous malice which the apostate
damned can feel, twang her destructive bow, and hurl
her deadly arrows at our breast?   No, none of these—
but, how astonishing! it is the hand of Britain that
inflicts the wound!"

Warren, viewed as he uttered the above sentiments in
"Old South," was a striking symbol of the revolt against
tyranny which he led.   Without any other weapon than
his eloquence, he boldly threw himself into the midst of
hostile legions, like a brave old paladin, defying whole
armies, alone.

> "Thou hast seen Mount Athos;
> While storms and tempests thunder on its brows,
> And oceans beat their billows at its feet,
> It stands unmoved and glories in its height.
> Such is that haughty man; his towering soul,
> Midst all the shocks and injuries of fortune,
> Rises superior, and looks down on Cæsar."

Indignant at the efforts made to stifle free discussion,
and to cheat the popular mind "of that liberty which
rarifies and enlightens it like the influence of heaven,"
he proclaimed the rights of man, undismayed by menace
and cheered on his patriotic brethren, while he awed

unprincipled sycophants into silence. His brave example and eloquent speech caused millions of hearts to beat
with a common sentiment of resistance. Every rock
and wild ravine was made a rampart to "the sons of
liberty," and their banner was on every summit un-
furled, inscribed in letters of fire, " *Resistance to tyrants
is obedience to God!*"

General Warren's speech resounds with the clash of
arms, and is imbued with a high spirit of chivalry and
faith. " Brief, brave and glorious was his young career," and while, by the fearful emergency in which his
country was plunged, he was compelled to tread "the
blood-shod march of glory," he was an upright and conscientious patriot, ready to receive "the deep scars of
thunder," and by his example to fortify the weak.
Warren knew that "'tis liberty lends life its soul of
light," and he was ready to immolate himself, if thus he
might win the boon for all mankind.

Says Edward Everett : "Amiable, accomplished, prudent, energetic, eloquent, brave ; he united the graces
of a manly beauty to a lion heart, a sound mind, a safe
judgment and a firmness of purpose, which nothing
could shake. At the period to which I allude, he was
but just thirty-two years of age ; so young, and already
the acknowledged head of the cause ! He had never
seen a battle-field, but the veterans of Louisburg and
Quebec looked up to him as their leader ; and the hoary-
headed sages who had guided the public councils for a
generation, came to him for advice. Such he stood,
the organ of the public sentiment, on the occasion just
mentioned. At the close of his impassioned address,

after having depicted the labors, hardships and sacrifices
endured by our ancestors, in the cause of liberty, he
broke forth in the thrilling words, "the voice of our fathers' blood cries to us from the ground !"   Three years
only passed away ; the solemn struggle came on ; foremost in council, he also was foremost in the battle-field,
and offered himself a voluntary victim, the first great
martyr in the cause.   Upon the heights of Charlestown,
the last that was struck down, he fell, with a numerous
band of kindred spirits, the gray-haired veteran, the
stripling in the flower of youth, who had stood side by
side through that dreadful day, and fell together, like the
beauty of Israel, on their high places !"

Warren was eminently chivalrous and brave.   Like
Louis XII. at Aignadel, he would exclaim to the timid :
" Let those who have fear, secrete themselves behind
me."   Or like the bold and generous Condé, he would
animate his countrymen in the darkest hour with the
cheerful cry, " Follow my white plume, you shall recognize it always on the road to victory."

In speech, as in action, he was sagacious and energetic.   His words teem with the sulphurous breath of
war, and are lurid with patriotic indignation, as if
coined at the cannon's mouth.   He seized his victim, as
a vulture grasps a serpent in his talons, and bearing him
aloft in triumph, tore him in fearless strength and scattered the fragments to the winds.   But this was the rage
produced by foreign aggression, and not the blind fury
of mad ambition.   Herein was Warren, like Washington, greater and nobler than Napoleon:

" The mighty heart that battled for the empire of the world,
And all but won, yet perish'd in the strife !"

Warren was a powerful orator, because he was a true man, and struggled for man's highest rights. Eloquence and liberty are the inseparable offspring of the same mother, nursed at the same breast; two beams from the same sun ; two chords of the same harp; two arrows from the same quiver; two thunderbolts twin-born in heaven, and most glorious in their conflicts and con-quests on the earth.

" 'Tis liberty alone that gives the flower
Of fleeting life its lustre and perfume,
And we are weeds without it. All constraint,
Except what wisdom lays on evil men,
Is evil; hurts the faculties, impedes
Their progress in the road of science ; blinds
The eyesight of Discovery ; and begets
In those that suffer it a sordid mind,
Bestial, a meagre intellect, unfit
To be the tenant of man's noble fcrm."

CHAPTER VII

JOHN ADAMS,

ORATOR OF BLENDED ENTHUSIASM AND SOBRIETY.

JOHN ADAMS was born at Quincy, then part of the old town of Braintree, October 19th, 1735. He was of Puritanic descent, his ancestors having early emigrated from England, and settled in Massachusetts. He was early noted for studious habits, and was placed under the classical tuition of Mr. Marsh, who was also the teacher of Josiah Quincy, Jr. Having been admitted to Harvard College, in 1751, Mr. Adams was graduated in 1755. In a class that was distinguished, he stood among the first. In 1758, he was admitted to the bar, and commenced the practice of law in his native town. The skill with which he conducted a criminal cause, at Plymouth, first gave him professional fame. His business increased with his reputation and ability until 1766, when he removed to Boston where he could enjoy a wider scope for his talents. In 1770, he had the boldness to undertake the defence of the British officers and soldiers, on account of the memorable massacre of the 5th of March. The result reflected honor upon himself and upon the jury who, in the midst of great exasperation, dared to be just in maintaining the supremacy of law.

In 1776, Mr. Adams was appointed Chief Justice of Massachusetts, but yielding to the ruling passion of his ardent and patriotic nature, he devoted himself almost entirely to politics. The impressions early made on his mind by James Otis in the famous argument against *Writs of Assistance*, seem to have given tone and direction to his whole subsequent career. Before twenty years of age he predicted a vast increase of population in the Colonies, anticipated their naval distinction, and foretold that all Europe combined, could not subdue them. His thoughts were early and sagaciously occupied on these topics. On the 12th of October, 1755, he wrote from Worcester as follows:

"Soon after the Reformation, a few people came over into this new world, for conscience sake. Perhaps this apparently trivial incident may transfer the great seat of empire into America. It looks likely to me; for, if we can remove the turbulent Gallics, our people, according to the exactest computations, will, in another century, become more numerous than England itself. Should this be the case, since we have, I may say, all the naval stores of the nation in our hands, it will be easy to obtain a mastery of the seas; and then the united force of all Europe will not be able to subdue us. The only way to keep us from setting up for ourselves is to disunite us.

"Be not surprised that I am turned politician. This whole town is immersed in politics. The interests of nations, and all the dira of war, make the subject of every conversation. I sit and hear, and after having

been led through a maze of sage observations, I sometimes retire, and laying things together, form some reflections pleasing to myself. The produce of one of
these reveries you have read above."

It has been said that "the true test of a great man—
that at least which must secure his place among the
higher order of great men—is his having been in advance of his age. This it is which decides whether or
not he has carried forward the great plan of human improvement; has conformed his views and adapted his
conduct to the existing circumstances of society, or
changed those so as to better its condition; has been
one of the lights of the world, or only reflected the borrowed rays of former luminaries, and sat in the same
shade with the rest of his generation at the same twilight
or the same dawn."

Tried by this test, it must be acknowledged that the
author of the above letter was among the wisest and
most provident seers of his day.

In 1765, Mr. Adams appeared before the public as an
author, in a work on the Canon and Feudal Law.

" The object of this work was to show that our New
England ancestors, in consenting to exile themselves
from their native land, were actuated, mainly, by the
desire of delivering themselves from the power of the
hierarchy, and from the monarchical and aristocratical
political systems of the other continent; and to make
this truth bear, with effect, on the politics of the times.
Its tone is uncommonly bold and animated, for that
period. He calls on the people, not only to defend, but
to study and understand their rights and privileges;

urges earnestly the necessity of diffusing general knowledge, invokes the clergy and the bar, the colleges and
academies, and all others who have the ability and the
means, to expose the insidious designs of arbitrary power,
to resist its approaches, and to be persuaded that there
is a settled design on foot to enslave all America. 'Be
it remembered,' says the author, 'that liberty must, at
all hazards, be supported. We have a right to it, derived from our Maker. But if we had not, our fathers
have earned it, and bought it for us, at the expense of
their ease, their estate, their pleasure and their blood.
And liberty cannot be preserved without a general
knowledge amoug the people, who have a right, from the
frame of their nature, to knowledge, as their great Crea-
tor who does nothing in vain, has given them understandings, and a desire to know; but besides this, they
have a right, an indisputable, unalienable, indefeasible
right to that most dreaded and envied kind of knowledge,
I mean of the character and conduct of their rulers.
Rulers are no more than attorneys, agents, and trustees
of the people; and if the cause, the interest and trust, is
insidiously betrayed, or wantonly trifled away, the people have a right to revoke the authority, that they themselves have deputed, and to constitute other and better
agents, attorneys and trustees.' "

In 1770, Mr. Adams was elected to the legislature by
the citizens of Boston. He took a deep interest in the
conflict with England, for which zeal he was especially
contemned by Governors Hutchinson and Gage.

By this time, impending dangers had so multiplied
that the united counsel of all patriots was demanded

A general Congress of delegates, to consider the affairs of the Colonies, having been decided upon, the legislature, on the 17th of June, 1774, elected James Bowdoin, Thomas Cushing, Samuel Adams, John Adams, and Robert Treat Paine, delegates from Massachusetts. The four last-named persons accepted their appointments, and took their seats in Congress, the first day of its session, September 5th, 1774, in Philadelphia. In this office Mr. Adams remained, till November, 1777, when he was appointed Minister to France. The year following, he was appointed Commissioner to treat of peace with England. Returning to the United States, he was a delegate from Braintree in the convention which framed the constitution of Massachusetts, in 1780. During the eight succeeding years, he was employed in the diplomatic service of the country, and resided at the various courts of Europe. In 1782 he concluded our first treaty with Holland. At a later period, he had the satisfaction of seeing the Minister Plenipotentiary of the Crown of England subscribe to the instrument which declared that his "Britannic Majesty acknowledged the United States to be free, sovereign, and independent." Returning to his beloved country in 1788, he was elected the first Vice President, a position which he occupied eight years, when he was raised to the Presidential chair, as immediate successor to the immortal Washington.

Leaving the illustrious subject of this sketch for a while in the most exalted political station man can ever hope to attain, let us attempt to analyze his character and describe his person.

Mr. Adams' individuality as a man and c'tizen, was strongly marked. We take him to have been the best specimen our early history affords of sobriety and en- thusiasm happily combined and wisely employed in promoting the public good. As a patriot he was firm, sagacious and persevering.

His firmness was indicated by the position he as- sumed as early as 1774, when, in company with three others named above, he was chosen by the Colony of Massachusetts, to represent them in the first Continenta! Congress. His friend, Sewall, who had taken the min isterial side in politics, and was at that time attorney-gen- eral of the province, hearing of his election, endeavored earnestly to dissuade him from his purpose of assuming the seat to which he had been appointed. He told him of the resolution of Great Britain to pursue her system with the greatest rigor ; that her power was irresistible, and would involve him in destruction, as well as all his associates. His response unfolds at once the dignity of his resolutions on contemplating this great and daring national movement.

"I know that Great Britain has determined on her system, and that very determination determines me on mine. You know that I have been constant and uni- form in opposition to her designs. Sink or swim, live or die, survive or perish, with my country, is my fixed, unalterable determination."

That this firmness was based on patriotic principle and inspired by it, is further indicated by what he said 'n a letter to his wife under circumstances of great pub- ic distress. He had heard of the attack made by the

British on Boston, of the dismay and ruin consequent thereon, but being not in the least daunted in his purpose, he wrote as follows :

" PHILADELPHIA, 20th September, 1774.

" I am anxious to know how you can live without government. But the experiment must be tried. The evils will not be found so dreadful as you apprehend them. Frugality, my dear, frugality, economy, parsimony, must be our refuge. I hope the ladies are every day diminishing their ornaments, and the gentlemen, too. Let us eat potatoes and drink water. Let us wear canvas and ˮundressed sheepskins, rather than submit to the unrighteous and ignominious domination that is prepared for us."

But Mr. Adams was a sagacious prophet in political matters, as well as a firm patriot. The celebrated letters of the 3d of July, 1776, abundantly prove this. A great living statesman has treated these letters in such a splendid manner in his eulogium on their author, that to quote them in their original shape, may indeed seem to destroy much of their effect. But we wish to contemplate the character of Mr. Adams through a medium of his own making; and shall here introduce the prophecy as he recorded it, in order to substantiate the position we have assumed.

" Yesterday, the greatest question was decided, which ever was debated in America, and a greater, perhaps, never was nor will be decided among men. A resolu tion was passed without one dissenting Colony, "that these United Colonies are, and of right ought to be, free and independent States, and as such they have and of right out to have, full power to make war, conclude peace, establish commerce and to do all other acts and things which other States may rightfully do." You will see, in a few days, a Declaration, setting forth the causes which have impelled us to this mighty Revolution, and the reasons which will justify it in the sight of God and man.

"When I look back to the year 1761, and recollect the arguments concerning Writs of Assistance in the Superior Court, which I have hitherto considered as the commencement of this controversy between Great Britain and America, and run through the whole period, from that time to this, and recollect the series of political events, the chain of causes and effects, I am surprised at the suddenness as well as greatness of this Revolution. Britain has been filled with folly, and America with wisdom; at least, this is my judgment. Time must determine. It is the will of heaven that the two countries should be sundered for ever. It may be the will of heaven that America shall suffer calamities still more wasting, and distresses yet more dreadful. If this is to be the case, it will have this good effect at least. It will inspire us with many virtues, which we have not, and correct many errors, follies and vices which threaten to disturb, dishonor and destroy us. The furnace of affliction produces refinement in States as well as individuals."

Then, speaking of the day on which the Declaration of Independence passed, he foretold that it would "be the most memorable epocha in the history of America.
8*

I am apt to believe that it will be celebrated by succeeding generations as the great anniversary festival. It ought to be commemorated, as the day of deliverance, by solemn acts of devotion to God Almighty. It ought to be solemnized with pomp and parade, with shows, games, sports, guns, bells, bonfires and illuminations, from one end of this continent to the other, from this time forward, forevermore.

"You will think me transported with enthusiasm, but I am not. I am well aware of the toil and blood, and treasure, that it will cost to maintain this Declaration, and support and defend these States. Yet, through all the gloom, I can see the rays of ravishing light and glory. I can see that the end is more than worth all the means; and that posterity will triumph in that day's transaction, even although we should rue it, which I trust in God we shall not."

We have said that Mr. Adams was firm, and that he was sagacious; we remark, thirdly, that he was ardent and energetic. His feelings were quick, and fully enlisted in the defence of his country; anything that reflected on her welfare was sure to arouse his indignation. Writing to his wife, he presents several instances in which his enthusiastic patriotism involved him in temporary confusion, such as on the following occasion, described in a letter, dated,

"FALMOUTH, 9th July, 1774.

"At another time, Judge Trowbridge said, 'It seems by Col. Barre's speeches, that Mr. Otis has acquired honor by releasing his damages to Robinson.' 'Yes,' says I, 'he has acquired honor with all generations.

Trowbridge—'He did not make much profit, I think.' Adams—'True, but the less profit, the more honor. He was a man of honor and generosity, and those who think he was mistaken, will pity him.'

"Thus you see how foolish I am. I cannot avoid exposing myself before these high folks; my feelings will at times overcome my modesty and reserve, my prudence, policy and discretion. I have a zeal at my heart for my country and her friends, which I cannot smother or conceal; it will burn out at times and in companies, where it ought to be latent in my breast This zeal will prove fatal to the fortune and felicity of my family, if it is not regulated by a cooler judgment than mine has hitherto been. Colonel Otis' phrase is, 'The zeal-pot boils over.'"

In all his public career, in perils the most imminent, and before foes the most mighty, Mr. Adams seems to have resolved on maintaining his position at any risk and, with this intent, to have ever sternly declared,

"Let them pull all about mine ears; present me
Death on the wheel, or at wild horses' heels;
Or pile ten hills on the Tarpeian rock,
That the precipitation might down stretch
Below the beam of sight, yet will I still
Be thus to them."

The coalition in Mr. Adams, of the three great attri- butes named above,—firmness, sagacity and fervor,— rendered him powerful in action and speech. Sound and substantial intellect must ever constitute the basis of true eloquence. It is this only that can sway the intellectual faculties of mankind, and take captive the judgment. In its deepest pathos and most impassioned appeals, this element must still predominate, or conviction that is enduring cannot be produced. Emotion is essential to deepen impressions and incite to action ; but in the most tumultuous agitations of both head and heart, the sovereignty of reason must be maintained, or the momentum derived from passion will only accelerate its victim to speedier disgrace and ruin. The great desideratum is, not to rely on intellect only, nor on feeling only, but appropriately to blend the two ; and thus by a natural and almost omnipotent process to grasp and control with spontaneous domination the feelings and understandings of men. The language of superior eloquence is nothing else than the enunciation of mind the most indomitable, earnest, and free ; and the highest power that the human spirit can possibly know may be thus expressed, since thought the most vast and comprehensive, as well as affection the most intense and inextinguishable, have their adequate expression in the vernacular of man, and, when honestly expressed, are instantly recognized and responded to by all mankind.

But this happy union of enthusiasm and sobriety is exceedingly rare, even in the first rank of orators. Sir James Mackintosh said that Fox was a speaker " the most Demosthenian since Demosthenes," because he was supposed to combine in his mental structure much of that reason, simplicity and vehemence, which formed the prince of ancient speakers. Others have insisted that the younger Pitt was endowed with a certain severe and majestic earnestness, a calm and self-balanceo energy, which rendered him even more like the mighty

Grecian than was the great parliamentary rival before named. Both these renowned Englishmen were certainly well qualified to debate great questions and sway the destinies of empires, but they were not orators of the most imperial power. Pitt especially failed in the poetic part of popular discourse, and Fox did not habitually manifest those splendors of imagination which constitute the most ethereal component of pure eloquence. One may be fertile in argument, and prolific in illustration,—memory may contribute innumerable facts, and invention may cunningly display vast resources of learned lore,—and yet, unless the speaker breathes a higher inspiration, the "third heaven" is never reached by his fancy, nor are intelligent crowds entranced by his tones. Such auxiliaries are like the wings of an ostrich, a profusion of showy but nerveless feathers which assist in running along the earth, but which are utterly unable to bear their cumbrous possessor in sublime flight to the skies. Where enthusiasm does not melt into reason and adorn its strength, a prosaic tameness is sure to characterize the printed page or spoken debate. •

John Adams was sometimes impetuous but rarely dull. When matters of great moment were at stake, he rose with a natural grandeur to a level with the emergency, and became master of the most violent storm. It was then that the *mens divinior*, the unquenchable flame of eloquence, seemed to expand his person and invest him with almost superhuman force. In such spontaneous bursts, as Jefferson declared, he raised his hearers from their seats. Swelling sympathy, irrepressible admiration and patriotic determinations, the most resolute and profound, filled every bosom and made sworn brothers of all. His speech was indomitable, because it was the inspiration at once of head and heart, the organs of a great soul fired with comprehensive and disinterested designs. He was luminous on the surface, because there was a perpetual and pure splendor within ; he was capable of a high polish, and endured without injury the severest shocks, because the substance of his eloquent nature was adamant of the finest and firmest grain.

> " He on whose name each distant age shall gaze,
> The mighty sea-mark of those troubled days !
> He, grand of soul, of genius unconfined,
> Born to delight, instruct, and mend mankind ;
> Adams ! in whom a Roman ardor glow'd,
> Whose copious tongue with Grecian richness flow'd,"

was the impersonation of fervid eloquence standing on the pedestal of solid judgment.

As was said above, it is seldom that we meet with great depth and acuteness in the same person; but in every such coalition, the result is genius. It is ever observant and meditative ; even while it seems to be in repose, it is in fact advancing by some secret path to great results. This is a power which cannot be altogether restrained. It is a vehement force, as irresistible to the mind of its possessor as it is potent on others ; it stimulates all contiguous faculties and insures success by the enthusiasm which always accompanies strong passions.

Genius is the constructive faculty of the mind, it is o accumulated erudition, and men of talents, merely,

what a skillful architect is to a mass of building matt-
rials lying inert before a body of plodding mechanics.

Oratorical genius has two organs of vision, observation and imagination. This double look, always fixed
on nature and humanity, is the inlet of that inspiration
peculiar to the gifted, and which adorns every thing
excellent in the department of eloquence and art. It
neither distorts nor falsifies the natural tone and qualities of the materials it employs, but simply does the
work of a wise lapidary who brings out many a hidden
vein and beauteous tint, thus raising to the rank and
value of gems what had often been discarded by the
unobservant traveller in the dusty highway of life.

Every masterly production of the mind is an aggregate of the sobriety and enthusiasm we have described,
it is the result of two intellectual phenomena, meditation
and enthusiasm. Meditation is a faculty mainly acquired; inspiration is a special and invaluable gift.
All men, to a certain degree, can meditate; but very
few are inspired. Meditation alone never wrote an Iliad,
nor drove back Xerxes; it never could break the
slumber of centuries, nor reform the world. In meditation, the spirit of man acts; in inspiration, it obeys; in
the first instance, the influence that impels is native
to man; in the other, it originates in a higher region,
and imparts to meditation its greatest force. It is the
amalgamation of these two faculties, meditation and
inspiration intimately allied, that constitutes the true
orator. He wins inspiration through meditation, as the
ancient prophets arose to extacy on the wings of prayer
In order that divine scenes may stand revealed to his

gaze, it is necessary that he should in a manner disrobe himself of material existence, and in calm silence gather up the loins of his mind. Thus isolated from the exterior life, he enjoys a plenteous development of the life internal; in the same proportion as the material world is withdrawn, the world of ideal beauty stands revealed. Holy and eloquent thought cannot spread its pinions and sublimely soar until it has laid off the gross burdens of earth. No healthful inspiration comes to the soul except as preceded by devout meditation. Among the ancient Jews, a people whose history is full of instructive symbols, when the priest had built an altar he kindled thereon terrestrial flames, and it was then only that divine rays descended from heaven.

They who most relish the ideal, and have the greatest facility in creating it, ever most enjoy the real. The refined artist, for instance, when abroad in the rough thoroughfares of life, will closely observe every changing aspect around him, and from the social confusion will elicit many a grace. In the street, on the strand, in the hovel, and under gilded domes, he culls with uniform skill and with equal success, everywhere gathering hints for his pencil and choice honey for the hive of his thoughts. In the rank mire of worldly strife, Dante and Milton selected pearls for the wreath of song; and Raphael found among dancing rustics and romping children the germs of many of his most magnificent creations. Look at Shakspeare's wonderful impersonations, and see how the actual and the ideal are closely conjoined. If at one moment he whirls you on high, and makes you dizzy and lonely in your sublime eleva tion, the next moment he opens a vista to earth again, and entrances the heart with feelings of home. A true man, one born to command the confidence and admiration of others through the medium of eloquent sentiments, is perpetually refreshed and invigorated by the inexhaustible resources which he seeks and enjoys in the play-grounds of the world. He is exhilarated by the streams that intersect the popular heart, just as by the mysterious attraction of nature the highest mountains draw up, through a thousand hidden tubes, the waters that thunder in the cataract and sparkle in beauty along the flowery plains.

This blending of enthusiasm with sobriety is the most prominent trait in the highest order of minds. Eccentricity is by no means a necessary concomitant of genius. Bacon, Milton, Newton, Locke, Bowditch, were the greatest geniuses and most sober men of their day. Genius is never more potent and useful than when chastened and restrained by reason, like the impetuous courser, Bucephalus, curbed and directed by the hand of Alexander. Men of the highest stamp unite in themselves the conformations of many subordinate grades; they who stand at the summit of the social pyramid are the exponents of the unbounded sentiments and passions which slumber in the masses beneath. Such was the natural position and rare endowments of John Adams. He was one of those energetic and audacious spirits who seem to be born expressly to revolutionize the world. They appear on the public stage robed and crowned with

" Truths serene,
Made visible in beauty, that shall glow
In everlasting freshness, unapproached
By mortal passion; pure amidst the blood
And dust of conquests;—never waxing old,
But on the stream of time, from age to age,
Casting bright images of heavenly youth."

We ought to expect that eloquence the most exalted would spontaneously emanate from such a soul. The orator, grand by nature, like the eagle, hovers above the clouds in the pure region of principles; while the mere haranguer, the demagogue, ruled by time-serving expediency, like the swallow, skims earth and sea, garden and swamp, making a thousand erratic turns, catching a few grovelling insects, and annoying the thoughtful traveller with its clattering wings. John Adams was the eagle of Colonial and Revolutionary eloquence in America, quick of eye and strong of wing, habitually calm in his grandeur, sometimes passionate and rapid in his course beyond all example.

He was an admirable model of *blended enthusiasm ind sobriety;* this constituted his individuality as a popular orator, and his consummate excellence as a statesman.

The marriage of the powerful Jupiter with the lovely Latona produced the graceful symmetry of Apollo—the happy combination of beauty, precision, agility, and strength—and these were the elements that composed the mental character of our great countryman. He resembled two of England's greatest forensic gladiators. Fox was a logician, Lord Chatham an orator. John

Adams combined in his eloquence much of the severe reason of the one, and the power of fascination so exuberant in the other. Arguments set forth by Fox were adapted to convince the reflecting; a speech from Chatham would impel all hearers immediately to action. John Adams was happily endowed to accomplish both results at the same time; his reasons for acting were as luminous as his appeals were exciting. Like the courser described by the classic poet:

> "His high mettle, under good control,
> Gave him Olympic speed, and shot him to the goal."

To think deeply and feel strongly, at one and the same time—to blend thought and emotion in luminous expression, and to concentrate both simultaneously on the audience in one blaze of argument and illustration—this is the means and guaranty of success, this is eloquence.

Herein consisted John Adams' great excellence. His head was cool, but his heart was ardent—a volcano beneath summits of snow—he projected his argument frigidly, in premeditated compactness, as if the fountain of emotion was entirely congealed in him; but when he arose in the eye of the nation, and began to feel the importance of his theme, he became lucid with the fires of patriotism, like the frenzied Pythoness, and seized possession of the general mind, with the authority of a master and a king. He clothed the bony substance of his dialectics with the flesh and blood of his ardent and spontaneous rhetoric ; he kindled the Continental Congress into a flame, because he was himself inflamed

He precipitated himself upon his hearers, without wan-
dering in extravagance, and commanded their feelings
with his pathos, without ceasing to rule their judgments
by the justness of his thought.   Sometimes, indeed, he
seemed to stagger under the weight and pungency of
conceptions which language could not express:

> "Low'ring he stood, still in fierce act of speech,
> Yet speechless."

His great talent lay in this: he intuitively saw to
what point in the minds of his audience to apply his
strength, and he sent it home there with the force of a
giant.

Mr. Jefferson has himself affirmed, "that the great
pillar of support to the Declaration of Independence,
and its ablest advocate and champion on the floor of
the House, was John Adams.   He was the colossus of
that Congress; not always fluent in his public addresses,
he yet came out with a power, both of thought and
expression, which moved his hearers from their seats."

Let us look back a moment and consider how the
great orators of the Revolution were disciplined, and
perfected for the sublime mission they performed.   They
were highly educated and classically refined ; but their
best weapons were forged in the presence of tyrants and
desperate toils.   Eloquence, to be affecting and grand,
must have perils to brave, the unfortunate to defend,
and daring honors to win.   Great trials and fearful conflicts make great orators.   The grammarians and the
musicians, the men who cured stammering, and taught
their pupil to pronounce the letter R distinctly, aided the

great Athenian much undoubtedly, but they created no nerve of his eloquence. Neither did his shaved head, his cave, his mouthful of pebbles, and his declamation by the sounding sea, inspire the imperial orator who fulmined over the world like a tropical storm. The mighty tempest of military force and political domination lowering on the hills of Macedon, and crashing on the plains of Chœronea—the fiery furnace of mental conflict, where the aspiring spirit is its own best instructor —the dread arena of physical battle with adverse legions, and lofty mental strife with malignant foes leagued to impel a falling state to ruin,—this was the school where Demosthenes was trained, and these were the means by which his eloquence was won.

And so of Cicero. Archias with his elegant learning, and Philo with his elaborate rhetoric,—the groves of Athens with all their philosophy, and the school of the Rhodián Milo, with all its gymnastic development,— formed not the master orator, potent alike in the fastidious Senate, or amid the tumultuous masses of that gorgeous pandemonium of imperial Rome,—the Forum. But to be the sport of rival chiefs and remorseless factions, hailed with a torrent of acclamations at one moment, and at the next drowned in the execrations of armed throngs,—to fight his way from the obscurity of an humble plebeian to the highest pinnacle of fame, and thence to be rudely dragged down to banishment, poverty, and popular odium by the traitorous Catiline and the accursed Clodius,—this was the source that inspired the Philippics, this was the school of Cicero's eloquence.

This first indication of mental freedom at the begin-

ning of the French Revolution, and the most remark
able department of intellectual improvement, was eloquence. The sudden expansion of senatorial oratory,
at that period, was a sure prognostic of rising liberty.
If a Barnave and his associates were virulent in their
attacks, and excited the populace to frenzy by their
stormy declamations, it was because the wrongs they
suffered were exasperating, and nothing but a tornado
could clear their path. Mirabeau was roused by seventeen *lettres de cachet*, directed against his own person ;
and under such motives to action he defended popular
rights with an energy that crushed a throne.

The discipline and destiny of an oratorical soul is
much like that emblem of freedom, the eagle. Dwelling
in the solitude of mountains, it seeks the highest summit, where with proud cry it hails the advent of morn,
and with eyes flashing fire outdazzles the sun. Its nest
is not lined with down nor encompassed with flowers;
but on some craggy height, where the thunderbolt has
scooped a hollow, the eaglet breathes his natal air, and
perpetually augments his strength, tossed by tempests
between gulfs below and sombre skies on high. He
hears the avalanche shoot and the thunders crash ; but
unterrified by the celestial flames that fringe the clouds
around 'him, and unexhausted by protracted toil, he
shakes rain and snow away, nourishes his famished
heart with fortitude, and turning a triumphant glance
towards receding storms, spreads his mighty wings and
sails in triumph through heavens purified by the war of
elements he has braved.

Effects are often mistaken for causes   Accidents

may sometimes develope great orators, but accidents never create them. Their high endowments come direct from God ; their best discipline is occasioned by the injustice of their fellow men. Philip, it has been said, formed Demosthenes. The dangers which he occasioned, developed the latent powers of the eloquent patriot. For example, look at the circumstances under which he delivered the great speech that brought about the alliance between Thebes and Athens, and led to the fatal battle of Charonea. He had warned his countrymen against Philip, but the tories of that day calmed the popular excitement. At length, late one evening, news arrived that Philip had seized Elatea, the key of Phocis and Bœotia, and might soon be expected before the walls of Athens. On the morrow, at dawn of day, the Senate met, and the people crowded into the assembly. The Prytanes reported the news. The herald himself was produced and made to recite from his own lips. Then the crier called aloud to the assembly, " Does any one wish to speak ?" None answered to the call; and it was repeated over and over again, until Demosthenes mounted the bema, and delivered that soul-stirring speech which made the assembly cry out, with one voice, " Let us march against Philip !" It is only this sort of men who reveal the full splendors of their native majesty, " on occasions calculated to strike and agitate the human soul." When consternation prevails in all common minds,—when the brave are dumb and the most resolute dismayed, those choice spirits intent on securing the common weal, exclaim, with Patrick Henry, " whatever others do, I'll fight ;" and with John Adams,

at the awful crisis of the vote of July, 1776, "Independence, *now ;* and INDEPENDENCE FOR EVER !"

The following is a specimen of Mr. Adams' style of
thought and composition, which we copy from an oration delivered before the citizens of Boston, on July 4th,
1793.

" We cherish, with a fondness which cannot be chilled
by the cold, inanimate philosophy of skepticism, the
delightful expectation, that the cancer of arbitrary
power will be radically extracted from the human constitution ; that the sources of oppression will be drained ;
that the passions, which have hitherto made the misery
of mankind, will be disarmed of all their violence, and
give place to the soft control of mild and amiable sentiments, which shall unite in social harmony the innumerable varieties of the human race. Then shall the
nerveless arm of superstition no longer interpose an
impious barrier between the beneficence of heaven and
the adoration of its votaries ; then shall the most distant
regions of the earth be approximated by the gentle attraction of a liberal intercourse ; then shall the fair
fabric of universal liberty rise upon the durable foundation of social equality, and the long expected era of
human felicity, which has been announced by prophetic
inspiration, and described in the most enraptured language of the muses, shall commence its splendid progress. Visions of bliss ! with every breath to heaven
we speed the ejaculation, that the time may hasten,
when your reality shall be no longer the ground of vo-
tive supplication, but the theme of grateful acknowledgment ; when the choral gratulations of the liberated

myriads of the elder world, in symphony, sweeter than the music of the spheres, shall hail your country, Americans! as the youngest daughter of Nature, and the first-born offspring of Freedom."

It would seem that, at a period somewhat later than the date of the above, this ardent and profound votary of Freedom had already realized much of his early and most enthusiastic desires. In one of the delightful letters written in the maturity of his eventful life, he says —" When, where, and in what manner we shall see the unravelling of the vast plot, which is acting in the world, is known only to Providence. Although my mind has for twenty years been preparing to expect great scenes, yet I confess the wonders of this Revolution exceed all that I ever foresaw or imagined. That our country, so young as it is, so humble as it is, thinking but lately so meanly of itself, should thus interest the passions, as well as employ the reason of all mankind, in its favor, and effect in so short a space of time, not only thirteen revolutions of government at home, but so completely accomplish a revolution in the system of Europe, and in the sentiments of every nation in it, is what no human wisdom, perhaps, could foresee."

True orators are character-born, or, as Napoleon said, they are victory organized. They make a disturbance in the scene where they appear, because they are both strong and new; they will have to encounter the force of love and hatred proportioned to their own originality. A massy and fleet man-of-war makes a wake as it ploughs the sea; the sixty-four pounder rakes the earth and shatters huge obstacles as it flies; and so does

a man like John Adams make impressions that agitate
the world around him. He fights the noblest battles
and wins the most enduring fame.

Says Fenelon, "Demosthenes moves, warms and captivates the heart. He was sensibly touched with the
interests of his country. His discourses gradually increase in force, by greater light and new reasons, which
are always illustrated by bold figures and lively images.
One cannot but see that he has the good of the republic
entirely at heart, and that nature itself speaks in all his
transports." Adams, we repeat, had much of the spontaneous passion of this great prototype, as well as much
of his premeditated wisdom. Happy is he who combines in his thought this double power of meditation
and inspiration. Sooner or later, whatever may be his
age, or rank, or preliminary suffering, his day will come;
and then, endowed and disciplined for his career, he will
rise boldly above the multitude, and "read his history in
a nation's eyes."

John Adams, in his day and for his country, was
second to no man that ever lived. Within his simple
exterior the divinity was concealed, not only latent, but
effective at will. If he did not appear before the world
with the insignia of Hercules, the shaggy lion's skin and
the knotted club, he bore a full quiver and the silver
bow of the god of the sun, and every shaft he loosened
from the string told with unerring aim at the heart of
his monster-foe.

Contemplate him as he appeared in the great debate
on the adoption of the Declaration of Independence,
standing, in that crisis of indescribable grandeur, like

Moses on the mount, encompassed with thunders and lightnings, bearing the tables of the law in his arms, his brow encircled with a halo of fire, and his eye gleaming with a prophetic view of a mighty nation soon to emerge from thraldom, and send generation after generation down through untold ages.

It was on the evening of that day on which the most momentous victory was won that history can ever record, that this champion, yet agitated by the storm and covered with the foam and dust of battle, retired in triumph from the field and wrote that glorious letter to his distant wife, beginning with the memorable words—" The die is cast. We have passed the Rubicon!"

Taking into account the circumstances under which Adams inscribed the above triumphant expression, and the patriotic valor therein contained, we are strongly reminded of an incident recorded in classic history. Immediately after the battle at Marathon, an Athenian soldier, still faint with the loss of blood, quitted the army, and ran to Athens to carry his fellow citizens the happy news of victory. When he arrived at the chief magistrate's house, he only uttered two or three words: "Rejoice, rejoice, the victory is ours!" and fell down dead at their feet.

As might be expected from the temperament and talents we have thus attempted to describe, the speeches and writings of Mr. Adams abound with brief but sig-nificant expressions. When the mind is free and thought is fearless, eloquence speaks in condensed and pointed terms, like arrows which are most sure when they are least encumbered and most swiftly winged

When the soul is heroic and its conceptions fervid, its corruscations bear the brilliant potency of lightning, ir- resistible to earthly obstructions, and terrible to guilt.

Cotemporaries say that John Adams was peculiarly luminous in his demonstrations—as if jets of light shot out from his eyes, his mouth, and his finger ends. He was not large in body, but his well-formed and expres- sive figure reflected all the passions of his soul. He was eloquent all over. He was a mental gladiator, a man of forensic war, and never was he more beautiful than when surrounded by the hottest flames of the fight.

On March 4th, 1797, Mr. Adams, then in his 62d year, was inaugurated President of the United States. A cotemporary, an intimate acquaintance of our re- nowned countryman, has told us that on that occasion he was dressed in a full suit of pearl-colored broadcloth, with powdered hair. He was then bald on the top of his head. The same writer observes, "Mr. Adams was of middle stature, and full person ; and of slow, deliberate manner, unless he was excited ; and when this happen- ed, he expressed himself with great energy. He was a man of strong mind, of great learning, and of eminent ability to use knowledge, both in speech and writing. He was ever a man of purest morals ; and is said to have been a firm believer in Christianity, not from habit and example, but from diligent investigation of its proofs."

But if the morning and noon of Mr. Adams' life were auspicious and splendid, the evening was full of the moral sublime. "Even when the brilliancy of reason's sunset yields to the advancing gloom, there is an indescribable beauty haunting the old man still, if in youth and vigor his soul was conversant with truth; and even when the chill of night is upon him, his eye seems to rest upon the glories for a while departed, or looks off into the stars, and reads in them his destiny with a gladness as quiet and as holy as their light. When our little day is folded up in shadows, the darkness must be deep indeed which does not reveal eternity by the rays of light that reach us from afar ; but the soul that can rise above the clouds of earth, can always behold the infinity of heaven, and perhaps every rightly taught man, before God takes him, ascends to a Pisgah of his own, from whence to look farewell to the wilderness he has passed in the leadings of Jehovah's right hand, and to catch a glimpse of the promised land lying in the everlasting orient before him."

It is well known that on July 4th, 1826, this great man, after a useful life found a peaceful death, breathing a blessing on the country which he had so eminently served, and exclaiming to the last, "independence for ever!"

Justice Story, another mighty name since inscribed by death high in the Pantheon of American renown, in allusion to Mr. Adams' departure from life, well said : " That voice of more than Roman eloquence, which urged and sustained the Declaration of Independence, that voice, whose first and whose last accents were for his country, is indeed mute. It will never again rise in defence of the weak against popular excitement, and vindicate the majesty of law and justice. It will never awaken a nation to arms to assert its liberties. It will never again instruct the public councils by its wisdom.

Bloomingdale Branch
WEST 100TH STREE

It will never again utter its most oracular thoughts in philosophical retirement." That great and pure spirit has departed, gone as a sunbeam to revisit its native skies—gone, as this mortal to put on immortality.

> " Ne'er to the chambers, where the mighty rest,
> Since their foundation, came a nobler guest;
> Nor ne'er was to the bowers of bliss conveyed
> A fairer spirit, or more welcome shade."

CHAPTER VIII.

THE PATRIOTIC PIETY OF '76.

THE original chart of American Liberty was drawn and signed in the cabin of the Mayflower. It was a civil compact, based on republican principles and sanctioned by religious faith. Such men as Carver, Bradford, Brewster, and Winslow, blessed our nation in its cradle, and patriotic teachers of religion have ever fostered its growth. At an early day, the acute and subtle Cotton, the erudite and energetic Hooker, and their associates, replenished the beacon-fires of learning, patriotism, and piety along our "rock-bound coast." Not a little did these men of God contribute to produce that state of things which prospectively seemed propitious, and in view of which they greatly rejoiced. In 1644, Cotton wrote to his friends in Holland, "The order of the churches and the commonwealth is now so settled in New England by common consent, that it brings to mind the new heaven and new earth, wherein dwells righteousness." Hooker was an apostolic hero, whose eye, voice, soul, gesture, and whole form were animated with the vital energy of primitive zeal. He was full of public spirit and active charity, serenely trusting in Providence with "a glorious peace of soul;" and,

"though persecutions and banisnments had awaited him
as one wave follows another," he adhered to the cause
of advancing civilization without wavering, and looked
for its ultimate triumph without a doubt. His cotemporaries placed him "in the first rank of men," and
praised him as " the one rich pearl, with which Europe
more than repaid America for the treasures from her
coast."

But such is the selfish tendency of our corrupt nature,
that even the best men are inclined to consolidate
power in themselves for the fortification of their favorite
creeds. Some of the leading Puritans early strove to
check the democratic tendency of colonial institutions.
On the election day, in May, 1634, Cotton preached to
the assembled citizens against rotation in office. But
the instinctive sense of political rights in the masses
prevailed; the electors, now increased to three hundred
and eighty, were bent on exercising their absolute power;
they reversed the decision of the pulpit, elected a new
governor and deputy, of congenial sentiments, and thus,
to use their own language, "the people established a
reformation of such things as they judged to be amiss in
the government." The dictation of popular rights by
aristocratic cliques was annihilated by popular discussion. " The freemen of every town in the Bay were
busy in inquiring into their liberties and privileges."
The principle of representative democracy was recognized and established as perfectly two centuries ago, as
it is to-day.

But there were two other elements not yet clearly
defined and popularly enjoyed—universal suffrage and

free toleration of religious sentiments. Who shall be the herald and type of these to the world? Let the best of American historians present him to your judgment and admiration. Says Bancroft, in the first volume of his History, "Roger Williams' mind had already matured a doctrine which secures him an immortality of fame, as its application has given religious peace to the American world. He was a Puritan, and a fugitive from English persecution; but his wrongs had not clouded his accurate understanding; in the capacious recesses of his mind he had revolved the nature of intolerance, and he, and *he alone*, had arrived at the great principle which is its sole effectual remedy. He announced his discovery under the simple proposition of *the sanctity of conscience*. This was the great tenet, which, with all its consequences, he defended, as he first trod the shores of New England; and in his extreme old age it was the last pulsation of his heart. He was the first person in modern Christendom to assert, in its plenitude, the doctrine of the *liberty of conscience*, and in its defence he was the harbinger of Milton, the precursor and superior of Jeremy Taylor."

Dr. Robertson, in his History of America, says, "Roger Williams' spirit differed from that of the Puritans of Massachusetts; it was mild and tolerating; and having himself to reject established opinions, he endeavored to secure the same liberty to other men, by maintaining that the exercise of private judgment was a natural and sacred right; that the civil magistrate has no compulsive jurisdiction in the concerns of religion; that the punishment of any person on account of his

9*

opinions was an encroachment on conscience and an act of persecution. These humane principles he instilled into his followers; and all who felt or dreaded oppression in other settlements, resorted to a community in which universal toleration was known to be a fundamental maxim."

The Puritans were a noble race. As Junius said to the king, " They left their native land in search of freedom, and found it in a desert." But they imported errors, and were imbued with the common imperfections of mankind; to correct which, Roger Williams was raised up by Providence, and early planted, with all his wealth of sublime principle and worth, in our infant land. It is worthy of note, that the sentiments respecting toleration which he first proclaimed, and for which he was severely persecuted by his fellow refugees, are now the unanimous opinions of this great nation, while those of the Puritans, on the same subject, have been discarded, as false in theory and oppressive in practice, and are at this moment obsolete in every free section of the globe. The germinal principle of religious liberty which first struggled into being under that great and good man's fostering care, amid bleak winters and savage tribes, has since grown to a mighty tree, under which the nations are beginning to worship in peaceful joy. And its growth is not yet consummated, thank God!

> " Millions of souls shall feel its power,
> And bear it down to millions more."

A careful perusal of our primitive annals will induce

a high appreciation of the patriotic piety and mutual sympathy between preachers and their flocks that then prevailed. Devoted ministers of religion, like Eliot and Wilson, shared in the hardships and dangers consequent on the early Indian wars. And when news first arrived in Boston of the menacing attitude assumed by England, prompt consultations were held for the common weal, and the boldest measures were projected. The fathers in Israel were all assembled, and " discovered their minds to one another." They voted unanimously against submission, and publicly declared, says Winthrop, " We ought to defend our lawful possessions, if we are able ; if not, to avoid and protract." Six hundred pounds were immediately raised in the poor settlements of the northern colony, and the fortifications were hastened by every kind of popular aid. The influence of the ministry was patriotic and conservative, at the South as well as around Plymouth rock. Smith, in his history of the colony at Jamestown, refers to the excellent Hunt, by whose " good doctrine and exhortation," popular vices were restrained, and the welfare of all promoted to the utmost extent.

The Revolutionary War was a struggle imposed on our fathers, not sought by them ; injustice was in their esteem a legitimate cause for resistance, and all willingly shared in the discharge of a duty which none could doubt. Those who led in the church, and those who led in the field, were impelled by one conviction and labored together with the same design. One taught the law of justice, the other defended it ; one was the voice of God, the other was His arm. Thus, the American

Colonies, confederated by patriotism and piety long before they were united under a written constitution, felt
that their resistance to oppression was a common cause,
and simultaneously grasped a sword which. had been
tempered in the fires of suffering and bedewed with the
tears of the sanctified.   Then were laity and clergy
distributed to all the posts of defence—the chamber of
council and the field of battle,—the rural church and
the martial camp,—and from each station of trust and
solicitude, fervent prayer ascended to heaven for favor
on our arms.

Burke said : "The Americans augur misgovernment
at a distance, and snuff the approach of tyranny in every
tainted breeze." The sense here described was most
acute in those whose faculties had been educated and
refined in the school of the Prophets.   As a hunter,
standing armed, listens at the foot of a tree to see
whence comes the wind, so they stood by the altars they
were appointed to guard, and listened attentively in that
direction whence wrong approached.   Considerations
of time, place, peril, or calling, impeded no one.   Men
of the greatest dignity, largest wealth, and most sacred
functions did not stop to compute profit and loss : blood
was poured out freely and poured for all.   The sainted
Robinson had magnanimously said to the voyagers in
the Mayflower, that he would not foreclose his mind to
the truth of God, even if it were new.   The new light
and liberties which our fathers had here learned to
enjoy, were deemed of too much value to be lightly sur
rendered to injustice or the miserable expediency of
false mercy   Conscience was their only compensation

on earth, and God on high. Hands consecrated to sacred service, breaking the bread of life and soothing
penitential sorrow, from the pulpit scattered profusely in
moral and martial tempests, seeds of patriotic piety
whose glorious harvests the whole world is yet destined
to reap in peace.

Prominent among the religious patriots who preceded
the Revolution, was the old President of Yale College,
Doctor Ezra Stiles. He was small in stature, but of
vast learning, undoubted piety and fervid patriotism.
On the occasion of the death of George II. and the accession of George III., he preached a sermon, in which
he admonished the latter against suffering any retrench-
ment of the liberties of New England. In his history
of the three judges of Charles I., (Whalley, Goffe and
Dixwell,) published long before our Revolution, he announced that the 30th of January, which was observed
by many Christians, in commemoration of the martyrdom of that king, "ought to be celebrated as an anniversary thanksgiving, that one nation on earth had so
much fortitude and public justice, as to make *a royal
tyrant bow to the sovereignty of the people.*" Let it be
added here, that another distinguished President of that
ancient seat of letters and religion, *Doctor Timothy
Dwight,* served with becoming zeal in the councils of
his country, and as a chaplain in her army.

Indeed, patriotism was a trait common to the great
majority of our clergy, both before and during the Revolution. They sided with their country in all the dis-
putes with Great Britain,—they prayed and preached in
favor of Independence, and in several instances went so

far as personally to take up arms. Jonathan Mahew, the famous leader of the Episcopal controversy, to whom Archbishop Secker and Dr. Johnson replied, was not only an ecclesiastic of great literary accomplishments, but a republican of the boldest port. On every hand, intelligent and patriotic pastors contributed powerfully to prepare the people for prompt and persevering resistance against every encroachment on their rights.

Rev. Samuel Davies, for some time a pastor in Virginia, and afterwards President of Nassau Hall, deserves especial notice. He was born in Delaware, Nov. 3d, 1724, and received his education in Pennsylvania. His grand characteristic, as a patriot and preacher, was boldness. This is a valuable attribute in every public agent. The great Lord Verulam declared, that "if he were asked what is the first, second, and third thing necessary for success in business, he should answer, bold-ness, boldness, boldness." Timid and effeminate efforts in the pulpit are as inefficient and more destructive than elsewhere. The stupid soul is startled into attention only by bold blows. Ministers may describe for ever the beauties of nature, the pleasures of virtue, the dignity of self-respect and the vulgarity of vice, but until more exalted motives are urged, and more potent influences are employed, few effects will follow that are either great or good.

Davies was the ablest Dissenter in the southern pio-vinces. His custom was to study his discourses with great care. Being pressed to preach on a certain occa-sion without his usual preparation, he replied : " It is a dreadful thing to talk nonsense in the name of the Lord."

But he was as prompt and fearless in any sudden emergency, as he was habitually deliberate and studious. Thanks to the movements in behalf of religious liberty made at the North, England granted the Toleration Act in favor of all the Colonies. Virginia, however, ruled by her Episcopal establishment, refused to admit that the Dissenters of their territory were included. Davies withstood all their forces alone, with Peyton Randolph at their head. He had made himself a thorough master of English law, civil and ecclesiastical, and always chose to meet every persecuting indictment in the highest courts with his own plea. So powerful was he in the capacity which the law of necessity compelled him to assume, that many of his friends, and even his foes were wont to exclaim, "*What a lawyer was spoiled when Davies took the pulpit!*" Spoiled, forsooth! As if the pulpit, with all its themes of eternal interest, was not the sublimest field for the development and exercise of eloquence ever vouchsafed to man.

Not satisfied with establishing his religious rights at the bar of colonial power, he went to England and obtained the explicit sanction of the highest authority with respect to the extension of the Toleration law to Virginia. It was during this mission that he gave another striking instance of his boldness. George II. and many of his court were in the congregation of this American Dissenter. His majesty, struck with admiration, or forgetting the proprieties of the occasion, spoke several times to those around him and smiled. Davies paused a moment, and then looking sternly at the king, exclaimed, "*When the lion roars, the beasts of the forest all tremble; and when King Jesus speaks, the princes of earth should keep silence.*"

Mr. Davies was tall, manly and dignified. A distinguished character of the day, on seeing him pass, said: "*he looked like the ambassador of some great king.*" His understanding was strong, his elocution graceful, and his address on some occasions was overwhelming. Patrick Henry was his neighbor and ardent admirer. It is believed that the renowned pupil was greatly indebted to this patriotic preacher, both for his sentiments and the invincible manner with which he enforced them.

During the gloomy period when the country was alarmed and distressed to the highest degree by the French and Indian war, Davies exerted himself constantly to mitigate the sufferings of the people and to disperse their fears. On the 10th of July, 1755, General Braddock sustained his memorable defeat, and the remnant of his army was saved by the courage and skill of Colonel Washington, then but twenty-three years old. On the 20th of the same month, our moral hero preached a sermon, "On the defeat of General Braddock, going to Fort Du Quesne." In this sermon, he calls on all his hearers, in the most impassioned and patriotic terms, to show themselves men, Britons, Christians, and to make a noble stand for the blessings they enjoyed." In the same year, he delivered a sermon before Captain Overton's company of volunteers, under the title of "Religion and patriotism, the constituents of a good soldier." It was in the discussion of this subject that

his famous prophecy occurred. Speaking of the encouraging fact, that God had "diffused some sparks
of martial fire through the country," said he, "as a
remarkable instance of this, I may point out to the
public that heroic youth, Colonel Washington, whom I
cannot but hope Providence has hitherto preserved, in
so signal a manner, *for some important service to his
country.*"

Sacred eloquence, in revolutionary times, is the chief
conservative of order and the grand solace of the popular mind. While it fortifies the patriot in his rebellion
against tyranny, it exhorts him to a patient endurance
of unavoidable wrongs. It alleviates as much as possible the pressure of the chain, by opening before the sufferer celestial horizons, fragrant with immortal ama-
rynths, and teeming with infinite beatitudes. Davies
was of this stamp, a bold patriot and a bold Christian

> " He had a twofold nature, and the one
> Was of a higher order, with the souls
> Who shine along the path of centuries
> In full and perfect brightness, standing forth
> In their own loftiness, the beacon lights
> By which the world is guided and upborne
> From its for ever downward tendency.

Another patriotic preacher fell a martyr to his zeal in
behalf of his country, at Elizabethtown, New Jersey.
On the 21st of January, 1780, the first Presbyterian
church was burned by the British, and in the following
November, they shot its minister, the *Rev. James Cald-
well.* He was a learned, pious, and devoted servant of

his country and his God. He embarked every thing in the holy cause he espoused, pouring his blood on the earth after they had burned the pulpit from which he had often poured his patriotic exhortations on the people's heads. " There were giants in those days;" and it is easy to explain the force of their language, and the fidelity of their actions. They preached in an age of revolution, a time of popular excitement and national transition, when there transpired in rapid succession changes more momentous than ever before agitated the world. Then every man was intensely absorbed in the general struggle ; feeling that the welfare of all was entrusted to each, every citizen was a consecrated soldier, in some form contending for freedom and national life at his appointed post in the very heat of the combat. Among the excited mass, ministers of the Gospel were by no means the least active or efficient. They extended the ægis of a divine religion over the battered and exhausted form of the colonial confederation, and inspired fortitude in all who were faint. They were agitated with a lofty inspiration, as the earth is shaken in the convulsions of an earthquake, not by the assaults of external power, but by the irrepressible fires of freedom and piety which burned within their patriotic hearts. It was for this reason that they had such a mighty influence on their hearers. True eloquence, like true religion, is a movement of sensibility as well as an act of reason. If one has " thoughts that breathe," you may be sure he will have " words that burn." If one is truly a patriot, in the pulpit or out of it, his conduct will comport with his professions, and his life will be at the service of his country as well as of his God.

Illustrious examples abound in every direction, but we will take our next in a region farther north. It was fitting that the first battle of the Revolution should be fought under the eves of the church at Lexington. It was in that vicinity that the Genius of Patriotism had long dwelt with her enthusiastic devotee.

The town records of Lexington contain many important documents which discussed the great questions involved in the national struggle for Independence. In 1765, the citizens vindicated the popular movement in respect to the Stamp-Act. In 1767, they unanimously concurred with the resolution of Boston, to prevent the consumption of foreign commodities. In 1768, they argued with great force against the right of Great Britain to tax America. In 1772, they resolved, in most thrilling terms, to seek redress for daily increasing wrongs; and in 1774, they took measures to supply themselves with ammunition, arms and other requisites for military defence. What hero drew those masterly papers, defended their principles, and fired the people at all hazards to defend them ? History has recorded the fact, that the *Reverend Jonas Clark*, was their author and chief defence. He was one of the many patriotic clergy of New England, who instructed their beloved flock in peace, and guarded them amid the dread necessities of war. "Mr. Clark," says Edward Everett, "was eminent in his profession,—a man of practical piety,—a learned theologian,—a person of wide, general reading,—a writer perspicuous, correct, and pointed, be-

yond the standard of the day,—and a most intelligent,
resolute, and ardent champion of the popular cause. He
was connected by marriage with the family of John
Hancock. Their connection led to a portion of the interesting occurrences of the 19th of April, 1775. The
soul-stirring scenes of the great tragedy which was
enacted on this spot, were witnessed by Mr. Clark,
from the door of his dwelling hard by. To perpetuate
their recollection, he instituted, the following year, a service of commemoration. He delivered himself a historical discourse of great merit, which was followed on
the returns of the anniversary, till the end of the Revolutionary war, in a series of addresses in the same strain,
by the clergy of the neighboring towns."

These were the brave men of prophetic eye who as-
cended the altars of God to proclaim in clear tones and
firm faith the future era of American democracy. They
had the disposition and capacity to take far-reaching and
comprehensive views. They were not content to con-
sume the passing hour, in amusing on the deck of the
ship of State, the audience that surrounded them with
applause; they knew the extent and the perils of the
sea upon which they were borne; they consulted the
currents of the tides and the ominous winds; equally
regardful of charts and guiding stars, they gave heed to
the reef on which their buffeted craft might suddenly
be dashed, and looked anxiously forward to a haven
where tempest-tossed humanity might in safety be
moored. But their solicitude, instead of impeding their
activity, inspired it. Animated by motives grand as the
liberties of a continent, these Christian soldiers illus-

trated, in their persons and work, how courage becomes
more firm when fortified by the principles of patriotic
piety, that a warrior is invincible when inspired by
faith, and when he can raise pure hands to the God of
battles, in whose name he fights.   It is under such circumstances and from such men that we may expect impressive preaching.   The eloquence of the pulpit is not
a festive pantomime, but a bold and rugged eloquence
that does battle with stern realities.   The weapons
which the preacher is called to use, like the sword which
guarded Eden's gate, must have the brilliancy of flame
as well as the force and edge of steel.   The era of '76
was favorable to the highest order of eloquence.   Every
youth came upon the public stage with the cap of liberty upon his head, and a passport to victory or death in
his hand.   Then the people assembled in their churches,
to invoke the blessing of God on their arms, while their
pastors preached to them under the frowns of power
and in the prospect of martyrdom.   This gave fervor
to their thoughts, depth to their sympathies, earnestness
and solemnity to their daring resolutions.   Outward
perils and inward solicitude invested the preacher with
the power of thrilling his audience through and through
with repeated shocks of mental batteries highly charged.
They did not fatigue with elegant inanity, nor stupify
with excessive prettiness.   Their soul teemed with an
intense virility, and their language was forked with terrific splendor.   They seemed more like prophets than
priests, master-spirits raised up to mould the destinies
of mankind; their attitudes were dignity ; their gestures
power. The functions they discharged were divine; their

tones were trumpets vocal with messages from heaven; their sentiments blazed like meteors prognosticating conflicts, conquests, and final doom.   Each one of those moral heroes who glorified the era of '76, was a co-lossus among ordinary men, and stood forth in native majesty, indomitable, unmoved, sublime.

A happy combination of piety and patriotism, consti-tuting the most useful private and public virtue, we have already found in different sections of our common country during the Revolution.   We have only to turn to the highest council of our infant nation, the most august assembly of men that ever congregated to declare themselves free, and we shall find another illustrious example in the person of *John Witherspoon.*

He was lineally descended from John Knox, the moral hero of Scotland, was born near Edinburgh, 1722, and, from the time he adopted America as his country, was as much distinguished as a preacher as a patriot. Dr. Witherspoon was one of the signers of the Declara-tion of Independence, which he eloquently defended; through a trying period of congressional responsibility he was a very efficient legislator; and for many years performed the duties of a laborious, erudite, and emi-nently successful president of Princeton College.   On taking his seat in Congress, he surprised his associates, as his brother Davies, who now sleeps by his side, had surprised the courts of Virginia, with his wonderful knowledge and skill as a civilian.   He was associated with Richard Henry Lee and John Adams on several important committees and himself drew many valuable

State papers. All his productions are marked oy wit,
energy, and eloquence.

Of his wit, one or two examples will suffice. Just
before the momentous decision of the fourth of July, a
distinguished member had said in debate, that we were
"not yet ripe for a Declaration of Independence." Dr.
Witherspoon responded, "in my judgment, sir, we are
not only ripe but rotting." Close and rigid argument
was his rule of debate, but corruscations of vivacious
fancy sometimes furnished amusing exceptions. He
had the tact to beguile an audience of weariness, by
indulging wisely in sarcastic mental frolics.

> "The humorous vein, strong sense, and simple style,
>   To teach the gayest, make the gravest smile."

For example : when Burgoyne's army was captured at
Saratoga, General Gates despatched one of his aids to
convey the intelligence to Congress. The officer indulged too freely in amusements by the way, so that the
news reached Philadelphia several days ahead of him.
Congress, however, principally for form's sake, proposed
to present him an elegant sword ; but Dr. Witherspoon
rose, and begged leave to move, that instead of a sword,
they should present him *a pair of golden spurs.*

This anecdote suggests a word or two with respect
to his energy. It was a trait which rendered him exceedingly useful as a patriot and preacher. In November, 1776, the army was in a deplorable condition for
want of necessary supplies. They were retreating,
almost naked and barefooted, in wintry cold, before a
numerous and well-appointed foe. Congress was in-

formed that the military force of the country was "much
more disposed to secure safety by submission, than to
seek it by a manly resistance." In this fearful crisis,
Witherspoon was appointed the chairman of a committee to repair to head-quarters, and co-operate with
Washington in redressing the grievances of the soldiers.
Triumphant success crowned their energy.

Numerous tokens of Dr. Witherspoon's eloquence
remain on the journal of Congress and in the literature
of the country. He usually wrote the main body of
his discourse with great care; but being a ready speaker,
and possessing a remarkable talent for extemporizing, he
could dexterously blend that which was premeditated and
that which was spontaneous, so as to give the aggregate
an air of great beauty and force. In one of his admirable rhetorical works he has himself said, "There is a
piercing heat and penetrating force in that which flows
from the heart, which distinguishes it not only from the
coldness of indifference, but also from the false fire of
enthusiasm or vain glory."

Excepting Washington, he is said to have possessed
more of what is called *presence*, than any other man of
his day. He was six feet high, nobly proportioned, and
remarkably impressive in voice, movement, and mien.
It was equally difficult for unruly students or thoughtless
men to trifle in his presence.

As soon as the liberties of the country were won,
Dr. Witherspoon gladly resumed his classical pursuits
and the work of the ministry. In a ripe and glorious
old age, he died in peace, having accomplished vastly
more than the Cardinal de Retz. "A man," said Bos-

suet, "who was so faithful to individuals, so terrible to the State; of so lofty a character, that it was impossible to esteem, to fear, to love, or to hate him in moderation. Firm in himself, he shook the universe, and obtained a dignity, which he afterwards wished to resign, as unworthy of what it had cost him; as an object beneath his mighty mind. But while he was in pursuit of what he was afterwards taught to despise, he shook every thing by his secret and powerful energies. Even in the universal overthrow of all around him, he appeared to suffice for his own support, and his intrepid aspect still breathed defiance to his adversary."

But the doctor's greatest forte was in the pulpit. He felt habitually, and especially in preaching,—a pursuit in his avowed opinion the most sublime of all,—that "it is not enough to speak, but to speak true." His vivacity, his fervid logic, his impressive manner, and spontaneous ease, all combined to make him a mode preacher, as well as model citizen. The ambassador for Christ, to be eloquent, must be true to the promptings of his nature when least shackled. It will not answer to conceal that which is intrinsically noble, for the purpose of conciliating the ignobly prejudiced. The inspired heart and the glorious gospel are both the creations of the same infinite hand, and, "being things so majestical," we should not "offer them the least show of violence." Let the preacher throw himself into the heart of his audience with all the brave confidence of spontaneous inspiration, then will the tones and emotions native to his soul awaken a sleeping echo in every other bosom. Delicate specimens of refined style are

10

usually the concomitants of languor and imbecility. They are often obtained at the sacrifice of those hardier felicities, which, like alpine flowers, adorn the inequalities of a more rugged and artless composition. It is not new arguments or novel images that are most demanded in the ordinary routine of modern pulpit ministrations, but that energy of soul which invests even feeble logic with startling power, and renders trite illustrations appalling to the aroused. We need more of that deep and strong feeling which melts into love, kindles into hope, or stiffens with despair. The mind of a pulpit orator should traverse the field of literary research and biblical exposition, as a potent angel careers through the unfathomed abyss of etherial space; now obscured in the dark recesses of thunder, and now shooting, in bold relief, through fleecy clouds of gold; now plunging to the remote horizon, as if to test the speed and power of his wing, and now floating in calm majesty through the infinite azure of untroubled sky. Such a man was

Dr. Samuel Stillman, of Boston. This distinguished patriot and divine was born in Philadelphia, but was removed early to Charleston, South Carolina, where he was educated, and where he was ordained, in 1759. He removed to Boston, 1763, and remained there until his death, 1806, the universally admired pastor of the First Baptist Church.

He was small in stature, but great of soul. His courtesy was proverbial, his accomplishments were diversified, his piety was undisputed by all, and his patriotic preaching unexcelled. He was explicit and bold in avowing his own peculiar views, but was exceedingly forbearing in his demeanor towards those who were conscientiously opposed. It was only the vicious and the recreant,— those who armed themselves with malignant hatred against the cross and his country,—that suffered beneath his scathing bolts. His ambition was that of a moral hero, who contended without anger, conquered without meanness, and accumulated triumphs without pride; habitually desirous of being governed by the golden rule, he fashioned his conduct under the influence of virtue and wisdom from above. Clothing his arms with light he fought against the powers of darkness ; at the same time contemplating with humble gratitude the miry pit from which he had emerged, and putting forth an active hand to rescue those who remained behind. He fostered every Christian enterprize, and neglected no effort that might contribute to instruct those whom prejudice had blinded, or set free from the thraldom of error those whom cupidity had long kept bound.

The respect which this admirable preacher won was most comprehensive and of the highest kind. Among refined gentlemen, liberal scholars, and eloquent divines, he ranked second to none of any section or name Standing in the presence of armed foes, he preached with a power that commanded respect, even when he could not create compunction. When the British took possession of Boston, and desecrated its sacred edifices some of the more skillful of their number, who had recoiled under Stillman's patriotic appeals, illustrated their spite by drawing a charcoal outline of the great divine on the plastered wall of his own pulpit, in all

the freedom of expressive gesture and eloquent denunciation.

It will not seem strange that Dr. Stillman's own
church was habitually thronged, or that whenever he
visited other cities his instructions were sought with
avidity by the most exalted minds. John Adams wrote
to his wife, thus:

"PHILADELPHIA, 4th Aug., 1776.

"Went this morning to the Baptist meeting, in hopes
of hearing Mr. Stillman, but was disappointed. He
was there, but another gentleman preached."

These letters of John Adams to his wife, abound
with intimations of the patriotism of the pulpit in those
days. In one, dated "7th July, 1775," he inquires:
"Does Mr. Wibird preach against oppression, and the
other cardinal vices of the times? Tell him, the clergy
here, of every denomination, thunder and lighten every
Sabbath. They pray for Boston and the Massachusetts. They thank God explicitly and fervently for
our remarkable successes. They pray for the American army. They seem to feel as if they were among
you."

The secular and the sacred patriots of that age labored, in different spheres, to fortify the two wings of the
same army. One promoted defence by martial force,
the other extended the interests of religion; one beat
down the ramparts of invading power, the other erected
the shrines of education and piety; one drove back the
Philistines from our shores, the other built pavilions
for Israel's God. When the battle was over and the
great boon of liberty was won, both parties were found

at the same altars, having toiled for one end, and
expressing gratitude for blessings dearly bought, and by
each equally prized.

Dr. Stillman was foremost among those who with one
hand discomfited the Amalekites, and raised the other to
implore divine benedictions. To the heroism of Joshua,
in the combat, he joined the faith of Moses upon the
mountain, beholding the goodly heritage which he had
panted to secure, and bearing under the arms of a warrior the heart and docility of a child. Always on the
field of battle, conquering souls for God or confounding
his foes, each step he took marked a new victory, and
at the end of his career he triumphantly grasped the
amarynth of immortal bliss.

"And now 'tis silence all—Enchanter, fare thee well!"

Archbishop Carroll was a devoted patriot and eloquent preacher. He was the first Catholic Bishop of
the United States. On the 22d of February, 1800, by
a solemn and admirable discourse, he commemorated
the character and services of General Washington, who
had died but a few months before. It has been said by
those who heard it, that when he recited the terrors, the
encouragements, the distresses, and the glories of the
struggle of Independence, he appeared to be laboring
under intense emotions correspondent to those topics—
to be swayed like the aged minstrel of the poet, with
contagious influences, by the varied strain which he uttered. Happy for our country and the world will it be,
if all our divines shall remain as loyal as these. A high
sense of national honor, that everlasting fire which alone

keeps patriotism warm in the hearts of its citizens, we cannot guard with a care too vigilant, and a jealousy too acute. A nation without the conservative influence of patriotic piety, may well say to corruption, thou art my father, and to the worm, thou art my mother and my sister. Every citizen, be his calling what it may, should bear the rose of heaven on his cheek and the fire of liberty in his eye.

The best orators of every age have been created by the oppressive circumstance, in the midst of which they have suddenly arisen with resistless power, as if they gathered strength and inspiration from the terrors of the storm. When the age needs great men it will find them —heroes not of the timid mimosa kind, who "fear the dark cloud, and feel the coming sound." Preachers in Revolutionary times are eminently practical; nature supplies them with abundant ammunition, and necessity teaches them expressly to load and fire. They are the flying artillery of " the sacramental host of God's elect." They are inspired by no fictitious goddess of the Aonian Mount, but by that Eternal Spirit who directed the pen of Moses, the fingers of David, and the tongue of Paul; they drink of no fancied Pierian spring, but at a purer and more exalted source.

The great Reformer said, " Human nature is a rough thing, and must have rough ministers to chastise it." Preachers who deal in sentimental commonplaces about the odor of roses and the blandishments of virtue, without enforcing the repugnant doctrines of transforming truth, are more recreant to duty and the welfare of man than was the tyrant Nero, when he despatched ships to

Egypt, the granary of the world, in quest of sand for his gladiators, at a time when Rome was starving with famine.

The most highly endowed among men are the chosen medium of communications from heaven. Such spirits are most numerous when most needed, and most powerful in the tempests which they are born to rule. The impressive march of events through which power on high is manifested to powers here below, the eternal unity of their cause and the solemn harmony of their results have an aspect that profoundly strikes the mind. Under such eliciting influences, that which is sublime and immortal in man clearly reveals itself, and listens to the voices that proclaim

> "A Providence that shapes our ends,
> Rough-hew them as we may."

The chosen ones of earth garner up these mysterious testimonies, and with them substantiate their faith. While Providence thunders in portentous events they fulminate with divine inspirations, and it is thus that celestial instruction is perpetuated and rendered intelligent to mankind. This was the mission which our patriotic fathers were raised up to perform; in every dread emergency, heroes like them are placed by Jehovah on the watch-towers of Jerusalem, and they are silent neither day nor night. They are the godlike, "who resist unto blood, *striving against sin.*" The banner of Constantine bore upon its folds a cross for a device, and the motto inscribed below, *Spes Publica.* Christian leaders have never been permitted to be mere carpet knights, effeminate actors in gay tournaments,—but masculine antagonists amid gigantic perils on a fearful battle-field.

Glance for a moment over the page of ecclesiastical history, and see how the noblest heroes have been educated and employed. Chrysostom, the most brilliant preacher of the ancient church, was compelled by duty to face Eudoxia as Latimer braved Henry the Eighth, or our own Davies awed into silence George the Second.

At a dark period of moral history, the preaching of Peter the Hermit and of Bernard induced multitudes to assume outwardly the symbol of the cross; and under more divine auspices, at a later period, a monk of the order of Augustine, transformed into something nobler, influenced the hearts of myriads to take up the true cross,—the truth that saves the soul. And who was this hero of the famous German Reformation? Frederic had power and wisdom; Reuchlin and Erasmus had talent and learning; Hutten had wit, and Sickengen courage; Cronberg had virtue of an exalted character, and Melancthon was endowed with almost every excellence that can belong to man. But these were all compelled to say, in respect to the needed strength, "it is not in me." Something mightier was needed than erudite scholars, accomplished princes, valorous warriors, and pedantic priests. Luther appeared, and brought with him, to use his own description, "that theology which seeks the kernel of the nut, the pulp of the wheat, the marrow of the bone." The world began to listen to preaching, strange indeed, but life giving. It was no longer a meretricious rhetorician nor a subtle schoolman that addressed them; it was a brother man who had felt the power of divine truth on his own heart, and whose impressive manner certified that he was intent on winning souls to Christ. A famous doctor, Meller-stadt, mixed in the crowds who attended on Luther's preaching. "This monk," said he, "will put all doctors to the rout; he will introduce a new style of doctrine, and will reform the whole church; he builds upon the word of Christ; and no one in this world can either resist or overthrow that word, though it should be attacked with all the weapons of Philosophers, Sophists, Scotists, Albertists, and Thomists."

The great maxim of Erasmus was "Give light, and the darkness will disperse of itself." Luther practised on that rule, and the light came. "I swear manfully to defend the truth of the Gospel," was the oath he took when he was made a doctor of theology. His words smote against the popular heart as mighty waves dash against the shore of the sea.

The American most like him was Samuel Davies. Said Luther, "If in my sermons I thought of Melanc-thon and other doctors, I should do no good; but I speak with perfect plainness for the ignorant, and that satisfies every body. Such Greek, Latin, and Hebrew as I have, I reserve for the learned. Nothing is more agreeable or useful for a common audience than to preach on the duties and examples of Scripture. Ser-mons on grace fall coldly on their ears." President Davies understood these maxims of common sense well, and reduced them to practice. He was undoubtedly one of the most accomplished and successful pulpit ora-

10*

tors of this or any other land. Though he died at thirty-six, he reared memorials of the power of his sacred eloquence, more precious and enduring than Pharaonic monuments.

" These stars have set; O, rise some other such !"

When the children of Israel were about to leave Egypt, Moses was afraid to take the command, because he felt the need of sovereign eloquence to sustain such an office. Jehovah, in his promise to supply the want of this exalted gift, acknowledged its importance as he answered, "Is not Aaron, the Levite, thy brother? I know that he can *speak* well, and he shall be thy spokesman unto the people." And as the tide of Reformation moved westward, observe how good speaking was, as ever, its herald and support. An impressive manner is always most conspicuous when it is most needed. The immense crowds that thronged around St. Paul's Cross, in London, and listened through successive hours in the open air to Jewell and Latimer, were not influenced by the artistic glories of magnificent architecture,—thrilling melody, breathing marbles, soaring arches, or the entrancing illumination of gorgeous windows,—and yet those motley multitudes were swayed to and fro by sacred eloquence, as a whirlwind bends forest boughs. Colet, the persecuted dean of St. Paul's, in 1505, was highly gifted in rhetorical excellence ; and so was the superlatively accomplished Andrews. Concerning the latter, the illustrious Sir Thomas More went so far as even to praise the language of his face. Of Donne, also dean of St. Paul's, in the reign of James I., the follow·

ing exquisite sketch is given by Walton: 'A preacher in earnest, weeping sometimes for his auditory; some-times with them; always preaching to himself, like an angel from a cloud, but in none; carrying some, as St. Paul was, to heaven in holy raptures, and enticing others by a sacred art and courtship to amend their ives; and all this with a most particular grace and an inexpressible addition of loveliness."

While the great theological contest was yet raging, it happened that Hooker was the master of the Temple-Church, and Travers the afternoon lecturer. It was with-in that exquisite edifice recently restored, that the author of the Polity delivered some of the noblest prose in the English language. But his manner was bad. He spoke with a feeble voice, and with his eyes fixed in a downward look, says Walton, "insomuch that he seem-ed to study as he spake." His opponent, Travers, on the contrary, was endowed with popular gifts; and it was not, as was often said, because they had Rome in the morning and Geneva in the afternoon, that the Temple was crowded in every part when Travers as-cended the pulpit. The preference, felt instinctively by all, will ever be given to the glowing utterance of thought and feeling, instead of the calm enumerations of frigid logic. Argumentative preaching is effective only as it is associated with the emotional part of reli-gion. Burke has said, "There is no heart so hard as that of a thorough-bred metaphysician," and he might nave added, there is no public talk so insufferably dull as metaphysical preaching. Studied nonsense in ser-mons is a more painful affliction than unstudied, since the latter has at least the mitigation of disgust which usually attends an extemporary effusion.

If we unite the solidity of Hooker and the practica. manner of Travers, the aggregate would be much like Witherspoon. Our renowned countryman was a kind of theologico-democratic compound; erudite and enthu- siastic, like Augustine; bold and patriotic, like Brutus. While in the President's chair at Nassau Hall, he shone pre-eminently as a scholar and divine; but in the im- passioned gladiatorship of Congress, the spirit of the Tribune predominated, and the patriotic priest bore no slight resemblance to the militant prelate of the middle ages, who, at the battle of Bouvines, would wield no other weapon than a mace, because his religion forbade him to shed blood, and who, in the midst of the conflict, blessed with one hand the numerous foes whom he crushed with the other. He was the devout cavalier of Liberty in her own temple of legislation.

It is not to be understood, however, that Dr. Wither- spoon, or his distinguished co-patriots in the pulpit, were religious or political fanatics. When a clergyman transforms himself into a phrenzied partizan, the dupe or champion of a local faction, he renders himself the more odious in contrast with the exalted profession he has disgraced. This is an instinctive feeling of the popular heart, and it is just; for what crime can be greater than to identify the things of earth with those of heaven, the illusions of time with the imperishable things of eternity? What can be more sacrilegious and fatal to human hopes than to place ar earthly pas- sion or human interest on the altar by the side of Christ, and sometimes even in Christ's own place? But the appropriate functions of a religious teacher do not forbid the duties of a patriot—they imperiously demand them. God designed that the minister of the Gospel should be the man of the people, the confidant of their miseries the balm of their secret griefs, the depositary of their tears, the interpreter of their necessities, their protector, friend and father, a living providence to all who hunger and thirst, a light to guide the benighted, and a beacon to warn those in danger of destruction.

It would be unjust to pass from the heroical age of pulpit eloquence, without adverting to that glorious man of God whose hallowed influence is flooding the world with ennobling power, *John Wesley*. Neither should we forget, that about the period we are now contemplating, Whitefield's glowing, impassioned, and awful eloquence—his incessant, daring, and quenchless enthusiasm—produced a profound and extensive impression on all classes of people in our land. But these allusions suggest topics quite too prolific to be broached fully at present. They richly deserve an extended article by themselves.

Before concluding, however, it will be well to remark that, all things considered, perhaps, the finest specimen of a captivating and profitable American preacher in Revolutionary times was the Boston pastor already described, *Dr. Stillman*. His views of pulpit ministrations were elevated and comprehensive. And what are they but to unfold the doctrines and explain the pure and sublime morality of the gospel, illustrating its tendency and diffusing its spirit—to exalt the aim of the soul and direct its aspirations toward immortal worth,—to proclaim the conditions of holy faith and enduring joy, exemplified in "the victorious agonies of saints and martyrs,"—to reveal that glorious and dread-ful destiny so intimately connected with every act of life, ascending with Milton to those immortal heights of light, love and glory :

> " The living throne, the sapphire blaze,
>   Where angels tremble while they gaze."

In efforts to do this, what stores of wealth are there in genius, eloquence, poetry, profound erudition, and sanc-tified embellishment, that may not be judiciously em-ployed ? When considered simply as a sphere for intellectual greatness and cultivation, how sublime is the station, and how glorious are the privileges which the Christian minister enjoys. But where are the zealous competitors whose chief ambition is to run for the prize of this high calling? Where are the men whose pas-sions are educated to fortify their understanding, and whose rational powers are penetrated and invested with heavenly grace, as the Shekinah burned in splendor ineffable, over and around the mercy-seat ?

The most effective preachers are not subtle dialecti-cians, nor the fastidious retailers of bigotted creeds. They do not always believe that it is indispensable to "explain upon a thing till all men doubt it." In their estimation it is desirable occasionally to take for granted what dubious metaphysicians and astute dogmatists deem it essential, as a primary step in all discourse, eternally to prove. Preachers like Stillman will make a better use of their powers. They will feel that they are employed in the divinest diplomacy; and, as ambassadors commissioned from heaven, they will exert every faculty in direct negociation for the salvation of souls. That is the best sermon which is easiest understood and longest remembered. The minister must be well-educated, but his education is for use and not for show. Preachers of the right stamp remember this and act accordingly. With the concentrated fires of an intelligent, enthusiastic, and ravishing eloquence, they impress transcendent worth upon the hearer, inflaming him with a passion for moral excellence, and imparting to him a vital impulse which, in virtuous habits and practical godliness, is perpetually reproduced.

The magnificent, equally with the majestic, is a source of power to the pulpit orator. Every kingdom of nature, every department of science, and every production of art,—philosophical research and patriotic disquisition,—whatever history has bequeathed, imagination invented, or fancy embellished,—may be appropriately employed in the foundation of the preacher's work, or as blandishments to adorn it. His audience yield to him this right willingly, and rejoice in its exercise, never more happy than when he snatches them "from Thebes to Athens, when and where he will." To him, at the head of all speakers, most legitimately belong the richest treasures of earth, air, and sea, the peculiar tint and tone of each clime, the mental wealth of each nation, and the accumulated wonders of the whole universe. He may revel in "gorgeous Ind," with her golden skies and glittering domes; "fanatic Egypt

and her priests;" the waving palms and wizard glens
of the South ; and the stern superstitions of the North,
with all its hills of snow and lucid air, "clad in the
beauty of a thousand stars." He may cull gems from
coral caverns, pluck flowers from sunny fields, and robe
himself in splendor from the radiant heavens; he may
lay all literature under contribution to illustrate his
theme, array all worlds around him as the theatre of his
discussion, and summon spirits from bliss, and devils
damned, to verify and enforce his thought.

Such a preacher was Stillman. The "truth came
mended from his lips." A few venerable persons yet
survive who remember his august and imposing action,
—that action which is the *soul* of thought. Nothing
ostentatious in the mode of his commencement indicated
premeditated display ; all was simple and sublime. His
figure was not corpulent, but it was compact and
graceful in an extraordinary degree. The full wig and
ample robes in which he was accustomed to preach
added to the nobleness of his exterior, while an air of
modesty and earnest candor augmented the force of his
speech. His voice was sweet, flexible, and sonorous,
but grave, firm, and masculine. His gestures, produced
without effort or affectation, moved simultaneously with
his mind, and both were animated, dignified, and persuasive. He occupied the same pulpit for many years,
under the scrutiny of a vast congregation, all of whom
found it difficult to decide which most to admire in
their preacher, his exemplary life, or his unequalled
eloquence ; the soundness of his doctrine, or the graces
of his delivery. Whenever his elegant form and ex

pressive features appeared in their presence, the vividness of his emotions and the pungency of his appeals
served to remind the classical hearer of that ancient
patriot who "*bore the republic in his heart.*"

CHAPTER IX.

PATRICK HENRY,

THE INCARNATION OF REVOLUTIONARY ZEAL

IF there be one attribute of man supreme in dignity and worth it is that of oratory. The illusions of the eye, combined with the enchanting power of music, constitute an influence less potent upon the imagination and will, than the spirit-stirring appeals of "eloquence divine." Other charms are mostly drawn from the external world, but this emanates from the unseen spirit within; its splendors gleam through animated clay and proclaim the superior majesty of immortal mind.

When men are exhilarated in the presence of excellence, when they are greatly moved by the power of cultivated speech, the imagination is more susceptible of receiving agreeable impressions, and the mind becomes insensibly imbued with the worth it in rapture admires

When the heart and fancy are thus taken captive by those sentiments which are addressed to our sensibilities, the better to move our reason, the severe rules which we impose on the frigid logician, become generously expanded. The orator feels no longer wounded by hypercritical restraints; more latitude is granted for the expansion of his genius, and in the moment of fortunate

PATRICK HENRY

THE NEW YORK
PUBLIC LIBRARY

ASTOR, LENOX AND
TILDEN FOUNDATIONS

daring, he creates happy emotions in others and fore-
tokens fame for himself.

The era in our history, now under consideration, was
exceedingly favorable for the cultivation of the most
exalted order of eloquence. It was a period when the
public mind was strongly agitated by the popular discussion of interests, the most comprehensive and enduring.

The war of 1776 was the Trojan war of America; it
diffused one impulse over our whole domain, united the
Colonies in one spirit of resistance against oppression,
and bound them together in one national bond. Moreover, it had the effect of the Persian war, when Miltiades
led the flower of Greece to Marathon, and a young, but
vigorous, nation could successfully compete with superior numbers and veteran skill. The different sections
of the country vied with each other in generous compe-
tition for precedence in facing a common foe, feeling
that stern conflicts and a glorious triumph were necessary to give them all a consciousness of their real
strength.

The period of our Colonial and Revolutionary history
was, in fact, an era of great superiority in eloquence, at
home and abroad. England then presented an array of
orators such as she has known at no other time. In
Westminster Hall, the accomplished Mansfield was constantly heard in support of kingly power, while the philosophic and argumentative Camden exercised his
mighty intellect in defence of popular rights. Burke
had awoke with all his wealth of fancy, daring imagination and comprehensive learning. Fox had entered the

arena of forensic and senatorial gladiatorship, with his great, glowing heart, and titanic passions, all kindled into volcanic heat. Junius, by his sarcasm and audacity, stung the loftiest circles into desperation. Erskine embellished the darkened heavens by the rainbow tints of his genius ; and Chatham, worthily succeeded by his "cloud-compelling" son, ruled the billowy sea of excited mind with the majesty of a god.

Against all that is powerful in mental energy and martial force, our fathers had to give battle under the most fearful odds. The chivalrous antagonists came into open field ; empires were at stake, and the struggle was worthy of the prize, as the result was glorious to those whom we delight to commemorate.

Eloquence in America then was a system of the most invigorating mental gymnastics. The popular orators hurled accusations and arguments into the bosom of the populace, and aroused universal rebellion against regal wrongs. Prominent among the mightiest of the " rebels," stood the subject of this sketch.

The ancients set up statues of renowned citizens in the most public resorts, to keep passing generations in remembrance of the worthies whose patriotism and piety they ought to emulate. Sometimes filial love would prompt admiring disciples to bring garlands, not with the vain hope of adding to the intrinsic worth, or external elegance, of the venerated form, but simply to wreathe round its brow a token of fond regard. In the present instance, our ambition "hath this extent, no more." We do not herein expect to elicit any new facts in the life of Patrick Henry, but shall attempt only to group, as comprehensively as possible, some of our views respecting the source and characteristics of his eloquence. The circumstances relating to his parentage, birth, and early history, have been carefully compiled by his biographer, Wirt, and are freely copied in the historical portion of the following sketch :

Patrick Henry, the second son of John and Sarah Henry, and one of nine children, was born on the 29th of May, 1736, at the family seat, called Studley, in the county of Hanover, and colony of Virginia. In his early childhood his parents removed to another seat in the same county, then called Mount Brilliant, now the Retreat; at which latter place, Patrick Henry was " raised" and educated. His parents, though not rich, were in easy circumstances ; and, in point of personal character, were among the most respectable inhabitants of the colony.

His father, Col. John Henry, was a native of Aberdeen, in Scotland. He was, it is said, a first cousin to David Henry, who was the brother-in-law and successor of Edward Cave in the publication of that celebrated work, the Gentleman's Magazine, and himself the author of several literary tracts : John Henry is also said to have been a nephew, in the maternal line, to the great historian, Dr. William Robertson. He came over to Virginia, in quest of fortune, some time prior to the year 1730, and the tradition is that he enjoyed the friendship of Mr. Dinwiddie, afterward the governor of the colony. By this gentleman, it is reported, that he was introduced to the elder Col. Syme, of Hanover, in whose family, it is certain, that he became domesticated during the life of that gentleman, after whose death he "intermarried" with his widow, and resided on the estate which he had left. It is considered as a fair proof of the personal merit of Mr. John Henry, that, in those days, when offices were bestowed with peculiar caution, he was the colonel of his regiment, the principal surveyor of the county, and, for many years, the presiding magistrate of the county court. His surviving acquaintances concur in stating that he was a man of liberal education ; that he possessed a plain, yet solid understanding ; and lived long a life of the most irreproachable integrity and exemplary piety. His brother Patrick, a clergyman of the Church of England, followed him to this country some years afterward ; and became, by *his* influence, the minister of St. Paul's parish, in Hanover, the functions of which office he sustained throughout life with great respectability. Both the brothers were zealous members of the Established Church, and warmly attached to the reigning family. Col. John Henry was conspicuously so : " there are those yet alive," said a correspondent in 1805, " who have seen him at the head of his regiment, celebrating the birthday of George III. with as much enthusiam as his son Patrick afterwards displayed, in resisting the encroachments of that monarch."

The mother of this "forest-born Demosthenes," was a native of Hanover County, and is said to have been eminently endowed with amiability, intelligence, and the fascinations of a graceful elocution. She had a brother who was one of the most effective orators of that day.

It is seldom, or never, that we meet with a man dis-

tinguished in any intellectual pursuit who had a num-
skull for a mother. How much does England and the
world owe to Alfred ? Liberty, property, laws, literature ; all that makes the Anglo-Saxon people what they
are, and political society so nearly what it ought to be
And who made Alfred all that he became to his own age,
all that he is destined perpetually to be ? She who
nursed his first thought and moulded his regal mind.
" The words which his mother taught him," the lessons
of wisdom she instilled into his aspiring soul, were the
germs of thought, genius, enterprise, action, every thing
to the future father of his country.   .

And to " Mary, the mother of Washington," whose
incomplete monument at Fredericksburgh lies shame-
fully neglected, we owe all the mighty debt due from
mankind to her immortal son. He has himself declared
that to her influence and early instruction he was indebted for all that was human in the direction of his fortunes.

Curran's mother was, comparatively, an obscure
woman, but one of strong original understanding and
glowing enthusiasm. In her latter years, the celebrity
of her son rendered her the object of increased attention ; and critical observers could easily discover, in the
irregular bursts of her eloquence, the primitive gushings
of the stream which, expanding as it descended, at length
attained a force and majesty that excited unbounded
admiration. Mr. Curran himself felt his indebtedness
for hereditary talent. Said he, " the only inheritance
that I could boast of from my poor father, was the very
scanty one of an unattractive face and person, like his
own ; and if the world has ever attributed to me some-

thing more valuable than face or person, or than earthly wealth, it was that another and a dearer parent gave her child a portion from the treasure of her mind." He attributed much of his subsequent success to the early influence of such a mother, and, to his latest hour, would dwell with grateful recollection upon the wise counsel, upon the lessons of honorable ambition, and of thorough piety, which she enforced upon the minds of her children. The mother of the Schlegels is said to have contributed greatly to form the character of her accomplished sons. We know that Canning, and Brougham, and Guizot, are indebted mainly to the same source of success.

The Scotch " gumption," and Virginia ardor, inherited from his parents, and so finely blended in his own mental organization, constituted a richer patrimony for Patrick Henry, than all the splendors of remote pedigree and ancestral fame.

The basis of Mr. Henry's character was acute common sense. His insight into the workings of human nature was early exercised to an extraordinary degree. In the common acceptation of the word, he was not educated ; like Shakspeare, according to Ben Jonson, he "knew little Latin and less Greek." But in the best sense of the term, he was superlatively disciplined for the mission he was destined to fulfil. His principal book was the great volume of human nature. In this he was deeply read ; and hence arose his great power of persuasion. The habit of critical observation formed in early youth went with him through life. Meeting, in a bookstore, with his friend Ralph Wormley, who, although a great book-worm, was infinitely more remark·

able for his 'gnorance of men than Mr. Henry was for that of books—" What, Mr. Wormley," said he, " still buying books?" " Yes," said Mr. Wormley, " I have just heard of a new work, which I am extremely anxious to peruse." " Take my word for it," said he, " Mr. Wormley, we are too old to read books; *read men*—they are the only volumes that we can peruse to advantage." But Mr. Henry neglected neither. From his earliest youth he studied both with care, though his education was desultory in the extreme. As early as most boys he had learned to read, write, and perform the ordinary tasks in arithmetic. At ten years of age he was taken home, and under the instruction of his father learned the elements of Latin and Greek.

Men of rare genius are generally fond of the extremes of existence—profound solitude or boisterous glee. Such was the case with Henry. While yet a youth, he would spend protracted seasons in silent meditation, and then with frenzied zeal would abruptly plunge into the greatest hilarity. He was much addicted to field sports, but these were employed as the occasions of mental discipline, rather than for purposes of dissipation. He was habitually frugal, though constitutionally sanguine and impetuous. If he freely used the angle and the gun for pastime, he assiduously pondered some great theme, or deduced an argument while a superficial observer would scarcely have supposed him to be at the same time employed in pursuits so widely diversified. His violin, his flute, a few favorite books, habitual and critical study of mankind, frequent ramblings in the wild woods, and profound meditations by

11

flowing streams, occupied the early years of his youth
The only science he loved was mathematics, and the
book he most read, among uninspired authors, was a
translation of "the pictured Livy." With respect to
reading, his motto seems to have been, "much, but not
many." He might have adopted Hobbes's opinion, "that
if he had read as much as other men, he should have
been as ignorant as they were." But the books he did
peruse, he digested thoroughly. He was not a thing
made up of fragments,—he was himself, a man self-de-
veloped,—he thought more than he read.

By this kind of severe self-tuition amid the beauties
and sublimities of nature, he cultivated a flexile majesty,
a natural grandeur of soul. It was not the artificial
groves of the Academy, the polished pavements of the
Portico, nor Grecian steeds constrained with bit and
curb, that listened to the harp of Orpheus, but the wild
trees of unfrequented haunts, the rocks of deserts un-
adorned, and the untamed tigers of the wood.

When fifteen years old, Mr. Henry was placed behind
the counter of a country store; but the hands destined
to forge thunderbolts, were unskillful in measuring tape
and hoarding worldly gains. Pegasus chafed in the
contracted sphere, and struggled for escape. By en-
larging the domain of more exalted excursions, however,
he ruined the petty profits of the shop. At the early
age of eighteen, he was married. This apparently in-
discreet act was probably an advantage in fact. It furnished him a secluded home of his own, a solace in
pecuniary trials, and a restraint on vicious indulgence.
Thus, in lonely studies, healthful toils and domestic joys,

he cultivated in deep obscurity the giant faculties of his soul.

> "There have been those that from the deepest caves
> And cells of night, and fastnesses, below
> The stormy dashing of the ocean-waves,
> Down, farther down than gold lies hid, have nursed
> A quenchless hope, and watch'd their time, and burst
> On the bright day, like wakeners from their graves!"

Fortunately for our hero, he was endowed with a fine flow of elastic spirits; with a noble fortitude he braced himself boldly against every disaster of life. Mr. Jefferson made his acquaintance in the winter of 1759-60, and has left us the following impressions respecting him. "On my way to the college, I passed the Christmas holydays at Col. Dandridge's in Hanover, to whom Mr. Henry was a near neighbor. During the festivity of the season, I met him in society every day, and we became well acquainted, although I was much his junior, being then in my seventeenth year, and he a married man. His manners had something of coarseness in them; his passion was music, dancing, and pleasantry. He excelled in the last, and it attached every one to him. He had, a little before, broken up his store, or rather it had broken him up; but his misfortunes were not to be traced either in his countenance or conduct." Says another cotemporary, "He would be pleased and cheerful with persons of any class or condition, vicious and abandoned persons only excepted; he preferred those of character and talents, but would be amused with any who could contribute to his amusement." Habitual cheerfulness is doubtless a mighty auxiliary to the mind, and happy is he who can rise above lowering storms and say,

> " I will dash these fond regrets to earth,
> E'en as an eagle shakes the cumbering rain
> From his strong pinion."

After a six weeks' preparation, he obtained a license to practice the law, being then twenty-four years of age, and almost entirely ignorant of the simplest forms of the profession he had embraced. For these facts we are also indebted to Mr. Jefferson. In the spring of 1760, he says, Mr. Henry "came to Williamsburg to obtain a license as a lawyer, and he called on me at college. He told me he had been reading law only six weeks. Two of the examiners, however, Peyton and John Randolph, men of great facility of temper, signed his license with as much reluctance as· their dispositions would permit them to show. Mr. Wythe absolutely refused, Robert C. Nicholas refused also at first; but on repeated importunities and promises of future reading, he signed. These facts I had afterwards from the gentlemen themselves; the two Randolphs acknowledging he was very ignorant of the law, but that they perceived him to be a young man of genius, and did not doubt that he would soon qualify himself."

Henry was one of those who are " victory organized," and will ever " find a way or make one." The same rule applies to all such, that was announced to the Directory by the principal in command, when young Napoleon first began to display his astonishing power,—" Promote this young man or he will promote himself."

For some time he was entirely unnoticed, but in his famous speech in *the parson's cause*, he at length began to engross public attention. As counsel for Mr. Dandridge in a contested election, he made a brilliant harangue on the rights of suffrage. Such a burst of eloquence from so plain and humble a man, struck the popular mind with amazement, and at once made the speaker an object of universal respect. The incident is described as follows, from the pen of Judge Tyler. It was the young advocate's first appearance in the digni- fied and refined society at Williamsburg, then the seat of lordly arrogance and colonial power. " The proud airs of aristocracy, added to the dignified forms of that truly august body, were enough to have deterred any man possessing less firmness and independence of spirit than Mr. Henry. He was ushered with great state and ceremony into the room of the committee, whose chair- man was Col. Bland. Mr. Henry was dressed in very coarse apparel ; no one knew any thing of him ; and scarcely was he treated with decent respect by any one except the chairman, who could not do so much vio- lence to his feelings and principles, as to depart, on any occasion, from the delicacy of the gentleman. But the general contempt was soon changed into as general ad- miration ; for Mr. Henry distinguished himself by a copious and brilliant display on the great subject of the rights of suffrage, superior to any thing that had been heard before within those walls. It struck the commit- tee with amazement, so that a deep and perfect silence took place during the speech, and not a sound but from his lips was to be heard in the room."

Let us at this point dwell a little on his personal ap‑
pearance and modes of address.

In his youth, Mr. Henry was exceedingly indifferent
to both costume and style, but as he rose in experience
and influence, he became more refined.   Through all
vicissitudes, however, his personal appearance was won‑
derfully impressive.   He was nearly six feet high ; spare
and raw‑boned, with a slight stoop of his shoulders.   His
complexion was dark and sallow; his natural expression
grave, thoughtful and penetrating.   He was gifted with
a strong and musical voice, often rendered doubly fasci‑
nating by the mild splendors of his brilliant blue eyes.
When animated, he spoke with the greatest variety of
manner and tone.   It was necessary to involve him in
some great emergency in order to arouse his more ster‑
ling qualities and then to the surprise of himself as
well as every body else, he would in the most splendid
manner develop,

> " A treasure all undreampt of :—as the night
> Calls out the harmonies of streams that roll
> Unheard by day."

Gleams of passion interpenetrating the masses of his
logic, rendered him a spectacle of delight to the friendly
spectator, or of dread to his antagonist.   He was care‑
less in dress, and sometimes intentionally and extrava‑
gantly awkward in movement; but always, like the
phosphorescent stone at Bologna, he was less rude than
glowing.   He could be vehement, insinuating, humor‑
ous, and sarcastic by turns, and to every sort of style he
gave the highest effect.   He was an orator by nature,

and of the highest class, combining all those traits of figure and intellect, action and utterance which have indissolubly linked his brilliant name with the history of his country's emancipation.

The true orator is not the actor of his subject, but its organ. With him who has something to say, under the importance of which he trembles, and is anxious to disburden his soul in the most direct and forcible manner, there will be no hollow wordiness, no gaudy decoration, no rhetorical sophisms, but a profound and manifest feeling of truth and honesty will gleam all over the speaker's person and fork the lightnings of his eloquence. The inspiration will be profound, the thought will be lucid, and the action natural ; looks, gestures, and tones will be such

> "As skill and graceful nature might suggest
> To a proficient of the tragic muse."

The etherial splendors which burned through Patrick Henry's words, were not elaborated, spark by spark, in the laboratory of pedantic cloisters. It was in the open fields, under the wide cope of heaven, full of free, healthful and livid atmosphere, this oratorical Franklin caught his lightnings from gathering storms as they passed over him ; and he communicated his charged soul with electrical swiftness and effect. *He was the incarnation of Revolutionary zeal.* He had absorbed into his susceptible nature the mighty inspiration which breathed throughout the newly awakened and arousing world. He tempered and retempered his soul in boiling premeditations against tyranny, as the cutler tempers a sword

by plunging it into water while yet red hot from the furnace.   The popular orator must be lucid if he would be
influential.   He must not be a metaphysician, an anti-
quarian, nor a pedant,

"Plunged to the hilt in musty tomes and rusted in."

He cannot have too much learning; but he must show
the edifice and not the scaffolding; or rather, he must
show nothing, but let all be seen without effort.   He
may possess subtle schemes and recondite erudition, but
these must be dragged from their obscurity into a full
blaze of light.   He may be skillful in fine theories and
cumbered with much learning, but they must be rendered
plain and prominent to common sense, or they have no
claims to the honors of eloquence.   That which cannot
be invested with a blaze of imagination and made palpable to the public gaze, is not a fit subject for the orator.   It is not meant by this that in order to be comprehended by the general mind one must be superficial;
on the contrary, nothing so soon palls on the popular
taste as shallowness, and nothing so soon disgusts as flip-
pant uniformity.   Affectation and common-place are as
loathsome to the masses as to the most refined individuals; and nothing will long interest them but deep
thought in clear expression, a compound of untamable
vigor, and daring originality.   Assembled multitudes
are enthralled by a style that is rich in meaning, vivid
in color, and varied in tone; its combinations must be
bold, unexpected, clearly significant, pertinent to the
topic in hand, and powerfully directed to one great end.

Mr. Henry's knowledge of legal science was quite

limited, but his great natural sagacity enabled him to make the most successful use of such resources as he possessed. His great forte lay in arguing questions of common law, or in the defence of criminals before a jury. " There, his intimate knowledge of human nature, and the rapidity as well as justness of his inferences, as to what was passing in the hearts of his hearers, availed him fully. The jury might be composed of entire strangers, yet he rarely failed to know them, man by man, before the evidence was closed. There was no studied fixture of features that could long hide the character from his piercing and experienced view. The slightest unguarded turn of countenance or motion of the eye let him at once into the soul of the man whom he was observing. Or, if he doubted whether his conclusions were correct from the exhibitions of countenance during the narration of evidence, he had a mode of playing a prelude, as it were, upon the jury, in his exordium, which never failed to " wake into life each silent string," and show him the whole compass as well as pitch of the instrument; and, indeed, (if we may believe all the concurrent accounts of his exhibitions in the general court,) the most exquisite performer that ever "swept the sounding lyre," had not a more sovereign mastery over its powers than Mr. Henry had over the springs of feeling and thought that belong to a jury. There was a delicacy, a tact, a felicity in the touch that was perfectly original, and without a rival. His style of address, on these occasions, is said to have resembled very much that of the Scriptures. It was strongly marked with the same simplicity, the same

11*

energy, the same pathos. He sounded no alarm, he made no parade to put the jury on their guard. It was all so natural, so humble, so unassuming, that they were carried imperceptibly along, and attuned to his purpose, until some master-touch dissolved them into tears. His language of passion was perfect. There was no word "of learned length or thundering sound," to break the charm. It had almost all the stillness of solitary thinking. It was a sweet reverie, a delicious trance. His voice, too, had a wonderful effect. He had a singular power of infusing it into a jury and mixing its tones with their nerves in a manner which it is impossible to describe justly; but which produced a thrilling excitement in the happiest concordance with his designs. No man knew so well as he did what kind of topics to urge to their understandings, nor what kind of simple imagery to present to their hearts. His eye, which he kept riveted upon them, assisted the process of fascination, and at the same time informed him what theme to press, or at what instant to retreat, if by rare accident he touched an unpropitious string. And then he had such an exuberance of appropriate thoughts, of apt illustrations, of apposite images, and such a melodious and varied roll of the happiest words, that the hearer was never wearied by repetition, and never winced from an apprehension that the intellectual treasures of the speaker would be exhausted."*

Henry exercised tremendous power over the people, because he was one of them—had studied their cha-

---

* This outline, drawn by Mr. Wirt, is a fine sketch of his own won derful abilities, as well as those of his admired predecessor at the bar

racter—was familiar with their habits of thought and action—had gained their confidence, and could conciliate their prejudice. He was skillful to ingratiate the affections of the popular heart, and could impel the convictions of all, before the current of his declamation and the fervor of his appeals. He smote right and left, like an invincible warrior armed with broadsword, hewing his way through opposing legions. Action was his forte rather than meditation. He was not adroit in fortifying a case with obscure precedents and subtle distinctions. He was little accustomed to hunt a principle through the musty alcoves of black-letter libraries; but his moral instincts were acute, his sense of justice as infallible as in the best of men, and the logic of his passionate soul commanded respect, if not conviction. Like Indian rubies of the finest water, he required no polish; his soul glowed with its own fire, and emitted a brilliancy that was native to the quarry. But the field of conflict, and not the quiet study, was his appropriate sphere; he was most splendid when in arms and involved in furious fight. Whenever his extraordinary faculties were aroused, he is reported by his cotemporaries to have been exceedingly fascinating. Judge Lyons said " that he could write a letter, or draw a declaration or plea, at the bar, with as much accuracy as he could in his office, under all circumstances, except when Patrick rose to speak; but whenever *he* rose, although it might be on so trifling a subject as a summons and petition for twenty shillings, he was obliged to lay down his pen, and could not write another word until the speech was finished."

On the contrary, the most distracting dangers of a tumultuous scene could not disturb the self-possession of Mr. Henry, nor shake the steadfastness of his purpose. It might have been truly said of him, "Half his strength he puts not forth, but stays his thunders in mid-volley." So firm and imperial was the control of his mind, that at any instant he could arrest the torrent of his fury, and, by a sudden change in its direction, overtake and scathe his foe. An exemplification of this will soon be quoted. In boldness of manner, and habitual self-command, that spirit of daring and confident reliance on internal resources which always commands attention and respect, our hero resembled Lord Chatham. It is related of the latter, that once in the House of Commons he began a speech with the words, "Sugar, Mr. Speaker," —and then, observing a smile to pervade the audience, he paused, looked fiercely around, and with a loud voice, rising in its notes, and swelling into vehement anger, he pronounced again the word "sugar" three times! and having thus quelled the House, and extinguished every trace of laughter, turned round and scornfully in quired, " Who will laugh at sugar now ?"

After Mr. Henry's death, there was found among his papers one sealed, and endorsed as follows, in his own hand-writing : " The within resolutions passed the House of Burgesses in May, 1765." They formed the first opposition to the Stamp-Act, and the scheme of taxing America by the British Parliament. All the Colonies, either through fear, or want of opportunity to form an opposition, or from influence of some kind or other, had remained silent. I had been, for the first time, elected a burgess a few days before, was young, inexperienced, unacquainted with the forms of the House, and the members that composed it. Finding the men of weight opposed to the opposition, and the commencement of the tax at hand, and that no person was likely to step forth, I determined to venture; and alone, unadvised, and unassisted, on the blank leaf of an old law book, wrote the within. Upon offering them to the House violent debates ensued. Many threats were uttered, and much abuse cast on me by the party for submission. After a long and warm contest, the resolutions passed by a very small majority, perhaps of one or two only. The alarm spread throughout America with astonishing quickness, and the ministerial party were overwhelmed. The great point of resistance to British taxation was universally established in the Colonies. This brought on the war, which finally separated the two countries, and gave independence to ours. Whether this will prove a blessing or a curse will depend upon the use our people make of the blessings which a gracious God hath bestowed on us. If they are wise they will be great and happy. If they are of a contrary character, they will be miserable. Righteousness alone can exalt them as a nation. Reader, whosoever thou art, remember this; and in thy sphere practice virtue thyself, and encourage it in others.

"P. HENRY."

The speech delivered by James Otis, in Boston, against " Writs of Assistance" made John Adams the orator. The eloquence of Patrick Henry, in the Colonial Assembly, at Williamsburg, May, 1765, created another college student, Thomas Jefferson, the patriot. This great statesman was young when the orator, whom he styled "the magnificent child of nature," first appeared in public with his famous resolutions against the Stamp Act, referred to in his own record just quoted. "The debate," to use Jefferson's strong language, "was most bloody," but torrents of indomitable eloquence from Henry prevailed, and the resolutions were carried.

Incidents which occurred during this famous debate indicated new features in Mr. Henry's oratorical character. A remarkable instance proved that his power of self-control was as great as that of his habitual impetuosity. As a courser of high mettle and pure blood suddenly reined in, stands on his haunches with every nerve trembling, so he could arrest the impetuous course of his eloquence, and turn in a moment to reply to any pertinent or impertinent interruption. The following illustration of this point is preserved to us by Mr. Jefferson. "I well remember the cry of 'treason' by the speaker, echoed from every part of the House, against Mr. Henry. I well remember his pause, and the admirable address with which he recovered himself, and baffled the charge thus vociferated." The allusion here is to that memorable exclamation of Mr. Henry : "Cæsar had his Brutus, Charles I. his Cromwell, and George III. —"Treason," cried the speaker, "treason! treason!" echoed the House—"may profit by the example," promptly replied the orator, "if this be treason, make the most of it."

It seems to be a fundamental law, that **moral courage**

should constitute the true basis of oratorical success as well as personal honor. "No slave can be eloquent," says Longinus, and all literary history shows that the highest attainments can be secured only by the union of the most unshackled and uncorrupted qualities of head and heart. To think vigorously, and fearlessly to say what you think, is the only way to be effective in the use of speech. The faculty of profound and penetrating thought was a distinguished feature in Henry's mental character, and the boldness with which he expressed his opinions at the hazard of personal convenience was equally remarkable. Exalted sentiment was the inform-ing soul which invested his person with an imposing grandeur; but the nobleness of his mien was enhanced by the perfect independence with which he employed his resources in defence of whatever he deemed essential to individual integrity or the public weal. His mind was ardent, and prolific of illustrations; it threw off a profusion of beauties in its progress as naturally as a current of molten iron glows and sparkles as it issues from the furnace. His eloquent soul was one of that elevated class that revels in the luxuriance of splendid imagery, in every succeeding sentence changing its hue and form with Protean facility, throwing out something original at each remove, and generally terminating the chain with a link more magnificent than all the rest.

Jefferson was present during the whole of the occa-sion alluded to above. He stood in the door of com-munication between the House and the lobby, where he heard the whole of the violent discussion. Like the boy, John Adams, he thenceforth consecrated himself to the service of his country. Scipio Africanus, while yet in his early youth, stood one day on a hill near Carthage, and looked down on a terrific battle-field where those veterans, Massanissa and Hamilcar, crushed through opposing legions in the tug of war. This chance view gave direction to his life. But Adams and Jefferson, in the presence of Otis and Henry, were inspired with loftier impulses, and for nobler ends.

On the fourth of September, 1774, the old Continental Congress of the United States met, for the first time, at Carpenter's Hall, Philadelphia. It is not our intention to dwell here on the wonderful effect produced by Mr. Henry's eloquence in that body in the opening of its solemn session. Neither at present do we more than simply allude to his still more extraordinary speech made in the convention of delegates which assembled on the 20th of March, 1775, in the old church at Richmond, Virginia.

Those were scenes of stupendous interest which have already been sketched in the opening chapter on *The Battle-Fields of Early American Eloquence*. It will be appropriate, however, in this place, to quote a portion of the Richmond speech, as a distinguished specimen of his style.

"He had," he said, "but one lamp by which his feet were guided; and that was the lamp of experience. He knew of no way of judging of the future, but by the past. And judging by the past, he wished to know what there had been in the conduct of the British ministry for the last ten years, to justify those hopes with which gentlemen had been pleased to solace themselves

and the House? Is it that insidious smile with which
our petition has been lately received? Trust it not,
sir; it will prove a snare to your feet. Suffer not
yourselves to be betrayed with a kiss. Ask yourselves
how this gracious reception of our petition comports
with those warlike preparations which cover our waters
and darken our land? Are fleets and armies necessary
to a work of love and reconciliation? Have we shown
ourselves so unwilling to be reconciled, that force must
be called in to win back our love? Let us not deceive
ourselves, sir. These are the implements of war and
subjugation—the last arguments to which kings resort.
I ask gentlemen, sir, what means this martial array, if
its purpose be not to force us to submission? Can
gentlemen assign any other possible motive for it?
Has Great Britain any enemy in this quarter of the
world, to call for all this accumulation of navies and
armies? No, sir; she has none. They are meant for
us; they can be meant for no other. They are sent
over to bind and rivet upon us those chains, which the
British ministry have been so long forging. And what
have we to oppose to them? Shall we try argument?
Sir, we have been trying that for the last ten years.
Have we any thing new to offer upon the subject?
Nothing. We have held the subject up in every light
of which it is capable; but it has been all in vain.
Shall we resort to entreaty and humble supplication?
What terms shall we find, which have not been already
exhausted? Let us not, I beseech you, sir, deceive our-
selves longer. Sir, we have done every thing that
could be done, to avert the storm which is now coming

on.   We have petitioned—we have remonstrated—we have supplicated—we have prostrated ourselves before the throne, and have implored its interposition to arrest the tyrannical hands of the ministry and parliament.   Our petitions have been slighted; our remonstrances have produced additional violence and insult; our supplications have been disregarded; and we have been spurned, with contempt, from the foot of the throne.   In vain, after these things, may we indulge the fond hope of peace and reconciliation.   *There is no longer any room for hope.* If we wish to be free—if we mean to preserve inviolate those inestimable privileges for which we have been so long contending—if we mean not basely to abandon the noble struggle in which we have been so long engaged, and which we have pledged ourselves never to abandon, until the glorious object of our contest shall be obtained —we must fight!—I repeat it, sir, we must fight!! An appeal to arms and to the God of Hosts, is all that is left us!"

John Randolph said of Patrick Henry, that he was Garrick and Shakspeare combined.   That was the most eloquent encomium ever pronounced on eloquence, and no doubt as much deserved by its object as by any human being.   His appeals to the heart were not less forcible than were the bolts of his invective or the deductions of his argument.

His style of thought and expression seems to have been formed much after the manner of the Hebrew prophets, and the unsophisticated orators of our western wilderness.   His most piercing expressions in the famous speech just quoted are borrowed from the Bible, and their suggestive trains of association, more grand and impressive even than those which he uttered, are much like the following extract from the Choctaw Chief, Pushmataha, who died at Washington, in 1824. "I shall die, but you will return to your brethren. As you go along the paths, you will see the flowers and hear the birds ; but Pushmataha will see them and hear them no more. When you come to your home, they will ask you, where is Pushmataha ? and you will say to them, he is no more. They will hear the tidings *like the sound of the fall of a mighty oak in the stillness of the wood.*"

Having previously held several high offices, both civil and military, Mr. Henry, on the 1st of July, 1776, was elected the first Republican Governor of Virginia, and was continued in that station, by an unanimous vote, until 1778. "On resigning the government," says his biographer, "he retired to Prince Edward County, and endeavored to cast about for the means of extricating himself from his debts. At the age of fifty years, worn down by more than twenty years of arduous service in the cause of his country, eighteen of which had been occupied by the toils and tempests of the Revolution, it was natural for him to wish for rest, and to seek some secure and placid port in which he might repose himself from the fatigues of the storm. This, however, was denied him ; and after having devoted the bloom of youth and the maturity of manhood to the good of his country, he had now in his old age to provide for his family He accordingly resumed the

practice of the law, in which the powers of his eloquence secured him constant employment."

Mr. Henry was actively occupied in patriotic and
professional toils through a long series of years.

In his habits of living he was severely temperate and
frugal. He seldom drank any thing but water, and furnished his table in the most simple manner. His morals
were strict; and as a Christian he was very decided, especially in his mature life.

Education among the Greeks was not effeminate.
Themistocles says of himself that he had learned neither
to tune the harp nor handle the lyre, but that he knew
how to make a small and inglorious city both powerful
and illustrious. He could not sleep for the trophies of
Miltiades. In his boyhood he shunned puerile sports,
and spent his time in severe self-discipline. Having
been a poor and disinherited child, he achieved the
highest honors in Athens, and for a season controlled
the destinies of the civilized world. In like manner,
Patrick Henry won, and worthily wore, the most exalted
honors. He collected the first corps of volunteers in the
South, after the battles of Lexington and Concord, and
was the most efficient patriot in his section of the land.

Probably no man ever passed through so long a series
of public services with a reputation less tarnished. In
the year 1794, he bade adieu to all professional toil, and
retired to the bosom of his family, attended by the gratitude, confidence, admiration, and love of his country.

"It is said that there stood in the court, before his
door, a large walnut tree, under whose shade it was his
delight to pass his summer evenings, surrounded by his

affectionate and happy family, and by a circle of neighbors who loved him almost to idolatry. Here he would
disport himself with all the careless gayety of infancy.
Here, too, he would sometimes warm the bosoms of the
old, and strike fire from the bosoms of his younger
hearers, by recounting the tales of other times; by
sketching, with the boldness of a master's hand, those
great historic incidents in which he had borne a part."
Thus employed, in his sixtieth year, disease met him
and began to waste away the mighty energies of his
body and mind. He sank rapidly, but in the placid confidence inspired by Christian hopes, and on the sixth of
June, 1799, a great man in Israel had fallen, Patrick
Henry was no more.

The great orator of Virginia, whose career we have
so rapidly delineated, never worried his prey by darting
on him javelins from afar ; he advanced directly up with
raised sledge, and smote his victim between his two
horns with a blow that felled him at once. The
effective speaker will be more intent on striking with
force than with elegance; wholly absorbed in his great
purpose, he will not stop to polish a phrase when he
should compel his antagonist to fall. He will make his
weapon keen rather than glittering.

There are two kinds of eloquence. The highest order
flows directly from the soul, as from a perennial and prolific fountain. Its current is incessant and irresistible ;
if opposed a moment, it accumulates its own chafing mass,
and will inevitably crush the obstacles by which it is impeded. The other multiplies its delicate threads around
its object, betraying him into the meshes of a skillful net,

by the fascination of a look, in the meantime strength‑ ening every tiny bond until the victim is secured and tortured to death by a thousand malignant stings.

Henry's mind was not disciplined into symmetry by severe science, nor was it embellished with the decora‑ tions of classical learning; but massy fragments of ori‑ ginal thought frequently appear in the progress of his speech, like shattered colonnades and broken statues, hurled from pedestal and base, buried in common dust. He was richly endowed with that permeating imagina‑ tion which gives vitality to the body of thought, and which makes the fortune of every great master in the divine art of eloquence. He was imbued with that ve‑ hemence of conviction, that oratorical action, which modulates the tones, and tinges the visage with irresisti‑ ble power, and suggests to the rapt listener more than articulated language can express. His soul melted when he spoke, and there were tears in his voice which no heart could withstand. His argument grew luminous as it arose, like a majestic tree on fire, and its com‑ bustion shone with a splendor inextinguishable and unexcelled.

The insipid prettiness of rhetorical mechanism no more resembles the soul of true eloquence, than the unconscious quiverings of galvanized muscles resemble the spontaneous throbs of a living and impassioned heart. Sampson chose an uncouth weapon, but three hundred Philistines felt its force.

It is necessary to bring into bold relief the natural grandeur of things by simplicity of expression. The orator must be familiar without vulgarity, original with‑

out eccentricity, natural and yet highly artistic,—in apparent carelessness "snatching a grace beyond the reach of art,"—fluent in language, but elaborate in thought, speaking at once to the instincts that are most profound, as well as to those that are most superficial. Ordinarily, Henry's style was the natural current of his thought, and glided along in limpid, glowing abundance, as if it reflected the still beams of the sun. But when some exciting crisis occurred, his speech became impetuous and rugged with scythes and daggers, like a Saxon war-chariot; then his flashing bolts shot off in every direction with the concussion of lightnings which in the same instant shine and kill. He drew the great masses of mankind closely around him by the exaltation of his sentiments ; he held them still more enthralled by the simplicity of his language.

The April shower is grateful to the soft herbage, and the still snow falls gracefully to earth, but neither of these produce strong impressions on the beholder On the contrary, when rugged clouds, fringed with electric fires, and buffeted by terrific winds, pour down piercing hail and torrent rain, intermingled with thunders that shake the skies and astound the earth, then do men tremble unbidden in the presence of natural sublimity.

Mr. Henry seldom used the pen, and has therefore left but little written eloquence authenticated by himself. To form our estimate of his powers, we have mainly to rely on the reports of those who had witnessed the wonders he wrought—those who had felt the magic of his action, trembled at the majesty of his voice,

and caught the flashings of his eye,—who had been fascinated by his smile, or repulsed by his terrific frown,
and who always found themselves incompetent to express
fully the power with which he impressed conviction.
When all his great attributes were fully aroused, his
language, like that of Pindar, burst forth with spontaneous force and splendid majesty.   Ordinarily, his reasoning was made obvious by the intense light of genius
with which it was invested; and if, sometimes, his judgment seemed bewildered, it was not so much from obscurity of perception, as from profuseness of emotion ;
like the throne of Milton's Heaven, his mind, when most
excited, would grow "dark from excess of light."   He
himself intimated that his chief lamp was the inward
light of reason, which is the brightest "affluence of essence increate."   When called upon the stage of public
life, he trusted to the guidance of truth, patriotism, and
justice, those primeval principles which "shine aloft as
stars."   The blazing brand of heaven which flashed
upon the earth, and arrested the careering steeds of
Diomed, was not more appalling to their affrighted
driver, than were the awful denunciations which Henry
hurled against tyranny and guilt.

Crattan said of the Irish orator, Malone, that "when
young, his eloquence was ocean in a storm; when old,
ocean in a calm ; but whether in a calm or storm, the
same great element, the sublimest and most magnificent
phenomenon of creation."   Tradition and history speak
in rapturous terms of Patrick Henry's eloquence, and
some of his speeches, reported by cotemporaries, substantiate his fame.   But as well might one attempt to

paint lightning with charcoal, as to delineate a soul like his in dull words. In order properly to appreciate his power, we

> "—Should have seen him in the Campus Martius,—
> In the tribunal,—shaking all the tribes
> With mighty speech. His words seemed oracles,
> That pierced their bosoms : and each man would turn,
> And gaze in wonder on his neighbor's face,
> That with the like dumb wonder answer'd him :
> Then some would weep, some shout, some, deeper touch'd,
> Keep down the cry with motion of their hands,
> In fear but to have lost a syllable."

We should have seen him when he knew that he spoke under the shadow of the scaffold,—when British cannon were booming in the North, and standing in the outlawed assembly of Virginia, like a lion at bay, he caught the first cry of distress from Lexington and Bunker Hill,—with a generous devotion that made no reserve, and knew no fear,—with a voice solemn, tremulous with patriotic rage, and swelling over the thrilled audience like a trumpet-call to arms, and with an eye flashing unutterable fire, he exclaimed—"Give me liberty, or give me death !"

CHAPTER X.

— ⁓⁓⁓⁓ —

RICHARD HENRY LEE,

THE POLISHED STATESMAN.

MR. LEE was a dignified citizen and scholar whose profound erudition and captivating rhetoric were rendered very efficient in moulding the early institutions of our land. He was born in Westmoreland County, Virginia, January 20, 1732. His juvenile studies were pursued in his father's house, but his more mature education was acquired in Yorkshire, England. Mr. Lee was noted for his assiduity as a student, and early became distinguished for his proficiency in the classics. He returned to his native land when about twenty years of age, and, as he possessed a large fortune, his time was mainly devoted to the improvement of his mind. Works of civil and political morality, history, law, and elegant literature were constantly perused by him with avidity, and their principles made effective in practical life.

The first public service which Mr. Lee attempted, was in the capacity of commander of the volunteer companies which were raised in 1755, for the purpose of aiding the expedition under General Braddock. In his twenty-fifth year, he was appointed to a civil office in his county, which attested the high personal consideration in which he was held. Soon after, he was chosen a delegate to the House of Burgesses, and. thus began the political career which gave his name its chief renown.

Mr. Lee was a republican of an early and rigid stamp. When, in 1764, the declaratory Act was passed in the British Parliament, claiming the right to tax America, he was the first to bring forward the subject to the notice of the Assembly of which he was a member. A special committee having, in consequence been appointed to draught an address to the King, a memorial to the House of Lords, and a remonstrance to the House of Commons, Mr. Lee, as chairman, prepared the first two papers. These, as his biographer remarks, "contain the genuine principles of the Revolution, and abound in the firm and eloquent sentiments of freemen." In 1765, Patrick Henry introduced in the Virginia legislature his famous resolutions against the Stamp-Act, which had just been passed by Parliament. Lee lent Henry's motion his zealous and powerful assistance. Shortly after the triumph gained on that occasion, Lee planned and effected an association "for the purpose of deterring all persons from accepting the office of vendor of stamp paper, and for awing into silence and inactivity those who might still be attached to the supremacy of the mother country, and disposed to advocate the right of colony taxation." This result the association bound themselves to attain. "at every hazard, and paying no regard to danger or to death."

The tax on tea, and the measure adopted by Pailia·
ment in 1767, "to make provision for quartering a part
of the regular army" at the expense of the colony, Lee
exerted himself every way to oppose, perceiving, as he
did, their despotic tendency, and feeling that a struggle
for freedom was inevitable. In 1773, a plan was adopted by the House of Burgesses, for the formation of corresponding committees to be organized by the legislatures
of the several Colonies, and also that of corresponding
clubs or societies, among the "lovers of liberty" throughout the Provinces, for the purpose of diffusing amongst
the people a correct knowledge of their rights, of keep-
ing them informed of every attempt to infringe them,
and of rousing a spirit of resistance to all arbitrary
measures. Of both these important suggestions Mr.
Lee was the author.

In 1774, the first general Congress assembled at
Philadelphia. Mr. Lee was a delegate from Virginia.
His labors during this session, and throughout his whole
Congressional career, were unremitting and invaluable.
In all the leading measures he took an active part, and
was not less influential in the appeals which went
abroad from his pen than in the counsels which came
iving from his lips. He was the author of many important State papers, and the resolute defender of the
boldest resistance against foreign aggression. The
great motion of June 7, 1776, "that these United Colonies are, and of right ought to be, free and independent
States ; that they are absolved from all allegiance to the
British crown ; and that all political connection between
them and the State of Great Britain, is, and ought to be

totally dissolved," was drawn, introduced, and ably supported by Mr. Lee.

The speech delivered by him in defence of this motion
is reported as follows:

"Ought I not to begin by observing, that if we have
reached that violent extremity, beyond which nothing
can any longer exist between America and England,
but either such war or such peace as are made between
foreign nations; this can only be imputed to the insatiable cupidity, the tyrannical proceedings, and the outrages, for ten years reiterated, of the British ministers.
What have we not done to restore peace, to re-establish
harmony? Who has not heard our prayers, and who is
ignorant of our supplications? They have wearied the
universe. England alone was deaf to our complaints,
and wanted that compassion towards us which we have
found among all other nations. And as at first our for-
bearance, and then our resistance, have proved equally
insufficient, since our prayers were unavailing, as well
as the blood lately shed; we must go further, and proclaim our independence. Nor let any one believe that
we have any other option left. The time will certainly
come when the fated separation must take place, whether
you will or no; for so it is decreed by the very nature
of things, the progressive increase of our population, the
fertility of our soil, the extent of our territory, the industry of our countrymen, and the immensity of the
ocean which separates the two States. And if this be
true, as it is most true, who does not see that the sooner
it takes place the better; and that it would be not only
imprudent, but the height of folly, not to seize the pre-

sent occasion when British injustice has filled all hearts
with indignation, inspired all minds with courage, united
all opinions in one, and put arms in every hand? And
how long must we traverse three thousand miles of a
stormy sea, to go and solicit of arrogant and insolent
men, either counsels or commands to regulate our domestic affairs? Does it not become a great, rich and
powerful nation, as we are, to look at home, and not
abroad, for the government of its own concerns? And
how can a ministry of strangers judge, with any discernment, of our interests, when they know not, and
when it little imports them to know, what is good for
us and what is not? The past justice of the British
ministers should warn us against the future, if they
should ever seize us again in their cruel claws. Since
it has pleased our barbarous enemies to place before us
the alternative of slavery or of independence, where is
the generous-minded man and the lover of his country,
who can hesitate to choose? With these perfidious
men no promise is secure, no pledges sacred. Let us
suppose, which heaven avert, that we are conquered;
let us suppose an accommodation. What assurance
have we of the British moderation in victory, or good
faith in treaty? Is it their having enlisted and let loose
against us the ferocious Indians, and the merciless soldiers of Germany? Is it that faith, so often pledged and
so often violated in the course of the present contest; this
British faith, which is reputed more false than Punic?
We ought rather to expect, that when we shall have
fallen naked and unarmed into their hands, they will
wreak upon us their fury and their vengeance; they

will load us with heavier chains, in order to deprive us not only of the power, but even of the hope of again recovering our liberty. But I am willing to admit, although it is a thing without example, that the British government will forget past offences and perform its promises, can we imagine, that after so long dissentions, after so many outrages, so many combats, and so much bloodshed, our reconciliation could be durable, and that every day, in the midst of so much hatred and rancor, would not afford some fresh subject of animosity? The two nations are already separated in interest and affections; the one is conscious of its ancient strength, the other has become acquainted with its newly-exerted force; the one desires to rule in an arbitrary manner, the other will not obey even if allowed its privileges. In such a state of things, what peace, what concord, can be expected? The Americans may become faithful friends to the English, but subjects, never. And even though union could be restored without rancor, it could not without danger. The wealth and power of Great Britain should inspire prudent men with fears for the future. Having reached such a height of grandeur that she has no longer any thing to dread from foreign powers, in the security of peace the spirit of her people will decay, manners will be corrupted, her youth will grow up in the midst of vice, and in this state of degeneration, England will become the prey of a foreign enemy or an ambitious citizen. If we remain united with her, we shall partake of her corruptions and misfortunes, the more to be dreaded as they will be irreparable; separated from her, on the contrary, as we are, we should neither have to fear the seductions of peace nor the dangers of war. By a declaration of our freedom, the perils would not be increased ; but we should add tc the ardor of our defenders, and to the splendor of victory. Let us then take a firm step, and escape from this labyrinth ; we have assumed the sovereign power, and dare not confess it; we disobey a king, and acknowledge ourselves his subjects ; wage war against a people, on whom we incessantly protest our desire to depend. What is the consequence of so many inconsistencies ? Hesitation paralyzes all our measures ; the way we ought to pursue is not marked out; our generals are neither respected nor obeyed ; our soldiers have neither confidence nor zeal : feeble at home, and little considered abroad, foreign princes can neither esteem nor succor so timid and wavering a people. But independence once proclaimed, and our object avowed, more manly and decided measures will be adopted ; all minds will be fired by the greatness of the enterprise, the civil magistrates will be inspired with new zeal, the generals with fresh ardor, and the citizens with greater constancy, to attain so high and glorious a destiny. There are some who seem to dread the effects of this resolution. But will England, or can she, manifest against us greater rigor and rage than she has already displayed? She deems resistance against oppression no less rebellion than independence itself.

The Americans may become faithful friends to the English, but subjects, never. And even though union could be restored without rancor, it could not withcut danger. And where are those formidable troops that are to subdue the Americans? What the English could not do, can it be done by Germans? Are they more brave, or better disciplined? The number of our enemies is increased; but our own is not diminished, and the battles we have sustained have given us the practice of arms and the experience of war.

America has arrived at a degree of power, which assigns her a place among independent nations; we are not less entitled to it than the English themselves. If they have wealth, so also have we; if they are brave so are we; if they are more numerous, our population will soon equal theirs; if they have men of renown as well in peace as in war, we likewise have such; political revolutions produce great, brave, and generous spirits. From what we have already achieved in these painful beginnings, it is easy to presume what we shall hereafter accomplish; for experience is the source of sage coun sels, and liberty is the mother of great men.

Have you not seen the enemy driven from Lexington by thirty thousand citizens, armed and assembled in one day? Already their most celebrated generals have yielded, in Boston, to the skill of ours; already their seamen, repulsed from our coasts, wander over the ocean, where they are the sport of tempests, and the prey of famine. Let us hail the favorable omen, and fight, not for the sake of knowing on what terms we are to be the slaves of England, but to secure ourselves a free existence,—to found a just and independent government. Animated by liberty, the Greeks repulsed the in

12*

numerable army of Persians; sustained by the love of independence, the Swiss and the Dutch humbled the power of Austria by memorable defeats, and conquered a rank among nations. The sun of America also shines upon the heads of the brave; the point of our weapons is no less formidable than theirs; here also the same union prevails, the same contempt of dangers and of death, in asserting the cause of our country.

Why then do we longer delay, why still deliberate? Let this most happy day give birth to the American republic. Let her arise, not to devastate and conquer, but to re-establish the reign of peace and of the laws. The eyes of Europe are fixed upon us; she demands of us a living example of freedom, that may contrast, by the felicity of the citizens, with the ever-increasing tyranny which desolates her polluted shores. She invites us to prepare an asylum, where the unhappy may find solace, and the persecuted repose. She entreats us to cultivate a propitious soil, where that generous plant which first sprung up and grew in England, but is now withered by the poisonous blasts of Scottish tyranny, may revive and flourish, sheltering under its salubrious and interminable shade, all the unfortunate of the human race.

This is the end presaged by so many omens; by our first victories, by the present ardor and union, by the flight of Howe, and the pestilence which broke out amongst Dunmore's people, by the very winds which baffled the enemy's fleets and transports, and that terrible tempest which engulphed seven hundred vessels upon the coast of Newfoundland. If we are not this day wanting in our duty to our country, the names of the American legislators will be placed, by posterity, at the side of those of Theseus, of Lycurgus, of Romulus, of Numa, of the three Williams of Nassau, and of all those whose memory has been, and will be for ever, dear to virtuous men and good citizens."

The address which, by the direction of Congress, Mr. Lee drew up in 1775, on behalf of the twelve United Colonies, to the inhabitants of Great Britain, is a masterly production, and will continue to the end of time an imperishable monument to his patriotism and eloquence.

Having enumerated the wrongs endured by the Colonies, and defended the measures of resistance by them employed, the Address closes with the following solemn adjuration :

"If you have no regard to the connection that has for ages subsisted between us; if you have forgot the wounds we have received fighting by your side for the extension of the empire ; if our commerce is not an object below your consideration ; if justice and humanity have lost their influence on your hearts ; still, motives are not wanting to excite your indignation at the measures now pursued; your wealth, your honor, your liberty are at stake.

" Notwithstanding the distress to which we are reduced, we sometimes forget our own afflictions, to anticipate and sympathize in yours. We grieve that rash and inconsiderate councils should precipitate the de-.

struction of an empire, which has been the envy and admiration of ages; and call God to witness that we would part with our property, endanger our lives, and sacrifice every thing but liberty, to redeem you from ruin.

" A cloud hangs over your heads and ours; ere this reaches you, it may probably burst upon us; let us entreat heaven to avert our ruin, and the destruction that threatens our friends, brethren, and countrymen on the other side of the Atlantic !"

As chairman of the committee appointed for that purpose, it was also Mr. Lee's privilege to furnish the commissions and instructions which invested George Washington with the command of the American army. In 1780, he retired from his seat in Congress, and declined returning to it until 1784. In the interval, he served in the Assembly of Virginia, and, at the head of the militia of his county, protected it from the incursions of the enemy. In 1784, he was chosen president of Congress by an unanimous vote, but withdrew at the end of the year. In 1792, his health compelled him to retire altogether from public life, and on June 19th, 1794, he died.

Mr. Lee was a polished gentleman. His mental accomplishments were richly diversified, and his manners were of courtly elegance. He had more talent than genius. In the pompous regularity of insipid elegance, and punctilious mediocrity, orators elaborated in the schools are more distinguished for the fewness of their faults, than the multitude and originality of their beauties. No enthusiasm, no blaze of imagination, no

weighty arguments irradiate their speeches with flashing splendors.

Lee's eloquence was like a beautiful river, meandering
through variegated and elegant scenes, but which never
inundates its banks nor bursts its barriers. He was
not, like Patrick Henry, a mountain torrent, springing
from exalted sources, and dashing away every thing in
its irresistible career.

But Lee was a fine rhetorician and a sagacious
debater. He had the happy faculty of throwing oil on
the agitated sea. When the Continental Congress met
in Philadelphia on the 5th of September, 1774, it is
said that silence, awful and protracted, preceded "the
breaking of the last seal," and that astonishment and
applause filled the house when this was done by Patrick
Henry. The excitement consequent on that wonderful
effort might have subsided into lassitude and despon-
dency, had not Mr. Lee perceived "the quiver on every
lip, the gleam in every eye." With the quickness of
intuition he saw the crisis and happily attempted to
turn the mass of agitated feeling to great practical
good. He arose, and the sweetness of his language,
and harmony of his tones, soothed, but did not suppress,
the tide of tumultuous emotion swelling in every breast.
With the most persuasive eloquence, he demonstrated
that there was but one hope for the country, and
that lay in the energy of immediate and united resistance.

Mr. Lee was undoubtedly a copious and eloquent
speaker. Some of his admirers called him "the American Cicero, but, unfortunately, none of his popular

speeches extant, justify this comparison.   He certainly occupied a high grade in oratorical excellence, but, perhaps, not the highest.

In the Gallery of Natural History at Florence, there is a fine Venus in wax, an elegant imitation of life, which you may deliberately take down in parts and study at your leisure, but in which model there is no throbbing heart.   Speakers abound of the same stamp. Their language is correct, but powerless; their illustrations are pretty, but dry.   There are polished phrases in abundance, but what is wanting is *animus*, soul The body of their speech bears no vital complexion, its circulation is water-colored, and not warm, vivifying blood.   Such a speaker does not animate his subject with the power of self-impulsion, but laboriously drags it after him, as one would a steamless locomotive.   He has not those powerful touches of deep feeling which act like a talisman upon the sympathies of an audience all aroused.   He lacks the inspiration of true oratorical genius, that earnestness and sincerity which often advantageously supply the place of copious erudition and elaborate finish.

Many speakers remind us of the Apollo Belvidere seen in a wintry morning, glittering all over with frost; it is a fine form, symmetrical as possible, and as cold. When a man withdraws himself from the direct agency of human affections, and lives in abstract intellect alone, he may be an adroit machinist in working out astute propositions, but he can never exert a wide and efficient control over the popular mind.   His is not that

"Eloquence, that charms and burns,
Startles, soothes, and wins, by turns."

He only is a true orator who has the power of commanding intellects and hearts with simultaneous influence on both; drawing them with the irresistible magic of sympathy—penetrating them with deep emo tion and lofty thought. Such an orator unites in himself all the blandishments of art, all the force of feeling, and all the dignity of wisdom. The spirit of eloquence is not limited to any particular form, but adapts itself to every variety of time, class, and occasion, With logicians, it argues; with mathematicians, it demonstrates; with philosophers, it teaches; with poets, it chants; with the mass of the people, it talks in language and sentiments graduated to the capacities and tastes of each. It can conceal the sternest truth under the veil of graceful allegory, or cause the repulsive skeletons of bony dialectics to assume the graceful form and hues of poetic life. Under all circumstances, the spirit we speak of is full of energetic vitality and is bodied forth in "action, utterance, and the power of speech, to move men's minds."

The above remarks would indicate the importance of uniting strong emotions to strong arguments. Mr. Lee was skillful in stating the terms of a question, and was often lucid in the exposition of facts, but his manner of address was not of that resistless order which makes the speaker and his speech to be forgotten in the subject. His fluency of language was almost preternatural; its

perpetual flow was like a river, and like Pactolus, its
current was often enriched with glittering gold. He
was not wanting in elegance, but perhaps he lacked
force. He was a great and useful patriot, but not of the
most exalted rank in the forum, who speak in tones
of power, as cataracts "blow their trumpets from the
steeps."

Eloquence is not something to be put on from without, but to be put out from within. It is manliness and
not mannerism that makes the orator. Manner is
something artificial, eloquence is natural, the external
manifestation of the inmost soul. When one feels deeply he will be felt; the popular mind will recognize and
revere him as quick as flesh feels fire. "The faculties
of the orator are judgment and imagination: and reason
and eloquence, the product of these faculties, must work
on the judgment and feelings of his audience for the attainment of his end. The speaker who addresses the
judgment alone, may be argumentative, but never can
be eloquent; for argument instructs without interesting,
and eloquence interests without convincing; but oratory is neither; it is the compound of both; it conjoins
the feelings and opinions of men ; it speaks to the passions through the mind, and to the mind, through ·the
passions; and leads its audience to its just purpose by
the combined and powerful agency of human reason
and human feeling."

It has been elegantly remarked that "a good style is
like the crystal of a watch, attracting attention, not to
itself, but to what is beneath it." Refined sensibility

aetracts nothing from the utility of rugged strength, but rather augments its worth; as Apollo found a rough shell on the sea-shore, and with a delicate fibre formed it into a lyre. Indeed, we know that it was the practice of some of the eloquent Romans, and of all Athenian speakers, to learn from dramatists and musicians to impart graceful ease to their delivery, and modulation to their periods.

> " Thus was beauty sent from Heaven,
> The lovely ministress of truth and good
> In this dark world; for truth and good are one,
> And beauty dwells in them and they in her,
> With like participation; wherefore then,
> O sons of earth! would ye dissolve the tie ?"

The triumphs of true eloquence, the most august manifestations of power on earth, are never seen except when the orator comes forth in the simple majesty of truth, overpowered with the weight of his convictions, and the momentous import of his theme. Under such circumstances neither speaker nor hearer is much occupied with polish and prettiness; the grand question is, what is to be said, and how shall it be most forcibly expressed. There will be a background of skillful arrangement, coloring and decoration, but that which is brought into boldest relief, and made to absorb the profoundest attention, is the matter at issue. Entering with whole heart and soul into the subject of his discourse, the speaker transports with his pathos, fascinates with the pictures of his imagination, melts masses of listeners with gushes of ten·

derness, and moves all before him on the impetuous and
resistless tide of his arguments.

"Now with a giant's might
He heaves the ponderous thought,
Now pours the storm of eloquence
With scathing lightning fraught.

THE
PUBLIC LIBRARY

ASTOR, LENOX AND
TILDEN FOUNDATIONS

ALEXANDER HAMILTON.

CHAPTER XI.

ALEXANDER HAMILTON,

THE MASTER OF POLITICAL SAGACITY.

PATRIOTS of exalted worth appeared in the Colonial period of our history, and signalized their respective merits in achieving enterprises of comprehensive and enduring utility. Their successors of Revolutionary renown were no less dignified in talent and untarnished in worth. Looking at the era of the formation and adoption of the Constitution of these United States, and the civil administration of Washington, next to the great President himself no name shines fairer than that of Alexander Hamilton. He was born January 11th, 1757, in the island of Nevis the most beautiful of the British West Indies. His father was a Scotchman, his mother a French lady, descended from that noble race, the Huguenots. This happy blending of contrasted elements in the original source of his blood and character, solidity and enthusiasm, sagacity to project theories and facility in their execution, will be exemplified in all his subsequent career. The father was a merchant, but his business was disastrous, and he died in penury at St. Vincents. The mother possessed elegant manners and a strong intellect, which made a vivid impression on her son, though she, too, died when he was but a child.

Like most men who are destined to become truly great, young Hamilton was early left to buffet adverse storms and in the midst of difficulties to be the architect of his own fortunes. By the favor of some persons related to his mother, the otherwise unprotected child was taken to Santa Cruz, where he received the rudiments of early education. He soon learned to speak and write the French language fluently, and was taught to repeat the Decalogue in Hebrew, at the school of a Jewess, when so small that he was placed standing by her side on a table. But his education at this period was conducted chiefly under the supervision of the Rev. Dr. Knox, a distinguished Presbyterian clergyman, who gave to the mind of his aspiring pupil a religious bias as lasting as his life. In 1769, he was placed as a clerk in the counting-house of Mr. Nicholas Cruger, a wealthy and highly respectable merchant of Santa Cruz. By his skill and assiduity as a clerk, young Hamilton soon won the attention and confidence of his patron, and at the same time betrayed in his favorite studies and private correspondence an ambition that soared far above his mercantile pursuits. Before he was thirteen years old, he wrote as follows to a young friend at school:

"I contemn the grovelling condition of a clerk, to which my fortune condemns me, and would willingly risk my life, though not my character, to exalt my station: I mean, to prepare the way for futurity."

Herein gleams the true fire of a noble youth, love of fame and the strongest attachment to untarnished integrity, guarantees of splendid success, which in this instance were never disproved by facts.

While in Mr. Cruger's office, the predestined statesman appropriated every hour he could command from recreation and repose, to mathematics, ethics, chemistry, biography, history, and knowledge of every kind. Some of his youthful compositions were published, and their promise was so extraordinary that his relatives and friends resolved to send him to New York for the purpose of maturing his education. He arrived in this country in October, 1772, and was placed at a grammar school in New Jersey, under the instruction of Francis Barber, of Elizabethtown, who afterward became a distinguished officer in the American service. At the close of 1773, Hamilton entered King's (now Columbia) College, where he soon "gave extraordinary displays of genius and energy of mind."

In college Hamilton never relaxed the severe application to study which his natural tastes and glowing ambition required; nor was he unmindful of the storm gathering beyond the quiet cloisters wherein he prosecuted scientific research and classic lore with hallowed delight. His penetrating mind, versatile pen, and powerful living tones were from the first employed in defending colonial opposition to the acts of the British Parliament. In December, 1774, and February, 1775, he wrote anonymously several elaborate pamphlets in favor of the pacific measures of defence recommended by Congress.

He suggested at that early day the policy of giving encouragement to domestic manufactures, as a sure means of lessening the need of external commerce. He anticipated ample resources at home, and among other things, observed that several of the southern colonies were so favorable in their soil and climate to the growth of cotton, that such a staple alone, with due cultivation, in a year or two would afford products sufficient to clothe the whole continent. He insisted upon our unalienable right to the steady, uniform, unshaken security of constitutional freedom; to the enjoyment of trial by jury; and to the right of freedom from taxation, except by our own immediate representatives, and that colonial legislation was an inherent right, never to be abandoned or impaired.

In this pamphlet controversy, young Hamilton encountered Doctor Cooper, principal of the college, and many of the most distinguished tories of the land. When the authorship of the youthful champion was proclaimed, all classes were astonished to learn such profound principles and wise policy from so young an oracle. By his extraordinary writings and patriotic influence he early deserved and received the appellation of the "Vindicator of Congress."

The country was at length compelled to plunge into war, and the struggle for emancipation from British domination had already commenced. The letter that announced the battle of Lexington to the New-Yorkers, concluded with these words: "The crimson fountain has opened, and God only knows when it will be closed."

Young Hamilton organized a military corps, mostly

of fellow students, who practised their daily drill early in the morning, before the commencement of their college studies. They assumed the name of "Hearts of Oak," and wore a green uniform, surmounted by a leathern cap, on which was inscribed " Freedom or Death." Early and late our young hero was busy, not only in promoting measures of resistance, but in mastering the science of political economy, the laws of commerce, the balance of trade, and the circulating medium; so that when these topics became prominent matters of speculation, in the light of new organizations for the general good, no one was more prompt and lucid in his demonstrations than Hamilton.

In March, 1776, he abandoned academic retirement, and entered the army as captain of a provincial company of artillery. In this capacity he brought up the rear of the army in the retreat from Long Island. He was in the action at White Plains, on the 28th of October, 1776 ; and with his company of artillery was firm and heroical in the retreat through New Jersey, on which occasion he repelled the progress of the British troops on the banks of the Raritan. He fought at the head of his brave company at Trenton and Princeton, and continued in the same command until the first of March, 1777, when, having attracted the admiration of Washington, he was appointed his aid-de-camp, with the rank of colonel. From this time, he continued until February, 1781, the inseparable companion of the Commander-in-chief, and was always consulted by him, and by all the leading public functionaries, on the most important occasions. He acted as his first aid at the battles of Brandywine, Germantown and Monmouth ; and at his own request, at the siege of Yorktown, he led the detachment which carried by assault one of the strongest outworks of the foe.

Many fine qualities were combined in Hamilton to render him useful to all, and especially to make him, in the service of Washington, what that great man declared he was, "his principal and most confidential aid." His accurate and comprehensive knowledge of military science, placed him in the first rank of tacticians ; his courteous manners rendered his general intercourse with the army a delight to all ; his familiarity with the French language won the especial attachment of all the French division of our army, making him the constant favorite in particular of the Marquis Lafayette and the Baron Steuben.

Never, perhaps, in the history of nations was a youth of twenty called to such precious honors and responsibilities as those which Hamilton, at that early age, was called to assume as the private secretary and confidential friend of Washington. On none did the arm of that great man more habitually lean for support than on this erudite and patriotic youth, and by no other earthly power was he more fortified than by him. It is in vain that we look through the gallery of universal history to find a fit companion to this picture of early wisdom and unblemished honor, standing forth as the palladium of national safety in the days of greatest peril. We do not mean that he stood alone, but only that he was unexcelled. Among the many willing and devoted hearts of that heroic age, in the camp and in the cabinet, patriots whom danger and suffering could not appall, nor treason or despair divert from their high enterprise, the fame of no one is brighter, and the path of none more exalted and pure, than that traced by Hamilton. This position we will attempt to substantiate by hastily reviewing first his merits as an orator, and secondly as a statesman.

Hamilton's first political speech to a popular assembly was delivered at "the great meeting in the fields," as it was called, and was occasioned by a call to choose delegates to the first Congress. At that time he was a student in King's College, and was every way exceedingly juvenile in appearance. Being unexpectedly called upon, his effort was unpremeditated, and at first he faltered and hesitated, overawed by the impressive scene before him; but his youthful countenance, his slender form and novel aspect awakened curiosity and excited universal attention. An immense multitude were astonished and electrified by "the infant orator," as they called him. After a discussion, clear, forcible, and striking, of the great principles involved, he depicted in glowing colors the long continued and constantly aggravated oppressions of the mother-country. Touching this point he burst forth in a strain of bold and thrilling eloquence.

"The sacred rights of mankind," were his words, "are not to be rummaged for among old parchments or musty records; they are written as with a sunbeam in the whole volume of human nature, by the hand of Divinity itself, and can never be erased or obscured by mortal power."

He insisted on the duty of resistance, pointed out the

13

means and certainty of success, and descr bed the waves
of rebellion sparkling with fire, and washing back on
the shores of England the wrecks of her power, her
wealth, and her glory.   Under this spontaneous burst
of mature eloquence from lips so youthful, the vast multitude first sank in awe and surprise, and then rose with
irrepressible astonishment :

> " Down sank
> Instant all tumult, broke abruptly off
> Fierce voice and clash of arms : so mute and deep
> Settled the silence, the low sound was heard
> Of distant waterfall, and the acorn drop
> From the green arch above."

The death-like silence ceased as he closed, and repeated huzzas resounded to the heavens.

Soon after this memorable event, young Hamilton
entered upon that military career which we have already
sketched down to the close of the Revolutionary conflict.   But the better qualities of his head and heart
were developed more especially in powerful speech,
during those five years of sorrow, and almost despair,
which succeeded, beginning with the close of the martial contest in 1782, and extending to the adoption of
the Constitution in 1787.   This period of our history is,
perhaps, least attractive to the general reader, but one
which in fact is most worthy of being explored
During these five years, Hamilton was a prominent
advocate for wise freedom in the four deliberative
bodies which most powerfully determined the future
destinies of the country.   These were the Congress of
the Confederation, in 1782 and 1783, which closed the

war and ratified the definitive treaty; the Convention
˄t Annapolis, in 1786, that laid the foundation of the
General Convention adopting the Constitution; the
Legislature of the State of New York in January, 1787,
in which the battle of State rights was fought against
the definitive treaty; and lastly, the General Convention which met in Philadelphia, in May of the same
year, and by which the Federal Constitution was constructed and adopted. In each of these great and
important bodies he appeared as an influential leader,
always relied on as among the most safe, and universally
esteemed for the clearness and force with which he
originated and sustained great measures of national
policy.

In December, 1780, Hamilton married the second
daughter of Major General Schuyler, and in the February following, he retired from the family of General
Washington, to become more completely absorbed
in forensic toil. He took his seat in Congress in
November, 1782. and continued there until the autumn
of 1783. The legislators of that body had many difficult and exhausting duties to perform. Army discontents were to be appeased; complicated claims to be
settled; and if possible, the half-pay of innumerable
patriots to be obtained. Hamilton renounced his own
demands, accruing from long martial service, that he
might freely plead the cause of his brethren in arms.
On the 6th of December, 1782, he moved and carried
an important resolution on national finance ; the beginning of his invaluable labors in behalf of an improved
revenue ; the sinking fund and assumption of the State

debts; a currency well defined and the establishment of a national coinage.

Immediately after Hamilton entered Congress all its proceedings assumed a more vigorous tone and exalted character. Grievances were redressed, and effective measures of general interest were promptly passed. His report in answer to Rhode Island, and many other documents and speeches in behalf of a more solid and effective union, gave a new and more cheering aspect to the whole face of public affairs. His influence in guiding the terms of peace was very great, and especially was he efficient in rendering the fruits of peace in the highest degree profitable to all classes of his countrymen.

In the brief *Convention at Annapolis*, Hamilton furnished the original draught of the report which was adopted and sent to the four States therein represented, namely, Virginia, Delaware, Pennsylvania, and New York.

In the New York Legislature of 1787, among other measures, we are told the following are due to him: The Bankrupt Act and amendment of its criminal code; the establishment of the State university and its general system of public instruction, then a novel scheme; and above all, his influence was pre-eminent in carrying into effect the provisions of the definitive treaty, in opposition to the dominant party, to many existing State laws, and to strong popular feeling against it.

In the Convention of 1787, his labors were undoubtedly the most important of all: to these we shall revert when we come to consider their author's statesmanship.

It is believed that Hamilton's eloquence consisted in a happy combination of a high sense of honor, a clear but energetic understanding, and an acute sensibility.

In the first place, he possessed a high sense of honor, which fortified all his powers, and crowned him with the majesty of a great and useful orator. We may apply to this master mind what Pope said of the distin-guished English statesman:

> " Argyle, the State's whole thunder born to wield,
> And shake alike the senate and the field."

The biographer of Hamilton, speaking of his father's powers as displayed in the Congress of 1782, laments, in common with the whole country, that so little remains to perpetuate the memory of it.

" Of the distinctive features," says he, " of that com-manding and winning eloquence, the wonder and delight of friend and foe, but of which no perfect reports are preserved, a delineation will not now be attempted. It suffices here to observe how deeply his modes of thinking imparted to the proceedings of this body a new tone and character. And those who re-mark in these pages the sentiments with which he regarded the demands of the army, how solemn his respect for the requirements of justice, how incessant and undespairing his efforts to fulfil them, can best image to themselves with what living touches and thrilling appeals he called up before this Senate their accumulated wrongs, and with what deep emotions and almost holy zeal he urged, he enforced, he implored,

with all the ardor of his bold and generous nature, an
honest fulfilment of the obligations to public faith."

But a clear and energetic understanding, vivified and
ennobled by acute sensibility, were traits equally prominent in the constitution of Hamilton's mind.   His
heart was as generous as his will was resolute.   He
seems to have ever been the object of passionate admiration to those who knew him best.   A senior officer in
Washington's staff conferred on him the epithet of
" The Little Lion," a term of endearment by which he
was familiarly known among his bosom friends to the
close of his life.

"Hamilton's great characteristics," says his son,
"were firmness and gentleness.   His spirit was as bold
as it was sympathizing.   He hated oppression in all its
forms, and resisted it in every shape.   Governed by the
highest principles, with them his lofty nature would admit no compromise ; for he was accustomed to view
infractions of them on all their remote consequences.
Hence his denunciations of tyranny were universal and
unsparing."   It was this "lion-like" fearlessness of heart
that infused into the whole of Hamilton's public life that
chivalric tone which so prominently marked it.   Whether
at the bar, in the cabinet, or on the field, he was still the
generous foe and the peerless knight, "*sans peur et sans
reproche.*"   Wherever wrong was to be redressed, or
rights vindicated, Hamilton stood foremost.   Wherever
the strong arm was needed, or the gallant heart, or the
eloquent tongue, to smite down the oppressor, or to raise
up the fallen, the first name invoked by the sufferer was
that of Hamilton.   It is one of the pleasing character-

istic incidents recorded by his son of his professional
career, that his very first appearance as an advocate
was in defence of one in name a foe, who, having been
through the war an adherent to the enemy, had fallen
under the hated proscription of the State itself. The
trial, too, was held under circumstances sufficient to have
daunted a less determined mind, irrespective of the inex-
perience of the pleader; "while the strife of the fierce contest was recent," are the words of his son, "in the midst
of a dilapidated and yet disordered city, where all around
were beheld the ravages of the invader, in a hall of justice desecrated and marred by the excesses of its late
occupants, a licentious soldiery. On one side was the ··
attorney-general of the State, armed with all its authority
to sustain its laws, representing the passions of an inflamed community. . . . On the other stood Ham
ilton, resting on the justice of this mighty cause, the
good faith of the nation. The result was honorable
alike to the court and the advocate. It was the triumph
of right over usurpation." But such triumphs were
often enjoyed in after life by this noble, dauntless, and
eloquent pleader. His son just glances at a celebrated
instance, when, in giving the touching history of his
father's return to the city of New York, after its evacua-
tion by the enemy, he says: "Cordial were the greet-
ings of this grateful city as it welcomed in its once
"stranger boy" the now powerful advocate of mercy to
its apprehensive denizens, hastening to shield them from
persecution for the venal offence of mistaken policy."
Thus, in the powerful eloquence of their strong foe, the
vanquished found a panoply to protect, where they

dreaded a destroying sword. It is added, that on his return from the seat of the legislature, whither he had hastened to defeat an unjust bill that would have brought ruin on the defenceless tories, he sternly refused from them a purse of some thousand dollars, made up for him in his absence by his grateful but unknown clients ; refused it with the magnanimous reply, that " the cause of national honor was not to be paid for." It was this happy union of largeness and loftiness of soul that made Hamilton the model-advocate of his own and of every age.

One who wrote on the character of this renowned statesman lawyer says : " He was a great favorite with the New York merchants ; and he justly deserved to be so, for he had uniformly proved himself to be an enlightened, intrepid and persevering friend to the commercial prosperity of the country. He was a great master of commercial law, as well as of the principles of international jurisprudence. There were no deep recesses of the science which he did not explore. He would occasionally draw from the fountains of the civil law, and illustrate and enforce the enlightened decisions of Mansfield by the severe judgment of Emerigon and the lucid commentaries of Valin. In short, he conferred dignity and high reputation upon the profession, of which he was indisputably the first of the first rank, by his indefatigable industry, his thorough researches, his logical powers, his solid judgment, his winning candor, and his matchless eloquence."

Colonel Hamilton was as forcible in speech as he was substantial. His arguments were like artillery of heavy calibre, planted on a commanding position, ind worked with an agility that captures or destroys every point. His ponderous metal, put into nimble and fatal execution, reminds one of Schiller's description :

> " Straight forth goes
> The lightning's path, and straight the fearful path
> Of the cannon-ball. Direct it flies, and rapid
> Shattering that it may reach, and shattering what it reaches."

The momentum of his thought was as great as its magnitude and value, all of which traits in him were seldom or never excelled. The severe grandeur with which he sketched the outline of his subject, and the elaborate beauty with which he wrought out its perfect execution, remind one of the rule which Tintoretto adopted : " I follow Michael Angelo for my designs, and Titian for my coloring." When impetuous feeling is the concomitant of lucid and legitimate argument, the passion of eloquence becomes contagious in its possessor, and is irresistible in its power of fascination. Hamilton's imagination " was strengthened by discipline and fed with truth ; the ardor of his heart melted his towering understanding into streams of inexhaustible richness and perennial flow ; so that his limpid and irresistible thought was poured forth like some majestic river, whose current, deep, vast and waveless, rolls past us silently, but will roll for ever."

Let us, in the second place, glance more particularly at the character of Hamilton, considered as a statesman. We have referred to the early period when he, then a stripling youth of seventeen, went forth to battle and

13*

spoke with so much success in the great meeting held where now stands the Park in New York. It was at the same period that he sent forth his first recorded appeals through the press, calling to union and pointing to glory "through," to use his own words, "the steady, uniform, unshaken security of *constitutional freedom;*" adding, with that noble enthusiasm which was his habitual inspiration and chief reward, "I would die to preserve the laws upon a solid foundation; but take away liberty, and the foundation is destroyed."

It would be difficult to over-estimate the value of Hamilton's services during the long period he acted as first aid and confidential secretary to the Commander-in-chief of the American army. The principal portions of the voluminous correspondence fell on him, and the most elaborate communications are understood to have been made essentially by his assistance. "The pen of our country," says Troup, was held by Hamilton; and for dignity of manner, pith of matter and elegance of style, General Washington's letters are unrivalled in military annals." The public documents drawn up by this secretary and by his associates richly deserve the encomium pronounced on them by Lord Chatham, in the House of Lords: "When you consider their decency, firmness and wisdom," said he, "you cannot but respect their cause, and wish to make it your own. For myself, I must declare and avow, that in all my reading, and it has been my favorite pursuit, that for solidity of reasoning, force of sagacity and wisdom of conclusion, under all the circumstances, no nation or body of men

can stand in preference to the general Congress at Philadelphia."

We have quoted the words of one who called Hamilton the *pen* of the Revolution. Others, with perhaps
still better reasons, have termed him the THINKER of that
momentous period ; and, as such, the prophetical patriot
who was above and beyond his age. It is certain that
he projected many plans which seemed to his cotemporaries impossible at first, but which were afterwards
demonstrated to be not only bold and majestic, but eminently sound and practical. His most difficult labors
were attempted and gloriously performed during the
gloomy period which extended from 1782 to 1787.
"Whatever," says Hamilton, "might be the future resources of this nation, whatever were the capacities of
the people, America now presented an unrelieved picture
of anarchy and disunion. Her public engagements had
nearly all been violated, her private resources appeared
either to be exhausted, or could not be called into action; and while the individual States were pursuing
measures of mutual hostility and detriment, the confederation was powerless over their laws, powerless over
public opinion." Nor was this the worst: "The general relaxation of morals, an usual and most lamentable
concomitant of war, was attended with a prevailing
disregard of, and disposition to question, the decisions
of the courts. In the political speculations to which the
Revolution had given rise, the sovereignty of the popular will, which was recognized as the basis of every
proceeding, was pushed to its utmost extremes in its

application; and wherever the operation of the laws
bore hard in the then unsettled relations of society, to
recur to elementary principles of government, and resolve every rule by its apparent adaptation to individual
convenience, was the prevailing tendency of public
opinion."

This great statesman felt the weakness of the existing
confederation, and saw how the national resources were
either utterly confused or exhausted. But, to use the
language of the historian of that period, " a new world is
seen rising into view; a world of hope; and as the
great lights that shine upon its morning path appear,
the grateful inquiry is: " Whose were those superior
minds that, amid the darkness of a chaotic confederacy,
combined the elements of social order, and formed them
into a vast majestic empire?"

Let us seek for a suitable response to that question in
the consideration of several facts.

When the enormous issues of paper-currency had involved the finances of the United States to the amount of
two hundred millions of dollars, and both the government and army were plunged into the greatest distress,
Hamilton set about discovering the best means of relief.
This was not to him an entirely new field of research,
and he explored most profoundly the complicated matters of finance, currency and taxation; studies which
soon invested him with the immortal honor of being
"the founder of the public credit of the United States."
In 1779 he addressed a letter to Robert Morris, detail-
ing a plan which he had projected for the restoration of
a depreciated currency, credit and confidence.   About

a year later he addressed a letter to Mr. Duane, a member of Congress from New York, on the state of the
nation. "This letter appears at this day,' says one,
"with all the lights and fruits of our experience, as masterly in a pre-eminent degree. He went on to show the
defects and total inefficiency of the articles of confederation, and to prove that we stood in need of a national
government, with the requisite sovereign powers ; such,
indeed, as the confederation theoretically contained, but
without any fit organs to receive them. He suggested
the idea of a national convention to amend and re-or-
ganize the government. This was undoubtedly the
ablest and truest production on the state of the Union,
its finances, its army, its miseries, its resources, and its
remedies, that appeared during the Revolution. It contained in embryo the existing federal Constitution, and
it was the production of a young man of the age of
twenty-three." In the winter of 1781-2, this indefatigable patriot continued his discussion of the same en-
grossing theme through a series of anonymous essays
published in the country papers of New York. In
brief, it was his pen that traced so early and so profoundly, with outlines the most clear and distinct, the
stupendous chart of empire then just opening on the
startled gaze of emancipated but feeble colonists. To
answer the question propounded above, we will ask
several more. From whose eloquent lips came so often
the thrilling cry of "union" and a "solid confederation ?"
—who wrote the "Continentalist ?"—who named the
'Federalist ?"—who was then stigmatized as the
"Unionist ?"—what mind roused the whole country to

reflection in the burning words of Phocion and Publius? —who fought its battles through good report and evil report, even from the very hour that the first blow was struck in the Colonial contest? These questions have been asked before, and may be answered, once for all— HAMILTON!

But after all that may be justly said in praise of this patriot as a popular orator, heroical soldier and polished writer, the most substantial service conferred on the country by his diversified and transcendent talents was performed by him in the character already referred to as the national financier. As Secretary of the Treasury he was the creative spirit that ruled the tempest and reduced chaos to form:

> "Confusion heard his voice, and wild uproar
> Stood ruled."

Being a member of President Washington's private council, he was one of the advisers of neutrality in April, 1793, when the proclamation was issued with respect to the war then raging between Great Britain and France. This neutral policy Hamilton aided much by his essays, under the signature of "No Jacobin," by the elaborate productions of "Pacificus," and still more by his advice in favor of the especial mission of Chief Justice Jay, as minister to England, in 1794.

In reviewing the life of Hamilton as a statesman, it should be remarked that he was fully equal to the highest stations he occupied, and that he honored them all. In this respect he resembled Edmund Burke. Owing nothing of his elevation to birth, opulence, or official rank he required none of those adventitious supports to rise and move at ease, and with instinctive power, in the highest regions of public effort, dignity and renown, the atmosphere of courts and senates was native to his majesty of wing. There was no fear that his plumage would give way in either the storm or the sunshine; those are the casualties of inferior powers. He had his share of both the tempest and that still more perilous trial which has melted down the virtue of so many aspiring spirits in the favor of cabinets. But he grew purer and more powerful for good; to his latest moment he continually rose more and more above the influence of party, until at last the politician was elevated into the philosopher; and fixing himself in that loftier region, from which he looked down on the cloudy and turbulent contests of the time, he soared upward calmly in the light of truth, and became more splendid at every wave of his wing.

Brougham thinks justly that Chatham's highest encomium rests on the fact that, " Far superior to the paltry objects of a grovelling ambition, and regardless alike of party and personal considerations, he constantly set before his eyes the highest duty of a public man, to further the interest of his species. In pursuing his course toward that goal, he disregarded alike the frowns of power and the gales of popular applause, exposed himself undaunted to the vengeance of the court, battled against its corruptions, and confronted, unappalled, the rudest shock of public indignation." That Hamilton actually pursued such a course as this, and was governed by such principles, is well known from cotemporaneous

history, and especially from his own pen in the opening
language of the "Federalist." "An enlightened zeal," he
observes, "for the energy and efficiency of government,
will be stigmatized as the offspring of a temper fond of
power and hostile to the principles of liberty. The consciousness of good intentions disdains ambiguity. I
shall not, however, multiply professions on this head.
My motives must remain in the depository of my own
breast; my arguments will be open to all, and may be
judged by all. They shall at least be offered in a spirit
which will not disgrace the cause of truth."

But by ingenuous and honest minds his integrity was
never suspected. His moral worth was of an exalted
character, and his varied services in behalf of his country and the human race can never be rated too high.
To him with the strictest propriety may be applied what
Mr. Burrowes said of Grattan : "His name silenced the
skeptic upon the reality of genuine patriotism. To
doubt the purity of his motives was a heresy which no
tongue dared to utter ; envy was lost in admiration, and
even they whose crimes he scourged blended extorted
praises with the murmurs of resentment. He covered
our then unfledged Constitution with the ample wings of
his talents, as the eagle covers her young ; like her he
soared, and like her he could behold the rays, whether
of royal favor or of royal anger, with undazzled, unin-
timidated eye."

To speak well and to write well are intellectual accomplishments every where considered of the highest
order, and in Hamilton the combination of these rare
excellences was strikingly exemplified. Like the re-

nowned Surrey, he was the most accomplished knight and the most accomplished scholar of his day:

" Matchless his pen, victorious was his lance,
Bold in the lists, and graceful in the dance."

In the hall, the camp and the forum, Hamilton was always employed in teaching the loftiest sentiments of patriotism and in executing the most generous deeds. When a whig student in college, he secured the tory president's safety at the risk of his own, even while the stubborn object of undeserved kindness cried out to the mob, " Don't listen to him, gentlemen! He is crazy! he is crazy!" And in all his subsequent career, we " find him thus fighting the cause of reason against popular passion, of the right against the expedient, and that, too, with the uniform and very natural reward of having his acts misconstrued, his motives misunderstood, his language misinterpreted, and himself held up, if not to public, at least to party odium, as a citizen without patriotism; an adopted but not a filial son of America; branded as a royalist, because he wrested from the law its sword of vengeance against the tories; as an Englishman, because he would not hate the ancestral land against which he was yet willing to shed his blood ; as a monarchist, because he loved not revolutionary France; as an enemy to the people, because he would save them from their own mad passions; and as a Cæsar in ambition, because he gave up his heart to his public duties, and ever labored in them as men do in that which they love. But popular fickleness and political rancor never moved him from his chosen and conscientious path. The motto that in the main governed his whole life, was, first, truth and honor, then the popular will."

In 1795, at the age of thirty-eight, Hamilton resumed the practice of law in the city of New York, where he continued in active professional pursuits until the close of life. His personal appearance at that time is represented as follows : He was under the middle size, thin in person, but remarkably erect and dignified in his deportment. His hair was turned back from his forehead, powdered, and collected in a club behind. His complexion was exceedingly fair, and varying from this only by the delicate rosiness of his cheeks. In form and tint his face was considered uncommonly handsome. When in repose, it bore a severe and thoughtful expression; but when engaged in conversation, it immediately assumed an attractive smile. His ordinary costume was a blue coat with bright buttons, the skirts being unusually long; he wore a white waistcoat, black silk smallclothes, and white silk stockings. His appearance and deportment accorded with the exalted distinction which, by his stupendous public services, he had attained. His voice was engagingly pleasant, and his whole mien commanded the respect due to a master-mind. His natural frankness inspired the most affectionate attachment; and his splendid talents, as is usual, elicited the firmest love and the most furious hate.

By nature Hamilton was a moralist and metaphysician. The axioms of political sagacity and the profusion of pointed and perspicuous reflections which flowed from his pen, as well as from his lips, gave an enduring value to his works. His great endowments of disciplined thought and energetic will imparted to his hastiest composition elaborate force and the grace of perfection. He could do that by intuition and a single blow which ordinary statesmen would require months to ponder and execute. Bold in his propositions, he was inexorable in his conclusions; grant him his premises, and the result was inevitable as fate. He did not fatigue himself with profuse skirmishes nor bewilder his mind in the labyrinth of a formal exordium ; but like an arrow impelled by a vigorous bow, he shot directly to the mark. One of the most enlightened critics of modern times has pronounced a worthy eulogium on him as the most eminent framer, most eloquent defender, and soundest expositor of the American Constitution. "Hamilton," says Guizot, in his late work on the character of Washington, "must be classed among the men who have best known the vital principles and the funda mental conditions of a government; not of a government such as this, (France,) but of a government worthy of its mission and of its name. There is not in the Constitution of the United States an element of order, of force, or of duration, which he has not powerfully contributed to introduce into it and caused to predominate."

Hamilton was the great master of the human heart. Deeply versed in its feelings and motives, he "struck by a word, and it quivered beneath the blow ; flashed the lightning glance of burning, thrilling, animated eloquence ;" and its hopes and fears were moulded to his wish. He was the vivid impersonation of political sagacity. His imagination and practical judgment, like two fleet coursers, ran neck-and-neck to the very goal of triumph. Military eloquence of the highest grade had its birth with liberty in the American Revolution. But the majority of our heroes were not adepts in literature. They could conquer tyrants more skillfully than they could harangue them. To this rule, however, Hamilton was a distinguished exception. He was the most sagacious and laborious of our Revolutionary orators. He anticipated time and interrogated history with equal ease and ardor. He explored the archives of his own land, and drew from foreign courts the quintessence of their ministerial wisdom. He illuminated the councils where Washington presided, and with him guarded our youthful nation with the eyes of a lynx and the talons of a vulture.

But we should give especial attention to Hamilton as a writer. Through the pen he wrought more extensively on the popular mind, perhaps, than by all the impressiveness of his living eloquence. He well understood the utility of this mighty engine for weal or woe. The ancient orators and writers, slowly transcribing their words on parchment, breathed in their little pipes a melody for narrow circles; but fame gives modern thought the magnificent trumpet of the press, whose perpetual voice speaks simultaneously to delighted millions at the remotest points.

It is of vast advantage to a nation that men of the most elevated positions in civil affairs should take a part in its literature, and thus, with their pen as well as by their patronage, foster its development and perfection. Æschylus, the oldest of the great tragedians of Greece, was himself a soldier, and fought with heroism in many of the glorious battles of his country, one of which furnished the theme of his most celebrated work. Herodotus was born only a few years before the great conflict with Xerxes; and Xenophon participated prominently in the remarkable military achievements he has commemorated. The profoundest scholars, acutest poets, most masculine heroes, the best writers and most sagacious statesmen are always polished into enduring elegance, and fortified with the best strength amid the stern realities of life.

Such was Alexander Hamilton. He was the indefatigable soldier of the press, the pen and the army; in in each field he carried a sword which, like the one borne by the angel at the gate of Paradise, flashed its guardian care on every hand. In martial affairs he was an adept, in literary excellence he was unexcelled, and in political discernment he was universally acknowledged to be superior among the great. We read his writings with ever-increasing zest, fascinated by the seductive charms of his style, and impelled by the opening splendors of his far-reaching and comprehensive thoughts. They accumulate with a beautiful symmetry, and emanate legitimately from his theme. They expand and grow, as an acorn rises into an oak, of which all the branches shoot out of the same trunk, nourished in every part by the same sap, and form a perfect unit, amid all the diversified tints of the foliage and the infinite complexity of the boughs. " That writer would deserve the fame of a public benefactor," said Fisher Ames, " who could exhibit the character of Hamilton with the truth and force that all who intimately knew him conceived it; his example would then take the same ascendant as his talents. The portrait alone, however exquisitely finished, could not inspire genius where it is not; but if the world should again have possession of so rare a gift, it might awaken it where it sleeps, as by a spark from heaven's own altar; for surely if there is any thing like divinity in man it is in his admiration for virtue.

"The country deeply laments when it turns its eyes back and sees what Hamilton was; but my soul stiffens with despair," continues Ames, "when I think what Hamilton *would have been*. It is not as Apollo, enchanting the shepherds with his lyre, that we deplore him; it is as Hercules, treacherously slain in the midst of his unfinished labors, leaving the world overrun with monsters."

It is unnecessary to dwell on the unrighteous and fatal event which robbed Hamilton of life—the duel with Aaron Burr at Hoboken, when

"A Falcon, tow'ring in his pride of place,
    Was by a mousing owl hawk'd at and kill'd!"

THE NEW YORK
PUBLIC LIBRARY

ASTOR, LENOX AND
TILDEN FOUNDATIONS

FISHER AMES,

CHAPTER XII

FISHER AMES,

ORATOR OF GENIUS AND ELABORATE BEAUTY.

In the progress of our national growth, there have been emergencies which demanded and received the patriotic support of extraordinary men. Of this charac-ter was the Colonial period, signalized by the eloquence and self-sacrifice of Otis, Quincy, Henry, Lee, and Samuel Adams. The era of the Declaration and War of Independence was one which demanded wisdom in council as well as valor in fight. It was then that such heroes as Washington, Warren, Hancock, and John Adams, appeared, and conducted the ship of State through terrific storms.

But of not less importance and difficulty was that portion of our history which dates from the peace of 1783, and immediately succeeds it. The independence of the United States was happily confirmed, but the dif ficulties which attended this conquest were far from being at an end. The new government went into ope ration under the pressure of an enormous debt, and with-out either a revenue, or the power of raising one. A long war had destroyed commerce, and fearfully con-

tracted the ordinary sources of national sustenance
The late army was unpaid, conflicts with the Indians
still raged, civil dissensions distracted the borders of the
country, and foreign politics exerted a threatening influence all over the land. It was a crisis which demanded
talents unlike, and, in their way, superior to any that
had ever before appeared. It was a period for ever memorable as having given employment and fame to those
kindred spirits of masterly endowments, Alexander
Hamilton and Fisher Ames.

In sketching the personal history of Mr. Ames, we
shall rely mainly for facts on President Kirkland, as he
has stated them in a biographical notice prefixed to the
great orator's collected works.

Fisher Ames was born on the 9th of April, 1758, at
Dedham, about nine miles from Boston. His ancestors
were distinguished in England, and his family was one of
the most respectable in his native State. Fisher was the
youngest of five children. His father died when he was
but seven years old, leaving widow and orphans in penury to be buffeted by the storms of the world. But the
mother, as if " anticipating the future lustre of the jewel
committed to her care," early resolved to struggle with
her narrow circumstances in order to give this son a
literary education ; and she lived to see his eminence
and prosperity, to receive the expressions of his filial
piety, and to weep over his grave.

Precocious talents are not usually the most auspicious
of enduring power, but in young Ames they were neither
feeble nor transient. He began the study of Latin
when but six years old. In 1770, soon after the com-

pletion of his twelfth year, he was admitted to Harvard College. With a mind too immature, perhaps, to receive the full benefit to bo derived from the collegiate course, his uncommon industry enabled him to outstrip many of his seniors, and he soon obtained a high standing. Even at this early period he was remarkable for the talent which afterwards constituted his principal claim to reputation. In a society formed among the students for mutual improvement in oratory, Ames was a favorite; and his declamation, says Kirkland, "was remarkable for its energy and propriety. His compositions at this time bore the characteristic stamp which always marked his speaking and writing. They were sententious and full of ornament. In 1774, he received his degree as Bachelor of Arts; but owing to the disturbed and excited condition of the country, his own youth, and the narrow circumstances of his mother, he did not enter at once upon the study of a profession. Meanwhile he was not idle; in teaching in one of the district schools of his native State, he at the same time obtained the means of maintaining himself, while leisure was left him for the prosecution of his favorite studies. All this time, he used afterwards to repeat, he read, with an avidity bordering on enthusiasm, almost every thing within his reach. He revised the Latin classics, which he had studied at College. He read works illustrating Greek and Roman antiquities and the mythology of the ancients; natural and civil history, and some of the best novels. Poetry was both his food and luxury. He read the principal English poets, and became familiar with Milton and Shakspeare, dwelt on their beauties, and

14

fixed passages of peculiar •excellence in his memoiy. He had a high relish for the works of Virgil, and at this time could repeat considerable portions of the Eclogues and Georgics, and most of the touching and splendid passages of the Æneid. This multifarious, though, for want of a guide, indiscriminate, and, probably, in sóme instances, ill-directed reading, must have contributed to extend and enrich the mind of the young student. It helped to supply that fund of materials for speaking and writing which he possessed in singular abundance ; and hence partly he derived his remarkable fertility of allu-sion, his ability to evolve a train of imagery adapted to every subject of which he treated."

Mr. Ames, having studied law in the office of William Tudor, Esq., of Boston, commenced the practice of that profession. at Dedham, his native place, in 1781. He entered warmly into the struggle for Independence, . although quite young, and his talents were soon both recognized and employed by his fellow citizens.

To devise some means for the relief of the general distress, occasioned by the great depreciation of the pa-per currency of that day, a convention of delegates from every part of the State assembled at Concord. Mr. Ames was chosen to represent his town at that meeting. In a lucid and eloquent speech he demonstrated the fu-tility of the measures at first proposed, and, at that early period, rendered himself a debater of much note.

The fame which followed his early efforts conduced to place him in the Massachusetts Convention for rati-fying the Constitution, in 1788. From this sphere, in which he made a deep impression by some of his speeches.

particularly that on biennial elections, ne passed to the House of Representatives in the State Legislature. Here, he soon became so eminent as an orator and man of business, that the voters of the Suffolk District elected him their first representative in the Congress of the United States. He had not been long in that assembly before his friends and admirers were satisfied that they had not overrated his abilities and claims on their support. He won there the palm of eloquence, besides proving himself equal to the discussion of the profoundest subjects of politics and finance, and the execution of the most arduous committee labors. He remained in Congress during the whole of Washington's administration, which he constantly and zealously defended.

Having thus rapidly traced Mr. Ames from his birth to the exalted position he in the maturity of his life attained, let us more minutely analyze and examine the elements of his character as an orator, a patriot, and a man.

Fisher Ames, among the great men of his day, was the orator of genius and elaborate beauty. Genius is the power of hard thinking. The two simple words which Newton employed to explain his own greatness, are "patient thought." The faculty of which we now speak, and which our countryman largely possessed, is an aggregate in which imagination, intelligence, and sentiment, are equally elevated and exactly combined. It is a soul whose glance penetrates exalted ideas, and whose skill can embody them in marble, in brass, in speech, and in writing; communicating to each offspring of the intellect a power from the heart, which, in turn, hurls it all living into the hearts of others. Genius is the most beautiful endowment, and the most indomitable force possessed by mankind; one can despoil man of rank, or of fortune, but genius is invulnerable. It is the greatest among finite powers; an intuition vast and subtle to perceive the relations that unite all gradations of being, a limpid lake wherein God and the universe are reflected with as much brilliancy of tint as splendor of light. When employed by those who are richly endowed, it is the faculty of rendering ideas visible to those who are not blessed with native vision to discover for themselves; it makes thought palpable in bold imagery, and imbues it with a power to touch, enlighten and subjugate, analagous to what one experiences when love comes to seize our attention and command our will.

In the ideals which genius creates, we meet with no dry mechanism, but an organic nature throbbing with the highest pulsations of life. Its offspring emanate from the inmost depth of the soul, and unfold with wondrous charms peculiar to each, like works fresh from the hand of God. Every mind endowed with high creative power, is a mystery standing by itself, a flower from Paradise, redolent of fragrance and perpetually blossoming with original charms, but for ever unmingled with others and unexplained. Who can ever mistake the spirit of beauty that hovers over Raphael's pictures, and who can ever analyze its power? Who has not been moved by the intellectual breath, the inner charm of soul, that reigns in Shakesperean creations, and yet who can define the influence which compels us to shudder or shout when we contemplate their features and feel their

touch? We believe that genius is taste in its greatest
perfection, formed by long practice on the best models
and so disciplined as to create excellence with spontaneous ease. Sophocles, speaking of his great predecessor in the tragic art, said very happily: "Æschylus does
what is right without knowing it." These few words
explain all that it is possible to understand respecting
powerful genius seemingly unconscious of its powers.

All ingenuous readers of the works of Mr. Ames, will
concur with those who heard him in public and in private, in accrediting to him a mind of high order, in
many respects of the highest, and that he has a just
claim to the honors of genius; that quality, to use his
own words, "without which judgment is cold and
knowledge inert; that energy, which collects, combines,
amplifies, and animates." In presenting his idea of this
power, he would not liken it to a conflagration on the
mountains, consuming its fuel in its flame; but would
represent it as a spark of elemental fire that is unquenchable, the cotemporary of this creation, and destined with the human soul to survive it. "Genius feels
the power it exerts, and its emotions are contagious because they are fervid and sincere. As well might the
stars of heaven be said to expend their substance by
their lustre, as that genius becomes exhausted by the
offshoots of its splendor."

But, while he could more safely trust to his native resources than most men, Mr. Ames never neglected to
subordinate the labors of other men to his use. "With
the dews of life in his brimming urn," he early formed
a passionate attachment to books; and this strong love

he cherished through his whole life. He was particularly fond of moral philosophy, but explored history with most enthusiastic zeal. He read Herodotus, Thucydides, Livy, Tacitus, Plutarch, and the modern historians of Greece and Rome. English history he studied almost constantly, and mastered beyond most men. Hence he possessed a great amount of historical information which was always at command both in writing and oral debate. His biographer says that "he was accustomed to read the Scriptures, not only as containing a system of truth and duty, but as displaying in their poetical parts, all that is sublime, animated, and affecting in composition." He was a devout admirer of the ancient classics, and especially of the poets. Homer he often perused, and read Virgil with constantly increased delight. Ames had all of Plato's admiration for the beauty of verse, but would have been less stern in legislating against the children of the muses. The latter banished poets from his ideal republic, but he directed that they should be crowned with flowers and conducted to the gates of the city, with the music of harps, in honor of that ray of divinity which they possessed, though he wished not to accept of their domination.

Sir Joshua Reynolds thought that excellence of the highest order may be acquired. But this theory of industry, so essential to genius, yet so useless without it, never produced a Correggio or Demosthenes. Still, nothing can be more incorrect than to suppose, that genius needs no study. Goethe rose early every morning, and studied closely the whole day. Leibnitz confined himself to his tasks for weeks together. Though it must be admitted that Shakspeare had not a complete education, his works show a vast amount of knowledge which must have cost him much research. He lived in an age highly favorable to poetry, and which cultivated the great poet much more than a practical age like ours. It was an era full of romantic thought and the quick instincts of this master of the heart readily absorbed its richest treasures.

The influence of genius pervades a wide area and effects all susceptible intellects according to the prevailing tendencies and peculiar endowments of each. In Elizabeth's day, the light of inspiration came from Italy, and it deeply *toned* the very atmosphere in which the literati breathed. More recently, the influence of Germany has gained ascendancy and has been reproduced in every department of literature. Genius was reflective with Coleridge, chivalrous with Scott, impassioned with Byron, and fiery to extreme in Campbell's thrilling melodies. But in every form, genius is the same—the ethereal soul of beauty and sublimity, which refines the gross and modulates the inharmonious, even as an Æolian harp arrests the vagrant winds and transforms them into enchanting strains. The atmosphere in which Ames was born and educated was fervid patriotism; this he imbibed into his fine-toned nature and reproduced in the loftiest and most elaborate eloquence

" Thy words had such a melting flow,
    And spoke of truth so sweetly well,
  They dropp'd like heaven's serenest snow,
    And all was brightness where they fell."

Being thus endowed, we can understand how it was

that Mr. Ames produced so many original combinations, resemblances and contrasts which none saw before, but on being presented, were immediately pronounced just and striking. Says President Kirkland:

"As a speaker and as a writer he had the power to enlighten and persuade, to move, to please, to charm, to astonish. He united those decorations that belong to fine talents to that penetration and judgment that designate an acute and solid mind. Many of his opinions have the authority of predictions fulfilled and fulfilling. He had the ability of investigation, and, where it was necessary, did investigate with patient attention, going through a series of observation and deduction, and tracing the links which connect one truth with another. When the result of his researches was exhibited in discourse, the steps of a logical process were in some measure concealed by the coloring of rhetoric. Minute calculations and dry details were employments, however, the least adapted to his peculiar construction of mind. It was easy and delightful for him to illustrate by a picture, but painful and laborious to prove by a diagram. It was the prerogative of his mind to discern by a glance, so rapid as to seem intuition, those truths which common capacities struggle hard to apprehend ; and it was the part of his eloquence to display, expand, and enforce them.

"His imagination was a distinguishing feature of his mind. Prolific, grand, sportive, original, it gave him the command of nature and art, and enabled him to vary the disposition and the dress of his ideas without end. Now it assembled most pleasing images, adorned with all that is soft and beautiful ; and now rose in the storm, wielding the elements and flashing with the most awful splendors."

Mr. Ames had a distinguished share in all the great measures which were discussed in Congress during the eight years of his membership. His speeches on Mr. Madison's resolutions, and on the appropriation for the British treaty, claim particular notice. The latter constituted the most renowned act of his life. His health was feeble, but the magnitude of the dangers which he believed threatened the country inspired him with extraordinary animation. The speech he then made abounded in the most elevated notions of national honor, and in the most impassioned appeals to the patriotism and reason of his hearers. During its delivery, a crowded house listened with the most profound attention ; and when in conclusion he alluded, in a touching manner, "to his own slender and almost broken hold upon life," the audience was moved to tears. As he took his seat, the question was loudly called for ; but the opposition dreaded the effects of a speech so hostile to their views, and one of its members moved that the decision of the question be postponed to the ensuing day, lest they should act under the influence of feelings which their calm judgment might condemn. The eloquence of Ames on this great occasion, and the motion in respect to it, were the same as in the famous instance of the great English orator at the close of his impeachment of Warren Hastings.

This speech on the British Treaty affords the best specimens of his style. He speaks of the power of pre-

14*

judiced nations as follows: "They are higher than a Chinese wall in truth's way, and built of materials that are indestructible. While this remains, it is in vain to argue; it is in vain to say to this mountain, be thou cast into the sea. For, I ask of the men of knowledge of the world, whether they would not hold him for a blockhead, that should hope to prevail in an argument, whose scope and object is to mortify the self-love of the expected proselyte? I ask further, when such attempts have been made, have they not failed of success? The indignant heart repels a conviction that is believed to debase it."

Instances of this sententiousness so peculiar to this orator frequently occur. As specimens, take the following: "Evil to a fatal extreme, if that be its tendency, requires no proof, it brings it. Extremes speak for themselves and make their own law."

"It is the prerogative of folly alone to maintain both sides of a proposition. Shame should blister their tongue, and infamy tingle in their ears."

Sometimes with a few strokes of his pencil, he suggests a fearful scene. For example: "Before we resolve to leap into this abyss, so dark and so profound, it becomes us to pause and reflect upon such of the dangers as are obvious and inevitable. If the assembly should be wrought into a tempest to defy these consequences, it is in vain, it is deceptive, to pretend that we can escape them."

Mr. Ames always entertained the most jealous fears with respect to the dangers of anarchy. Speaking on that topic, he presents a specimen of the highly figurative style in which it was so natural and common for him to indulge. "A mobocracy is always usurped by the worst men in the most corrupt times; in a period of violence by the most violent. It is a Briareus with a thousand hands, each bearing a dagger; a Cerberus gaping with her thousand throats all parched and thirsting for fresh blood. It is a genuine tyranny, but of all the least durable, yet the most destructive while it lasts. The power of a despot, like the ardor of a summer's sun, dries up the grass, but the roots remain fresh in the soil; a mob-government, like a West India hurricane, instantly strews the fruitful earth with promiscuous ruins, and turns the sky yellow with pestilence. Men inhale a vapor like a Sirocco, and die in the open air for want of respiration. It is a winged curse that envelopes the obscure as well as the distinguished, and is wafted into the lurking places of the fugitives. It is not doing justice to licentiousness, to compare it to a wind which ravages the surface of the earth; it is an earthquake that loosens its foundations, burying in an hour the accumulated wealth and wisdom of ages. Those, who, after the calamity, would re-construct the edifice of the public liberty, will be scarcely able to find the model of the artificers, or even the ruins. Mountains have split and filled the fertile valleys, covering them with rocks and gravel; rivers have changed their beds; populous towns have sunk, leaving only frightful chasms, out of which are creeping the remnant of living wretches, the monuments and the victims of despair."

This profusion of imagery may offend the taste of phlegmatic persons. It is not uncommon for frigid critics to be dissatisfied, while enthusiastic throngs are charmed. In the productions of Mr. Ames, it is certain that there was great energy and quickness of conception, an inexhaustible fertility which sometimes superabounds in ornament. A wise reviewer has said:

" Image crowded upon image in his mind, he is not chargeable with affectation in the use of figurative language; his tropes are evidently prompted by imagination, and not forced into his service. Their novelty and variety create constant surprise and delight. But they are, perhaps, too lavishly employed. The fancy of his hearers is sometimes overplied with stimulus, and the importance of the thought liable to be concealed in the multitude and beauty of the metaphors. His condensation of expression may be thought to produce occasional abruptness. He aimed rather at the terseness, strength, and vivacity of the short sentence, than the dignity of the full and flowing period. His style is conspicuous for sententious brevity, for antithesis and point. Single ideas appear with so much lustre and prominence, that the connection of the several parts of his discourse is not always obvious to the common mind, and the aggregate impression of the composition is not always completely obtained. In those respects where his peculiar excellencies came near to defects, he is rather to be admired than imitated."

But fire and fancy are not incompatible with truth and wisdom. Lord Chatham's reply to Mr. Pelham, when taunted on this ground, was very just. " What the gentleman on the other side means by long harangues, or flowers of rhetoric, I shall not pretend to determine ,

but if they make use of nothing of the k md, it is no very
good argument of their sincerity, because a man who
speaks from his heart and is sincerely affected with the
subject upon which he speaks, as every honest man
must be when he speaks in the cause of his country,
such a man, I say, falls naturally into expressions which
may be called flowers of rhetoric, and, therefore, deserves
as little to be charged with affectation as the most stupid
serjeant-at-law that ever spoke for a half-guinea fee."

It is evident that Mr. Ames was better adapted to
the senate than the bar. "It was easy and delightful to
him to illustrate by a picture, but painful and laborious
to prove by a diagram." Genius sees by intuition,
illustrates by pictures, and speaks in music. The
phraseology in which its sentiments are clothed, is not
a kind of patch-work laboriously tagged together, but is
part and parcel of the thought, and is born mature and
splendid, like Minerva glittering from the brow of Jove.
But of the great effects produced by Mr. Ames through
his living tones and impressive action, we can form no
adequate conception from the comparatively lifeless
matter of his printed works.

> " There's a charm in deliv'ry, a magical art,
>   That thrills, like a kiss, from the lip to the heart;
>   'Tis the glance—the expression—the well-chosen word—
>   By whose magic the depths of the spirit are stirr'd—
>   The smile—the mute gesture—the soul-stirring pause—
>   The eye's sweet expression, that melts while it awes—
>   The lip's soft persuasion—its musical tone :
>   Oh! such were the charms of that eloquent one!"

We have glanced at Fisher Ames as an orator, let us

in passing, contemplate him a moment in the character
of a patriot. He very early became distinguished, not
less by the power of his pen than by the splendor of his
living eloquence. Abhorring the excesses of the French
Revolution, he feared the hold which France had upon
the sympathies of America. He foresaw the downfall
of the federalist party, to which he was zealously
attached, and he dreaded lest the country should perish
with it. But time has shown that his fears, and the
fears of many other good men, on this score were
unfounded. Repeated experience confirms the belief
that changes of party tend to preserve the Union rather
than destroy it.

If Mr. Ames was excessively fearful as to the purity
and permanency of the young republic, it ought not on
this account to be inferred that he was insincere or
wanting in patriotism. Such an imputation is disproved
by his own strong and explicit declaration. "I detest
the man and disdain the spirit, which can bend to a
mean subserviency to any foreign nation. It is enough
to be Americans; that character comprehends our
duties, and ought to engage our attachments." He did
not love his own country less, but he hated foreign
politics more. He beheld, he said, in the French Revolution, a "a despotism of the mob or the military from the
first, and hypocrisy of morals to the last." Impelled by
a zeal that was doubtless honest, though sometimes
gloomy to excess, he kept his pen busy in the defence
of his political views, even when sickness had withdrawn
him from forensic strife. In the character of " Lucius
Junius Brutus," he wrote a series of powerful essays to

animate the government of his country to decision and energy; and after the Revolutionary storm subsided, as "Camillus," he taught the nation to profit by the dangers it had passed. The eloquence of the tongue and the pen are not often combined in the same man; but Ames was alike eminent in both.

We have already presented several extracts from his great speech on the British Treaty, as specimens of his style and eloquence. We will draw still farther from the same source, in order to present in Mr. Ames' own language one or two exemplifications of his spirit as a patriot. Said he, " A treaty of amity is condemned, because it is not made by a foe, and in the spirit of one. —I like this, sir, because it is sincerity. With feelings such as these, we do not pant for treaties. Such passions seek nothing, and will be contented with nothing, but the destruction of their object. If a treaty left King George his island, it would not answer; not if he stipulated to pay rent for it. It has been said, that we ought to rejoice if Britain were sunk in the sea ; if where there are now men, and wealth, and laws, and liberty, there were nothing more than a sand-bank for the sea-monsters to fatten on; a space for the storms of the ocean to mingle in conflict."

Ames entertained exalted and worthy views respecting political integrity and national honor. " If," said he " there could be a resurrection from the foot of the gallows, if the victims of justice could live again, collect together and form a society, they would, however loath, soon find themselves obliged to make justice, that justice under which they fell, the fundamental law of their State. They would perceive it was their interest to make others respect, and they would therefore soon pay some respect themselves to the obligations of good faith." It is thus that he goes on to deprecate the existence of bigotry and intrigue in our relations with foreign nations. "For," exclaims he, "What is patriotism? Is it narrow affection for the spot where a man was born? Are the very clods where we tread entitled to this ardent preference because they are greener? No, sir, this is not the character of the virtue, and it soars higher for its object. It is an extended self-love, mingling with all the enjoyments of life, and twisting itself with the minutest filaments of the heart.

It is thus we obey the laws of society, because they are the laws of virtue. In their authority, we see, not the array of force and terror, but the venerable image of our country's honor. Every good citizen makes that honor his own, and cherishes it not only as precious, but as sacred. He is willing to risk his life in its defence, and is conscious that he gains protection while he gives it.

For, what rights of a citizen will be deemed inviolable, when a State renounces the principles that constitute their security? Or, if his life should not be invaded, what would its enjoyments be in a country odious in the eyes of strangers, and dishonored in its own? Could he look with affection and veneration to such a country as his parent? The sense of having one would die within him; he would blush for his patriotism, if he retained any, and justly, for it would be a vice. He would be a banished man in his native land."

At the close of the session, in the spring of 1790, Mr. Ames travelled in Virginia for his health. At this time the college of New Jersey expressed their estimation of his public worth by conferring on him the degree of Doctor of Laws. He gained sufficient strength to attend the next session of Congress, though with rapidly decreasing health. He was chairman of the committee which reported the answer to Washington's speech. This answer contained a most affectionate and appropriate allusion to the President's declaration, that he now stood for the last time in their presence. In conclusion, it said; "for your country's sake, for the sake of republican liberty, it is our earnest wish, that your example may be the guide of your successors, and thus, after being the ornament and safeguard of the present age, become the patrimony of our descendants."

The session being terminated, Mr. Ames, having declined a re-election, retired to his favorite residence at Dedham, to enjoy repose in the bosom of his family, amid those rural occupations in which he greatly delighted.

Having rapidly sketched the character of Fisher Ames as an orator and patriot, it remains briefly to speak of him as a man. Kirkland says: "Happily, he did not need the smart of guilt to make him virtuous, nor the regret of folly to make him wise. His spotless youth brought blessing to the whole remainder of his life. It gave him the entire use of his faculties, and all the fruit of his literary education. Its effects appeared in that fine edge of moral feeling which he always pre served ; in his strict and often austere temperance ; in his love of occupation, that made activity delight; in his distaste for public diversions, and his preference of simple pleasures. Beginning well, he advanced with unremitted steps in the race of virtue, and arrived at the end of life in peace and honor. The objects of religion presented themselves with a strong interest to his mind. The relation of the world to its author, and of this life to a retributory scene in another, could not be contemplated by him without the greatest solemnity. He felt it his duty and interest to inquire, and discovered on the side of faith a fullness of evidence little short of demonstration. At about thirty-five he made a public profession of his belief in the Christian religion, and was a regular attendant on its services.''

In 1804, Mr. Ames was chosen president of Harvard College,—an honor which ill health compelled him to decline. When Washington died, he was appointed to pronounce his eulogy before the legislature of Massachusetts, a duty which he performed with distinguished success. The theme seemed to inspire him with a primitive glow of eloquence. It was almost the last public service he performed, and a fitting close to a brilliant and useful career. His energies rapidly declined, until, after an extreme debility for two years, death at length ended his sufferings. He expired, July 4th, 1808. His remains were carried to Boston, where they were interred with honors such as had never before been accorded to a private citizen. To such a man, having performed such services,

" Death is the crown of life :
Were death denied, poor man would live in vain
Death wounds to cure : we fall, we rise, we reign ;
Spring from our fetters, fasten to the skies,
Where blooming Eden withers from our sight.
This king of terrors is the prince of peace."

Those who were familiar with the person of Mr. Ames, represent him as being above middle stature, and well formed. His features were not strongly marked. His forehead was neither high nor expansive. His eyes were blue and of middling size ; his mouth was handsome ; his hair was black, and short on the forehead, and, in his latter years, unpowdered. He was very erect, and when speaking he raised his head. His expression was usually complacent, when in debate, and if he meant to be severe, it was seen in good-natured sarcasm, rather than in acrimonious words. It was said that the beautiful productions of his pen were the first flow of his mind, and hardly corrected for the press. " In public speaking he trusted much to excitement, and did little more in his closet than to draw the outlines of his speech and reflect on it, till he had received deeply the impressions he intended to make ; depending for the turns and figures of language, illustrations and modes of appeal to the passions, on his imagination and feelings at the time. This excitement continued, when the cause had ceased to operate. After debate his mind was agitated, like the ocean after a storm, and his nerves were like the shrouds of a ship torn by the tempest." Such, in brief, were the appearance and mental habits of the great man,

" Whose eloquence brightening whatever it tried,
    Whether reason or fancy, the gay or the grave,
    Was as rapid, as deep, and as brilliant a tide,
    As ever bore freedom aloft on its wave !"

The training preparatory to public life which Fisher
Ames experienced, was thorough and comprehensive.
In moral worth he was excelled by no statesman of his
day. His youth was studious, and his whole life was
consecrated to the highest cultivation. He has himself
said, " The heart is more than half corrupted, that does
not burn with indignation at the slightest attempt to
seduce it."

He excelled all his cotemporaries in the fascinations
of conversation, even more than he was superior to
most persons in public debate. He quailed before none
amid the severe splendors of the rostrum, but he turned
with hearty delight and unequalled attractiveness to the
more genial charms of social life, of which he was very
fond. " The value of friends," he observes, " is the most
apparent and highest rated to those who mingle in the
conflicts of political life. The sharp contests for little
points wound the mind, and the ceaseless jargon of hypocrisy overpowers the faculties. I turn from scenes
which provoke and disgust me, to the contemplation of
the interest I have in private life, and to the pleasures
of society with those friends whom I have so much reason to esteem."

He who pulls but one string, will ring but one bell ;
ne who has not his whole nature cultivated, will be nar-
rowly restricted in his influence on mankind. We
reach the passions only through the passions ; we impel

in others only that which is identical with what we first move in ourselves. The great orator must be "many-sided" and variously educated. He must grow up like the mountain oak, which, from unfolding germ to matured development, feeds as it grows on every kingdom of nature—taking in strength of heart, vigor of limb, and that ruggedness to endure which is perpetually appropriated from rocky earth and genial dews, from summer zephyrs, and wintry storms.

Fisher Ames was the orator of genius among our Revolutionary patriots. He was impelled in his oratorical career by those mighty wings vouchsafed to few, but which re-appearing from time to time in aid of the choicest minds, are necessary to bear Truth through the sea of time. He united the substantial and ornamental,—the multiflora rose-bush in full bloom wreathed round a column of granite,—the decorations welling up from the fount of fine emotion, and lending vividness and momentum to the penetration and judgment which always constitute the basis of a great character. He was fond of patient investigation, when required; but was more skillful in that prophetical sagacity of mind which lays hold of remote consequences with the force and accuracy of intuition. He seems to have meditated without effort, and to have produced without exhaustion.

The sublime in speech is nothing else than that which true genius discovers beyond the hackneyed regions of ordinary ideas. The impressive orator must plunge in the deep mines of thought, and not be content to gather the brilliant grains of sand which cover the profounder veins of massy gold. He must leap beyond vulgar conceptions, and create his thought in those pure regions which extend between the extremes of trite prettiness and vapid exaggeration. The popular speaker must develope in their splendid magnitude the harmonious and imposing forms of expression which give to eloquence its force, its dignity, its vehemence, its gradation of thought and majestic movement. "The fulminating arrows of Demosthenes," says Cicero, "would strike with much less power, if they were emitted with less rythm and impetuosity."

Acute sensibility, the inseparable concomitant of genius, and potent auxiliary of reason, was finely developed and copiously abounded in Fisher Ames. A mind kindled with enthusiasm unfolds its grandeur in the light of its own flames, as the sea is never more grand than at night when it heaves, storm-tossed and brilliant, with the illumination of its own phosphorescence. When fully aroused in debate, Ames frequently trembled from head to foot; he wept in irrepressible emotion, and paused in the struggle to embody the inarticulate eloquence of his heart. He bent under the reflex passions he aroused in others, and then in turn bowed them under the augmented weight of his own.

The great orators of antiquity labored long and passionately to develope their own sensibilities, and, in speaking, to make their heart a mighty auxiliary to their intellect. They strove to feed the fires of their eloquence with the choicest materials, selected from the most glowing sources; not as dry quotations, frigid ornaments tagged to the limping dullness of their own stupid thoughts, but as spontaneous contributions of volcanic heat and power, kindling where they fell and blending with the flames they augmented. Their minds were rich with the selectest stores of elegant literature, and as some pertinent maxim or splendid illustration occurred in extemporaneous discourse, the gem grew suddenly brilliant amid the corruscations of inflamed fancy, while the orator poured his whole soul into his quotation, and sent it, revivified and blazing to every enraptured bosom. This power of reproducing familiar thoughts with all their original inspiration and effect, is a rare gift, and was constantly improved by Fisher Ames. He possessed the power of striking those delicate notes of soul-harmony which a sympathetic audience always repeat with rapture in their own hushed hearts. He diffused a charm around him, like ambrosia evaporating from an open vase, and which was worthy to be served at the table of the gods. He was not simply a rhetorician, or an adept in metaphysics, he was an orator by the true passion of eloquence; he was a musician in his tones, and a poet in his expressions.

Ames was a sound reasoner, but his style of argument was harmonious with the constitution of his mind. The logic that is most felt is least seen, as the cannon-ball that rends the target is not visible in its flight. True force should be measured by its efficiency, rather than by the manner in which its results are executed.

Popular eloquence must be rich in colors, simple in subject, sparkling with light, palpable in premises, bold in deduction, and varied in tone, in order to please the multitude and convince all. As in nature there are some prominent objects which can be seen from far, as a house, a tree or a mountain, so there are but a few reasons so obvious as to strike the common mind. That which a philosopher comprehends by an argument, the mass of the people comprehend in an image. It is indispensable to use variety. The ear is soon pained with sameness of tone, and the soul loaths a perpetual string of syllogisms.

Ames in this respect was a master. He was easily excited, but exercised a sovereign power of self-control. He knew that it was necessary to be master of his own passions, in order to govern those of others. He assumed diversified forms and hues with Protean facility. Now he skims the ground and obscures himself in smoke; anon he darts through the empyrean with coruscations of flame, and with resplendent light illuminates the waters, the earth and the heavens.

> " The rapid argument
> Soar'd in gorgeous flight, linking earth
> With heaven by golden chains of eloquence,
> Till the mind, all its faculties and powers,
> Lay floating self-surrendered in the deep
> Of admiration."

His imagination was imperial. The whole universe of nature and art were at its control and subordinated to its use. The beautiful and the sublime, those two great pulses of eloquence, he felt deeply and could embody in multifarious forms. There were many stops of great power in the organ of his soul, and he could touch them all in a manner to suit his purpose and the time,—now piping in tender pathos, like night-winds sighing among reeds over a fountain in a lonely dell, and, on more fearful occasions, crashing on the startled ear like bursting tempests, or distress-guns booming amid the awful magnificence of elemental storms.

His power of giving a rapid sketch of a comprehensive and diversified field, is exemplified in the following paragraph. He is speaking of the ambition of a nation whose infidelity he dreaded. "Behold France, conducting her intrigues and arraying her force between the arctic circle and the tropics; see her, in Russia, the friend of despotism ; in Ireland, the auxiliary of a bloody democracy; in Spain and Italy, a papist ; in Egypt, a mussulman ; in India, a bramin ; and at home, an atheist ; countenancing despotism, monarchy, democracy, religion of every sort, and none at all, as suits the necessity of the moment."

As an example of his illustrious imagination, take the following. He is speaking of England as a model of national industry to be imitated, rather than the nations on the continent. Among the latter he proceeds to say: "Commerce has not a single ship; arts and manufactures exist in ruins and memory only; credit is a spectre that haunts its burying-place ; justice has fallen on its own sword ; and liberty, after being sold to Ishmaelites, is stripped of its bloody garments to disguise its robbers."

Mr. Ames habitually dealt in a copious use of figures of speech. In his eulogy on Washington, he discourses as follows:

"Great generals have arisen in all ages of the world, and perhaps most in those of despotism and darkness.

15

In times of violence and convulsion, they rise, by the force of the whirlwind, high enough to ride in it, and direct the storm. Like meteors, they glare on the black clouds with a splendor, which, while it dazzles and ter- rifies, makes nothing visible but the darkness. The fame of heroes is indeed growing vulgar; they multiply in every long war; they stand in history, and thicken in their ranks, almost as undistinguished as their own sol- diers.

"But such a chief magistrate as Washington appears like the pole-star in a clear sky, to direct the skillful statesman. His Presidency will form an epoch, and be distinguished as the age of Washington. Already it assumes its high place in the political region. Like the milky way, it whitens along its allotted portion of the hemisphere. The latest generations of men will survey, through the telescope of history, the space where so many virtues blend their rays, and delight to separate them into groups and distinct virtues. As the best illustration of them, the living monument, to which the first of patriots would have chosen to consign his fame, it is my earnest prayer to heaven. that our country may subsist, even to that late day, in the plenitude of its liberty and happiness, and mingle its mild glory with Washington's."

But, after all, the chief excellence in Mr. Ames, and one that renders him a worthy model to be emulated by all public speakers, was his great industry and care in improving to perfection the chaste beauty of his style. As a specimen of his elaborate composition, and at the same time the very best description of himself

we will take the following extract from his encomium on
Alexander Hamilton :

" It is rare that a man, who owes so much to nature,
descends to seek more from industry ; but he seemed to
depend on industry, as if nature had done nothing for
him. His habits of investigation were very remarkable ;
his mind seemed to cling to his subject, till it had exhausted it. Hence the uncommon superiority of his
reasoning powers, a superiority that seemed to be augmented from every source, and to be fortified by every
auxilary, learning, taste, wit, imagination, and eloquence.
These were embellished and enforced by his temper and
manners, by his fame and his virtues. It is difficult, in
the midst of such various excellence, to say in what
particular the effect of his greatness was most manifest.
No man more promptly discerned truth ; no man more
clearly displayed it : it was not merely made visible—it
seemed to come bright with illumination from his lips.
But prompt and clear as he was, fervid as Demosthenes,
like Cicero, full of resource, he was not less remarkable
for the copiousness and completeness of his argument,
and left little for cavil, and nothing for doubt. Some
men take their strongest argument as a weapon, and
use no other ; but he left nothing to be inquired for
more—nothing to be answered. He not only disarmed
his adversaries of their pretexts and objections, but he
stripped them of all excuse for having urged them ; he
confounded and subdued, as well as convinced. He
indemnified them, however, by making his discussion
a complete map of his subject ; so that his opponents
might, indeed, feel ashamed of their mistakes, but they

could not repeat them. In fact, it was no common effort that preserved a really able antagonist from becoming his convert; for the truth, which his re- searches so distinctly presented to the understanding of others, was rendered almost irresistibly commanding and impressive by the love and reverence, which, it was ever apparent, he profoundly cherished for it in his own. While patriotism glowed in his heart, wisdom blended in his speech her authority with her charms."

We have said that Fisher Ames, among our Revo- lutionary statesmen, was the orator of genius. We mean by this that he possessed something higher and better than mere talent.

Genius is the native breath of the most richly endowed, luxuriating in every thing beautiful and fair,—the inspired vision which makes the future present, and the distant near,—a lingering reminiscence of the infinite ocean from which we all emerged, and a vivid prognos- tic of an eternity to come. It is a rare possession, the line of demarcation between the highest form of the intellectual, and the lowest form of the divine, causing its possessor to be a "maker" of things, most like God; a "declarer" who speaks the highest law in tones like the sound of many waters, and with a splendor as pure and pervading as the light of heaven.

It is the quality of genius to flow, while plodding talent has a constant tendency to freeze. He who is blessed with the first, passes through life as a broad and placid river traverses continents, and, in its calm but irresistible course, reflects every natural charm. Ben Jonson possessed an extraordinary opulence of thought:

but it was the produce of the amassing power of talent, not, as in Shakspeare, the creative power of genius. Materials, which, in the hands of talent, are but herbs and crude metal,—papyrus and bronze,—by the magical touch of genius are elevated into stupendous architecture, temples that outlive the Pyramids, around which the deluge of ages roars in vain.

Talent accomplishes results with slow toil, like Caliban ; while genius works its spontaneous wonders like the wand of Prospero. The traces of talent are discovered by the searcher after excellence; but genius strikes us like the lightning, without the eye being obliged to look for it. It illumines every thing with its own broad clear flash. Genius is daring, thinks for itself, and pursues its ends out of the beaten track ; while talent plods on after the manner and dictum of others, and is applauded only by critics of the same taste and mental calibre.

Talent takes impressions from beautiful objects; genius creates its own originals. Talent collects data and from them deduces conclusions; genius overleaps the intermediate process and reaches the same result by intuition. Newton had genius, and it discovered the law of gravitation; he also had talent, and with this he proved it. The higher attribute is necessary to render one great in his own presence; the other must be employed to render one useful to the world. Without the sun, the universe is a chaos ; genius kindles an original flame, and talent walks in the light thereof.

Exact definitions of these qualities are difficult, but Ames was certainly not entirely wrong when he said that. "talent might be compared to a bee, gathering honey from every flower, but creating none ; while genius is like a spider, it spins from its own bowels." We may add that genius is insatiable, and becomes vigorous in proportion as it is appropriately fed.   Like the Phœnix, which rises renovated from its own ashes, or the vitals of Prometheus which grew as fast as the vultures devoured them, the finer powers of the soul become purified by the flames they traverse, and are strengthened by the struggles they endure.   Lord Brougham is an orator of talent, but Fisher Ames was the orator of genius

CHAPTER XIII.

WILLIAM PINKNEY,

THE ACCOMPLISHED COUNSELLOR.

SERJEANT TALFOURD, one of the most elegant scholars
and able lawyers now practising in Westminster Hall,
has said that there is no pursuit in life which appears
more captivating at a distance than the profession of the
bar. "It is the great avenue to political influence and
reputation ; its honors are among the most splendid
which can be attained in a free State; and its emolu-
ments and privileges are exhibited as prizes, to be contested freely by all its members. Its annals celebrate
many individuals who have risen from the lowest ranks
of the people, by fortunate coincidence, or by patient
labor, to wealth and station, and have become the
founders of fortunate families. If the young aspirant
perceives, even in his hasty and sanguine glance, that
something depends on fortuitous circumstances, the conviction only renders the pursuit more inviting, by adding
the fascinations of a game of chance to those of a trial
of skill. If he is forced to confess that a sacrifice of
principle is occasionally required of the candidate for
its more lucrative situations, he glories in the pride of

untempted virtue, and pictures himself generously resisting the bribe which would give him riches ana
authority in exchange for conscious rectitude and the
approbation of the good and the wise. While he sees
nothing in the distance, but glorious success, or more
glorious self-denial, he feels braced for the severest exertion ; nerved for the fiercest struggle ; and regards every
throb of an impatient ambition as a presage of victory."

Among the early, persevering and triumphant devotees at the shrine of Themis, in America, William
Pinkney, of Maryland, stands pre-eminent. He was
born at Annapolis, on the 17th of March, 1764. His
father was an Englishman and a tory; but the son early
avowed his ardent attachment to republican liberties,
and to the last struggled for the independence which in
boyhood he espoused.

He commenced his law studies in the office of Justice
Chase, in 1783, and was called to the bar in 1786. His
first efforts commanded public admiration, and to the
minds of the sagacious foretokened eminent success.
At that time the law of real property, and the science of
special pleading, were the two great departments of
legal study, and in these he was considered accurate
and profound. "His style of speaking," says Wheaton,
"was marked by an easy flow of natural eloquence and
a happy choice of language. His voice was very melodious, and seemed a most winning accompaniment to
his pure and effective diction. His elocution was calm
and placid—the very contrast to that strenuous, vehement, and emphatic manner, which he subsequently
adopted."

In 1786, M: Pinkney removed to Harford County, where he practiced his profession, and in 1788, was elected a delegate to the State Convention which ratified the Constitution of the United States. In the same year, he was elected to represent the county of Harford in the House of Delegates, which position he continued to occupy until 1792, when he removed to Annapolis. In 1789, he married Miss Ann Maria Rodgers, sister to Commodore Rodgers, the celebrated ornament of our navy.

While in the State legislature, Pinkney distinguished himself in several important debates. In 1789 he made an admirable speech on the voluntary emancipation of slaves, nearly the whole of which has been preserved. The following are brief extracts which illustrate his character and exemplify his style:

" The door to freedom is fenced about with such barbarous caution, that a stranger would be naturally led to believe that our statesmen considered the existence of its opposite among us as the *sine qua non* of our prosperity ; or, at least, that they regarded it as an act of the most atrocious criminality to raise an humble bondsman from the dust, and place him on the stage of life on a level with their citizens.

"Eternal infamy awaits the abandoned miscreants, whose selfish souls could ever prompt them to rob unhappy Afric of her sons, and freight them hither by thousands to poison the fair Eden of liberty with the rank weed of individual bondage!

"Sir, it is really matter of astonishment to me that the people of Maryland do not blush at the very name of

15*

freedom. That they who have, by the deliberate acts
of their legislature, treated her most obvious dictates
with contempt ; who have exhibited for a long series of
years, a spectacle of slavery which they are still solicit-
ous to perpetuate; who, not content with exposing to
the world for near a century, a speaking picture of
abominable oppression, are still ingenious to prevent the
hand of generosity from robbing it of half its horrors;
that *they* should step forward as the zealous partizans of
freedom, cannot but astonish a person who is not cas-
uist enough to reconcile antipathies

"For shame, sir! let us throw off the mask, 'tis a cob-
web one at best, and the world will see through it. It
will not do thus to talk like philosophers, and act like
unrelenting tyrants; to be perpetually sermonizing
with liberty for our text, and actual oppression for our
commentary."

In 1792, Mr. Pinkney was elected a member of the
Executive Council of Maryland, in which office he remained until November, 1795, when he resigned his
seat as President of the Board, to assume still higher
functions to which he had been appointed. During all
this time he was exceedingly assiduous in study, and rose
rapidly to the head of the bar, and to a distinguished
rank in the public councils of his native State. Mr.
Walsh, speaking of this period of Pinkney's life, says,
"His acuteness, dexterity, and zeal in the transaction of
business; his readiness, spirit, and vigor in debate; the
beauty and richness of his fluent elocution, adorned
with the finest imagery drawn from classical lore and a
vivid fancy; the manliness of his figure and the energy

of his mien, united with a sonorous and flexible voice, and a general animation and graceful delivery, were the qualities by which he attained this elevated standing."

In 1796, he was selected by President Washington as one of the Commissioners on the part of the United States, under the 7th article of Jay's treaty with Great Britain. After some hesitation he accepted the trust, and embarked for London, where he arrived in July, 1796. His services abroad were of a difficult character, but were executed with great care and success. In 1804, he returned to his country, and with enlarged capacities and renewed zeal entered again upon the toils of his profession. During his diplomatic mission abroad, he was far from relaxing his forensic studies. Like Homer's hero, though withdrawn from the field a while, his arm was not in the slightest unnerved by indolent repose. He obtained in retirement a full suit of Vulcanian armor, and renewed the conflict with fresh strength, with a facility and force of action more propitious to the combatant than unremitted battle might have proved. He returned to the American bar and Senate, to " shed lustre upon letters, renown upon Congress, glory on the country."

Soon after Mr. Pinkney's return from England, he removed to Baltimore, and commenced attending the Supreme Court at Washington. In 1805, he was appointed Attorney-General of Maryland, and may be considered as having then entered upon the widest sphere of professional honor and emolument. At this point, let us more minutely analyze his character, and consider the instrumentalities he employed.

Like all proficients in every profession who win a wide and enduring fame, Pinkney laid his foundation deep and strong in a truly liberal education. In early manhood his classical training was imperfect, but in mature life he abundantly repaired all deficiencies. An anecdote is related of him which strikingly illustrates his character in this respect. When at the Court of St. James, he was dining in company with Burke, Sheridan, Fox, and a host of great names, when a discussion arose upon a passage in Virgil. All of the guests expressed their opinions but Mr. Pinkney, and as he had said nothing, *pro* or *con.*, they appealed to him as umpire. He had to confess his ignorance of the Latin language ; but when he left the company, he sent immediately for a teacher, and commenced the study of it. The result was, that, amid all the tumultuous cares of exalted stations, he continued to prosecute the study of ancient literature and became an accomplished classical scholar. He accustomed himself to acute observation and untiring application. Abroad, as well as at home, he emulated the best models, and was ambitious of the highest honors. He was as unremitting in his search for the elements of oratorical power and professional celebrity, as ever was alchymist in pursuit of his golden secret. This is always a happy omen, since, as Johnson has said, " Men's ambition is generally proportioned to their capacity. Providence seldom sends any one into the world with an inclination to attempt great things, who has not likewise abilities to perform them."

But our renowed countryman's heart did not only run o'er in silent worship of the great of old ;" he was

assiduous in winning excellence from the most prominent among his cotemporaries. His residence in London, in intimate connection with the most distinguished
masters of the bench and bar, was of great service in
consummating Mr. Pinkney's forensic education. Whenever his diplomatic duties allowed, he was constant in
attendance in all the higher courts, and critical in his
analysis of all the proceedings. Hence, when he returned to the American bar, it was observed that he had
lost nothing in legal attainment by absence, but had
gained immensely. He resumed his position in the lists,
completely armed at every point.

The two men abroad who stood highest in Pinkney's
esteem, and the latter of whom he not only admired but
imitated, were Sir William Scott, and Mr. Erskine.
According to the following estimate of Scott, by Lord
Brougham, no jurist was worthier of being emulated.
"Sir William Scott's learning, extensive and profound
in all professional matters, was by no means confined
within that range. He was amply and accurately endowed with a knowledge of all history of all times;
richly provided with the literary and the personal portion of historical lore ; largely furnished with stores of
the more curious and recondite knowledge which judicious students of antiquity, and judicious students only,
are found to amass ; and he possessed a rare facility of
introducing such matters felicitously for the illustration
of an argument or a topic, whether in debate or in more
familiar conversation. But he was above the pedantry
which disdains the gratification of a more ordinary and
every-day curiosity. No one had more knowledge of

the common affairs of life ; and it was at all times a current observation, that the person who first saw any sight exhibiting in London, be it production of nature or of art or of artifice, was Sir William ·Scott—who could always steal for such relaxations an hour from settling the gravest questions that could be raised on the rights of nations or the ecclesiastical law of the land. Above all, he was a person of great classical attainments. Of diction, he was among the greatest masters, in all but its highest department of energetic declamation and fervent imagery."

Probably few devotees ever adored and emulated the "god of their idolatry," so passionately as did Mr. Pinkney his friend, the great forensic orator, Erskine. He had learned much from the severe dialectics of Scott; he was thoroughly enraptured by the masterly arguments and appeals of Erskine. He had often heard him in his happiest efforts, and seems never to have lost the inspiration which he imbibed as a spectator of the splendid strife. Nothing is more natural to gifted minds than insensibly to imitate what they habitually admire. Intentionally or unintentionally, it is well known that Pinkney had caught many of the peculiar airs of his great model. Talking one day to a fellow practitioner about Erskine, he started up and said, "I'll give you a specimen of his manner." "And," says his brother lawyer, "it *was* an admirable specimen——of Mr. Pinkney."

Emulation of living masters is doubtless a good practice, when the best models are selected, and their faults are avoided. But, unfortunately, the excrescences

wh'ch are most prominent and least valuable, are ordinarily the first copied. Herein is the danger, since no
one can ever be great by imitation alone. Mr. Pinkney,
however, possessed extraordinary natural abilities, and
did not incur dangers so great as those that threaten
mediocrity whenever imitation is indulged. Moreover,
the model he chose to adopt, was second to none then
extant. "The eloquence of Lord Erskine," says a
distinguished critic, "was of a very high order. Though
never deficient in any of those qualities, it was not
indebted for its excellence either to beauty of diction,
or to richness of ornament, or to felicity of illustration ;
—it was from its unrivalled strength and vigor that it
derived its superior character. The intenseness, the
earnestness, the vehemence, the energy of the advocate,
were ever present throughout his speeches, impressing
his arguments upon the mind of the hearer with a
force which seemed to compel conviction. Throughout
even the longest of his speeches there is no weakness,
no failing, no flagging; but the same lively statement
of facts, the same spirited and pointed exposition of
argument. He never gave way to what he has happily
termed "the Westminster Hall necessity"—of filling up
his speech with common-places; but invariably presented his subject in some striking or brilliant light,
which never failed to rivet the attention, and to work
upon the convictions of his audience."

Mr. Pinkney possessed uncommon powers, cultivated
with incessant care, and directed always toward the
the grand aims of his profession. He had great power
in dealing with facts, a facility in arraving and sifting

evidence, and in arguing upon probabilities, which few or none could either anticipate or subvert. Among other eminent attributes, he was especially distinguished for one which a high authority has declared that even Burke did not possess,—fierce, nervous, overwhelming declamation, and close, rapid argument. His career as an orator was a brilliant commentary on the lines of Percival :

> " Men are made to bend
> Before the mighty, and to follow on
> Submissive where the great may lead—the great,
> Whose might is not in crowns and palaces,
> In parchment rolls or blazoned heraldry,
> but in the power of thought, the energy
> Of unsupported mind, whose steady will
> No force can daunt, no tangled path divert
> From its high-onward purpose."

The ambition which always seemed to actuate this great man at the bar was complex interest in the fate of his client, and the promotion of his own fame. Undoubtedly, he was ambitious, as who that is worthy of esteem and destined to win it is not? But his aspirations were honorable, and bent towards the goal of untarnished glory, rather than to the accumulation of sordid pelf. In his letters on the study of History, addressed to the great grandson of the Earl of Clarendon, Bolingbroke, after speaking of the profession of the law as " in its nature the noblest and most beneficial to mankind, in its abuse and debasement, the most sordid and the most pernicious," makes the following remarks, both eloquent and true : " There have been lawyers that were orators, philosophers, historians,—there have been Bacons and Clarendons, my lord. There will be none such any more, till, in some better age, true ambition, or the love of fame, prevails over avarice, and till men find leisure and encouragement to prepare themselves for the exercise of this profession, by climbing up to the 'vantage ground,' so my Lord Bacon calls it, of science; instead of grovelling all their lives below in a mean, but painful application to all the little acts of chicane. Till this happen, the profession of the law will scarce deserve to be ranked among the learned professions; and whenever it happens, one of the 'vantage grounds,' to which men must climb, is metaphysical, and the other historical, knowledge."

Mr. Pinkney's mind was sufficiently acute to master the nicest metaphysics of law, and in this department he greatly excelled. Early in life, special pleading was his forte, and to the last he encountered no superior. He was often most eloquent on questions the most abstruse, as in the elucidation of great principles which involved black-letter precedents and feudal lore. Of his personal appearance and professional excellence, no one was better qualified to speak than Justice Story, and the following is his estimate of Mr. Pinkney's character :

"For the last ten years of his life, he was never supposed, by any one, to be excelled by any other advocate, and rarely deemed to be equalled. His person was strong, compact, and muscular, exhibiting great vigor of action, with no small grace and ease of move-ment. His countenance, without being strikingly interesting for its intelligence, or suavity, was manly and open ; and, when excited by any discussion, was capable of the most powerful and various expression, suited, at once, for the playfulness of wit, the indignation of resentment or the solemn dignity of argumentation. His mind was singularly subtle and penetrating, equally rapid in its conceptions, and felicitous in the exposition of the truths which it was employed to develope or analyze. In native genius, or, in other words, in the power to invent, select, illustrate, and combine topics for the purposes of argument, few men have been his superiors. But he did not rely exclusively on the resources of his genius. He chastened, improved, and invigorated it by constant study, and laborious discipline. He was from early life a diligent student, not only of the law, but of general literature, and especially of classical literature. He was ambitious to be not only a good, but an exact scholar; not only a persuasive, but an elegant writer ; not only a splendid, but a solid speaker; full of matter, as well as of metaphor ; able to convince, as well as to instruct and please. His professional learning was very extensive, deep, and accurate. It was the gradual accumulation of nearly forty years' steady devotion to the science, as well as practice, of jurisprudence. He possessed a minute acquaintance with the ancient common law. Its technical principles, and feudal peculiarities, its quaint illustrations, its subtle distinctions, and its artificial, but nice logic, were all familiar to his early thoughts, and enabled him, in the later periods of his life, to expound the abstruse doctrines of modern tenures and titles, with great facility and perspicuity. But his studies were not confined to mere researches into the doctrines of the old law. His reading was very extensive in all the departments of modern jurisprudence; and his practice, which was, perhaps, more various than that of any other American lawyer, led him to a daily application of all his learning, in the actual business of the forum. Few men, in our country, had attained so exact, thorough, and methodized a knowledge as he of the general principles of the Law of Nations; of the doctrines of the Prize and Admiralty Courts; of the broad and various foundations of equity, jurisprudence, and of the admirable theories, as well as practical developments, of all the branches of Maritime and Commercial Law."

Justice Story goes on to speak of Mr. Pinkney's thorough mastery of Constitutional Law, and of his frequent exemplifications of exalted patriotism, but our limits will not admit of farther quotation, except a few sentences on his oratorical manner. " It was original, impressive, and vehement. He had some natural and some acquired defects, which made him, in some degree, fall short of that exquisite conception of the imagination, a perfect orator. His voice was thick and guttural. It rose and fell with little melody and softening of tones, and was, occasionally, abrupt and harsh in its intonations, and wanting in liquidness and modulation. These, however, were venial faults, open to observation, indeed, but soon forgotten by those who listened to his instructive and persuasive reasoning; for no man could hear him for any length of time without being led captive by his eloquence. His imagination was rich and inventive, his taste, in general, pure and critical; and his memory uncommonly exact, full, and retentive. He attained a complete mastery of the whole compass of the English language; and, in the variety of use, as well as the choice of diction, for all the purposes of his public labors, he possessed a marvelous felicity. It gave to his style an air of originality, force, copiousness, and expressiveness, which struck the most careless observer. His power of amplification and illustration, whenever these were appropriate to his purpose, seemed almost inexhaustible; though he possessed, at the same time, the power of condensation, both of thought and language, to a most uncommon degree."

It would be easy to adduce passages from Mr. Pinkney's printed remains to justify the above remarks on the substance and manner of his speech. Take the following from his celebrated reply to Mr. King on the Missouri Question: "Time, that withers the strength of man and 'strews around him, like autumnal leaves, the ruins of his proudest monuments,' produces great vicissitudes in modes of thinking and feeling. It brings along with it, in its progress, new circumstances—new combinations and modifications of the old—generating new views, motives, and caprices—new fanaticisms of endless variety—in short, new every thing. We ourselves are always changing—and what to-day we have but a small desire to attempt, to-morrow becomes the object of our passionate aspirations.

"There is such a thing as enthusiasm, moral, religious, or political, or a compound of all three;—and it is wonderful what it will attempt, and from what imperceptible beginnings it sometimes rises into a mighty agent. Rising from some obscure or unknown source, it first shows itself a petty rivulet, which scarcely murmurs over the pebbles that obstruct its way—then it swells into a fierce torrent, bearing all before it—and then again, like some mountain stream which occasional rains have precipitated upon the valley, it sinks once more into a rivulet, and finally leaves its channel dry. Such a thing has happened. I do not say that it is now happening. It would not become me to say so. But if it should occur, woe to the unlucky territory that should be struggling to make its way into the Union at the moment when the opposing inundation was at its height, and at the same instant this wide Mediterranean of discretionary powers, which it seems is ours, should open all its sluices and, with a consentaneous rush, mingle with the turbid waters of the others."

The best preserved argument ever delivered in the Supreme Court, by Mr. Pinkney, was the famous one in the case of the ship Nereide. It was evidently prepared with great care, and surviving witnesses attest that it was delivered with great effect.

> " With menacing hand,
> Put forth as in the action of command,
> And eyes, that darted their red lightning down."

We are told that Lord Erskine, like many other characters of uncommon acuteness, had a morbid sensibility to the circumstances of the moment, which sometimes strangely enfeebled his presence of mind; any appearance of neglect in his audience, a cough, a yawn, or a whisper, even among the mixed multitude of the courts, and strong as he was there, has been known to disturb him visibly. Pinkney had much of this acute sensibility, and something of its weakness ; but in him it was manifested in an extraordinary attention to the elegancies of dress. When he had a cause of momentous interest to conduct, he elaborated every thing beforehand with the utmost care, and came before the supreme tribunal chastely, but richly adorned within and without. Conceive him, dressed in the top of fashion, perfumed, and gloved, in oratorical attitude, with the most imperious air, delivering the following passage, while the foam starts at his mouth and adds terror to his action and look : "I entreat your honors to endeavor a per- sonification of this motley notion, and to forgive me for presuming to intimate, that if, after you have achieved it, you pronounce the notion to be correct, you will have gone a great way to prepare us, by the authority of your opinion, to receive as credible history the worst parts of the mythology of the Pagan world. The Centaur and the Proteus of antiquity will be fabulous no longer. The prosopopœia to which I invite you is scarcely, indeed, within the power of fancy, even in her most riotous and capricious mood, when she is best able and most disposed to force incompatibilities into fleeting and shadowy combination, but if you can accomplish it, it will give you something like the kid and the lion, the lamb and the tiger portentously incor- porated, with ferocity and meekness co-existent in the result, and equal as motives of action. It will give you a modern Amazon, more strangely constituted than those with whom ancient fable peopled the borders of the Thermodon—her voice compounded of the tremendous shout of the Minerva of Homer and the gentle accents of a shepherdess of Arcadia—with all the faculties and inclinations of turbulent and masculine War, and all the retiring modesty of virgin Peace. We shall have in one personage the *pharetrata Camilla* of the Æneid, and the Peneian maid of the Metamorphosis. We shall have Neutrality, soft and gentle, and defenceless in herself, yet clad in the panoply of her warlike neighbors—with the frown of defiance upon her brow, and the smile of conciliation upon her lip—with the spear of Achilles in one hand and a lying protestation of innocence and helplessness unfolded in the other. Nay, if I may be allowed so bold a figure in a mere legal discussion, we shall have the branch of olive entwined around the bolt of Jove, and Neutrality in the act of hurling the former, under the deceitful cover of the latter."

The above is a fine instance of the transformation of metaphors into arguments; for as copious as the figures are, it will be found, on consulting the matters under discussion, that none of them are impertinent, provided the position assumed is correct. This, unfortunately for the eloquent advocate in this instance, was not the fact. The ethereal intellect of Chief Justice Marshall detected the sophism, and beautifully interpreted the law in its relation to this case. But the magnificence of the speech overruled imparted something of its charms to the judgment of the court, as it was rendered by its chief in language like the following:

"With a pencil dipped in the most vivid colors, and guided by the hand of a master, a splendid portrait has been drawn, exhibiting this vessel and her freighter as forming a single figure, composed of the most discordant materials of Peace and War. So exquisite was the skill of the artist, so dazzling the garb in which the figure was presented, that it required the exercise of that cold investigating faculty which ought always to belong to those who sit on this bench, to discover its only imperfection—its want of resemblance.

"The Nereide has not that centaur-like appearance which has been ascribed to her. She does not rove over the ocean, hurling the thunders of war, while sheltered by the olive branch of peace. She is an open and declared belligerent; claiming all the rights, and subject to all the dangers, of the belligerent character. The characters of the vessel and cargo remain as distinct in this as in any other case"

Mr. Pinkney was every way a patriot. When the British, under General Ross, meditated an attack on Washington, he accepted the command of a volunteer corps, and marched to Bladensburg, where he was severely wounded.

In March, 1816, he was again called to the diplomatic service of his country, being induced to accept the appointment of Minister Plenipotentiary to the court of Russia, and of special Minister to that of Naples. Soon after this double mission had been conferred upon him,

in a conversation with one of his friends, he said·
"There are those who wonder that I will go abroad,
however honorable the service. They know not how I
toil at the bar; they know not all my anxious days and
sleepless nights; I must breathe awhile; the bow for
ever bent will break;" "besides," he added, "I want to
see Italy; the orators of Britain I have heard, but I
want to visit that classic land, the study of whose poetry
and eloquence is the charm of my life; I shall set my
foot on its shores with feelings that I cannot describe,
and return with new enthusiasm, I hope new advantages,
to the habits of public speaking."

This is the language of a true man and a true devotee
at the shrine of excellence. He who does the most, is
the least vain of his work. Genius, like the Apostle
Paul, looks beyond the present, and sees things indescri-
oable. The Iliad, the Parthenon, York Minster, the
Transfiguration of the Vatican, and the Oratorio of
Creation, when executed, were thrown behind their
authors as incomplete embodiments of their thought.
No true orator yet was ever satisfied with his best
achievements. The greatest triumphs never make the
onsummate hero vain, for he has a vivid perception of
he immense interval that lies between what he does,
and what he conceives ought to be done.

In 1818, Mr. Pinkney solicited his recall from Russia,
which, being granted, he entered with fresh zeal upon
the practice of his profession in the Supreme Court.
In 1820, he took his seat in the American Senate, where
he displayed extraordinary abilities, while he still conducted an immense law business. " The success which

16

attended him every where," says his biographer, "was as much the effect of extraordinary diligence and labor as of his genius and rare endowments of mind. He was never satisfied with investigating his causes, and took infinite pains in explaining their facts and circumstances, and all the technical learning connected with them. He constantly continued the practice of private declamation as a useful exercise, and was in the habit of premeditating his pleadings at the bar, and his other public speeches,—not only as to the general order or method to be observed in treating his subject, the authorities to be relied on, and the leading topics of illustration, but frequently as to the principal passages and rhetorical embellishments. These he sometimes wrote out beforehand; not that he was deficient in facility or fluency, but in order to preserve the command of a correct and elegant diction."

Mr. Pinkney continued his professional labors at the session of the Court in 1822, with the intensest application and desire of success. On the 17th of February, he was attacked by a severe indisposition, brought on, doubtless, by great exertion in preparing for an important debate. On the 25th of the same month he expired, and was entombed in the Congressional burying-ground. Richard Henry Wilde, a great and good man, recently a victim to the pest in New Orleans, thus speaks of him in his "Stars of the Fourteenth Congress." "There was a gentleman from Maryland, whose ashes now sleep in our cemetery. It is not long since I stood by his tomb, and recalled him, as he was then, in all the pride and power of his genius. Among the first of his countrymen and cotemporaries as a jurist and statesman, first as an orator, he was, if not truly eloquent, the prince of rhetoricians. Nor did the soundness of his logic suffer any thing by a comparison with the richness and classical purity of the language in which he copiously poured forth those figurative illustrations of his argument, which enforced while they adorned it. But let others pronounce his eulogy. I must not. I feel as if his mighty spirit still haunted the scene of his triumphs, and, when I dared to wrong them, indignantly rebuked me."

Awed by this solemn dissuasive from a critical judgment on the merits of the departed master whose professional character we have attempted briefly to delineate, it is indeed difficult any farther to proceed. But it is because the subject of this sketch was so admirable as a whole, that we should the more carefully scan the degree and complexion of his faults. No one is perfect, and the imperfections of the best are the most instructive of all. It was not from the productions of mediocrity, but from the master-pieces of Euripides and Phidias, that the refined critics of Greece took their examples of error. " Go to the Parthenon," said the sculptor to his aspiring pupil, "and find not what bunglers but what great men have left undone."

We have seen that after Mr. Pinkney's long residence in London, and habitual attendance in Westminster Hall, he adopted a mode of address much more violent than that which graced the beginning of his public career. In the opinion of many judicious persons, the change was no improvement, and the elegance of his elocution did not keep pace with the augmentation of his intellectual stores. One who studied him much and wise y, has said that "his mind was of an order that could rather acquire than create. Argumentative and subtle; his figures of speech, his flights of fancy, cost him more labor than his argument; he almost always wrote them out, and committed them to memory. His fancy did not grow out of his subject, like the leaf from the summer bough; it was rather stuck on it, like a flower in a cap, for display; and a certain chilliness reminded us that it was a hot-house plant—a forced cultivation. Yet as a lawyer, I know not his superior; and no man could do better than to confide his case to Mr. Pinkney—because he never neglected it, through indolence, pleasure, or inattention; and, if he took it in hand, he attended to it, not more for emolument, than for success and fame." This is explicit, and, without doubt, just. From all we can learn, he was generally most frigid when he was most vociferous. This is usually the case. Unlike the dread scene at Sinai, the lightnings blaze and the thunders crash, but no law is delivered. Like begets like. When noisy declamation proceeds from the head rather than the heart, it is the head only that it will reach. He was erudite in legal knowledge, ingenious and stringent in argument, sometimes fanciful to excess, but not often truly impassioned. His tumult was more like the falling of an avalanche than the bursting of a volcano.

The practice of accurate premeditation and careful composition, we have several times observed, was habitual with Mr. Pinkney. In this respect he was directly opposed to that great master of the English forum, whom in many traits he resembled, Charles James Fox. Brougham says of the latter that, "One of his worst speeches, if not his worst, is that upon Francis, Duke of Bedford; and it is known to be almost the only one he ever much prepared, and the only one he ever corrected for the press." But that such careful preparation offers no necessary impediment to the most enrapturing oratory is evident from the example of Sheridan. It is notorious that he never made a speech of any importance, without first writing out its main points and most thrilling passages over and over again. Indeed, when his affairs became so deranged as to forbid such minute and elaborate preparation, he ceased to speak in public altogether. Still, in the instance of our countryman, the fastidiousness of his taste may have chilled the fervor of his emotions. That which serves best in a written disquisition is often least effective in spoken discourse. It has been said that a didactic poet is a contradiction in terms; the remark is equally true in respect to didactic eloquence. In a popular audience, it is never permitted to make the hearer a mere passive listener; his presence must be felt by the speaker, and he must not only be identified with the passing scene but kindled into sympathy by direct personal appeals.

Aristotle, speaking of certain old philosophers, compared them to undisciplined gladiators, who strike at random instead of right forward, and therefore fight with little effect, though they may occasionally deal a powerful blow. Our hero was too well trained to strike much at random, and he had too much force in all his well-aimed blows to fail in felling his unwary antagonist to the ground. From the ordinary placidity which characterizes the forensic eloquence of our age, Pinkney as widely differed, as the style of Addison differs from that of Dryden. The former has been likened to a clear and transparent stream, whose motion is too gentle to ruffle the surface or sully the purity of its waters; whilst that of Dryden "has the impetuosity of a torrent, which often tears the weeds from its banks, and stirs up the ooze from the bottom of its channel; but that ooze is mixed with grains of precious gold, and those weeds contain amongst them flowers of the most delightful hue and odor; whilst the very swiftness of the current fixes our regard more intensely than the tranquil surface of the gentler stream. He seems to have principally aimed at being strong and forcible, and to this object every minor consideration is sacrificed."

After all is said, it must be acknowledged that the faults of Mr. Pinkney's manner were lost in the effulgence of his matter, as the fervor of the sun hides its own spots. There was a vast body as well as momentum in his argument; a power that generates success, daunts opposition, and annihilates resistance. Like the giants of ancient mythology, he was in his sphere and mode an ideal of strength. For ever should he be admired for his industry and patriotism. With all the advantage of uncommon outward talents, so intense and habitual was his love of intellectual improvement, that he considered every hour deducted from study as worthy of a black pebble. Titus never more deeply mourned the loss of a day. What the greatest of Irish orators said of the best of English statesmen may not unjustly be said of Pinkney, and to have deserved the encomium is an honor sufficient to prompt and reward the ambition of any man. "No state chicanery, no narrow system of vicious politics, no idle contests for mere party victories, regardless of principle, ever sunk him to the vulgar level of *hr. so* called great."

CHAPTER XIV.

WILLIAM WIRT,

THE ELEGANT ADVOCATE.

ELOQUENT and upright lawyers have ever been among the first to resist oppression and promote human weal. Demosthenes, who roused the Athenians to resist the tyranny of Philip, was an advocate. Cicero, the antagonist of oppressors and the savior of his country, was an advocate. When Charles the First commenced his despotic exactions, it was the advocates of England who first breasted the torrent. France was revolutionized by advocates; and her best patriots at this moment are the ablest leaders at her bar. When the enormities of Great Britain threatened subjugation to her colonies in the west, it was the voice of such advocates as Otis, Henry and Adams, that, like a Paladin's horn, roused the people of America to conquest and liberty. From the first planting of republican institutions in our land, advocates have perpetually kindled the beacon-lights of patriotism and law—"hope of the fettered slave and glory of the free." Prominent in this noble class was

William Wirt. His parents were a Swiss and a

German, who resided, at the time of his birth, Nov. 8th, 1772, at Bladensburg, near Washington. His father died when he was an infant ; and his mother when he was but eight years old. Like most great men, he was early left orphaned of every thing but resolution and hope, to antagonize with worldly adversity, and, in the midst of storms, to build his fortunes.

After suitable preparatory studies, he went to Leesburg, Virginia, and when seventeen years old, com: menced the study of law in the office of Mr. Swann. He seems to have prosecuted his studies with great diligence and success. Among other good influences under which his mind was there developed, he was ever of the opinion that he derived much advantage from the beauty and sublimity of the natural scenery which encompassed him. Undoubtedly, his conclusion on that point was correct. There is always a striking resemblance between the predominating character of local scenery and the minds matured under its influence. Edmund Burke grew up amid the most gorgeous scenery of Ireland, and Daniel Webster was cradled in the bosom of the White Mountains of New Hampshire, where all in nature is cool, colossal, sublime.

Mr. Wirt obtained his license to practice law in 1792, a few days before he was twenty years old. The first cause in which he was engaged was in Culpepper County, on which occasion his argument is said to have been firm, collected and successful.

For several years, he resided in the family of Dr. G. Gilmer, whose daughter he married in 1795. The Doctor had a high professional and classical reputation.
16*

and was on familiar terms with the first men of the day. Here Wirt became acquainted with Monroe, Madison, Jefferson, and other eminent citizens, whose learning he emulated, and in whose society he greatly improved.

After the death of his wife, in 1799, he was elected Clerk of the House of Delegates of Virginia, which brought him into the sphere of some of his greatest achievements. His first appearance in Richmond, as a speaker, was upon the 4th of July, 1800, and in the celebrated trial of Callender. In 1802, he was elected Chancellor of the Lower District of the Chancery Court, held at Williamsburg. In the autumn of that year he married Miss Gamble, who survived him. During thirteen years, the time of his residence at Richmond and Norfolk, he conducted a great many civil and criminal causes, and competed successfully with the Tazewells, Taylors, Wickhams, Randolphs, and other distinguished men who adorned the Virginia bar.

One of the first trials which engaged his attention, after his return to Richmond, and which gave him a wide reputation, was the prosecution of Aaron Burr, in 1807. To him, as much as to any of the counsel engaged, belonged the commendation of the court, that " a degree of eloquence, seldom displayed on any occasion, embellished solidity of argument and depth of research."

In 1808, Mr. Wirt was elected to the House of Delegates from Richmond, and during that year drew up several important State papers. The British Spy was written in 1803 ; the Old Bachelor, in 1812; and in 1817, he published the Life of Patrick Henry.

In 1816, Mr. Madison appointed Mr. Wirt District-Attorney for Virginia ; and in the following year, at the age of forty-five, he was appointed by Mr. Munroe, Attorney-General of the United States. Unlike his predecessors, he removed permanently to Washington, and continued there throughout eleven years and four months, more than twice the time the office had been held by any other. He was very strict in his attention to official duties, and exceedingly laborious. He instituted a new practice in the office, and not only filed every document for future reference, but made a regular record of every official opinion and letter he wrote Three large volumes of this kind he left for the use of the future historian of the jurisprudence of the country, more valuable material, no doubt, than can be gathered from all the previous incumbents of his office since the government was formed.

In 1826, at the request of the citizens of Washington, he delivered an eulogy on Adams and Jefferson. It was deemed one of the most masterly productions which that melancholy event occasioned. In the winter of 1822, he was severely attacked by a disease resembling apoplexy, and was compelled to resign his position as Attorney-General.

But he did not cease to prosecute with ardor the duties of his profession. His aid was sought by individuals, by corporations, by States, and even by the government itself, in matters of the greatest importance. He visited every part of the Union, in his professional capacity, and every where commanded admiration by his great legal and personal worth.

Having now glanced over the greater part of his career as an advocate, we propose in ampler detail to delineate his character and examine his claims on our regard.　Let us inquire into his scholarship, his efficiency as a lawyer, and his excellence as a man.

Mr. Wirt enjoyed no collegiate course of studies in early life, but from the first he was habitually studious, and before the meridian of his manhood he had become a ripe proficient in the classics, both ancient and modern.　Horace, Virgil, Cicero, and Seneca, were his favorite Latin authors ; the first was a constant inmate of his valise in all his visitations to county courts, and often his companion late at night.　His juvenile tastes inclined to works of fiction ; but in maturer life he preferred Bacon, Boyle, Locke, and Hooker.　His reading was incessant, discriminating, and comprehensive.　He ranged over the whole domain of letters and science with irrepressible ardor.　It was his custom to prosecute the study of the philosophy of law always in connection with the philosophy of mind.　He mingled the investigation of material sciences with the highest spiritual truths.　Astronomy, with the natural phenomena connected therewith, was a favorite theme with him, but moral science was his master passion.　He garnered rich stores of diversified knowledge, much of which was contributed by the graceful Nine under Apollo's care ; but, in general his weapons were of a sterner kind, many of the most potent shafts of his quiver being drawn from the glorious armory of Hooker and Chillingworth. About the time some poetical extracts from Wirt's famous speech against Burr were widely published, an eminent jurist expressed to one of his most intimate and learned friends a doubt as to his possessing much abstruse legal erudition. " Your estimate is wrong," was the reply. "His true character is that of a laborious, profound lawyer, more conversant with the *black letter* than even with works of taste, poetry, and fiction."

It is believed that Mr. Wirt, was, indeed, liberally educated to an eminent degree. His knowledge of history, of the ancient and modern classics, and of legal science, was varied and profound, while his political information and sagacity equalled his other accomplishments. A mere acquaintance with the technicalities of the law will not constitute a successful lawyer in America. Eloquence goes far to make the powerful advocate here. To this primary requisite, extensive learning of a general character, and elegant acquisitions which shall fortify and adorn that eloquence, must harmoniously unite. His outfit for professional strife must be practical as well as profound. " He who has collected his knowledge in solitude, must learn its application by mixing with mankind," said Doctor Johnson. On reviewing Mr. Wirt's qualifications as an advocate, and the successful use he made of his powers, we think that it may be said of him justly, as was said of George Canning, whom, in certain points he greatly resembled: " He was any thing rather than a mere scholar. In him were combined, with a rich profusion, the most lively, original fancy—a happily retentive and ready memory—singular powers of lucid statement—and occasionally wit in all its varieties, now biting and sarcastic to overwhelm an antagonist—now pungent or giving point to an argument—now playful for mere amusement, and bringing relief to a tedious statement, or lending a charm to dry chains of close reasoning."

It is rare that genius is not conscious of its own latent powers. However discouraged and prostrate the aspirant may be at the outset, every great man experiences moments when he rises in dignified pride against those who persecute or forget him, and, without waiting for the commemorative statues which admiring posterity are sure to erect, confidently crowns himself with his own hands.

> "There have been those that from the deepest caves,
> And cells of night, and fastnesses, below
> The stormy dashing of the ocean-waves,
> Down, farther down than gold lies hid, have nurs'd
> A quenchless hope, and watch'd their time, and burst
> On the bright day like wakeners from their graves."

Wirt wrote the "British Spy," while he was a student, or immediately after he commenced the practice of his profession. His eloquent description of the *novi homines*, the new men, was to no one more applicable than himself. The magnificent yearnings embodied in the essays written in early manhood on the means and purposes of eloquence, betrayed his prevailing tastes and foretokened his success. "Genius," says Du Bos, "is an aptitude, which man has received from nature to perform well and easily, that which others can do but indifferently, and with a great deal of pains. We learn to execute things for which we have a genius, with as much facility as we speak our own mother tongue." There can be no doubt that Wirt's genius was of the highest order, but he began and continued through his whole splendid career under the deep and abiding conviction that eminent success depended on the most assiduous self-cultivation. His favorite pursuits indicated his native capacities, and his extraordinary industry justified the glowing prophecies of his most sagacious friends. Every person who has decided tastes and fervid aspirations, in other words, who has a strong individuality of his own, will be forcibly moved by corresponding traits in the objects he contemplates and the excellence he adores. A man's favorite pursuits and most admired authors, even the works of art he most enjoys, are a sure index to the calibre and complexion of his mind. The peculiar delight felt in a given pursuit or recreation, if carefully analyzed, will be found mainly to depend on the resemblance between the object admired and the mental character of the devotee.

What Mr. Wirt's prevailing passion and pursuits were we may easily learn from the following extract from an admirable letter of advice he wrote in the maturity of his life to a young gentleman engaged in the study of law. His benevolence and wisdom are therein signalized. "It requires a previous acquaintance with the student, to ascertain the natural condition of his various powers, in order to know which requires the spur and which the rein. In some minds, imagination overpowers and smothers all the faculties; in others, reason, like a sturdy oak, throws all the rest into a sickly shade. Some men have a morbid passion for the study of poetry—others, of mathematics, &c., &c. All this may be corrected by discipline, so far as it may

be judicious to correct it.   I believe in all sound minds
the germ of all the faculties exists, and may, by skillful
management, be wooed into expansion ; but they exist
naturally in different degrees of health and strength,
and as this matter is generally left to impulses of nature
in each individual, the highest and strongest germs get
the start—give impulse and direction to the efforts of
each mind—stamp its character and shape its destiny.
As education, therefore, now stands among us, each
man must be his own preceptor in this respect, and by
turning his eyes upon himself, and describing the comparative action of his own powers, discover which of
them requires the most tone—which, if any, less.   We
must take care, however, not to make an erroneous
estimate of the relative value of the faculties, and thus
commit the sad mistake of cultivating the showy at the
expense of the solid.

"A brave and pure spirit is worth more than '*half the
battle*,' not only in preparing for life, but in all its conflicts.   *Take it for granted, there is no excellence without great labor*.   Wishing, and sighing, and imagining,
and dreaming of greatness will never make you great
If you would get to the mountain's top on which the temple of fame stands, it will not do to *stand still*, looking,
admiring, and wishing you were there.   You must gird
up your loins, and go to work with all the indomitable
energy of Hannibal scaling the Alps.   Laborious study,
and diligent observation of the world, are both indispensable to the attainment of eminence.   By the former,
you must make yourself master of all that is known of
science and letters ; by the latter you must know *man*.

at large, and particularly the character and genius of your countrymen. You must cultivate assiduously the habits of *reading, thinking, and observing.* Understand your own language, grammatically, critically, throughout; learning its origin, or, rather, its various origins, which you may learn from Johnson's and Webster's Prefaces to their large dictionaries. Learn all that is delicate and beautiful, as well as strong, in the language, and master all its stores can teach. You must never be satisfied with the surface of things; probe them to the bottom, and let nothing go till you understand it as thoroughly as your powers will enable you. When you have mastered all the past conquests of science, you will understand what Socrates meant by saying, that he knew only enough to be sure that he knew nothing. Seize the moment of excited curiosity on any subject to solve your doubts; for if you let it pass, the desire may never return, and you may remain in ignorance. The habits which I have been recommending are not merely for college, but for life. Franklin's habits of constant and deep excogitation clung to him to his last hour. Form these habits now; learn all that may be learned at your university, and bring all your acquisitions and your habits to the study of the law, which you say is your profession:—and when you come to this study, come resolved to master it—not to play in its shallows, but to sound its depths. Resolve to be the first lawyer of your age, in the depth, extent, variety, and accuracy of your legal learning. Master the science of pleading—master Coke upon Littleton— and Coke's and Plowden's Reports—master Fearne on

Contingent Remainders and Executory Devises, till you can sport and play familiarly with its most subtle distinctions. Lay your foundations deep, and broad, and strong, and you will find the superstructure comparatively light work. It is not by shrinking from difficult parts of the science, but by courting them, and overcoming them, that a man rises to professional greatness. There is a deal of learning that is dry, dark, cold, revolting—but it is an old feudal castle, in perfect preservation, which the legal architect who aspires to the first honors of his profession will delight to explore and learn all the uses to which the various parts used to be put; and he will the better understand, enjoy, and relish the progressive improvements of the science in modern times. You must be a master in every branch of the science that belongs to your profession ; the laws of nature and of nations, the civil law, and the law merchant, the maritime law, &c., the charte and outline of all which you see in Blackstone's Commentaries. Thus covered with the panoply of professional learning, a master of the pleadings, practice, and cases, and at the same time *a great constitutional philosophic lawyer*, you must keep way, also, with the march of general science. Do you think this is requiring too much ? Look at Brougham, and see what man can do if well armed and resolved.—You must, indeed, be a great lawyer! but it will not do to be a mere lawyer— more especially as you are properly turning your mind, also, to the political service of your country, and to the study and practice of eloquence. You must, therefore, be a political lawyer and historian; thoroughly versed in the Constitution and laws of your country, and fully acquainted with *all its statistics*, and the history of all the leading measures which have distinguished the several administrations—you must study the debates in Congress, and observe what have been the actual effects upon the country of the various measures that have been the most strenuously contested in their origin. You must be a master of the science of political economy, aud especially of *financiering*, of which so few of our countrymen know anything.

But it is time to close this letter. You may ask for instructions adapted to improvements in eloquence. This is a subject for a treatise, not for a letter. Cicero, however, has summed up the whole art in a few words; it is *"apte—distincte—ornate—dicere"*—to speak to the purpose—to speak clearly and distinctly—to speak gracefully:—to be able *to speak to the purpose*, you must understand your subject and all that belongs to it:—and then your *thoughts and method* must be *clear in themselves, and clearly and distinctly enunciated:*—and lastly, your voice, style, delivery and gesture, must be *graceful and delightfully impressive.* In relation to this subject, I would strenuously advise you two things: *Compose much, and often, and carefully with reference to this same rule, "apte, distincte, ornate,"* and let your *conversation* have reference to the same objects. I do not mean that you should be *elaborate and formal* in your ordinary conversation. Let it be *perfectly simple and natural,* but *always in good time,* (to speak as the musician,) and well enunciated.

With regard to the style of eloquence that you sha'l

adopt, that must depend very much on your own taste
and genius. You are not disposed, I presume, to be a
humble imitator of any man. If you are, you may bid
farewell to the hope of eminence in this walk. None
are mere imitators to whom Nature has given original
powers. If you are endowed with such a portion of
the spirit of oratory as can advance you to a high rank
in this walk, your manner *will be* your own. I can only
tell you that the *florid and Asiatic style* is not the taste
of the age. The *strong*, and the *rugged and abrupt*,
are far more successful. Bold propositions, boldly and
briefly expressed,—pithy sentences—nervous common
sense—strong phrases—the *feliciter audax*, both in language and conception—well-compacted periods—sudden
and strong masses of light—an apt adage—a keen sarcasm—a merciless personality—a mortal thrust—these
are the beauties and deformities that now make a
speaker the most interesting. A gentleman and a Christian will conform to the reigning taste so far only as his
principles and habits of *decorum* will permit. We require that a man should *speak to the purpose and come
to the point*—that he should *instruct and convince*. To
do this, his mind must move with great strength and
power; reason should be manifestly his master faculty—
argument should predominate throughout; but these
great points secured, wit and fancy may cast their lights
around his path, provided the wit be courteous as well
as brilliant, and the fancy chaste and modest. But they
must be kept well in the back-ground, for they are dangerous allies; and a man had better be without them,
than to show them in front, or to show them too often.'

We are not aware that a better code of precepts than the above of the same length exists. How far Mr. Wirt governed himself by his own rules, will be indicated, as, in the second place, we proceed to inquire into his efficiency as an advocate.

In his personal appearance, he had much about him to propitiate popular favor. He possessed a fine person, manners remarkably conciliating, and colloquial powers of the highest order. The most casual glance upon him in repose or action, impressed the beholder with an instinctive sense of his superiority. His natural air was dignified and commanding; his countenance was broad, open, manly and expressive; his eye was full of fire and feeling; his mouth denoted mingled humor and firmness; and his whole appearance was truly oratorical. His frame was large, but agile; his nose was Roman, his complexion pale and marked with lines of thought; his forehead was not high, but broad; his hair was sandy, and his head bald on the top. He had great original powers of action, but spoke with a chastened dignity which commanded respect bordering on awe. Of him it might have been said, as Dryden in his time declared of Harte, that "kings and princes might have come to him, and taken lessons how to comport themselves with dignity." Wirt's impressiveness resulted from the aggregate of a Ciceronian person, a Chatham face, the voice of Anthony, and the mental qualities of Irving and Bowditch,—a model of grace and a master of dialectics,—poetry and philosophy combined. He had much of the acuteness of Marshall, and all the intrepidity of Pinkney; but in his composition, there was no want of fluency, and no insolence or exultation of manner. Judgment and imagination lay in the balance of his mind in such delicate and equal proportions that the scale seldom trembled, and the splendors that encompassed the glorious combination in his mature life were never obscured.

Such an advocate will be heard. The envious and fastidious may pronounce him vague, impalpable or diffuse, and yet all are compelled to listen to him with that spell-bound emotion which is always produced by noble and harmonious eloquence emanating from an honest and impassioned heart. Wirt was not a stranger to the popular esteem which such talents command.

His pathos was refined and thrilling. He could subdue all his admirable powers of mind and voice to those delicate tones which go directly to the heart, like zephyrs changed to angelic strains as they traverse Æolian strings. Such was his power when he described female innocence and beauty abandoned by him who had basked in her smiles, and who should have prevented the winds of heaven from visiting her too roughly, now left "shivering at midnight on the winter banks of the Ohio, and mingling her tears with the torrent, which froze as they fell."

> " Never tone
> So thrilled through nerve, and vein, and bone,
> His eyebrow dark and eye of fire
> Showed spirit proud and prompt to ire ;
> Yet lines of thought upon his cheek
> Did deep design and counsel speak."

Those who were familiar with the clearness, melody,

and flexibility of Mr. Wirt's voice when at the height
of his fame, and his distinct, emphatic, and unembarrass-
ed pronunciation, may be surprised to learn that when
he entered on the practice of his profession, "his utterance was thick—his tongue clumsy, and apparently too
large—his pronunciation of words clipping—and, when
excited by feeling, his voice unmanageable; sometimes
bursting out in loud, harsh, indistinct, and imperfect
articulation." All this he overcame through persevering cultivation. The miracle of the pebbles performed
by Demosthenes was repeated in his own person. In
all his life he was a passionate and persevering votary
of elocution in the broadest sense of the term. First, as
to language, as Dryden said, in one of his criticisms,
"the third happiness of this writer's imagination is elocution, or the art of clothing or adorning that thought
so found and varied, in apt, significant, and sounding
words." But over and above the mere verbiage of his
spoken thought, he gave great attention to gesture,
which is the language of the body. "The hands are the
common language of mankind," said Cicero, and another
distinguished Roman orator was accustomed to declare,
that "he was never fit to talk, till he had warmed his
arm." So important is a graceful manner in public address, that the prince of ancient rhetoricians laid it down
as a primary maxim, that "it is this alone that governs
in speaking; without which the best orator is of no
value, and is often defeated by one, in other respects,
much his inferior."

"Action is eloquence, and the eyes of the ignorant
More learned than the ears."

The art with which Mr. Wirt came at length to conceal his art was consummate—it was carried, perhaps,
to a fault.   He became so fastidious as to the perfection
of his oratorical manner that he too sternly repressed
those natural outbursts of emotion which constitute the
principal source of eloquence.   It required the most
sagacious eye to detect the artifice, but a master would
see it—or, we should say, the fault was felt rather than
seen.   What was wanting in his ordinary efforts, was
the talismanic power of evoking and controlling the profounder passions of our nature.   Not altogether inappli-
cable to Wirt is the criticism which an English critic
applied to Canning, whom we have already intimated
he resembled: "His declamation, though often powerful, always beautifully ornate, never deficient in admirable diction, was certainly not of the very highest class.
It wanted depth; it came from the mouth, not from the
heart; and it tickled or even filled the ear rather than
penetrated the bosom of the listener.   The orator never
seemed to forget himself and be absorbed in his theme:
he was not carried away by his passions, and carried
not his audience along with him.   An actor stood before us, a first-rate one, no doubt; but still an actor; and
we never forget that it was a representation we were
witnessing, not a real scene.   The Grecian artist was
of the second class only, at whose fruit the *birds* peck-
ed; while, on seeing Parrhasius's picture, *men* cried out
to draw aside the curtain "

But there was no radical deficiency in Mr Wirt of
acute sensibility and refined imagination.   His mind

originally was like a prism of a thousand angles, through which every ray of thought was made to dazzle the spectator with innumerable resplendent beams. In his early productions, he resembles the gorgeous bird of Juno that exhibits with ostentation its plumage all bedecked with emerald, sapphire and gold. When there is an excess of rhetorical ornament, the superfluity palls on the taste, like a surfeit of honey. Fires that burn with steady and perpetual flame are impressive, as well as useful; but one is soon rendered cold and discontented in the presence of transient coruscations, the result of idle pyrotechnic skill, which flash for a moment in gaudy hues that obscure the stars, and the next moment are lost in the deepened gloom of night. Natural and impassioned eloquence speaks in the lucid vernacular of all men, and is comprehended by all; while that which is artificial, be it never so polished, is with difficulty understood; one recites its formal prettiness on the brink of the abyss where truth lies drowning; the other descends with energy and averts her fate. The effectiveness of poetry and painting consists in their power of moving and pleasing; and eloquence, a kindred art, is valuable in proportion as it persuades. To insure the desired result, the production must possess merits beyond those of mere elegance and regularity. Connoisseurs never examine the works of the old masters without perceiving that they evidently considered the graces of execution not as the ultimate end of their art, but only as means for displaying excellences of a far superioı kind. The grand aim of an orator is not to be com-

17

mended for the symmetry and beauty of his discourse, things that have comparatively little persuasive virtue, but to convince our judgments by the force of his arguments, and to move our hearts by the pathos of his appeals. The sources of these indispensable materials must be native to the soul, while art can only supply their judicious arrangement and economical use. In the highest order of eloquence, the powers of language, music and painting are combined; and even this concentration of forces is augmented by the momentum which natural emotion and appropriate gesture impart to it. We are not so much roused and inflamed by what a great original mind tells us, as by what he enables us to tell ourselves. No intelligent listener ever heard a first rate speaker, without bearing away with him the consciousness of abilities he never felt before. The oration will seem not to have been very remarkable, since it was so natural; and the hearer who came without an idea in his head, goes away quite fluent with admirable comments on the theme. The truth is, his torpid nature has been vitalized by coming in contact with an ardent heart; his senses have been enlivened, his intellect has been invigorated, and the stagnant fountain of his affections has suddenly sprung up responsive to the call of generous sentiments.

The limited views of persons prejudiced and dwarfed in their own character, do not allow them to comprehend that universality of talent which distinguishes men of the highest order. When they observe the presence of the agreeable, they exclude the substantial;

when they discover dexterity, agility, and other physical graces, they cannot admit, as compatible with
these, the more severe and effective graces of the mind.
Persons of one idea, and accustomed to single and exclusive views, find it hard to credit the historical fact,
that Socrates, the prince of philosophers, was skillful in
the dance; they are equally unwilling to believe that
elegant accomplishments may be intimately associated
with attributes the most vigorous and profound. Such
used to be the imputation cast upon Mr. Wirt, but
nobly, on a memorable occasion, did he repel and dis-
prove it. The passage is well worthy of careful perusal,
as it illustrates many of its author's qualities—his imagination—his fluency—his sarcasm giving force to his
logic—his noble bearing and indignant eloquence.

To the insinuating depreciations in which Mr. Wick-
ham had indulged, in the trial of Burr, Wirt replied as
follows : " I shall now proceed to examine the motion
itself, and to answer the argument of the gentleman
who opened it. I will treat that gentleman with candor.
I will not follow the example which he has set me on a
very recent occasion. I will not complain of flowers
and graces where none exist. I will not, like him, in
reply to an argument as naked as a sleeping Venus, but
certainly not half so beautiful, complain of the painful
necessity I am under, in the weakness and decrepitude
of logical vigor, of lifting first this flounce and that
furbelow, before I can reach the wished-for point of
attack. I keep no flounces or furbelows ready manufac-
tured and hung up for use in the millinery of my fancy,

and if I did, I think I should not be so indiscreetly impatient to get rid of my wares, as to put them off on im-
proper occasions. I cannot promise to interest you by
any classical and elegant allusions to the pure pages of
Tristram Shandy. I cannot give you a squib or a
rocket in every period. For my own part, I have
always thought these flashes of wit (if they deserve that
name), I have always thought these meteors of the brain
which spring up with such exuberant abundance in the
speeches of that gentleman, which play on each side of
the path of reason, or sporting across it with fantastic
motion decoy the mind from the true point in debate,
no better evidence of the soundness of the argument
with which they are connected, nor, give me leave to
add, the vigor of the brain from which they spring, than
those vapors which start from our marshes and blaze
with a momentary combustion, and which floating on
the undulations of the atmosphere beguile the traveller
into bogs and brambles, are evidences of the firmness
and solidity of the earth from which they proceed. I
will endeavor to meet the gentleman's propositions in
their full force and to answer them fairly. I will not, as
I am advancing towards them with my mind's eye,
measure the height, breadth and power of the proposition, if I find it beyond my strength, halve it; if still
beyond my strength, quarter it; if still necessary, sub-
divide it into eighths ; and when by this process I have
reduced it to the proper standard, take one of these sections and toss it with an air of elephantine strength and
superiority. If I find myself capable of conducting, by

a fair course of reasoning, any one of his propositions to an absurd conclusion, I will not begin by stating that absurd conclusion as the proposition itself which I am going to encounter. I will not, in commenting on the gentleman's authorities, thank the gentleman with sarcastic politeness for introducing them, declare that they concluded directly against him, read just so much of the authority as serves the purpose of that declaration, omitting that which contains the true point of the the case which makes against me ; nor if forced by a direct call to read that part also, will I content myself by running over it as rapidly and inarticulately as I can, throw down the book with a theatrical air, and exclaim, ' just as I said,' when I know it is just as I have not said. I know that by adopting these arts, I might raise a laugh at the gentleman's expense, but I should be very little little pleased with myself if I were capable of enjoying a laugh procured by such means. I know, too, that by adopting such arts, there will always be those standing around us, who have not comprehended the whole merits of the legal discussion, with whom I might shake the character of the gentleman's science and judgment as a lawyer. I hope I shall never be capable of such a wish, and I had hoped that the gentleman himself felt so strongly that proud, that high, aspiring and ennobling magnanimity, which I had been told conscious talents rarely fail to inspire, that he would have disdained a poor and fleeting triumph gained by means like these."

It is a fine trait in Mr. Wirt, that his mind became greatly enriched and chastely splendid, as he advanced

in years. His oratorical talent was none the less valuable for being developed in the vigor of manhood ; like
the blossoming of the aloe, although long delayed, the
unfolding of his riper genius was marvelous. At the
period when ordinarily the animal spirits flag, and fancy
grows dim, his intellect blazed out, like the sacred flame
on the altar of the fire-worshipper, at the very moment
of threatened extinction. In this respect, he resembled
Edmund Burke, and the most eloquent of the Hebrew
prophets, Isaiah. He was to the last accustomed to
invest the most grave and important topics with a
graceful and charming spirit, and yet he was one of the
most thoroughly practical men of his day. The flowers
with which he adorned his discourse were as strong of
stem as they were beautiful and full of odor. The
results of the most comprehensive and judicious reading
were constantly poured forth through his pen and living
voice. Imagination blended with reason and enhanced
its force. Running through his elaborate masculine
composition,

> "Its veins like silver shine,
>   Or as the chaster hue
> Of pearls, that grace some sultan's diadem."

He never allowed indolence to "hang clogs on the
nimbleness of his soul," but by constant struggles
upward, he "plumed his feathers and let grow his
wings." Every theme he touched he adorned. Even
Burr's infamy was glorified by the oratory which
detailed and avenged it. It is the prerogative of
patriotic impeachment to perpetuate the memory of

those who would otherwise soon perish in ignominous oblivion. Philip and Catiline, Verres and Hastings, owe their most enduring fame to the accident of being scathed by the bolts of immortal eloquence. This great prerogative Wirt possessed in an eminent degree. In original and striking combinations, rich perspectives, dramatic groupings, and the happy union of rigid argument and elegant illustration, he was hardly excelled. The secret of this extraordinary power lay in his love of research, and fidelity to his profession.

Says Mr. Southard: "His labor was without limit. I know of but one individual (Pinkney) who in this respect equalled him. They both improved steadily and rapidly, to the last moment, as advocates, counsellors, and scholars; exhibiting to the young aspirant after fame the true and only road to eminence; and proving to demonstration, the error of the common opinion, that the mind attains its usefulness, and vigor, and abundance, before the age of forty or forty-five; and that the struggle afterwards is to maintain its strength and acquirements, and to use them for the individual and public benefit. Their progress in intellectual wealth, and its active use, was at no period more rapid than the last fifteen years of their lives."

The devotion of Mr. Wirt's whole soul to the interests of his clients was proverbial. A lawyer who does not believe in his heart that the man for whom he pleads ought to have a verdict, will be very likely not to obtain one. His own unbelief will be the first thing lodged in the bosoms of the jury, and no perfunctionary protestations will remove it. Swedenbourg professed to

have seen in the spiritual world a group of persons endeavoring in vain to express a proposition which they
did not believe; but they could not, though in repeated
attempts they distorted their lips with indignation.

As an instance in which it is well known his private
friendship gave additional force to his professional
energy, take the following description by an eye-witness,
Mr. Thomas. It also illustrates this elegant advocate's
happy tact in quotation.

"One of the most interesting cases ever witnessed at
the Baltimore bar was a trial in a mandamus case, in
which the right to a church was contested. Mr. Duncan had been established in the ministry, in Baltimore,
by a number of Scotch Presbyterians, in an obscure
edifice. His talents drew such a congregation that it
soon became necessary to build a larger one. It was
done; and in the progress of events the pastor preached
a more liberal doctrine than he had at first inculcated.
His early supporters remained not only unchanged in
their faith, but they resolved to have it preached to
them by one with whom they could entirely agree upon
religious matters. The majority of the congregation
agreed with Mr. Duncan. A deep schism arose in the
divided flock which could not be healed, and which was
eventually, by a writ of mandamus, carried before a
legal tribunal. Mr. Taney was counsel for the old
school side, and Mr. Wirt for the defendants. The
court-room, during the trial, was crowded with the
beauty and fashion of the monumental city. It was
such a display of eloquence, and a full appreciation of
it, as is seldom witnessed. Mr. Wirt was always happy

in making a quotation, and in concluding this cause he made one of his happiest. After alluding to the old school members, who, it has been said, were Scotchmen, and after dwelling upon the tragedy of Macbeth, the scenes of which are laid in Scotland, he described their preacher as being in the condition of Macbeth's guest ; and said, after a stern rebuke upon them, that though they should succeed in their cause, which he felt confi-dent they would not, they would feel like the guilty thane.

> "This Duncan,
> Hath borne his faculties so meek, hath been
> So clear in his great office, that his virtues
> Will plead like angels, trumpet-tongued, against
> The deep damnation of his taking off."

"The quotation was made with such oratorical effect, that there was a deep silence when Mr. Wirt took his seat, which was succeeded by repeated outbreaks of ap-plause." He gained the case.

A few words only must suffice in relation to Mr Wirt's character as a man. His principles of conduct were of an exalted order, guided by strict integrity, and crowned by the purest moral worth. He never gave, nor willingly received, offence. The querulous, in dealing with him, found themselves in the predicament described by Dr. Johnson, when he said of Sir Joshua Reynolds, that he was one of those men with whom, if a person desired to quarrel, he would have been most at a loss how to abuse.

Above all, Mr. Wirt was a humble and consistent Christian. He had thoroughly examined the evidences of our holy religion and openly became one of its

17*

brightest ornaments. The last acts he performed, on the day he was seized with his fatal sickness, were those of private and public devotion. It was the Sabbath. He lingered a few days in severe physical suffering, and then expired in the calm grandeur of triumphant faith.

CHAPTER XV.

THOMAS ADDIS EMMET,

THE ORATOR OF DEEP FEELING

IRELAND, in its natural features, national spirit, and moral history, is a land of strange contrasts. Ancient sovereignty and modern servitude, the noblest virtues and most ignoble vices, intellects of the greatest splendor and hearts of the warmest affection, alas ! often blinded with excess of passion and chilled under tyrannic wrongs,—these are some of her national peculiarities and mental traits. Her poets are among the oldest and the best ; her literati shine brightly amid the chief (fairest) luminaries of art and science ; her martial heroes have never been excelled ; and of her statesmen it is enough to say, that for centuries they have been what they now are, the mightiest leaders of Parliament. While they had national councils of their own, they shone supremely in legislative wisdom and justice · when forced into alliance with England, they eclipsed the splendors they encountered. The brightest names in English literature and generalship, science and jurisprudence, are Irish.

But it is in eloquence, especially, that Ireland may

safely challenge the most refined nations of modern times. Like all things human, it has its faults, some-times seen in a superabundance of imagery, and more often expressed in exaggerated sentiments; but its merits predominate, and are supassingly grand, in force, fervor, passion, imagination and argument. An un-broken series of consummate orators illuminate the dreary history of injured and abused Ireland, like so many pillars of fire. Prominent among these stands the name of Thomas Addis Emmet.

He was born in the city of Cork, in 1765. His parents were highly respectable inhabitants of that city. At an early age, the son was placed at the University of Dublin, and designed by his father for the profession of medicine. Having completed his classical course, he was removed to Edinburgh, where he pursued his medi-cal studies. On the death of his elder brother, who was a member of the Irish bar, his parents wished him to change his professional studies; to which desire he as-sented. He went to London, read two years in the Temple, and attended the courts at Westminster. Hav-ing prosecuted his preparatory studies with great care, he returned to Dublin, and commenced practice. His talents, natural and acquired, were seen to be of a high order, and he soon obtained distinction and business.

It was at this period that a spirit of rebellion against regal oppression shook Ireland to the centre. Emmet was too ardent in character, and too enthusiastically attached to his country to remain indifferent. He deeply imbibed the indignant resentment which every where prevailed against British connection and control.

When, in 1795, the societies of united Irishmen were revived, Emmet not only joined them, but soon became a prominent leader. Their avowed object was revolution, and independence for Ireland. He boldly acted as one of the grand executive committee of the societies, when they were computed as consisting of at least five hundred thousand men. On March 12, 1798, he was arrested and committed to prison at Dublin, as a conspirator. In July, after a severe confinement, an interview took place between Emmet and Lord Castlereagh, at Dublin Castle, and it was agreed that he and the other State prisoners should be permitted to go to the United States, as soon as they had made certain disclosures of their plans of revolution, in respect to the alliance which it was supposed had been projected between the united Irishmen and France. A memoir of disclosures was delivered, August 4th, but all names involved were inflexibly withheld. Further examinations took place, and Mr. Emmet was, as he supposed, discharged. Instead, however, of being sent to the United States, he and nineteen more were, early in 1799, landed in Scotland, and incarcerated in a fortress of Nairn, called Fort George. This new imprisonment lasted three years. At the expiration of that term of injustice, pardons arrived for all except Mr. Emmet. The governor of the fortress, however, took the responsibility to release him, when, with his admirable wife, who had shared unremittingly his reverses and imprisonment, both in Ireland and Scotland, they were landed at Cuxhaven, spent the winter of 1802 in Brussels, and that of 1803 in Paris. In October, 1804, they sailed from Bordeaux for this country, and arrived in New York on the eleventh of the next month. Emmet was then forty years old. He was well qualified for both the professions of medicine and law, and hesitated which to adopt in the new world; but his friends induced him to resume practice at the bar. His original intention was to remove at once to Ohio, but the then governor of the "Empire State," George Clinton, prevailed on him to settle in New York. By special dispensation, he was admitted to the bar without delay, and by indefatigable industry rendered doubly efficient by fervent eloquence, he rose rapidly to the first rank of his profession. It is said that in the course of a very few years, he was not surpassed in business and fame by the most eminent lawyers in America.

Having thus briefly glanced at Mr. Emmet's career, up to the time of his landing on our shores, we will examine more minutely into his qualifications, his personal appearance, his progress in public favor, and the peculiarities of his eloquence.

We have seen that Mr. Emmet was early and thoroughly disciplined in classical erudition and professional training at the best institutions of the three kingdoms. In every field he explored, he was distinguished for patient toil, critical observation, and rapid conquests. The variety of his studies, connected with opposite professions, probably had a happy effect in liberalizing his mind with diversified and comprehensive views. As has been already noted, it was the unhappy loss of his distinguished and eloquent brother that induced Mr. Emmet to abandon the practice of medicine and aspire after forensic glory. He entered upon this career at a later period in life than is usual with aspirants after excellence in the rugged and thorny path of the law. But his maturity was no impediment to ultimate success. His mind had become so well accustomed to the generalizations of science, that in about two years he reduced the chaotic mass of English law to an organized creation. Early in life he had formed the habit of recurring to first principles, and this often led him to those sources of legal knowledge of which Coke, Hale, and Mansfield had drunk. His intellect was naturally inquisitive and eager of acquisition; and his natural tastes, as well as cultivated habits, prompted him at the outset to lay a broad and firm foundation of general jurisprudence, such as is seldom formed by the effeminate and timid hands of ordinary students. Instead of being an injury to him, it was undoubtedly an advantage of the highest order to have been variously trained before he came to make his first efforts at combination among the distracting and endless distinctions of law. Such would be our inference from the discipline and professional success of the first orators of every age. Demosthenes, Cicero, Lord Erskine, and Patrick Henry, were each about twenty-six years old when they commenced their forensic labors. Sir James Mackintosh and Mr. Emmet were still later in their studies, and were both for some time educated for another profession. But whatever may be our inferences, there can be no dispute touching the fact as to Mr. Emmet's great and invaluable qualifications for the office he finally assumed and zealously prosecuted until death. He stored his mind with a profusion of knowledge, profounder and richer than was possessed by the great majority of his competitors ; and though he was never ostentatious of science, it imparted a reach of thought, variety of illus tration, and energy of expression, which, aided by the bold and flowing elocution so native to the land of his birth, constituted him one of the most agreeable speakers, and certainly one of the most powerful lawyers, ever heard.

Mr. Emmet was mainly anxious to be thoroughly grounded in the substantial attributes of education, but he did not entirely neglect the decorative. He was eminently accomplished for the duties of his calling, but it was not altogether through his having " yellowed himself among rolls and records." He had an eye voracious of every thing beautiful, and a soul capacious, for every thing grand. His education was liberal, in the noblest sense, a stupendous, but symmetrical tem- ple, " built with the riches of the spoiled world." The most eminent lawyers have ever been distinguished as devotees of elegant letters as well as for skill in rigid dialectics. Lord Hardwicke and Lord Mansfield had great fondness for the lighter productions of the imagi- nation ; Justice Story is well known to have been a poet in temperament, taste, and practice, and so was his great master, Chief Justice Marshall. Shiel and Talfourd, the two brightest ornaments now living of the Irish and English bar, are as distinguished for dramatic excellence, as for being learned and brilliant advocates. Emmet was skilled in that erudition which is the result of long continued and comprehensive studies. From the beginning, and all through life, he mingled constant practice with copious acquisition. It was thus that he learned to execute with facility whatever duty required or his fancy could suggest : "He read to learn, and not to quote ; to digest and master, and not merely to display." This blending of substantial and ethereal elements in the nutriment of his mind, inspired within him a vigorous and perennial fountain of impetuous thought. He was no mere passive vehicle of inspiration, but an active votary who beat out much oil for the sanctuary in which he adored. He studied patiently, meditated profoundly, investigated minutely, till intuitive, and acquired knowledge became wedded to his habitual feelings, and obedient to its master's call, burst forth in every emergency with that invincible and enrapturing power which rendered him great in the foremost rank of men.

But perhaps the best lessons Mr. Emmet ever learned were acquired in the severe school of adversity. Under the iron hoof of tyranny, and in dungeon glooms, his youthful aspirations had been repelled and his patriotism scorned. Our best strength is generated in storms rather than in the calm. The only spiritual engine that can be wielded, so as to make all iniquitous powers tremble on their accursed thrones, is that which they most fear, an independent and eloquent soul. This, and this alone, can arraign all principles, and all tyrants before the tribunal of eternal right, and its greatest triumphs are always won in the sternest conflicts   The waters must have frequently gone over the soul, before it wins the powel·

ful suppleness to dart with fortitude under the billows or float in triumph amid their foamy crests. No
one will be likely to think either with depth or precision,
until he has been made strongly to feel. Like the precious gems and varied merchandize cast by wild waves
upon the strand near which some richly freighted ship
has been wrecked,—such is the spoil won by reflection
and stored in the exalted regions of the mind, when the
tumultuous passions which occasioned the conquest are
calmed.

The following sketch of Mr. Emmet's personal appearance is the combination of various outlines from
different hands. He was of the ordinary height, possessing a body compactly formed, and stooping a little
in the shoulders. He bore a frank and open countenance, strongly expressive of that native good nature,
which it is so notorious he constantly exemplified. He
was somewhat short sighted, but this did not in the least
diminish the fascination of his clear, bright, blue eyes.
Justice Story first made his acquaintance when a little
more than fifty years old. The lines of care were then
deeply traced upon his face; the sad remembrances, it
was conjectured, of past sufferings, and of those corroding anxieties which eat their way into the heart. There
was a pensive air about him, which suggested to the
observer other solicitudes than those which belonged to
mere professional life. "He was cheerful, but rarely, if
ever, gay; frank and courteous, but he soon relapsed
into gravity, when not excited by the conversation of
others."

But mental stimulus was essential to the development

and display of Mr. Emmet's nobler and more commanding traits, as light is necessary to unfold the beauty and
grandeur of a landscape. When his soul was thoroughly
aroused, his figure assumed a majestic mien, every motion of which was graceful; an expressive countenance
was lit up by a sparkling and piercing eye, that almost
commanded victory, while it "spoke audience ere the
tongue." While thus invested with the robes of splendid intellect, his person seemed made to contain his
spirit; his spirit filled and animated his person. His
look answered to his voice, and both spoke with simultaneous power to the soul. He was crowned with the
diadem of mental majesty, and stood forth a monarch in
the realms of eloquence. He sounded the full diapason
of the human spirit, touched every chord of passion in
himself and others, and yet, like some tall cliff around
which the storm roars, with its head reposing in the blue
serene, he preserved a stern self-control amid all the tumult
as it raged. He combined the utmost energy with every
variety of expression His transitions were rapid, and
sometimes extreme, but the all-absorbing intensity of his
feelings forced them into unity and gave them breadth.
He produced extraordinary effects by a look, a tone, a
gesture. By nature and consummate art, he was admirably endowed for forensic war. He had neither the
wart of Cicero, nor the stammer of Demosthenes; he
had healthful lungs and graceful limbs, melodious tones
and a hardy soul, revivified by an impassioned organization as vigorously developed as it was rigidly controlled.

Since there was such a happy coalition of extraordinary mental and physical qualities in Mr. Emmet, it

cannot be a matter of surprise that his progress in popular estimation was both rapid and triumphant. In 1812, he was appointed Attorney-General of the State of New York; and, in 1815, began to practice before the supreme tribunal at Washington. To succeed in this most exalted forum of the nation, requires the exercise of the ripest knowledge of jurisprudence and the clearest logical acumen. "Before such a bar, as adorns that court, where some of the ablest men in the Union are constantly found engaged in arguments, it is difficult for any man long to sustain a professional character of distinction, unless he has solid acquirements and talents to sustain it." But Emmet's success was founded on a power superior to the ordinary gifts that command popular favor—to undoubted genius there was superadded that moral interest which irresistibly commands the best sympathies of an audience. He had conducted himself with such gentleness and dignity through all the vicissitudes of adversity, persecution, imprisonment, and exile, that every generous heart took pleasure in contemplating the splendor of his talents as he exercised them without ostentation on the serene heights of prosperity and fame. Justice Story presents us the following interesting statement in point:

" It was at this time that Mr. Pinkney, of Baltimore, one of the proudest names in the annals of the American bar, was in the meridian of his glory. Mr. Emmet was a new and untried opponent, and brought with him the ample honors, gained at one of the most distinguished bars in the Union. In the only causes in which Mr. Emmet was engaged, Mr. Pinkney was retained on the other side ; and each of these causes was full of important matter, bearing upon the public policy and prize-law of the country Curiosity was awakened ; their mutual friends waited for the struggle with impatient eagerness ; and a generous rivalry, roused by the public expectations, imparted itself to their bosoms. A large and truly intelligent audience was present at the argument of the first cause. It was not one which gave much scope to Mr. Emmet's peculiar powers. The topic was one with which he was not very familiar. He was new in the scene, and somewhat embarrassed by its novelty. His argument was clear and forcible ; but he was conscious that it was not one of his happiest efforts. On the other hand, his rival was perfectly familiar with the whole range of prize-law ; he was at home, both in the topic and the scene. He won an easy victory, and pressed his advantages with vast dexterity, and, as Mr. Emmet thought, with somewhat of the display of triumph. The case of the Nereide, so well known in our prize-history, was soon afterwards called on for trial. In this second effort, Mr. Emmet was far more successful. His speech was greatly admired for its force and fervor, its variety of research, and its touching eloquence. It placed him at once, by universal consent, in the first rank of American advocates. I do not mean to intimate that it placed him before Mr. Pinkney, who was again his noble rival for victory. But it settled henceforth and for ever, his claims to very high distinction in the profession. In the course of the exordium of this speech, he took occasion to mention the embarrassment of his own situation, the novelty of the forum, and the public expectations, which accompanied the cause. He spoke with generous praise of the talents and acquirements of his opponent, whom fame and fortune had followed both in Europe and America. And then, in the most delicate and affecting manner, he alluded to the events of his own life, in which misfortune and sorrow had left many deep traces of their ravages. 'My ambition,' said he, ' was extinguished in my youth ; and I am admonished by the premature advances of age, not now to attempt the dangerous paths of fame.' At the moment when he spoke, the recollections of his sufferings melted the hearts of his audience, and many of them were dissolved in tears."

We will now enter into a more critical analysis of Mr. Emmet's eloquence. It is to be regretted that we have neither the space nor ability to present copious extracts characteristic of this great orator's composition. But few of his happier efforts were ever reduced to writing, and almost none are now extant. In this respect he much resembles the most renowned of his predecessors in the best age of Irish eloquence. No full record has preserved to us the rhetorical wealth of the fascinating and silvery eloquence of Hussey Burgh. Only a few fragmentary remains have come down to us of the massive oratory of Yelverton. The reports were never full and faithful until the times of Plunket, Sheridan, Burke, Curran, Grattan, O'Connel and Shiel. The original grandeur of the temple can hardly be estimated by a few shattered bricks ; but as we wander amid the scenes of primitive greatness, and catch the few antique t)nes that still linger there, we remember that even the shepherds were once melodious on those glorious hills, and learned to attune their souls to lofty airs on pipes formed of the eagle's wing.

From all that can now be gathered from Mr. Emmet's recorded works, and reputation with cotemporary critics, we infer that his eloquence was ardent and national, original and graceful, sober and substantial, and always studious of the good and the just.

In the first place he was evidently full of ardor and deep national feeling. The circumstances which developed these classes of emotion so strongly in our orator, we have already glanced at in considering his early life. No doubt he verified most acutely the sentiment of Cowper:

> "'Tis *liberty* alone which gives the flower
> Of fleeting life its lustre and perfume,
> And we are weeds without it."

In all speakers of the first class, the most predominant quality is force. The greatest ability in one who addresses a popular audience does not consist in the power of plunging deep in science or soaring high in poetic inspiration, but in walking firmly on the solid earth, swaying the masses of men before him as he goes. He must know how to touch and inflame the sympathies of mankind, conscious that whatever is not allied to these, is foreign to his purpose. His first duty is to be understood by all; and this end he will never attain. until he can pour himself into the general heart through the channels of deep feeling in language which all instinctively comprehend. So intimate and sagacious are the ties of sympathy which bind all hearts, that the most ignorant person will immediately detect the hollowness of false pathos whenever its imposition is attempted. Transitions the most abrupt, and language the most extravagant, are sufferable when listeners are once imbued with the fires of sincere emotion, as the smith buffets the mass of iron at discretion and with perpetual effect when at a welding heat. To take such liberties with an assembly on the dead level of ordinary feeling, would be something worse than folly. It is much easier to compel laughter and weeping in rapid alternation, when hearers are once excited, then it is to create the slightest ripple of emotion at the first attacks on the frigid sea of mind.

The only true basis of sterling eloquence is severe reason : but the imagination is always a grateful accompaniment, and the heart a most powerful aid. Their skillful combination constitutes consummate excellence ; as the combined attributes of Seraphim and Cherubim —the knowing ones and the loving ones—signalize the highest bliss of heaven. Grace and harmony are essential to effective speech, since they strengthen the ideas of the speaker and give energy to his expression. It is a primary requisite that he should invigorate the sinews and muscles of his mind, and fortify all the powers of will with a masculine firmness ; but the articulations of bony and sinewy strength must be rounded into symmetry and beautified with the attractive lines of supple life. Pope's description of beauty is equally applicable to eloquence. It is not the eye or the brow that we call beauty; and it is not the exertions of intellect or the evolutions of the body, separately considered, that we call eloquence, " but the full force and just effect of all." When a speaker is deeply absorbed in his subject, and pours himself forth in a tide of glowing emotion, the awkwardness of his gesture is lost in the fascination of his honest feeling, but no artificial elegance of the outside can ever be substituted for the rugged and sincere workings of the heart. Emmet, in his better moments, wrought in the creation of oratorical armor like a god.

Some of his paragraphs are the embodiments of the most powerful conceptions in the most vivid language ever forged in the blazing furnace of impassioned mind.

Lord Erskine, himself an admirable proficient in eloquence, said in a letter introductory to the speeches of Fox, that "intellect alone, however exalted, without strong feelings—without even irritable sensibility— would be only like an immense magazine of powder, if there were no such element as fire in the natural world. It is the heart which is the spring and fountain of all eloquence." To be efficient in the use of speech, one must be himself moved, must be sincere and in earnest. Within, the fires of logic, fed by passion, must keenly burn ; without, an air of conviction and forgetfulness of self, must mantle the speaker and augment his power. A cold-blooded retailer of hackneyd phrases and empty tropes, who contemplates his delicate hand as he waves it in effeminate prettiness, and recites his pointless periods in tones as insipid as their author's spirit, will never attract a crowd and kindle in them the healthy excitement of fervid sensibility. A man

18

may convince a few, and even induce many to act, by mere reason and argument. But that kind of oratory which commands universal admiration, and stamps its author a master among men, is never divorced from great warmth of conception and manner of expression. Passion, when it rouses and kindles the mind, without disturbing the power of self-possession, always substantiates and exalts the associated powers of the mind. The fervid inspiration of the heart renders the intellect more enlightened, vigorous, penetrating, and imperial, than it is in the calm of indifference. Thus prompted, the speaker is in no loss for words, or apt deductions. Through the lucid medium of contagious sympathy, he transmits to others the glowing sentiments he feels; his looks, tones, gestures, are all persuasive, and nature in every such instance, shows herself infinitely more powerful than art.

Eloquence, so far as it is excellent and true, will be national—it will be characterized by the most prominent features of the nation by whom and for whom it is produced. Every judicious speaker will consult the taste of his audience; in doing this he will designedly or by instinct catch the tone of the inclinations he consults, and will shortly come to possess the character he has assumed. This law of assimilation is as venerable as human nature itself, and the recognition of its power in forensic life is certainly as old as Cicero Said he, " The eloquence of orators has always been governed by the taste of the hearers. He who is desirous of being heard with approbation, naturally consults the dispositions of those whom he has to address, and in all respects conforms himself to their will and pleasure." Emmet was rocked in the cradle of liberty, and grew in one continued struggle for human rights. Every faculty he possessed had been tempered in the flames of persecution abroad, ere he came to be pro- tected and matured by the Genius of Liberty at her great western shrine. Providence created and trained him for great and noble deeds.

In the second place, Mr. Emmet was original and graceful to an uncommon degree. Originality is one of the best traits of Irish eloquence. It is unique both in its good qualities and its bad; it strikingly exemplifies the temperament and mental structure of the people of the "Emerald Isle." To attain excellence in oratory of a high order, originality is pre-eminently demanded. The speaker must yield to the potent impulses of his own spirit, rather than conform to the cold rules not in- digenous to the soul and soil of his father-land. Per- severing practice may produce the frigid uniformity of a fluent harangue; but it is only when God's creative breath fans the fires of patriotism in the soul sublimely endowed, that a true orator is fashioned for sovereignty over the hearts of mankind. Mechanism is of great utility in reducing powerful elements to practical use, but mechanism has no power to create the etherial spirit of omnipotence it struggles to employ.

Originality is not extravagance, nor need one be un- couth in order to be strong. Indeed, as Carlyle has said, "it is a fundamental mistake to call vehemence and rigidity strength. A man is not strong who takes convulsion fits; though six men cannot hold him then

He that can walk under heaviest weight without staggering, he is the strong man." The most rugged and refined qualities were combined in Mr. Emmet's composition. Fervid passions and resistless energies lay folded within him, like latent lightnings in a summer cloud; but over these accumulated stores of power, affection, "soft as dews on roses," spread a graceful mantle, shrouding what on fitting occasions burst forth in fire-showers to blast wherever they fell. Like all regal spirits of the rostrum, he always excelled with greatest certainty where his sympathies were most aroused. Marinus, speaking of old Proclus, the commentator on Plato, says, that "he did not seem to be without divine inspiration. For words similar to the most white and thick-falling snow, proceeded from his wise mouth; his eyes appeared to be filled with a fulgid splendor, and the rest of his face to participate of divine illumination." The allusion here is undoubtedly to the beautiful description of Ulysses in the third book of the Iliad, which is paraphrased as follows by Pope:

> " But when he speaks, what elocution flows !
> Soft as the fleeces of descending snows
> The copious accents fall with easy art;
> Melting, they fall and sink into the heart."

Emmet had much of that enthusiastic suavity,—that humor combined with pungency so peculiar to his countrymen,—that knowledge of human nature, and tact in controlling it, which Croly has so graphically described as the leading quality in Sheridan : "Of all great speakers of a day fertile in oratory, Sheridan had the most conspicuous natural gifts. His figure, at his

first introduction into the House, was manly and striking; his countenance singularly expressive, when excited
in debate; his eye, large, black, and intellectual; and
his voice, one of the richest, most flexible, and most
sonorous, that ever came from human lips. Pitt's was
powerful, but monotonous; and its measured tone often
wearied the ear. Fox's was all confusion in the commencement of his speech; and it required some tension
of ear throughout to catch his words. Burke's was
loud and bold, but unmusical; and his contempt for
order in his sentences, and the abruptness of his grand
and swelling conceptions, that seemed to roll through
his mind like billows before a gale, often made the
defects of his delivery more striking. But Sheridan, in
manner, gesture, and voice, had every quality that
could give effect to eloquence. Pitt and Fox were listened to with profound respect, and in silence, broken
only by occasional cheers; but from the moment of
Sheridan's rising, there was an expectation of pleasure,
which, to his last days, was seldom disappointed. A
low murmur of eagerness ran round the house; every
word was watched for, and his first pleasantry set the
whole assemblage in a roar. Sheridan was aware of
this, and has been heard to say, "that if a jester would
never be an orator, yet no speaker could expect to be
popular in a *full house* without a jest; and that he
always made the experiment, good or bad, as a laugh
gave him the country gentlemen to a man." Mr.
Emmet may not have equalled his great countryman
in the talent of humor and story-telling, but in all the
more elevated qualities of an orator, he was rarely

excelled. Science had well trained his reasoning powers,
and the graces adorned with their zone every passion
of his breast. He conceived his argument strongly,
and having clothed his thought in the choicest phraseology,

> "He said and *acting* what no words could say,
> He sent his soul with every lance he threw."

We remark, thirdly, that Mr. Emmet, as an orator,
was both sagacious and substantial. Many persons
doubt that great elegance and utility can be combined.
It is sometimes supposed that a forensic hero must be
ugly in order to be useful. If his weapons are polished
and chastely adorned, however massive, their beauty
and brightness raise suspicions as to their durability
and strength. Since gravity is usually the cloak of
wisdom, the undiscriminating world not unfrequently
forget that many exceptions exist, where dullness is
clothed in robes the most demure. Hence the general
disposition to depreciate any example of uncommon
brilliancy, as tending to demonstrate by its glowing
substance, that insipidity and reason are not always
inseparable companions. Gold is not the less valuable
when superbly wrought into artistic shapes, elegantly
burnished and embossed. The solidity of a temple's
substructure is not weakened by the grandeur of its
colonnades and the graceful swell of the dome; nor is
he the strongest of intellectual beings whose arid reason
is the only faculty with which he is endowed. The
power of a well-balanced mind is augmented by the
energies of the heart and imagination which approxi·

mate the prerogatives of omnipresence and unbounded love.

Exuberance of fancy is certainly a defect, but when properly employed, it is an attribute essential to an orator. Devoid of the ideal which imagination creates, the speaker sinks to a mere dry arguer, the most repulsive of public men; the plodding mason, but not the inspired architect; he breathes not that divine life which imparts to dull matter animation and soul. But Mr. Emmet never restricted himself to a narrow range of action or thought. He could conciliate attention in notes as soft and gentle as birds "singing of summer in full-throated ease;" or, if necessary, with equal facility he assumed the thunderer's attitude and arms, hurling down those bolts that "make flexile the knees of knotted oaks." In some of his bolder personifications, he sometimes trod the dizzy verge that marks the boundaries of the sublime; but he trod it like a god. The ballast of his intellect gave stability and use to the towering sails which deep feeling spread. He had stored his memory with noble sentiments, striking images and graceful expressions; and these were rendered effective by a perpetual enthusiasm for liberal pursuits, elegant letters, and lofty freedom. He did not horde wisdom for selfish ends, but to guide the public weal, educate the people, elevate the national taste, and conduct his adopted country, our glorious republic, to the head of the mightiest nations on earth.

This leads us to remark, in conclusion, that Mr Emmet seems ever to have been studious of the just and the good. Justice Story speaks of this, in the

following general comments on his character: " His
mind was quick, vigorous, searching, and buoyant. He
kindled as he spoke. There was a spontaneous combustion, as it were, not sparkling, but clear and glowing.
His object seemed to be, not- to excite wonder or
surprise, to captivate by bright pictures, and varied
images, and graceful groups, and startling apparitions ;
but by earnest and close reasoning to convince the
judgment, or to overwhelm the heart by awakening
its most profound emotions. His own feelings were
warm and easily touched. His sensibility was keen,
and refined itself almost into a melting tenderness. His
knowledge of the human heart was various and exact
He was easily captivated by a belief that his own cause.
was just. Hence, his eloquence was most striking for
its persuasiveness. He said what he felt; and he felt
what he said. His command over the passions of others
was an instantaneous and sympathetic action. The
tones of his voice, when he touched on topics calling for
deep feeling, were themselves instinct with meaning.
They were utterances of the soul, as well as of the lips."

No man was better qualified to put a just estimate
upon Mr. Emmet, than the great and good judge whose
judgment has just been quoted, and who, alas! has now
followed Legare, Wirt, Pinkney, Emmet, Marshall, and
others, to the great tribunal. Of Pinkney's great force,
but lack of feeling, we have already spoken. His
exhibition sometimes resembled splendid winter scenery,
gorgeous forests and mountains glittering with sleet,
and brilliant with innumerable gems, but cold as the
material of which their beauty was formed. But in the

scenes which Emmet evoked, the spectator beheld a summer prospect of natural luxuriance and verdure, less dazzling, but infinitely more replete with charms. His mind was chaste and fair, "as the leaves of the spring's sweetest book, the rose ;" and it was destitute of no element of either natural or acquired strength. His industry was perpetual and elevated. Even amid the fires of persecution, like the sacred bush, he burned but was not consumed. While imprisoned at the fortress in Scotland, he wrote a work on the history of his abused country, which was printed in New York, in 1807.

Before Emmet was exiled from his native land, his most intimate associate at the bar, and noble rival, was Curran, of whom Lord Byron said, that he had spoken more poetry than any man had ever written. The two young heroes were in many respects alike, and both were fine exemplifications of great suppleness combined with great power to resist. Judge Robinson, the author of several stupid, scurrilous pamphlets, on a certain occasion cast a sneer on Curran's poverty, by the brutal remark that he "suspected his law library was rather contracted." "It is very true, my Lord," replied the indignant barrister, "that I am poor, and the circumstance has somewhat curtailed my library : my books are not numerous, but they are select, and I hope they have been perused with proper dispositions. I have prepared myself for this high profession rather by the study of a few good works, than by the composition of a great many bad ones. I am not ashamed of my poverty ; but I should be ashamed of my wealth, could

18*

I have stooped to acquire it by servility and corruption.
If I rise not to rank, I shall at least be honest; and
should I ever cease to be so, many an example shows
me that an ill-gained elevation, by making me the more
conspicuous, would only make me the more universally
and the more notoriously contemptible." With all such
burning indignation towards arrogance, tyranny, and
servile meanness, Emmet profoundly sympathized. His
private life was irreproachable, and his professional
career was ever characterized by a noble demeanor,
patient investigation, and untarnished integrity. As a
patriot, Mr. Emmet was worthy to take the place he
has won among the choicest spirits of our race. He
loved freedom, as his dear brother Robert loved his
broken-hearted betrothed, to whose father he wrote
from prison as follows; "I would rather have had the
affections of your daughter in the back settlements of
America, than the first situation this country could
afford without them." At twelve o'clock on the day of
execution, the same hand wrote its last lines thus:

"My love, Sarah! it was not thus that I thought to
have requited your affection. I did hope to be a prop
round which your affections might have clung, and
which would never have been shaken; but a rude blast
has snapped it, and they have fallen over a grave.

"This is no time for affliction. I have had public
motives to sustain my mind, and I have not suffered it
to sink; but there have been moments in my imprisonment when my mind was so sunk by grief on her
account, that death would have been a refuge.

"God bless you! I am obliged to leave off immediately.

" ROBERT EMMET."

The enthusiastic patriotism which allured him to his destiny, and fortified him in all the tempest he endured of withered hopes and accursed tyranny, enabled him, it is said, to write the above lines with composure, and immediately after to meet his fate with unostentatious fortitude. The two brothers were alike, fearless of aristocratic or regal malice, and ready to die at any moment rather than be recreant to duty. Such is the inspiration which the good and the true imbibe at the shrine of righteous liberty.

In the van of a glorious morn not yet risen to ful. day, Thomas Addis Emmet was dragged from dungeon to dungeon, hunted from continent to continent, athwart seas and oceans, until he found a safe and honorable protection under the ægis of America. Here he pursued a long and glorious career. His death took place in the sixty-third year of his age, in a manner somewhat remarkable. November 14th, 1827, while conducting an important case at New York, in the Circuit Court of the United States, he was seized with an apoplectic fit, which put an end to his existence the following night. He was thus suddenly cut down in the fullness of his virtues, strength, and fame. It was only on the day preceding the fatal attack, that he had delivered a most powerful address to a jury in a cause of the greatest difficulty and importance. The whole nation mourned his fall. Precious and splendid tes timonials immediately indicated the high place he occupied in popular regard.   Nor was the respect thus proffered a transient emotion.   In the crowded thoroughfare of Broadway, the admirers of genius and exalted worth may still be often seen to pause and contemplate the noble monument to his memory in St. Paul's church-yard.

This perpetuity of admiration mingled with grief, comports well with the character of the man we have attempted to describe.   He was as fascinating in private life, as he was splendid in the forum.   His manners were conciliating and attractive to an extraordinary degree, blending the dignity and urbanity of the gentleman with the cordiality and playfulness of the friend. Like Hector, setting aside his crested helmet, that he might not frighten his boy, he laid aside all perfunctionary austerities, and put every person in his presence at confiding ease.   Politeness in him was of the truest type, and flowed from its only true source—a noble, warm, and magnanimous heart.   For whatever was amiable in childhood, or venerable in age—lovely in woman, or heroic in man—lofty in principle, endearing in friendship, or praise-worthy in enterprise, he had an instinctive capacity to appreciate, and spontaneous sympathies to embrace.

THE NEW YORK
PUBLIC LIBRARY

ASTOR, LENOX AND
TILDEN FOUNDATIONS

JOHN RANDOLPH.

CHAPTER XVI

JOHN RANDOLPH,

THE IMPERSONATION OF SARCASM.

ONE of the most remarkable men that ever lived was John Randolph, of Roanoke. He was born on 2d of June, 1773, at Matoax, the seat of his father, three miles above Petersburg, Virginia. In his veins were blended the aristocratic blood of England and the blood royal of primitive America. His lordly bearing, aboriginal descent, eccentric career and extraordinary eloquence, early fastened the attention of his countrymen upon him, and through many years engrossed popular regard to a wonderful degree.

The progenitor of the Virginia Randolphs was William of Yorkshire, England, who settled at Turkey Island, on the James River. William married Mary Isham, of Bermuda Hundred. Several of their sons were distinguished men : William was a member of the House of Burgesses, from Goochland, 1740, and Adjutant-General of the Colony. Richard was a member of the House of Burgesses, 1740, for Henrico, and succeeded his brother as treasurer. Sir John was Speaker of the House of Burgesses and Attorney-General. Peter son of the 2d William Randolph, was Clerk of the House of Burgesses and Attorney-General. Peyton, brother of John, was Speaker of the House of Burgesses and President of the first Congress held at Philadelphia. Thomas Mann Randolph, great grandson of William, of Turkey Island, was a member of the Virginia Convention, 1775, from Goochland. Beverly Randolph was Member of Assembly, from Cumberland, during the Revolution, and member of the Convention that formed the Federal Constitution, and of the Virginia Convention that ratified it, Governor of the State of Virginia and Secretary of State of the United States. Robert Randolph, son of Peter; Richard Randolph, grandson of Peter ; and David Meade Randolph, son of the 2d Richard, were cavalry officers in the War of the Revolution.

John Randolph, of Roanoke, was grandson of the 1st Richard. Many distinguished families in Virginia, including Thomas Marshall, father of the Chief Justice, were descended from Randolph of Turkey Island.

Jane Bolling, great-grand-daughter of Pocahontas, married Richard Randolph, of Curles. John Randolph, Jr., of Roanoke, seventh child of that marriage, married Frances Bland, and our hero, John Randolph, of Roanoke, was one of the children of this union.

The Randolphs were proud of their patrician blood, and named their respective seats with sounding titles of distinction ; such as Thomas, of Tuckahoe ; Isham, of Dungeness ; Richard, of Curles ; and John, of Roanoke. Other branches of this famous family had their splendid mansions at Turkey Island. Bremo, Varina, Wilton, and

Chatswort, venerable localities eagerly contemplated by
the curious traveller on James River. The crest of the
arms of the Virginia Randolphs is an antelope's head.

John Randolph's early education, according to his
own account, was very irregular. He was sent to a
country school at an early age, where he acquired the
rudiments of the Latin and Greek languages. His
health failing, his mother sent him to Bermuda, where
he remained more than a year, losing all his Greek, but
reading with great avidity many of the best English
authors. After his return to the United States, he was
sent with his brother Theodorick, to Princeton College,
where they commenced their studies in March, 1787.
In the year 1788, after the death of his mother, he was
sent to college in New York, but returned to Virginia,
in 1790. In the same year he went to Philadelphia, to
study law in the office of Edmund Randolph, then recently appointed Attorney-General of the United States.
But his law studies scarcely extended beyond the first
book of Blackstone. He became of age in June, 1794,
up to which time he appears to have led an irregular,
desultory life, with a residence as fluctuating as his
object of pursuit was undecided.

In Greek literature, John Randolph never was a proficient; in Latin he was better read, and quoted its
treasures with promptness and accuracy. But with the
best English classics he was thoroughly and comprehensively acquainted. In his "Letters to Dudley," he
speaks of his education as follows: "I think you have
never read Chaucer. Indeed, I have sometimes blamed
myself for not cultivating your imagination when you

were young. It is a dangerous quality, however, for the possessor. But if from my life were to be taken the pleasure derived from that faculty, very little would remain. Shakspeare and Milton, and Chaucer and Spencer, and Plutarch, and the Arabian Nights' Entertainments, and Don Quixote, and Gil Blas, and Tom Jones, and Gulliver, and Robinson Crusoe, 'and the tale of Troy divine,' have made up more than half my worldly enjoyment. To these ought to be added Ovid's Metamorphoses, Ariosto, Dryden, Beaumont and Fletcher, Southern, Otway, Pope's Rape and Eloisa, Addison, Young, Thompson, Gay, Goldsmith, Gray, Collins, Sheridan, Cowper, Byron, Æsop, La Fontaine, Voltaire's Charles XII., Mahomet and Zaire, Rousseau's Julie, Schiller, Madame de Stael, but above all, Burke. One of the first books I ever read was Voltaire's Charles XII. ; about the same time, 1780–1, I read the Spectator, and used to steal away to the closet containing them. The letters from his correspondents were my favorites. I read Humphrey Clinker, also, that is, Win's and Tabby's letters, with great delight; for I could spell at that age pretty correctly. Reynard the Fox, came next, I think ; then Tales of the Genii and Arabian Nights. This last, and Shakspeare, were my idols. I had read them, with Don Quixote, Gil Blas, Quintus Curtius, Plutarch, Pope's Homer, Robinson Crusoe, Gulliver, Tom Jones, Orlando Furioso, and Thompson's Seasons, before I was eleven years of age ; also Goldsmith's Roman History, and an old history of Braddock's War. At about eleven, (1784–5,) Percy's Reliques and Chaucer became great favorites, and

Chatterton and Rowley I then read Young and Gay, &c. Goldsmith I never saw till 1787."

Mr. Randolph made his first appearance in public life, in 1799, as a candidate for a seat in Congress, and was elected. He was indebted to his eloquence for success in this early contest, as he was without family influence in the district, and was a mere boy in appearance. His antagonist was the veteran statesman and orator, Patrick Henry. The exciting questions which arose out of Mr. Madison's famous resolutions of 1798, were the chief matter in debate. On the alien and sedition laws, and other exciting topics of that day, the contest ran high. An anecdote has been preserved strongly characteristic of both combatants. Mr. Randolph was addressing the populace in answer to Mr. Henry, when a comrade said to the latter, "Come, Henry, let us go—it is not worth while to listen to *that boy.*" "Stay, my friend," replied the sagacious patriot, "there is an old man's head on that boy's shoulders."

When he entered Congress, his youthful aspect, among other striking traits, attracted universal surprise. As he presented himself at the clerk's table to qualify, the official demanded his age. "Ask my constituents," was the characteristic reply.

Mr. Randolph soon became a marked man in the national councils. His fearless thought, pungent language, withering sarcasm, and general power as a prompt and passionate debater, attracted the admiration as well as excited the dread of all parties within Congress and without. He was frequently chairman of important committees, participated in almost all the chief debates,

and amid one continued whirl of changes and contra-
dictions, acted the hero and the buffoon for many years
on the public stage.

Let us attempt to delineate his person, analyze his intellect, and describe somewhat minutely his strange career.

John Randolph was about six feet high. He had
elevated shoulders, a small head, and a physiognomy all
the parts of which were entirely unintellectual, except
his eye. His hair was dark, thin and lank, and lay
close to his head. His voice was shrill as a fife, but its
clear shrieking tones could be distinctly heard by a
large audience. The muscles and skin about his face
were shrivelled and cadaverous, like wrinkled parchment; and his whole form was so attenuated and meagre
that tall as he was, his acquaintances supposed him not
to weigh more than a hundred and thirty pounds.

The author of Clinton Bradshaw, who enjoyed a favorable opportunity of observing this strange being, has
given us the following graphic description of his person,
habiliments and manners: "His long, thin legs, about
as thick as a stout walking cane, and of much such a
shape, were encased in a pair of light small clothes, so
tight that they seemed part and parcel of the wearer.
Handsome white stockings were fastened with great
tidiness at the knees by a small gold buckle, and over
them, coming about half way up the calf, were a pair of
what, I believe, are called hose, coarse and country
knit. He wore shoes. They were old-fashioned, and
fastened also with buckles—large ones. He trod like an
Indian, without turning his toes out, but planking them
straight ahead. It was the fashion in those days to

wear a fan-tailed coat, with a small collar, and buttons
far apart behind, and few on the breast. Mr. Randolph's
was the reverse of all this. Instead of its being fan-
tailed, it was what I believe the knights of the needle
call swallow-tailed ; the collar was immensely large, the
buttons behind were in kissing proximity, and they sat
together as close on the breast of the garment as the
feasters at a crowded public festival. His waist was
remarkably slender : so slender that, as he stood with
his arms akimbo, he could easily, as I thought, with his
long bony fingers, have spanned it. Around him his coat,
which was very tight, was held together by one button,
and, in consequence, an inch or more of tape, to which
the buttons were attached, was perceptible where it was
pulled through the cloth. About his neck he wore a
large white cravat, in which his chin was occasionally
buried as he moved his head in conversation; no shirt
collar was perceptible : every other person seemed to
pride himself upon the size of his, as they were then
worn large. Mr. Randolph's complexion was precisely
that of a mummy—withered, saffron, dry, and bloodless,
you could not have placed a pin's point on his face
where you would not have touched a wrinkle. His
lips were thin, compressed, and colorless; the chin,
beardless as a boy's, was broad for the size of his face,
which was small; his nose was straight, with nothing
remarkable in it, except, perhaps, it was too short. He
wore a fur cap, which he took off, standing a few moments uncovered. Fancy a dead man struck into life
by lightning, and all his life in his eye, and you have a
picture of John Randolph."

It would be difficult, we think, to present a more striking portraiture of one's exterior, than the one we have just quoted. A still more difficult task remains to present in detail the elements of his mental and rhetorical power.

Humor, wit, and sarcasm are legitimate and effective tools when adroitly used in oratory. There is no malignity in true irony. If that which is intrinsically absurd, is made to appear ludicrous, when sketched by a sagacious master, the ridicule belongs to the subject, and not to the artist. Bland humor is almost always associated with great intellectual strength. Says a distinguished Edinburgh reviewer, "Men of truly great powers of mind, have generally been cheerful, social, and indulgent; while a tendency to sentimental whining, or fierce intolerance, may be ranked among the surest symptoms of inferior intellects. In the whole list of our English poets, we can only remember Shenstone and Savage—two, certainly, of the lowest—who were querulous and discontented. Cowley, indeed, used to call himself melancholy; but he was full of conceits and affectations, and has nothing to make us proud of him. Shakspeare, the greatest of them all, was evidently of a free and joyous temperament : and so was Chaucer, their common master. The same disposition seems to have predominated in Fletcher, Jonson, and their great cotemporaries. The genius of Milton partook something of the austerity of the party to which it belonged, and of the controversies in which it was involved ; but even when fallen on evil days and evil tongues, his spirit seems to have retained its serenity as well as its dignity ; and in his private life, as well as in his poetry, the majesty of a high character is tempered with great sweetness and practical wisdom."

But Randolph was not of this stamp. He possessed little of that delicate and courteous humor which "gives ardor to virtue, and confidence to truth." When irony is refined and sparingly employed, it produces a pleasing excitement of mind in all who can perceive the significant force latent in every delicate allusion. But when those personalities are palpable and poignant, as was the custom with Randolph, they leave an irritating sting in the wound, which breeds death. The dealer in such wares is justly dreaded by all, for it is impossible to tell who next will be made to bleed under the keen dagger of unscrupulous sarcasm. With malignant delight, such antagonists occupy themselves incessantly in sharpening their arrows, and in pluming them for attack. Armed with weapons which, like vipers, though small are too deadly to be contemptible, these mental dwarfs rendered effective by their venom rather than by their reason, scornfully overleap opposing arguments which have been elaborated with care, and by sudden stings inflict wounds on some sensitive but unguarded part, and thus destroy the equanimity of the giant whose deductions they cannot subvert. One thus tormented by ignoble foes will painfully verify the sentiments of Southey's hero :

> " Quick am I to feel
> Light ills—perhaps, o'er hasty : summer gnats,
> Finding my cheek unguarded, may infix
> Their skin-deep stings to vex and irritate :

But if the wolf or forest-boar be nigh,
I am awake to danger. Even so
Bear I a mind of steel and adamant
Against all greater wrongs."

Carlyle has said that " true humor springs not more
from the head than from the heart ; it is not contempt
—its essence is love ; it issues not in laughter, but in
still smiles which lie far deeper. It is a sort of inverse
sublimity, exalting, as it were, into our affections what
is below us, while sublimity draws down into our affections what is above us." But of this amiable, vivacious
excellence, Randolph had little or none. His humor
was not mere pleasant, pungent railery, but generally
darkened into ferocious vituperation. He was as fickle
as the wind, implacable as the storm, and scathing as
lightning :

"One of that stubborn sort was he,
Who, if they once grow fond of an opinion
They call it honor, honesty, and faith,
And sooner part with life than let it go."

Satire, in the person of one who has a shrewd eye to
observe, and a graphic pen to describe, is a mighty
agent for good in the literary and moral world. Whose
heart does not echo back the brief and pungent exclamation of the prince of dramatists ?

" Life's a poor player,
Who frets and struts his hour upon the stage,
And then is heard no more !"

Pope has sarcastically amplified this thought, and, at
the same time, added a solemn view to the subject :

" Behold the child, by nature's kindly law,
  Pleas'd with a rattle, tickl'd with a straw !
  Some livelier plaything gives our youth delight,
  A little louder, but as empty quite :
  Scarfs, garters, gold, our riper years engage ;
  And beads and prayer-books are the *toys* of age !
  Pleased with his bauble still as that before,
  Till tir'd we sleep, and *life's poor play is o'er*."

If it is correct to say that a good style resembles the
crystal of a watch, attracting attention, not to itself,
but to what is beneath it ; then a judicious infusion of
the bitter-sweet of humor into the milk of human kindness in composition, will be an advantage rather than
otherwise, since it will excite expectation and command
respect.   In the almost universal skill of pedantic dog-
matism which prevails in modern society, we have little
of the genuine Socratic irony which once instructed
Athens and improved the world.   Frederick Schlegel
has a pertinent remark on this topic : " We also find in
the classical works of antiquity, at a time that depth of
a loving sentiment was not so generally revealed, this
same phenomenon amidst the highest spiritual clearness
and serenity, in the most charming attire of exquisite
language.   I mean that characteristic irony which belonged to the discourses and instructions of Socrates,
as exhibited in the Platonic writings.   I must here,
however, observe that this word, in the modern usage,
has sunk to a degree lower than its original meaning :
insomuch, that it now only signifies common mockery,
and certainly does not fulfil Aristotle's idea, when he
says that it makes manners gracious.   True irony is
the irony of love."

We have endeavored to show that Mr. Randolph was greatly deficient in humor ; his wit was more abundant, but not more amiably employed. Satire is undoubtedly a potent ordnance with which one may " shoot folly as it flies." But is it noble to be inclined to ridicule, rather than admire, and is that a manly sensitiveness which resents a burst of enthusiasm as an offence against the decorum of enlightened society—a fastidious and effeminate taste which represses all outpourings of generous thought in which glowing passion impels the imagination, and exalted sentiment is steeped in fancy? True wit is fearless, frank, and jocund, giving and taking hits with equal magnanimity. But Randolph was captious, acrimonious, and snarly, never sparing his foes, and often dreaded by his friends. The scourge with which he unmercifully lashed his victim was composed of thongs that cut deeply and left corroding gangrene in the wounds they made.

We have seen that humor is the genial oil and wine of every festival, without which there is no jovial fellowship. Wit, on the contrary, is a tart, pungent ingredient, much too acid for ordinary stomachs. Its legitimate use lies in the encouragement of timid merit, and the discomfiture of insolence. Many crude theories and impracticable systems are more successfully attacked by ridicule than by reason. Satire, wisely used in the promotion of public morals, and even in the defence of religion, will do more good than a formal discourse; since this sort of remedy is grateful to the popular taste, whilst at the same time it imparts reproof and excites fear :

"Of all the ways that wisest men could find,
To mend the age and mortify mankind,
Satire, well writ, has most successful prov'd,
And cures, because the remedy is lov'd."

But we never heard of any one who had a particular
affection for Randolph's sarcastic wit. His withering
spirit was not of the kind that sportively would "break
a butterfly upon the wheel," but a demoniac passion
that is sure to blast whatever embodiment of beauty or
strength it scornfully condescends to touch. Had he
restrained himself within reasonable bounds and subordinated his great powers to noble ends, he might have
accomplished an immense amount of good. Shallow
pretenders to wisdom, and ostentatious charlatans of
divers sorts infest society, every where prompt only to
distract and destroy; to unmask the hideous features
of such, and to deride their boastful meanness, is the
prerogative of men endowed like the satirist of Roanoke.
But in painting in vivid and perhaps exaggerated colors,
the "fears of the brave and follies of the wise," or in
shipping off the disguise of some glittering exterior in
order to "bare the mean heart that lurks beneath a
star," his object should be not so much to diminish our
respect for a particular class of men, as to augment our
love for all mankind. If the wise reprover of popular
or personal faults would banish the false glare that
plays around bold but barren summits, it is only that
through a clearer medium and over a wider area, we
may extend our view in the exercise of beneficent
regards. The most forcible and useful satirists have
ever been at heart the best-natured men. In them the
19

essence of generosity was much more abundant than the bitter ingredient in which, for exalted purposes they sometimes dipped their pen, and it is by virtue of their kindlier elements that their influence continues alive.

There are a plenty of "cooing, insipid lack-a-daisical moralities" in the world, fair game for the caustic lampooner, and an occasional scourging at his hand will do no harm. There are many popular errors so supremely ridiculous that their folly could only be exceeded by an attempt to reason them down. "A man might as well drag up a forty-two pounder to overthrow *a lodge in a garden of cucumbers.* By bringing a grave syllogism against a supreme absurdity, we make it more respectable than it can be by its native merits. The best thing is to knock it over with ridicule." Follies that are fortified by fashion are most effectually attacked by turning them into burlesque, after the style of Don Quixote. This is to reform evils without augmenting them. But there are other minds, of darker tone, who ever seek matter of pleasantry in things serious, and are never contented except as they can cause the ridiculous to emanate from the sublime. They corrupt, if possible, what is intrinsically elevated and pure, by the fantastic medium through which they cast their cynical look. But this is the cruel gayety of the shallow buffoon, rather than magnanimous satire seasoned with attic wit. Such ignoble spirits have neither the disposition nor ability to soar in the regions of lofty thought, but their descent is facile, clinging to the accessories of things but never appreciating their substance. They haunt the domain

of moral excellence only as unquiet ghosts, and through
the bowers of beauty and magnificence drag their loathsome slime, not because such regions are most congenial
to their native tastes, but because they therein find an
abundance of worth which they are ambitious to degrade
rather than enjoy.

Ridicule is a potent weapon in the hands of evil men;
but principles which are not substantial enough to withstand the basest marauders, even when they employ the
basest tools, deserve to fall.   Plutarch, in his life of
Fabius Maximus, says, "as Diogenes, the philosopher,
when one said, 'They deride you,' answered well,
'But I am not derided;' accounting those only to be
ridiculed, who feel the ridicule and are discomposed at
it; so Fabius bore without emotion all that happened to
himself, herein confirming that position in philosophy,
which affirms that *a wise and good man can suffer no
disgrace.*"

But that man's sensibilities must have been indeed
obtuse who did not writhe under the hand of John Randolph, and he was, indeed, fortunate who did not long
bear the marks of his blows.   He had the infernal
power of investing a fair name with ludicrous associations as lasting as life.   He could at will transfix a
tender heart with fiery-forked antitheses, or brand his
victim with scorching epithets that eat like aspics to
the soul.   There are some diseases that will yield to
nothing but the caustic; but he would be a terrible
practitioner who should resort to this remedy in every
case.   Sometimes burning indignation is demanded

reply to tyrannic arrogance; and is the only kind of response in which generous and patriotic bystanders can sympathize. Such an instance occurs in the history of Irish eloquence. The supercilious Fitzgibbon—Lord Clare—had made a domineering and unmanly attack on Mr. Grattan, in his absence. The eloquent and noble-hearted Yelverton immediately replied to the titled but base calumniator as follows: "If my learned friend were present, the honorable gentleman would take some time to consider before he hazarded an encounter with his genius, his eloquence, and his integrity. The learned gentleman has stated what Mr. Grattan is—I will state what he is not. He is not styed in prejudices —he does not trample on the resuscitation of his country, or live like a caterpillar on the decline of its prosperity; he does not stickle for the letter of the Constitution with the affectation of the prude, and abandon its principles and spirit with the effrontery of a prostitute."

Randolph had all this energy of contempt, but not always equal suavity of language. When fully aroused, he would not condescend to steep his sting in honey. He neglected the advice of that courtly gentleman, Sir Lucius O'Trigger: "Let your courage be as keen, out at the same time as polished, as your sword." He would not only cut, but hack and mangle his victims by the fierceness of his invective. It was utterly impossi-ble either to avoid the lacerating edge of his scathing ideas or be tranquil under the pangs they were designed to inflict. Like St. Anselm, he should have prayed God to take away obstinacy from his sentiments and rudeness from his manners.

JOHN RANDOLPH. 447

As a specimen of the unamiableness of his wit, take the following : The Honorable Peter ——, who was a watchmaker, and who represented B—— County for many years in Congress, once made a motion to amend a resolution offered by Randolph on the subject of military claims. Mr. Randolph rose up after the amendment had been offered and drawing out his watch from his fob, asked the Honorable Peter what o'clock it was. The honest and unsuspecting member told him. "Sir," replied the scornful orator, "you can mend my watch, but not my motions. You understand *tictics*, sir, but not tactics."

Sometimes he served his purpose with apt quotations which he hurled full of venom at whole bands of antagonists. His self-control and defiance were invincible. Once when beset by almost the whole House in boisterous debate, he turned to his foes with a look of ineffable contempt, and then cried out to the Speaker, "Sir, I am in the condition of old Lear—

> " The little dogs and all,
> Trey, Blanche, and Sweetheart,
> See, they all bark at me."

The power of ridicule is very great, but its habitual use by no means indicates a good heart. He who is copiously endowed with extraordinary qualities will signalize his superiority over common men, by using his wit oftener in friendship than in enmity. But John Randolph chose to fight habitually with the weapon of contempt; a weapon which the malignant gladly substitute for argument, since it inflicts most pain. He pronounced ridicule to be the keenest weapon in the whole parliamentary armory, and he learned most skillfully to cut and thrust with it, but never played with foils. Conflict with him was no sham, but a war to the knife, and knife to the hilt. But this is power which ought to be despised rather than admired. In the code of Charondar, at ancient Sparta, public ridicule was assigned as the penalty to be inflicted only on the adulterer and busy-body, the sycophant and coward. This indicates the range such wit holds in dignity, as well as the measure of its force. "The very life of such characters," says Moore, "is their licentiousness, and it is with them, as with objects that are luminous from putresence—to remove their taint is to extinguish their light."

In tender strains of eloquence Randolph never was a master. He had too little generous humor and too frigid sensibilities for that. The only time he was ever known to attempt the pathetic with success was when he moved an adjournment to attend Commodore Decatur's funeral. It is said that his expressions of grief on that occasion were deep and tragical. He invoked the national sorrow for the fall of the brightest star in the constellation of our naval glory, and elicited sad notes from the Orphean lyre, which might draw "iron tears down Pluto's cheek." But the pathetic was not his forte. He had not that irresistible inspiration of a tender heart which enables its ardent possessor to play with the feelings of great multitudes, as Ariel sported with Caliban and Trunculo; sometimes diving into the billows, sometimes playing in the plighted clouds. He had a plenty of fickleness in his character, but no great versatility of talent. His imagination was vivid—for

much of his life active to a degree of downright insanity
—but there were few gentle, attractive hues in his
wildness. His wit was always tinged with sarcasm, or
debased into gloomy invective. His intellect was brilliant, but its effulgence was borrowed of passions the
least amiable, ever ready to blast where it shone. As
he advanced in life, the currents of his heart seem to
have merged into a single channel, and that ran profusely with gall. Irony to intimidate the feeble, and
invective to harass the strong, were the resources
most husbanded by him and constantly employed :

> "Like two dark serpents tangled in the dust,
> That on the paths of men their mingling poisons thrust."

In mental character and manner of speech, Randolph, in several particulars, was much like a distinguished living statesman of France. A recent
listener to the latter, describes the scene as follows:
"At length silence is re-established ; the orator is about
to speak ; listen, or if your organization is at all delicate
and musical, begin by stopping your ears, and open
them by degrees, for the voice you are going to hear is
one of those shrill, screeching, piercing organs which
would make Rubini shiver, and give Lablanche a fit. It
is something equivocal, anomalous, amphibious, neither
masculine or feminine, but rather appertaining to the
neuter gender ; and strongly flavored, moreover, with a
provincial accent.

"And, yet, this little man, without appearance, without dignity, without voice, is none other than M.
Thiers, one of the most eminent personages of the

epoch, and one of the most powerful orators of the Chamber. Those shrill lungs emit sounds almost always listened to with favor, and often applauded with phren-zica enthusiasm ; from that nasal throat issues a flow of words transparent as crystal, rapid as thought, sub-stantial and compact as meditation itself."

If the Frenchman and American resembled each other in the traits above named, their power of tor-menting an opponent was absolutely identical. Con-tinues the writer just quoted : "Have you ever seen a bull endeavoring vainly to get rid of a gad-fly, which fixes itself upon his sides, his eyes, his ears, his nostrils and stupifies the beast with his buzz—the infuriate animal bellows, foams, twists, and rolls itself about, but unable to free itself from its indefatigable foe, terminates the contest by plunging headlong down an abyss?" This sketches Randolph to the life. His cynical soul fastened itself at different points on his antagonist, like a vampire, and the victim was not abandoned till all vital blood was destroyed. His attacks had much of the condensed bitterness of Junius, and were not often more gross. But when most restrained there was still a tendency in the evil spirit to escape; you might hear the growls through the thongs of the muzzle. His hints and insinuations, accompanied by significant glances and sneering tones, were enough to disturb ordinary equanimity; but the withering power of his more direct invective was insufferable to the last degree.

Of the new Constitution of Virginia, he said, "It was brought into life with the *Sardonic* grin of death upon its countenance." In that expression he has given us the outline and tone of his own portrait. His language was pointed and severe, full of condensed fire and inhuman energy. His oratory was Spartan in brevity and force; his words fell like vipers among his hearers, and stung them into fiery excitement. He was morbid and morose to excess; but his gloom was volcanic heat, ready to explode at any moment and in any direction. Suddenly, his stoical nature would become possessed as by a demon, and his cold, sinister eye blazed with splendid fires, and radiated from his hueless face like a wintry sky flashing with lightning. A political opponent boasted on the stump, that if his mind was not naturally as strong as that of the Orator of Roanoke, he had done his best, by an arduous collegiate course, to improve it, &c. " Not the first weak soil, gentlemen," exclaimed Randolph, interrupting him, " that excessive cultivation has reduced to barrenness :—let him stay at home—let him lie fallow, fallow."

We have sketched John Randolph's person and mental constitution ; let us now glance at the use he made of his powers in his public career. He entered public life in 1787. In 1806, he declared open hostility to the administration of Jefferson, and from that time seems to have quarrelled with every public measure and every prominent man. In 1811, those paroxysms of insanity began to appear, of which in his Letters to Dudley, he says he had a lurking consciousness, and which, in the form of hypochondria, was the great malady of his life. It was in this year that his *Anglomania* developed itself so strongly, which led him on the 10th of December so violently to oppose the war

19*

an opposition perpetually renewed, as on the resolution he offered, May 29th, 1812. "That under existing circumstances it is inexpedient to resort to war against Great Britain." It was in the angry debate connected with this resolution that his animosity became fully aroused against Mr. Clay.

In 1822, he visited England, Ireland, and Scotland, countries of which he had previously acquired a wonderfully minute and correct idea from conversation and books. The attention he received abroad was very great, his eccentricity was in no way abated, and he returned to figure a while longer with aggravated vexation on the public stage.

It is easy to perceive from Randolph's letters, as well as from his speeches, that he read immensely, and had a strong memory to retain what he had once mastered. He was the demon of cleverness. He had almost every subject at the very end of his fingers, and could, if the fit pleased him, converse admirably on every intelligent theme. He had a vast amount of miscellaneous knowledge, but little scientific discipline. He was ready for every occasion, could declaim better than any body else on every thing, but was elaborate and sound in nothing.

Randolph's most extensive and critical knowledge lay in the department of old English literature. Evidently he was chaste in language, and exceedingly fastidious in the selection of words. He was feudal in taste and anti-republican in education. Foreign books, baronial castles and ducal pedigrees, filled his imagination and formed his manners. By profession, he was a democrat;

in spirit and practice he was an ultra aristocrat. He
disliked and opposed every administration from Washington to Jackson ; in every thing and towards every
body, he was "a good hater." His tongue was "a
chartered libertine," steeped in the poison of asps, and
ready to impede any step of popular progress. He con-
fided in no one, and was distrusted, if not despised by
all. The curse-book of Pandemonium was condensed
by him into epigrams and antitheses of malignant contempt, and hurled like double-headed shot at all whom
the whim of the moment marked as his foes. He took
his old books to England to be bound, rather than have
them repaired north of Mason and Dixon's line, and it
is believed, with the same hatred of every thing noble
beyond the contracted sphere which his own contemptible prejudices had formed, he would have fed his enmity
at the expense of all the freedom of our land.

It has been said of Fox's speeches, that " they are full
of impressive allusions ; they abound in expositions of
the adversary's inconsistency ; they are loaded with
bitter invective ; they never lose sight of the subject ;
and they never quit hold of the hearer by the striking
appeals they make to his strongest feelings and his
favorite recollections : to the heart, or to the quick and
immediate sense of inconsistency, they are always
addressed, and find their way thither by the shortest and
surest road ; but to the head, to the calm and sober
judgment, as pieces of argumentation, they assuredly
are not addressed. But Mr. Fox, as he went along, and
exposed absurdity, and made inconsistent arguments
clash and laid bare shuffling, or hypocrisy, and showered

down upon meanness, or upon cruelty, or oppression, a
pitiless storm of the most fierce invective, was ever
forging also the long, and compacted, and massive chain
of pure demonstration."

John Randolph possessed the erratic qualities attributed
above to the eloquence of Charles James Fox, without
its higher attributes. He was poorly fitted to rebuke
inconsistency in others, as of all statesmen that ever
lived he was most vacillating and inconsistent himself. He was utterly devoid of stability of character.
His positions were changed so rapidly, that it was impossible to tell where he would next appear, and what
new mode of attack he would next employ. No public
man ever frittered away time so uselessly, and expended
his resources with such abortive aims. "Watch him in
any one of his set speeches, and it will be a question
whether in any other spectacle whatever you can discover so great a waste of power. Every succeeding
paragraph has a different design from those which preceded it; and from the utter confusion and opposition
of the integral forces, the aggregate energy is destroyed.
You will see him at one moment sedulously hunting
with a pack of allies to whom the glow of a common
hatred has united him, but in the next instant, if a cross
scent strikes him, he will be found scampering off, in
hot haste, and will return before long, loaded with the
trophies of a victory over his own associates. This
extreme fickleness and oddity doubtless very much contributed to his success. He kept his hearers in constant suspense, watching for the next vagary that might
appear. Like Dean Swift, he would often make a re-

mark, much like a compliment, and then transform it
into a sarcasm, or he would abruptly utter a sarcasm,
and with ambiguous malice qualify it into a compliment.
Those who were most familiar with Randolph's mode
of debate, were accustomed to take him in a sense
opposite to his apparent design. If he began by treating his antagonist with unwonted respect, it was easy
to see that the kindness was unnatural, and that his
assumed flattery was portentous. His fitful courtesy in
the forum was never real, but a hollow air put on for
the moment,

> " With smooth dissimulation skill'd to grace,
> A devil's purpose with an angel's face."

The ample folds of hypocritical complacency with
which he occasionally condescended to drape his foe, to
the infinite dismay of the victim, would soon kindle
into the fierce torture of the shirt of Nessus, and burn to
the quick.

Randolph prepared himself for forensic strife in a
way as peculiar to himself as it was characteristic of
every thing he attempted to perform. In the first place,
he made himself familiar with the private history, peculiar temperament, and personal foibles of every man
with whom he was associated. Then, as soon as he
conceived the purpose of making a speech, his mind
went to work to collect, arrange, and prepare his materials. Every thing strong and stinging that could be
wrought into his intended harangue, was carefully can-
vassed, and if found worthy, was put down in his random notes. But it was only on the point of some

epigram, the "*sting in the tail*" of a sarcasm, as he himself declared, that he bestowed especial care. The chain of his argument was left for the chances of the occasion to forge; but the perpetual accompaniment of ridicule was anxiously and maliciously premeditated. He carried these sharpened missiles about with him constantly, and if the fitting occasion did not soon occur to disgorge himself in public, he would often rehearse his oratorical points in private conversation. Says one of his acquaintances, "I remember particularly the last speech he made in the House of Representatives. He had been waiting the opportunity to make it for ten days: and in that interval, I am inclined to think, I heard from him, in private, almost every brilliant thought contained in the speech." With his wide scope of personal acquaintance, and with his habits of prepared onslaught, his rising to address the House was a signal for universal dread and commotion. Piquant allusions, epigrammatic phrases, malicious anecdotes, scornful and withering quotations, brief but most excrutiatingly pertinent to the persons before him, flew off in every direction like sparks from Vulcan's forge, and, like the bolts of Jupiter, shivered wherever they fell. He knew the vulnerable part of every character, and often hurt the most when the popular eye least saw the blow. It has been well remarked that he used his tongue as a jockey would his whip; hit the sore place till the blood came, and there was no flourish or noise in doing it.

Many survive Randolph who remember the aspect

he presented in Congress, and the effects he wrought. In the language of Wordsworth, he was one of those

> " Dire faces, figures dire,
> Sharp-knee'd, sharp-elbow'd, and lean-anckled, too,
> With long and ghastly shanks, forms which once seen
> Could never be forgotten."

His tones were as unearthly as his look. His gesture was chiefly with his long and emaciated finger, more like the talon of a vulture than the member of a human form. The impressiveness with which he used this in debate was proverbial. There was a great deal of heedless power and striking caprice in his manner of address. He was attractive as an orator, on the same principle that the cell in the *Jardin des Plantes*, at Paris, closely glazed and guarded with iron net-work without, is perhaps the most popular show-room in the world, because it contains the most destructive serpents and deadly creatures any where to be found. Randolph was a perturbed spirit, and, like Milton's monarch-fiend, seems to have thought it " better to reign in hell than serve in heaven." He was possessed by the intemperate fury of Diomede, a passionate love of battle, which no consideration of subject or place could curb:

> " Creature of one mighty sense,
> Concentrated impudence."

Randolph formed the acquaintance of a prominent bookseller in Baltimore, of whom he made several purchases, and with whom he was wont freely to converse. At a subsequent period, being in Washington with a

friend, he saw Randolph approaching him, and proposed
to introduce his companion to that famous man. But
his friend declined, knowing something of the wayward
hero whose brutal rudeness he did not wish to incur.
" Well," said the quondam friend and confident book-
vender, " I'm sorry you will not be introduced. I'll go up
and give him a shake of the hand, at any rate." Up he
walked, with familiar air and cordial salutations. The
aristocratic republican immediately threw his hands be·
hind him, as if scorning to touch plebeian flesh, and with
a look as searching as his tones were impudent, exclaimed,
" Oh, oh! you are Mr. ——, from Baltimore ?"   " Yes,
sir," was the reply.   " A bookseller ?"   " Yes, sir," was
the second response.   " Ah! I bought books from you ?"
" Yes, sir, you did."   " Did I forget to pay you for
them ?"   " No, sir, you did not."   " Good morning,
sir!" said the cynic, lifting his cap with offended dignity, and hurrying on.

It was his custom and delight, in public and private
life, to deal out the contents of the bitter urn profusely.   His most moderate style was bitter-sweet ;
from this he rose or sank into the pure bitter, and if
the matter in hand was important, and his antagonists
dignified, he invariably ended with vinegar distilled,
thickened with deadly drugs.   Like the urchin of mis-
chief in the " Lay of the Last Minstrel," he used fairy
gifts with a spirit of deviltry, ever prompt to provoke,
to annoy, and to injure, no matter whom he wounded,
or when, or where.   His personal resentments led him
away from every consideration, save that of how he
could best mutilate and silence his adversary.   His in

vectives were fearful, not so much from the grandeur
of his mien, or the dignity of his talents, but from the
acuteness of his weapons, and the condensed venom
they infused. He easily intimidated all but the most
fearless, and even they were not ambitious of encoun-
tering him, since it was not a battle with a lion but a
viper. A distinguished statesman and orator from
Rhode Island, known as " the Bald Eagle of the House,"
was the only antagonist who effectually silenced this
forensic Thersites after his own manner. When this
gentleman publicly rendered thanks to God that in
anomalous creatures there is a physical law which pre-
vents the perpetuation of their own species, the allusion
would have been too atrocious if directed against any
one besides John Randolph.

He was not indifferent about the selection of his
victims, but with a choice husbandry of his resources,
he seemed to take special delight in setting up the fairest
personages as a target for his wit-bolts. And whoever
he pounced upon found the process no holiday sport.
Before ordinary harlequins of the forum, dignified
personages might composedly sit, " wrapt in rich dullness, comfortable fur," consoling themselves with the
remark of Shakspeare, "If a man will be beaten
with brains, he shall wear nothing handsome about him."
But not so in the presence of Randolph. When summoned to the rack, the candidate for torture was bound
to go and have his vitals torn by demon vultures. Contempt, says an oriental proverb, pierces even through
the shell of a tortoise ; one needed a panoply strong
indeed to shield him from the personal javelin hurled by

Randolph's hand. He labored most earnestly to impeach Judge Chase, but failed in his effort, and came out of the contest without a single laurel.

It would be unjust to deny that Mr. Randolph possessed great powers of eloquence of their kind. He could hold an audience for a long time enthralled by his speech. Speaking of his own opposition to the Bankrupt Bill, he said, "How delighted I am to think that I helped to give that hateful bill a kick,—yes, sir, this very day week I spoke for three hours against it, and I assure you that whilst I was speaking, although the northern mail was announced, not a single member left his seat to look for letters, a circumstance that had not occurred during the session!" But he had more talent than courtesy or self-respect. He contemplated the suffer· ings he produced with as much complacency as the artist who wished to delineate the agonies of martyrdom, and studied the contortions of the shrieking model on a rack. In some of his better inspirations, there are beautiful gleams of truth, impressed in graceful and energetic language, "like orient pearls at random strung;" but ordinarily his snatches of truth wear an infernal aspect, and convulse us with dread, without touching the finer chords of the heart.

"The flesh will quiver where the pinchers tear,
The blood will follow where the knife is driven."

Some persons combine in themselves the attributes of the toad and the salamander; they imbibe no aliment from earth but its poisons, and they breathe naturally only in fire. They are of the class described by Burke, in allusion to the French Revolution. "They have tigers to fall upon animated strength. They have hyenas to prey upon carcasses. The national menagerie is collected by the first physiologist of the time · and is defective in no description of savage nature. Neither sex, nor age—nor the sanctuary of the tomb, is sacred to them."

John Randolph was the Sagittarius of the American Congress, "armed at point," and letting fly on all occasions his dart with terrific power. He was king Scapin, and could at any moment invest his subjects with the air and honors of infinite contempt. Whenever he saw fit to level his long, ghastly finger, at the head of any one, with the ominous shrill cry of "Mr. Speaker!"—it was the signal for all the risibles in the house to relax, and the prelude of roars of laughter at the poor victim's expense. The famous "Yazoo claim," was for many years a bone of contention, annually defended by Randolph in a series of speeches, which some think are destined to "stand the test of time, of scrutiny, and of talent." Battling one day against some of the strongest men of the nation, he made the withering remark which at the time rung all over the union. Shaking that claw-like finger of his in the face of his opponents, he exclaimed, "*Mr. Speaker, I hope, sir, to see the day when a Yazoo claimant and a villain, will be synonymous terms.*"

The best scholars of our universities, the first leaders in our State legislatures, and the master-spirits in every walk of forensic gladiatorship, trembled at the necessity of a rencontre with John Randolph on the floor of Congress. He was always ready to meet every new-comer and at once to annihilate his pretensions, or cover him with disgrace. However potent their talents, and however righteous their cause, they needed to keep in mind the caution addressed of old to the Archangel:

> " I forewarn thee, shun
> His deadly arrow; neither vainly hope
> To be invulnerable in those bright arms,
> Though temper'd heavenly; for that fatal dint,
> Save Him who reigns above, none can resist."

Undoubtedly a brilliant flame burned amid the attenu-ated and deranged fibres of Randolph's intellect, but it did not quicken his pulse, nor kindle his frigid nature into genial warmth. His sarcasms were as stinging and adhesive as the burr or nettle that annoys the lover of quiet nature in his woodland rambles. He not only smote his victims with blows that keenly kill, but like the Levite described in the Bible, he cut the carcass into fragments and scattered them to the winds. Rude-ly to attack and savagely to demolish was his vocation.' What Burke said of the Constituent Assembly of France, in the days of her phrenzy, was eminently true of John Randolph: "He could not build—he could only pull down—he was the Vitruvius of ruin." In vain shall we search for any memorial that attests any bene-fit resulting from the influence of his life. He is the parent of no law, the author of no treatise, and the builder of no valuable institution. If his name was not written in water, it was inscribed in darker hues on the memory of mankind.

Aristophanes and Juvenal were feared while alive, but the worthies whom they ridiculed were the only ones destined to receive posthumous esteem. To mutilate the monuments that gratitude has erected to genius, and so extinguish the lamp lighted by devotion over against the image of love, can be the ambition of no tender heart or exalted intellect. If it is disgraceful thus to dishonor the dead, it is something worse to destroy the peace and deface the fair character of the living. He who shall make this the business of his life, must hereafter expect the retribution which the malignant can never escape. A man in Bengal was long distinguished for skill in hunting the tiger. His adroitness in the chase won him much agreeable exercise and reputation. A length he came near losing his life by his daring, and relinquished the sport with this remark, " Tiger hunting is very fine amusement, so long as we hunt the tiger; but it is rather awkward when the tiger takes it into his head to hunt us." The tiger at length turned upon Randolph, and held him awfully at bay.

In the spring of 1824, he repeated his visit to England; and, in 1830, was appointed Minister to Russia, where he remained but a short time. On the 20th of May, 1833, Mr. Randolph came from Virginia to Philadelphia, on his way to New York, where he intended again to embark for Europe in search of health. It was

here that the melancholy drama of his life came to a
solemn close, as described by his physician, Dr. Parrish.

"For a short time he lay perfectly quiet, his eyes were
closed, and I concluded he was disposed to sleep. He
suddenly roused from this state, with the words 'Remorse, Remorse.' It was twice repeated; at the
last time at the top of his voice, evidently with great
agitation, he cried out, 'Let me see the word.' No
reply followed: having learned enough of the character
of my patient to ascertain, that when I did not know
exactly what to say, it was best to say nothing. He
then exclaimed, 'Get a dictionary—let me see the
word.' I cast my eyes around me and told him I believed there was none in the room. 'Write it down,
then—let me see the word.' I picked up one of his
cards from the table, 'Randolph of Roanoke,' and
inquired whether I should write on that. 'Yes, nothing
more proper.' Then with my pencil I wrote Remorse.
He took the card in his hands in a hurried manner, and
fastened his eyes on it with great intensity. 'Write it
on the back,' he exclaimed. I did so, and handed it to
him again. He was excessively agitated at this period
—he repeated, Remorse! you have no idea what it is,
you can form no idea of it whatever ; it has contributed
to bring me to my present situation ; but I have looked
to the Lord Jesus Christ and hope I have obtained pardon.' He then said, 'Now let John take your pencil
and draw a line under the word ;' which was accordingly done. I inquired what was to be done with the
card ; he replied, 'Put it in your pocket; take care of
it ; when I am dead look at it.'

"This was an impressive scene. All the plans of ambition, the honors and the wealth of this world, had vanished as bubbles on the water. He knew and he felt that his very moments were few, and even *they* were numbered." In a few hours after this scene, on the 23d of May, 1833, John Randolph was dead. · His remains were removed to Roanoke and there, in a lonely dell, amid venerable trees, without a monument, without an epitaph breathing affection, and with not even a fragrant shrub planted in the arid soil to indicate the remembrance of some friendly hand, in solitude and neglect his dust awaits the resurrection morn.

John Randolph at one time was regarded, and perhaps still is by some persons, as the prince of American orators. We have no disposition to depreciate his merits, nor would we uncharitably "draw his frailties from their dread abode." We leave him in the hands of the benign Sovereign of all, without the slightest desire either to aggravate his faults or pronounce their doom. In this review of his career we have to do with his character only as an orator, and not with his eternal destiny. Viewing his merits in the light of his public deeds, we think that if an apotheosis is to be granted to him at all, it should be in company with such men as Warren Hastings. Speaking of the latter, Burke said that he knew something of the Brahmins. He knew that as they worshipped some gods from love, so they worshipped others from fear. He knew that they erected shrines not only to the benignant deities of light and plenty, but also to the fiends who preside over smallpox and murder. Nor did he at all dispute the claim

of Mr. Hastings to be admitted into such a Pantheon."
Perhaps the moral sense of enlightened nations, estimat-
ing a man's claims to perpetual esteem according to
the beneficent influence of his life, will assign to John
Randolph a like position in the temple of righteous fame.

www.ingramcontent.com/pod-product-compliance
Lightning Source LLC
Chambersburg PA
CBHW022016110726
47901CB00006B/1544